DEFYING DOOMSDAY

EDITED BY
Tsana Dolichva
& Holly Kench

First published in Australia in May 2016
by Twelfth Planet Press

www.twelfthplanetpress.com

Cover art by Tania Walker
Design by Tehani Wessely
Typeset in Sabon MT Pro

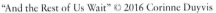

National Library of Australia Cataloguing-in-Publication entry

Title:	Defying Doomsday
	Tsana Dolichva, Holly Kench, editors,
ISBN:	978-1-922101-40-2 (paperback); 978-1-922101-41-9 (hardcover)
Subjects:	Short stories.
	Disabilities—Fiction.
	Judgment Day—Fiction.
Other Creators/Contributors:	Kench, Holly, author.
Dewey Number:	A823.408

Table of Contents

Introduction

Robert Hoge

People with disability already live in a post-apocalyptic world.

Stairs remain at stubborn right angles. Communications can wash over us, unheard, unseen. Some social interactions elude—a millimetre away, a mile away. Impairment and chronic illness can make negotiating the everyday world that little bit more difficult.

So much of our world is a not-made-for-us space that disaster may as well have already struck. And that's exactly what makes the stories in this anthology so crunchy and interesting—we are already fighting and thriving in interesting and diverse ways. When the apocalypse comes, we've got a head start.

Defying Doomsday is an anthology that demonstrates characters with disability and difference have far more interesting stories to tell in a post-apocalyptic setting than have been told before.

Literature has a long history of singling out people with impairment as objects of interest. In William Goldman's *Lord of the Flies*—essentially a post-apocalypse story itself—three characters who have impairments are picked off by other boys on the island. Piggy, who is short-sighted, has asthma and is overweight, has the worst of it. He puts up a strong, reasoned fight before he is eventually killed.

A century earlier, Charles Dickens gave us *A Christmas Carol*. In it we are introduced to Tiny Tim, a saintly, young cripple, suffering on his crutch and steel frame, seemingly defined solely by his impairment.

Tsana and Holly have included in *Defying Doomsday* wonderful stories that feature characters with all kinds of disability. The breadth of the stories these authors have told is as important as it is worthy. But it's their depth we should be most impressed with. These characters are not a burden. They're active participants negotiating their way through a world that is degrees harder than it was before. They are not just saints, not just sinners. These characters are not a burden, set solely in a story to slow others down. They are decisive, interesting, fun. They are deep.

Anyway, enough from me. Go and read these great stories. Just over the page, doomsday is beginning. And the amazing characters you are going to meet are only just starting to defy it.

And the Rest of Us Wait

Corinne Duyvis

We were among the earliest to arrive at the shelter—a day and a half before impact—and it still took two hours for the volunteers to process us. My parents and I stood on one side of a long desk in a low-ceilinged office, the muffled noise from the shelter hallway outside growing louder the more people joined the line behind us.

They scanned us for contaminants. They scanned our bags. They double- and triple-checked our blood, our IDs, and our shelter assignment letters. They squinted at our faces to match the photos, and I waited for a glimpse of recognition as they placed my face and accent, but nothing came. They asked me to explain my cathing equipment and leg braces. They asked where we were from (Riga, Latvia), how long we'd been in the Netherlands (seven weeks), where we'd stayed (twenty minutes outside Amsterdam); I couldn't tell if they were verifying their information or making small talk. Right when I thought they were ready to let us go, they went through our bags again, which contained spare clothes and little else.

"No food?" the shelter volunteer asked in thickly accented English.

Mum shook her head. "We spent the last five weeks in a refugee centre."

"Should've saved food."

Mum opened her mouth and shut it again.

"There's food here. Right?" Dad's lips twitched. "They said…"

The woman shrugged. "We have food, but it's tight. Better if people bring their own."

"We'll remember that for the next apocalypse," I said.

Afterwards, as we sat down on the creaky beds we'd been assigned in a sea of camping beds, bedrolls, and stretchers, Mum leaned in. "Careful, Iveta," she whispered. "Don't stand out."

Dad scanned the hall, as though the other families hesitantly testing their beds would descend on us at any moment. We weren't the only ones who'd arrived early. I recognised others from our refugee centre: from Finns to Belarusians, from Ukrainians to Romanians, even a stray Bulgarian and Turkish family, although most people that far south had fled to Africa rather than Western Europe.

People looked up as I stalked through the narrow aisle between beds. During my few weeks in the country, the only Dutch people I'd interacted with were the refugee centre volunteers. Still, I could recognise the language, and the moment I heard an older couple talk in hushed Dutch, I stopped by their cots. They'd seen me coming. Mum could warn me not to stand out all she wanted, but I was hard to miss: I walked with a waddling limp, my hips seesawing fiercely.

"Question," I said in English. "Did you bring any instruments?"

They gave me a confused look.

"For music." I mimicked playing the piano.

"No, we...of course not. We only brought the supplies we needed. Why?"

I swept an arm at the hall, which was three or four times the size of my high school gym. They couldn't have designed it any plainer if they'd tried: nothing but pillars and beds and cold lighting, and the pale green walls were bare aside from the occasional water fountain and posters displaying shelter rules in a dozen languages.

"What else is there to do while we wait?"

Cot by cot, the shelter filled up.

People arrived by the busload that day and the day after. I trailed the aisles, hitting up other Dutch families I found. I didn't need to identify them by their speech anymore. They were the ones with the bulging backpacks, the uncertain look about them, while those of us from the refugee centres carried narrow sacks and looked weary more than anything else.

I explored the rest of the shelter and found myself lingering outside the main halls, glad for the relative silence. It was too easy to get a headache in the murmur and anxiety permeating the shelter, and the last thing I needed was to worry about minor headaches.

Aside from the five sleeping halls, there were two smaller halls, the walls soft blue and every inch filled with mismatched chairs and tables instead of beds. Packets of playing cards and old books were strewn around the tables. Some of the kids' tables had crayons, pencils, paper.

No instruments.

"Not impressed?" a voice behind me said. "It's only for three days."

I turned, facing a girl a few years older than me— early twenties, probably—with a prettily patterned hijab framing a narrow face.

"And afterwards we can all go home, right?" I said, sceptical.

"That...would be nice. Iveta?"

Had someone finally recognised me? There were a lot of Baltic curly blondes around, but people always said I looked unique, with narrow blue eyes and a wide forehead made wider by the way I pulled those curls behind my ears. I was never a huge name outside of Latvia, but I'd done a handful of European shows, and I'd expected more people to recognise me. It was the lack of wheelchair, I figured: even if people recognised my face, they might not recognise it atop an upright body.

"Iveta. That's me," I said.

"Samira. I'm helping shelter management. Our medical information on the refugees assigned here is incomplete. I'm trying to fill it up."

"This late in the game?"

"We still have a few hours before impact." She smiled an almost-genuine smile. She was trying; I gave her that much. "They didn't even realise they missed this information until I pointed it out."

"It's been chaotic," I said airily, which was an understatement the size of the comet that was about to hit us.

"So you're from Latvia?"

"Yes."

"I'm sorry."

I leaned against a table. The room was surprisingly empty—most people were guarding their bags in the sleeping halls. "Yeah, well." I scratched at the table, seeking resistance and finding only smooth surface. "We might survive all right."

The comet had been announced in July 2034, half a year ago. They hadn't been certain where it would hit: Eastern Europe was their best guess. It might hit south of that, near the Middle East, in which case my words to Samira might be true; it might hit north of that, near Scandinavia, in which case Samira's sympathies were justified but nowhere near enough.

Latvia wouldn't be the only casualty. The Netherlands wouldn't stay intact, either. No place would. Not with impact dust masking the sun for at least a year, not with wildfires and earthquakes and more. Millions—perhaps billions—of people had already left on generation ships or taken shelter in permanent basements deep underground. The rest of us only had these temporary government shelters to outlast the initial impact. Afterwards, we'd flood back onto the surface and fend for ourselves.

But even if the Netherlands didn't stay intact, it would *exist*.

Latvia might not.

"Did you bring any instruments?" I asked abruptly. "Or do you sing?"

Her head cocked. "Badly enough to make my fiancé leave the room."

I exhaled with a whistle. "All right. What do you need to know?"

For the next ten minutes, I told her about my spina bifida and all that came with: from my club foot to my partially paralysed legs, from my spinal implant against chronic pain to my shunt to manage my hydrocephalus.

"What does that implant run on?"

"Body heat. We got the latest and greatest." Money had been one of several upsides to my bout of fame. I'd made enough to move my family into an accessible apartment and buy a brand-new wheelchair for shows and long distances. It had gotten stolen on the long, crooked escape from Latvia to the Netherlands.

"Good. We can charge prosthetics and equipment, but the more power we save, the better."

We'd sat down at a table in a quiet corner. Normally, people got weirded out when presented with my laundry list of conditions. Samira hadn't batted an eyelash. She'd asked all the right questions, too, but for the sake of completeness rather than prying.

"How much do you know about KAFOs?" I knocked on my leg braces.

"Sorry?"

"You're a doctor. It's not exactly the flu or messing with organs, but how good are you with orthotics?"

"I'm just a volunteer. I'll ask Dr Kring, but he's been busy. Some of the refugees arrived with severe malnutrition."

At least someone was looking after them. The refugee centre volunteers had tried to help, but doctors—like food—were a rare commodity. Too many medical professionals had left on generation ships or moved into permanent shelters.

Again: just like the food.

Samira leaned in as though confiding in me. "I'm... really just a medical student. I simply volunteered when I saw how overworked Dr Kring was."

I scratched at the table and was left just as unsatisfied as before. "All right."

"What's the matter with your orthoses?"

I stood. "It's not urgent. Like you said: we've got all the time in the world."

"I said we have three days."

My smile was steady. "Same thing, isn't it?"

Any minute now.

I didn't know what I was supposed to feel.

I sat on the bed, Mum on one side, Dad on another, both leaning into me as though that would help. Someone from shelter management had given a speech about what we'd need to do around impact time, and they'd repeated themselves on the intercom system.

The instructions were clear: *stay on your cots; stay calm; we'll update you when we can.* We'd feel shaking, but they didn't know how strong or how long for. We might hear something, but they doubted it.

I thought half a year would've been enough to prepare me, but it still hadn't sunk in. Mum stared stoically ahead. Dad had tear tracks on both cheeks. Me—I didn't know whether to panic or cry, and in the end, I did neither. Instead, my mind wandered off, tweaking lyrics in Latvian and English both. I reached for my wrist only to find it empty, our wrist tabs bartered for food weeks before.

Mum took my hand, squeezed it. "We'll be fine," she whispered.

I squeezed back and hoped she didn't expect me to believe her.

The lights flashed bright and crackled for a flash of a second.

Then they went out.

Gasps. Beds creaked as people sat upright. Someone called out in Dutch. Next, a high-pitched voice spoke in Russian. Then, a pained groan.

My eyes were still adjusting, blinking rapidly in a desperate attempt to find *some* source of light that was just too faint for me to have clung onto yet. Didn't some people still have their tabs? Shouldn't there be light coming from underneath the doors?

Nothing.

Experimentally, I raised my hand in front of my face. I didn't see a thing. I couldn't remember darkness like this since—since ever.

"What's happening?" someone called in English. "No one warned us about this!"

Dad grabbed my hand. At the same time, Mum stood. I could only tell because the bed veered up below me and her clothes brushed past mine.

The yells layered into each other, near and far, angry and frightened, in languages I didn't even recognise. All of a sudden, I missed home with a passion. I missed my room, the Dauvaga Promenade, Grandma's mushrooms, performing at Kalnciema Quarter, a quiet mind and not translating every word and *music*—

"This wasn't supposed to happen," Mum insisted, yanking me back to the dark. "They have enough battery power for days. And the shelters are shielded against EMPs."

"Maybe they turned off the lights as protection," Dad said.

I didn't bother to shake my head. They wouldn't see. "Shelter management would've warned us." Governments had announced months in advance why and when they'd be deactivating the power plants, to give time to prepare. There was no chance shelter management would've so thoroughly informed us about our rations and the bathroom policy, but neglect to mention turning off the lights.

I peeled Dad's hand from mine and stood, feeling Mum's presence by my side. "Does anyone have a tab?" I called in English. "We could use the light to—"

"Tabs aren't working!" someone shouted back. "Mine was fully charged—"

"Mine just turned off—" someone else added.

"Doctor!" someone screamed. It might've been in Dutch, but if so, the word was similar enough to leave no doubt. "*Doctor!*"

Snippets of shouts. I caught a word here—*heart*—and there—*help*—which was enough.

Lights out. Tabs dead. Sudden heart attacks.

"The shielding didn't work," I said.

Abruptly, it hit me what that meant. If there was an EMP, it meant the comet had hit, that it really had *happened* after all these months, and Latvia was—

The notion slipped away.

"Help me onto the bed," I said. There was no use in theorising and panicking. Everyone else was doing a fine job of that already. I groped in the darkness for Mum's arm, then used it to steady myself and climb on. My legs buckled once or twice, the soft mattress too unsteady, but once I stood, I remembered a dozen concerts I'd given, and a dozen smaller shows besides. I remembered crowds hanging on my every word. I got them to scream at the top of their lungs, and to go so quiet a moment later that they could've heard me whisper even without the microphone. I got them to shout in support of deregulated Internet and better accessibility and against Russia's latest stunts.

At home, I'd been Iveta, teen novelty. Here, I was just another refugee.

Let's see if I can still pull it off.

I braced myself against Mum and called out, "*Listen up!* Get on the beds! Keep the paths clear!" I wished my accent when speaking English didn't mark me as a refugee so clearly. I kept shouting, again and again, until it shut up the panicked voices around me. "Keep the paths clear! Keep quiet! If your neighbour is hurt, help them to the exit. Keep the injured in the hallway until someone finds a doctor—"

"I'll find someone!" a voice from near the exit called.

Around us, I heard the shuffle of people climbing onto their beds, shouts in other languages that I was half-sure were people repeating my instructions.

I let Mum help me sit, already aching from exertion.

"Good," Dad murmured. "That was good."

"Not exactly lying low like Mum said." A nervous laugh escaped me. People passed by in a rush of air and footsteps and urgent Dutch words. I wiggled my fingers under the KAFO to massage my calf, which hovered between numb and painfully tingly.

Mum tugged lightly at a curl of my hair. "My daughter would never listen to such silly advice."

God, that tingling was annoying—it reminded me of forgetting to take my pain meds and—

My fingers curled tight as the realisation hit.

"The EMP," I whispered. "My spinal implant died."

"Oh." Mum pulled me in close. She made another small sound: *oh*.

I couldn't tell if the pain was worse than before or if, after a year of blissful nothing, every small prick simply felt like a stab.

It made it impossible to sit still. So I didn't.

People had found candles by now. Flickering flame lit up the broad central hallway, which contained an urgent mess of people slipping into different rooms to seek familiar faces or staff and tossing out occasional half-shouts of "keep your bags close!"

Every now and then, a rumble went through the walls and floor. I groped the wall for stability. The first big shakes had been enough to knock people down, but now, it was just occasional trembles.

I didn't want to think about what the world above looked like. What buildings that *hadn't* been built with a comet impact in mind looked like.

There should have been an announcement by now. Why hadn't shelter management stepped up?

I wasn't the only one wondering. I caught snippets of Russian and English. Something about the EMP. About Dr Kring. About death.

Goosebumps shuddered across my skin. I stayed close to the walls, ready to grab them for balance in the push-and-shove of the crowd and the inconstant tremors. I scanned the dimness for familiar faces. Samira, shelter management, neighbours from the refugee centre.

"Listen, listen!"

It was a male voice, his English tinged with a Dutch accent. He stood so tall above the crowd that he must've been standing on a chair. He held a candle in one hand, lighting him in eerie yellow.

"I wanted to update...My name is Ahmed. I'm with the Amsterdam police." If his name made the murmur increase, his job had people quieting down a little. Relief flashed over his face. "It looks like an EMP hit us."

Someone shouted in Dutch. For a moment, I worried I'd lose track of the conversation, but Ahmed responded in English without missing a beat. "Yes, the shelter was shielded. It must not have held. What we know is that our generator…stopped working. Several people were injured putting out the fire. Lights, tabs, radio equipment, much of the kitchen—anything electrical is gone. We may have functional flashlights, but we're not sure."

He repeated the answer in Dutch, but was quickly drowned out by further questions.

"What about the doctor?"

"What about fresh air? Will we be okay without electricity?"

"Why are *you* talking to us? Where's shelter management?"

Ahmed's candle flickered beneath his face. "Between, ah, pacemakers failing and the generator fire, not all of shelter management has survived." He rattled off a list of names, some deceased, others—like Dr Kring—injured. "The rest of management is discussing options. Others are helping the injured, including Sam—including my sister-in-law. Anyone with medical know-how, come to the med bay."

"There won't be other *doctors*. We were lucky to have Kring!"

So much for Kring looking at my KAFO, I thought, jittery. Without a doctor—with amateurs looking after a dozen injured people—my situation became a lot less urgent. What if the pain worsened? What if I got headaches? Nausea?

"Can we eat okay? Without the kitchen equipment?"

"We don't know yet. If—"

Voices surged. A burly Russian man nearby argued with someone by his side. I picked up just enough to know that his wife was one of those with a pacemaker. I chose the opportunity to wobble through the crowd towards Ahmed.

He spoke louder. "Anyone who knows about engineering or air ventilation systems, come talk to me."

He stepped off the chair just as I broke through the crowd. I wasn't the only one trying to talk to him, but I *was* the only one he happened to stand right in front of. "Samira?" I called.

He frowned, half annoyed, half distracted.

"Your sister-in-law! Samira? Tell them she's a doctor." I struggled to speak loudly enough to be heard, let alone keep his attention.

"She's not—" He stepped past me.

I followed him through the crowd. We reached a less packed part of the hallway, and I took the opportunity to surge closer and talk privately. "End on a positive note. Public speaking 101. Back when I—never mind. You had bad news. People are panicking. Lie—give them *something*."

"I shouldn't even be doing this. If I lie…"

"Shelter management doesn't know about that speech? What are they *doing*?"

"Panicking," he said wryly. "Get to your cot. That's all anyone can do right now."

*

The pain was a vindictive thing. I lay flat on my bed, arms under my back, knuckles pressing into my skin.

Shelter management didn't serve dinner that night. Once they got their act together, they rattled off the state of things and encouraged us to eat and share whatever food we'd brought. People did share, to their credit, but only with those they knew.

Us refugees only knew each other.

Management promised we'd have breakfast by morning, once they'd spent the night organising the remaining food and staff. They'd brought in more candles, and a handful of body heat flashlights from properly shielded cases in storage.

"But why wasn't the full shelter shielded?" Inga said. She was a fifty-something Latvian-Russian woman from Salaspils, outside Riga. She'd been at a refugee centre on the Dutch coast, waiting on a boat to England that never came. Now, she sat cross-legged on the ground by our beds, along with two near-identical girls my age and a Finnish male couple she'd befriended at her shelter.

"There were a lot of shelters to build in a very short time," Dad said. "These temporary shelters, the permanent ones, the ships. They might've made a mistake, or there weren't enough supplies."

"Bet there were supplies for those ships and permanent shelters, though." I pushed my thumbs deep into the fleshy parts on either side of my spine. I wished I could reach in and around, cutting off the pain signals the way my implant was supposed to.

"They cut corners," Mum said from the foot end of my bed.

"They wouldn't. *Not* with lives at stake." One of the Finnish men was sitting up all prim and proper.

"If our lives mattered, we'd be on a ship." I turned my head to face them properly and pulled my lips into a distorted grin. "Sucks being left behind. Doesn't it?"

It was one of my lyrics. Apparently, that did the trick: Inga's daughters went *oh!*

"Iveta?" one said.

"Aren't you? You are! I knew I recognised you."

"I am."

"I thought you'd be on a generation ship…"

"Me too." I faked that same grin. It was nice being recognised, I had to admit. The novelty had worn off quickly for those at our refugee centre. I guessed that mimicked my career: from one day to the next, hundreds of thousands of people had known my name. *That cute blonde girl in the wheelchair on that talent show from, what was it, Latveria? Did you see her audition footage? Holy shit, right?*

Just as quickly, it dropped off. I'd floundered for a bit, but rather than push on in desperation, I had claimed to want to focus on school, and promised to pick up my career again at eighteen, when people might take me more seriously. I never imagined doing anything else.

Then July 2034 happened, and I found out the

world would end three weeks before my seventeenth birthday.

I'd done free pop-up concerts in every major town from Riga to Amsterdam. I'd told the audience I wanted to offer a distraction—*we need music at the end of the world, am I right?*—and told my parents one of my fans might find us a spot somewhere permanent. Except no one did. The final truck we hitchhiked on dropped us off in the Netherlands, and not a single boat would take us further towards safety.

The girls crept closer while the adults talked. "Where's your wheelchair?" one asked, switching to Latvian.

"Got stolen. I mostly used it during performances, anyway."

She faltered. "You're not really...?"

"I used it during *performances*, so I could *save energy*, and not have to worry about *falling over*." I'd been lying down for the past hour, so they couldn't have seen my unglamorous waddle, but even then, my shoulders were crooked as hell. You'd think that would tip them off I wasn't faking.

"Oh," she said quietly. "Oh, okay."

I pushed upright and grimaced. As if the pain wasn't enough, my stomach was rumbling uncomfortably too. "Sorry. I'm being snippy."

"I wondered because..." She pulled up her left sleeve. In the candlelight, I saw shining metal, matte plastic. A prosthesis.

"The EMP busted it," her sister chimed in.

"I'm uncoupling it soon. Too heavy to carry around for nothing. I just hoped…"

I looked closer at the robotic arm. It hung heavily, limply, by the girl's side.

"I couldn't remember if your chair was electric. I was worried it might've broken down too. I saw someone else with that problem earlier." She blushed, tugging the sleeve back down. "I can't believe we didn't recognise you. Without the chair, and in this light, and—"

"And under these circumstances. I'm not expecting to run into any colleagues. I get it."

"I'm Ginta."

Her sister added, "I'm Vera. We love your music. We went to two of your concerts."

"Yeah?" My head tilted as I regarded them. "What about *playing* music?"

I woke early.

My parents were still asleep. All around were whispers, isolated pools of light. I gestured at someone a few beds down to shine their flashlight at me so I could light our candle. I put on my KAFOs, grabbed my cathing gear, and headed to the bathrooms.

I supposed the pain itself wasn't so bad. It hurt, yes, but it was easy enough to cope with if I focused on something else. The problem was, I could only focus on something else for so long. The pain was too constant, like a fly whizzing around my head. Inevitably, the buzzing grated enough to become thunder.

The line to the bathrooms was short, twenty minutes at most. Afterwards, I lingered outside the med bay. I tried the handle. Locked. I knocked.

A baggy-eyed Samira opened the door. "Look, we'll update you if...oh. You."

"Me," I confirmed. "Do you have a minute? I have a...problem."

She stepped aside.

Inside, scattered flashlights lit the room from bizarre angles. Slowly, my eyes focused. A dozen people were laid out side by side. Some sat upright, reading a book; others were sound asleep. One woman rocked back and forth, the bed creaking underneath, as she sewed up a coat—at least, I thought she was; her hands holding the needle and thread were frozen still.

The door shut, locking away the noise. She breathed in shakily and resumed her sewing.

"It's so *quiet*," I marvelled.

"Meet my assistant." Samira gestured at an older, severe-looking man holding a book that he paid no attention to. If not for the white coat, I'd have pegged him a patient.

"Ex-military. No formal medical training, but I improvise." He offered a nod in greeting.

"And we have two physical therapists and a trainee EMT volunteering."

"That's pretty good," I said, relieved.

The man nodded a second time. "If only it convinced Samira to take a break."

"You didn't sleep?" I asked her.

"I napped." She guided me into an open office so we could talk semi-privately. "What do you need?"

"My spinal implant…"

It took her a second. "Crap. How bad is it?"

"Not heart-attack bad. But not pleasant." I described it—pricking nerve pain, centred around my lower legs—and Samira frowned.

"Is that part of the spina bifida?"

"My doctors were never sure. Just one of those things."

"Well, I might have something mild to take the edge off. You'll have to ration it." She pointed a flashlight at a desk and started rifling through a stack of paper. "Dr Kring is recovering. If you still want to ask about your KAFOs, the physical therapists could help."

I hesitated. "They don't fit well. They might need readjustment."

"Did you lose weight?" Samira grimaced. "That's a silly question. I'll ask the physical therapists."

She found a form with my name on it and ran her index finger down the page, where her handwriting got increasingly squiggly to fit everything on. I assumed she was checking the information I'd given her to determine the medication, but the longer her finger paused at the bottom of the page, the less sure I was.

"Impressive list, right?" I said, an unsubtle prod.

"That's not it."

"Then are you thinking about how screwed I am?"

Her head dipped. I almost expected her to blush. "It's just—"

"Samira?" Military Guy stuck his head around the corner. "Breakfast arrived for the patients. I'll ask them to bring us some."

"No, I'll grab my own. Did they get the portions right?"

"Surprisingly, yes." He retreated again.

"Shouldn't be that surprising." Samira sighed to herself. "I gave specific instructions about everyone's needs. Anyway..." She looked back at the sheet.

"You were thinking about how screwed I am," I said helpfully. "Until yesterday, I'd have said my implant wasn't a concern, but that EMP proved me wrong. Instead, I get to worry about running out of whatever medication you give me. Or my cerebral shunt clogging and my hydrocephalus killing me with no one around to replace the shunt. Or being unable to disinfect my catheter and getting a UTI with no antibiotics around, or my KAFOs breaking with no one to repair them, or my scoliosis getting worse with no one around to build a brace."

The scoliosis was a best-case scenario. It meant there'd be time for it to get worse.

Samira seemed unsure of what to say. For a moment, I wanted to leave it at that. Make her feel even a fraction of my dread. Make her prove me wrong.

Then I just wished I hadn't said anything at all; it wouldn't make a difference.

I stood. "I should get my ID papers if I want breakfast. People are already queueing." In the time it would take to grab my ID, stow my cathing gear, and perhaps replace the sloppy clothes I'd used as pyjamas, I bet that line would grow twice as long.

"Come see me at noon. I'll have that medication, and I'll have talked to the physical therapists."

Noon. I could last that long, especially once I got some food in me. My stomach groaned in anticipation.

Samira hesitated. "Do you want to talk…?"

"I've had half a year to consider my odds." I gave a one-shouldered shrug. "We're all doomed. Some of us are simply more doomed than others."

The line for breakfast was huge. I thought it was just the number of people, but the closer I got, the more I realised it was something else: at the big counter between the hall and kitchen, volunteers were rifling through files the same way Samira had done.

"You're *kidding* me."

Manually looking up each individual. Checking their dietary needs and allowances. Marking off breakfast. For *hundreds* of us. No wonder it took so long.

Finally, after an hour and a half, I managed to walk away with an apple, a protein bar, and vitamin-boosted water, and thumped onto my bed where Vera and Ginta waited in the near-dark.

"Sorry. I got in line late." It was nice switching back to Latvian. I bit down, savouring the apple's sweet, sticky freshness. Maybe I should have eaten the protein bar first, get something solid in, but actual flavour couldn't be beaten.

"You said you had a song in mind? From your album, or...?" Vera looked at me with eager eyes.

"Something newer." Bite, chew, swallow. Even the needling in my legs felt less urgent. "I performed it on the way here."

"Wish we could've seen those concerts," Ginta said wistfully.

"Now you'll be in one." I reached into my bag for a few torn pieces of paper. I'd jotted down lyrics with a stubby pencil. I put them under the light Ginta was holding. "Here's the chorus. I need back-up voices for this part, and this...Vera, did you get those drums?"

"The kitchen gave me some containers. Not the same, but I can build a rhythm." Excitement coloured her cheeks. "I only played in the school band so far. Backup."

"Can you do something like this?" I hit my thighs with flat palms, creating a quick rhythm that was a pale imitation of anything my old band could've done. The thwacks doubled as welcome distractions from the pain, numbing my skin for half-moments.

Vera mimicked the rhythm on her own thighs, nodded.

"Okay, so the English chorus goes like..." I sang a fast version, emphasising the key line, which was in spiteful-enough-to-spit Latvian: "*But you made up your mind, one look was enough*—Ginta, can you sing that line, but kind of quieter..."

Ginta mimicked me. It took a few tries to get the right tone. It wasn't the way I'd done it originally—more subdued—but her quieter version made the line all the more venomous.

"Yes! That, *that*!" I bounced from excitement, my apple nearly rolling from my lap. I'd almost forgotten about it. I took another bite, my mind working overtime to incorporate Ginta's approach into the rest of the song. I missed my producer for a fierce second, but shoved that feeling into a dark corner alongside the stabbing in my legs and my maybe-headaches and the thought of home.

"So, first refrain. Originally, I had it like this." I launched into the old version, but didn't get far.

"Do you mind?" someone hissed in English.

The sisters turned as one. "Sorry, we'll keep it down," Ginta said.

The man shone his flashlight from a few beds away. I squinted at the glare. "How can you be singing at a time like this?"

"You're welcome." I planned to say more, but clenched my jaw as sudden pain jolted through my right calf.

"Have some respect. We're trying...trying..."

"I'm glad you girls are having fun," a neighbouring woman pitched in, "but this isn't the time."

"We'll go somewhere else," Vera said.

I'd have given them the finger, so I guessed it was a good thing Vera got there first.

At noon sharp, I knocked on the medical bay entrance. The door opened, revealing that military guy from this morning. He looked wary. "Yeah?"

I peered past him. More people sat upright than last time, and some beds were empty. "Samira said I should come by."

One patient—a woman Mum's age—laughed weakly. "Samira? Good luck with that." She sat on the edge of a high stretcher, a flickering candle beside her and a loose-leafed paperback in her lap.

I stepped inside. "What do you mean?"

"She's just talking to her fiancé," Military Guy said.

"Pft. Samira'll be gone the moment that fiancé finds a shelter with electricity." The woman's English was solid—smoother than mine—but I detected an accent I couldn't place. "I overheard them talking, you know. He went outside."

"Outside?" I said. Outside was ruination. The dust cloud was so thick you'd need an air filter to breathe. The minimal shaking we'd felt would have had far worse results topside. It was only another twenty-four hours before the shelter was supposed to empty out, but anyone sensible would make of those twenty-four hours what they could.

I planned to.

"To find *help*," Military Guy said.

"You think she wouldn't stay gone? Find a shelter with fresher air, lights that work, hot food? Fewer refugees, pre-starved, pissed off, and needy as hell?" She gestured at herself and sneered. "Ha!"

"You need to lie down and stop talking nonsense." Military Guy pointed at the patient. "At least you're getting stronger."

"Damn right."

"'Cause of Samira. She hassled a lot of people to get you that diet. So have faith, will you? And *you*." He turned his pointed finger at me. "Samira got your meds ready."

"How fast do they work?" I asked. "I'm giving a show—tomorrow morning, right before we leave."

The woman laughed, but Military Guy only shook his head. "Follow me."

I didn't feel pre-show jitters the way I used to. Perhaps it was the medication. It felt like lying down after a long day on tour, finally letting my muscles relax. No frantic back-and-forths, no triple-checking my equipment, no peeks at the audience.

That would've been difficult, anyway: only a handful of people knew we planned to perform in an hour.

"It's almost nice, knowing no one gives a damn," I told Vera and Ginta. We each had a container-turned-drum in our laps and were scribbling on them with black markers. Professionalism was too much to aim for, but we could at least avoid advertising frying oil and salted peanuts. While Vera and I went for all-black containers, Ginta clamped hers between her knees and used her one arm to black out the logo and draw elaborate patterns on the remaining white areas. Her shoulder kept jolting forwards when the container shifted, as if to reach for it, but she didn't say a word.

"Are you sure no one…" Vera's words faded.

Our flashlight was trembling. Just a quiver. I wouldn't have noticed if the light beam didn't amplify the movement. Another quake? I thought they'd tapered off by now.

The flashlight's trembling worsened. It skittered sideways across the table, a gentle *rat-rat-rat*. Across the room, something fell. A muted sound rumbled in the far distance.

"Are earthquakes this constant?" Vera asked.

"At least we're holding up okay," I said. Others seemed to come to the same conclusion; some had rushed to their cots and families, but most were talking in curious tones.

Ginta looked at the ceiling. "I wonder what it'll look like later. Outside."

"Did you hear?" Vera said. "The doctor's boyfriend and two others got special permission to scout outside.

They weren't supposed to tell anyone, but I heard—"

"I heard a hundred different things," I cut in. The ground was covered in rocks and dirt, no, the ground was cracked all over; not a single building remained upright, no, they were still standing, just broken skeletons; it was pitch dark, no, it was gloomy, no, you could see by the lightning storms and wildfires—

We'd find out in a few hours. That was soon enough.

I went back to scribbling on my container. "Let's just get ready."

Forty minutes later, a woman from shelter management climbed atop a table and asked us to gather round. "Nearly fifty minutes ago," she said, "we had to lock down the central air vents. Because…"

The room was mouse quiet. I sat upright, stretching as though it would let me hear her better.

"Because salt water was coming in via the vents." She cleared her throat. "The dunes and dikes must have given in. We're under—"

I couldn't hear the word "water" in the sudden screams.

But I didn't need to.

The good part was that we were no longer leaving the shelter that day.

The bad part was everything else.

We huddled together near the sisters' and their mother Inga's cots, clutching our few possessions tight as the shelter blurred in panic.

"Please!" someone shouted every few minutes. "Go to your beds and *wait*!"

"How long will the air last?"

"How much water are we talking about? Can we get to higher ground?"

Inga shook her head in disbelief. "Higher ground? Half this country is below sea level."

"How long are we *staying*? Is there enough food?"

"We'll have to ration even—"

"Is anyone coming?"

"Is it the entire coastline? My brother's in—"

"The oxygen!"

"Do the permanent shelters know? Does the government—"

"*Government*." Mum barked a laugh. "As though there still is one."

"There is," I said, "in those ships and shelters."

For all those screaming for answers, there were enough families just like us. Clustered together, quiet, nervous. A teen boy and his little brother leaned into each other. Their mum squeezed the younger boy's shoulder so tight it had to hurt.

I thought of the rations, barely sufficient to sustain and never enough to satisfy. Of candles shrinking into stubs, of flashlights starting to flicker. Only devices that ran on body heat would last.

We could ration flashlights. We couldn't ration air.

"Below sea level," Mum scoffed, "and they build underground shelters? How are we supposed to reach dry land? How far *is* dry land?"

"Tens of kilometres. A hundred? We don't know how far the water went." Dad shook his head. "We knew the risks when we decided to go the Netherlands."

Given the certainty of debris and earthquakes and the sun disappearing behind dust, we hadn't worried about the relatively slim chance of a flood—even then, it'd been worth being so far from the impact site and any volcanoes or fault lines. No other country would've taken us, besides. France and Switzerland had closed their shelters to refugees, so once we'd realised we couldn't reach England, it was too late to risk going south.

I supposed being stuck inside with limited food was better than being stuck outside where we'd need to scavenge for any food at all. But at least outside, there was a chance in the long run.

In here, there wasn't.

From the eyes of those two boys and their mother, I could tell they'd come to the same conclusion.

I abruptly stood. "Let's get ready."

My parents looked up.

"To leave?" Vera said.

"Nope."

Ginta had been talking to her mum in soft tones, but now glanced sideways. "You're joking."

"I'm not. Vera, where'd you leave those containers?"

*

Our audience-to-be had the same idea as Ginta.

Not at first. At first, they didn't even realise what was happening. But by the time we'd shoved a handful of similar-sized tables together to form an impromptu stage, climbed up, and Vera started hitting the containers, "you're joking" seemed to be the general impression.

Vera led us in, starting with a slow rhythm.

I wished I had a microphone to dramatically grab. Instead, I stepped forwards. My foot came down hard on the table. I raised my voice, kept it harsh and even for the intro, with Ginta providing a background hum.

Three times last night I woke
Three times last week I cried
Three times last month I fought
Three times in life I nearly died

A single slap on a container for emphasis. People were staring, grimacing, disbelieving. "Get off there!" someone called. I called back:

But: one too-short skirt I wear
and you know all there is to know
Nah: two crutches in my hands
and you know there's nothing left to know

"The hell is wrong with you?"

I missed amplification; an outfit that had been washed at any point in the past weeks; fans' joyful screams.

Here's what I had, though: those two boys staring, transfixed; Ginta backing up the next verse; my *own* screams.

Afterwards, I collapsed onto the nearest chair. "I miss my wheelchair," I huffed.

"No one's clapping." Vera stared at the audience. Most people had started ignoring us halfway through.

Ginta leaned against the table. "That was so cool."

"You were awesome. Both of..." I trailed off. My parents were elbowing through the still-anxious crowd towards us. Two others did the same: the woman who'd given the announcement earlier, and Ahmed, Samira's brother-in-law. Neither looked happy.

"Did you like the show?" I asked innocently.

"That was *not* appropriate," the woman said.

"I made sure the language was fine for kids. Can't people use a distraction?"

Ahmed eyed me sharply. "Keeping order in a place like this is difficult enough without"—he gestured at the tables—"*this.*"

"Especially after news like today's!" the woman added. "Any other time would've been fine, but this... this was..."

"Don't do it again," Ahmed said.

*

"We're doing it again, right?" I asked the sisters in line for lunch the next day.

Things had quieted down since the announcement that the water levels had stabilised and our air vents were no longer underwater.

We had air. But we were just as stuck, and just as hungry. The flood had left something tense and restless and scared in the atmosphere. It was one thing to wait—it was another thing to wait without knowing what you were waiting for, without knowing when or if or how it would even come.

I wanted to do more than *wait*.

"We totally are." Vera nodded vehemently. "Yesterday was great, but we can do better."

"You just want applause," Ginta teased.

My head snapped up at a commotion further down the line. Not that we had a "line"—more of an uncoordinated mess of people, with those who'd already gotten their food disappearing into a hall on the right, and everyone else pressing closer to the counters where volunteers were putting marks by our names and handing out our rations.

Near those counters, people were pushing and shouting. The rest of us surged back. I grabbed Vera to steady myself. There had been other scuffles—mostly people mad at others cutting in line—but the handful of volunteers standing on chairs and overlooking the hall kept an eye on those.

"'Scuse me? Sir?" I asked in English, tugging at the sleeve of the man ahead of us. "What's going on? We can't understand them."

"Nothing to worry about." He stared across the crowd with a frown. "I think there's a woman who got a different lunch from everyone else. They're saying she might've—ah—bribed people."

"I thought lots of people get different rations," I said. "If they have some sort of condition."

The man offered a sympathetic smile. "That might be it." He winced—as did the three of us—at a particularly loud shout. "But, well...they can't exactly get special meals once they leave, either. It's kind of a waste, isn't it?"

He turned back as the line surged forwards. I watched him fade into the crowd, and was still biting my lip when Vera said, "Same song, or did you have something else in mind?"

Afterwards, I spoke to Samira—who seemed glad to answer questions *other* than about what her fiancé had seen outside—and asked whether she'd be able to check for hydrocephalus better than my parents and I could.

"Not without equipment. Do you have a headache? Nausea?"

"Not really." I hesitated. "I wanted to know. In case."

"How's the pain?"

"Not gone, but *so* much better. But let's talk about something else"—I gave a quick drumroll and ba-*tish* on an imaginary drumset—"can I extend a personal invitation for my show later today?"

After a few hours of practice, we performed "The Yes and the No", which the sisters knew almost by heart, and which people in the hall knew, too. I assumed they did, anyway: some mouthed along, and others looked up, surprised, as though they'd heard their name being called.

"*Again?*" someone shouted. "Do you even realise—"

Conveniently, my next line had the word *jackass*. I placed extra emphasis on it.

I didn't know whether I expected applause this time. But when Samira—standing a dozen feet from the stage—started whooping and bouncing at the end of the song, I couldn't help a crooked smile.

Others hesitantly joined in. A few claps. A shout, "*Nice!*"

One person called out, "Are you that singer from Lithuania?"

"Latvia!" I shouted back. "And damn right I am. So are these two!" I swept an arm at Vera and Ginta.

Samira put her hands by her mouth and let out another whoop, though that wasn't enough to distract me from a pissed-off Ahmed stalking closer. He threw up his hands. "Come on. We asked you—"

"—to not perform right after bad news." I let Mum help me climb down. "You *did* say any other time would've been okay."

"Will you perform again?" While my parents and I stood in line for dinner, a lanky woman by Dad's side had kept glancing over. It looked like she'd finally scrounged up the courage to say something.

"You think we should?" I asked. My publicist would've been proud. *Turn back the question, keep your fans involved.* If I weren't stuck with a hundred others in a sweat-stenched, candlelit hall, waiting for a meal that would've barely passed as a healthy snack last year, I'd almost have felt like I was backstage in the Arēna Rīga again, signing autographs for eager fans.

"It's not really my kind of music. It's not bad... just...just young. But my daughter was in line for the bathroom at the time, and she was so mad she missed it."

"We'll do another one," I promised.

"Oh! She'll be thrilled. Let us know when?" She gave the location of their cots. "I'm Mandy, by the way."

"Line seems to be moving faster," Dad observed, in English so as to not be rude.

Mandy nodded, glancing from him to me as if confirming we were together. "They split things up. Parents with young kids have a separate line. So do people with different diets. And I think they asked anyone over fifty-five, or who can't handle crowds, to wait until after eight thirty to get in line."

"About time they figured that out," Dad said.

"'Can't handle crowds?' Oh, come *on*," a woman on the other side of Mandy scoffed. "I heard they're even delivering special meals to the med bay."

"Well, people are in there for a reason." Mum scrunched up her nose. "I heard there was a fight at lunch about a different diet. That must be why they split us up."

"It's such nonsense. Special diets? Come on. It's the end of the damn world. If even one percent of us ends up surviving, I'd call it a win."

I was glad to be hidden from the woman's sight behind my parents. She was right, of course. That was the whole problem.

She was right.

Dad didn't seem so convinced. Before he could say anything, the woman continued, on a roll. "I don't like it either, but you *know* those people will die within a week of setting foot outside. A day! What's the point in coddling them? We don't have enough food for everyone. We should set priorities, right? Focus on people with half a chance of surviving? I mean, look at those sick girls wasting energy on silly teen music— like there aren't more important—"

"Sick?" Dad said.

Silly? I mouthed.

Mandy stepped back, as if out of the line of fire.

"Well, you know! One of them was missing her arm. Another one, she could barely walk, and her shoulders were all..." I imagined the woman dropping one shoulder to form an uneven line.

"Stop talking," Mum said.

"I'm not saying—they're just teenagers, it's not like they *deserve* what's gonna happen, but we should be realistic—"

"No," Dad said. "Stop. *Talking.*"

Mum gripped my shoulder tight. I wanted to listen to her for once. Hide, not get involved, and not replay those words over and over.

Instead, I shoved past her until I could look the woman in the eye.

She froze.

"We're doing another show tomorrow. You should come. We all deserve some music before we die." I snapped my fingers. "Wait, you'll be with that surviving one percent, right? *So* sorry, your highness, truly. Didn't mean to lump you in with food hogs like me. Really, I ought to be lying down and dying for your convenience."

"I wasn't—" She seemed torn between apologising and digging in further. "I'm just *pragmatic.*"

"And that makes it okay. I completely understand." I offered her a spiteful-sweet smile. "I'm gonna enjoy wasting this meal on my crippled ass *so* bad."

*

That night, Mum and I bowed over my bare legs, holding a candle close.

I always had to check for injuries I might not feel, but normally, I did it in the privacy of my shower seat. Perhaps I should've cared that a hundred people could turn to see me half-nude on the bed; once, I would have. I'd have felt insecure over skinny, ghost-pale legs, over my KAFOs' imprints, over being unable to stand.

Now, I stared across the hall and idly thought, *I wonder where they got the supplies for that mural.* All across one wall stretched wild blotches of deep green forest. The rays of a setting sun cut between the trees, lighting up rough earth. Still-wet paint glistened in the candlelight.

"There's a cut here." Mum tapped the back of my calf.

I ran my fingers over it. A faint feeling of pain registered, almost like a bruise.

"You should get that doctor girl to disinfect it."

We finished checking the rest—nothing—then Mum grabbed the KAFOs again. With one of them in hand, she paused. She turned it over, fiddled with the knee joint. "What that woman said...in line for dinner."

I was still studying the mural. "She was charming, right?"

"You'll have it harder than most people once we leave, yes, but...it doesn't mean that..." Mum chewed her lip, for once at a loss for words.

"I know you won't make promises you can't keep."
I finally tore my eyes away, taking the KAFO from
Mum. "Thanks."

"I just *hate*..."

I'd had a lifetime of people looking at me in horror
or pity or with too-friendly smiles, or trying hard to
not look at me at all. Only the occasional person would
lean in and confide: *I couldn't deal. I'd kill myself if I
were you. How do you do it?*

That meant only the occasional person was
misguided enough to say it to my face. Didn't mean
no one else had that same thought, talking with their
friends over dinner: *You know, if it were me...*

The woman's words weren't news to either of us.
She was just the only person in the shelter to say it out
loud.

I looked past Mum at a dozen whispering families
clustered together in their beds.

"I know," I told her.

"You're doing *what*?"

"Shh, shh!" Samira looked into the main med bay to
see if I'd woken anyone. "You'll be fine without me. Dr
Kring is still weak, but he's sharp enough to give advice."

"Go back to the part where you're leaving the
shelter tonight. I thought outside was—"

"Parts of the shelter—like the air vents—reach
above the water level. We can exit safely."

"*Safely*! Nothing about that is safe!"

"The shelter has an inflatable raft. Ahmed has a hunch where we can find even better transport. If we reach other shelters, we can trade for food, flashlights—"

"They might've been badly shielded too. And they'd be just as stuck. Why would they have *food* left?"

"They could have working radios," Samira insisted.

"Radios." I blinked. Damn it—she was right. "Why you?"

"Because I won't let my fiancé go alone. And because we need to be able to trade something—like medical assistance."

"Well…you'll miss our next show."

Samira laughed and held up a medical spray. "Haul up your pant leg."

Word spread quickly.

By mid-afternoon the next day, everyone knew the following things:

Three people had killed themselves.

The med bay had been raided by someone convinced they had a food stash.

A young couple had left the shelter to seek help.

Those Latvian girls had another performance at five o'clock, in the sitting hall behind the kitchen.

"I don't know about this," Ginta said. "Maybe they're right. Is it in poor taste?"

Vera shook her head. "You kidding? Look, people

are already staking out spots. It might be their last chance to see a show. Besides, we're not the only ones performing. I saw these fifteen-year-old twins doing magic tricks for the kids, and a woman in the hall across sang opera this morning."

"Was it any good?" I asked.

"*Awful*," Vera said. "Just awful."

I smiled.

"Why the smile? Less competition?"

"It's…just nice to picture."

"Maybe we inspired her." Vera beamed. "See. Helping."

"You just want applause." Ginta sounded quietly annoyed.

"If I do," Vera said, "it's 'cause applause is a good indication that people are happy."

"It's fine if you just like applause, too," I said. "Any reason is fine."

"I don't even know mine." Ginta played with her empty sleeve. "I didn't have anything else to do. Is that awful? I enjoyed it, really, I just—"

"You're *good*," Vera said. "You really are."

I nodded. "You are. But if you weren't…"

Ginta glanced over.

"That opera singer didn't let it stop her, either."

Ten minutes before the show, Ahmed pulled me aside to speak with the woman from management.

"You can't cancel us," I said. "People are excited. We prepared a whole new song—"

Ahmed shook his head. "No, no. We need your help. You heard about what happened last night?"

"The med bay break-in?"

"Among other things. We were supposed to have left days ago. We're stretching food we barely have. We thought...you mentioned public speaking. You could help with an announcement about the rations. We won't last the way we've been going."

Eyes ceilingwards, the woman said, "We're not lasting anyway unless your brother finds help." She looked back at me. "An announcement would look better coming from—"

Ahmed cut her off with a glare.

"You could help," she amended.

I frowned. "I'm supposed to tell everyone they'll be even hungrier...so they won't get pissed at *you*?"

"That's not it." She hesitated. "People are agitated. There are fights, break-ins. The meal lines take forever. We're not simply cutting back, we're streamlining: everyone will get the same."

"What?"

"You wanted to keep people calm, right? Making exceptions doesn't help. It's not fair to everyone else. These shelters were built on a principle of equality—"

I laughed, short and high-pitched. The shelters' very existence proved the opposite. "I'm sorry. Okay, let's ignore anyone who's already underfed, ill, or injured, has diabetes or anaemia...I'm with you."

"Look, we can't help—if they—everybody should receive the same treatment."

"Except it's not the same if it hurts some but not others, is it? But I said I'm with you. *Do* go on."

Her lips pressed together. "Do you want to actually help? Or just keep yelling from atop a table?"

I stared at her long and hard. "You can come on stage after the show. But I'm *not* making your announcement."

Ginta dropped out. "I can't focus. I'm sorry. I'll cheer really loudly, though."

Vera would take over for the few lines that needed backing vocals the most. Her voice wasn't as good as Ginta's, and she was overexcited, rattling off the lines too fast.

"Don't worry about that, okay?" Mum said before helping me on stage. "People won't even notice."

"I wasn't worried," I said.

"Oh. Forget I said anything, then."

"Is that weird?" I wondered suddenly. "We're doing this for them. Shouldn't I care more about what they think?"

"Are you?" she asked. "Doing it for them?"

At a loss for an answer, I let her help me onto the table.

"Go. Kick ass," Mum said. "And enjoy."

On stage, Vera and I looked out at the crowd. A few dozen people stood near the tables. Even behind them, people had gone quieter than usual. Many looked up with interest.

I took a deep breath. "Shelter management has an announcement after the show. Stick around."

A few people murmured to each other. Vera was eying me, waiting for the signal—a flick of my hand—to begin. Previously, we'd dived right in.

I didn't give the signal. "So...some of you were already familiar with my music. A lot of you probably didn't want to be, but were stuck in the room yesterday. Hope you're converts now. P.S., buy my album."

Scattered laughter sounded at the back of the room.

"Yes, thank you. That was, indeed, a joke." I gestured at a laughing person, who might've been Ginta. "If you listened to the lyrics—I promise it's not *just* yelling—you'll know where I stand on the idea of equality." I sought out the woman from management in the crowd. When our gazes locked, I offered a nod.

She nodded back, encouraging.

"Equality means that...even if we're not the same, we get the same chances.

"But here's the thing. People like me, or like those in the med bay—I'm not confident about our survival chances. I know you aren't, either." I shifted my weight. "You can't promise us we'll live. I get that. But you *can* promise us that, if we *don't* survive, it's not 'cause you didn't give us an equal chance. It's not 'cause you sped it along."

My parents were restraining the management woman from coming towards me. My chin jutted out. A grin spread across my lips. I didn't know if my words would change the rations, if they would rile people up further, if they would make any difference at all.

What I did know was this: "I'm not writing us off."

I gave a flick of my hand and plunged us into music.

To Take into the Air My Quiet Breath

Stephanie Gunn

A priest once told my sisters, Annalee and Eliza, that God put flowers in their lungs to make them beautiful.

Roses, he'd said, sixty-five of them. He smiled at Mama, as if to say: look, see how I understand that they are too young to pronounce cystic fibrosis.

That night, Eliza woke screaming, babbling about roses growing in her lungs, thorns tearing at her throat. One long scream twisted into a wet gurgle, then blood gushed from her lips.

As her sister fought for breath, Annalee slipped her small hand into mine. Her fingers were cold, her nails blue. She was careful not to lean on my scarred right arm.

"Georgie," she said, "why would God put flowers in our lungs, if it makes it so hard for us to breathe?"

Eliza's phone rings, waking me from a restless sleep.

It's that awful ring tone the kids were all

downloading before the flu: the sound of a British air raid siren from World War II.

Eliza is awake, her eyes wide. The phone's light catches on her nasal cannula, on the tubing feeding into it from her oxygen concentrator. She's sixteen years old and every breath of every one of those years has been a struggle.

It's been a good night, at least. She managed to get to sleep without her CPAP, a machine that delivers constant air pressure to keep her clogged lungs open. We might finally have beaten her latest infection.

The air raid siren sounds again. Across the room, Annalee sleeps on, her breathing deep and clear. For once, she was out working on the farm all day, and is too exhausted to wake, I suppose.

Eliza picks up the phone just as it falls silent. "No signal now. Caller unknown."

She coughs, the sound congested and wet. Swearing beneath my breath, I pull myself out of bed, find the wind-up torch. The air in the room is warm and close, and the fabric of my long-sleeved nightgown clings to me, damp and sweat-sour. I envy the twins their sleeveless nightgowns, light clothes which are not an option for me.

"Have you slept at all?" I ask Eliza as I set up the CPAP.

Eliza's only answer is continued coughing.

"Another course of IVs." I hand Eliza the CPAP mask, start with the IV. At least I can run antibiotics via the portacath in Eliza's chest, rather than attempting her scarred veins. "This will clear it. I promise."

Eliza has to know I'm lying. Before, she'd planned on applying for medical school if she got a lung transplant, and she knows her disease through and through. But she nods and smiles as I start the IV.

From the other side of the room comes Annalee's voice, "It was the black phone, wasn't it?"

Eliza has two phones. Her pink one is identical to the one Annalee uses only for listening to music now. The second, plain and black, Mama bought for communication with the lung transplant centre. A call on that phone would only come if the hospital had lungs for Eliza.

When the networks went down, Eliza stopped charging her pink phone. She always keeps the black phone charged.

I climb back into bed. "The hospital stopped running months ago. It was probably just the phone glitching."

Annalee turns towards the wall, scratches at the scars beneath her breasts. A year ago, Annalee was the one holding the black phone. After it rang, the doctors sawed through her ribs, opened up her chest like the petals of a flower, planted a dead man's lungs in her. Saved her life.

It's a long time that night before I can sleep properly again. I keep starting awake, thinking that I hear an air raid siren echoing through the darkness.

*

The basket, heavy with eggs and tomatoes, strains my good arm as I lift it onto the kitchen bench. It's hot, and I'm sweating in my jeans and jacket. I drink a glass of water to cool down, glad for the bore and tanks that keep us supplied.

My right arm aches badly this morning, pain a tight band around my elbow. The scarring spirals around the joint, thickened skin and muscle contractures keeping me from fully straightening my arm. More than once I've been tempted to slice through the scars, just so I could stretch properly.

I crack eggs into a bowl, wondering how Annalee will reject them this morning. Yesterday she wanted potato chips, the day before it was Coke and Tim Tams. Anything but what we have.

As though summoned by my thoughts, Annalee pads into the kitchen. She's developed the habit of wearing Bryce's old clothes, and she swims in the oversized T-shirt and shorts. As always during waking hours, her earbuds are in, noise leaking out.

Predictably, she makes a face at the eggs.

"There's bread," I say. "Butter and preserves."

"*Goat* butter," she says without removing her earbuds. "And it's *damper*, not bread. Can we at least have tea?"

"If you want tea, you make it."

Annalee's eyes slide to the starburst of scars on my right cheek, the only part of my scars that she and Eliza have ever seen. She makes no move towards the kettle.

"If you want to help, you can slice the tomatoes," I say.

The big chef's knife sits on the side of the sink. Annalee looks at it, quickly turns away. "My hands hurt from Eliza's therapy."

Eliza's physiotherapy loosens the thick mucus in her lungs, making it easier for her to cough up and clear her airways. She used to have a vest that achieved the same effect, but the motor burned out a week into our isolation. Now, it's manual therapy only: an hour or more of pounding on her chest and back several times a day.

Annalee picks up a tomato. They grow soft in the heat, and juice pools around her fingers when she presses them in. "We should go into the city. If the phones are working, other things might be back. There might be *real* food."

I crack another egg. This one has two blood spots in the white, the spots joined by a thin thread. "Have you checked everything?"

Annalee slumps. One of the few duties she doesn't shirk—along with Eliza's therapy—is checking all forms of communication every morning. Her reaction tells me that everything is silent, as it has been for months.

"The last thing the emergency channel said was for people to stay inside and wait." I whisk the eggs, pour them into a pan. "Mama and Bryce said the same. We wait here until someone comes or we hear something official."

"But we didn't even get sick when—"

"I don't want to hear it!" I pick up the knife, try to ignore the way the steel always feels greasy beneath my fingers, no matter how much I wash it. "We just have to wait."

Annalee's eyes fix on the ghost gums visible through the kitchen window. The trees sway in a breeze that doesn't reach the house. "I've spent my whole life waiting. For a cure. For a transplant. And for what?"

Her fingers tighten on the tomato. The skin breaks with a wet pop, seeds and juice squirting onto the bench. Annalee lets the tomato fall into its own spilled guts and leaves the room, shaking seeds from her fingers as she goes.

I stare at the fallen seeds, then set to scraping them up so they can be replanted. Some of them have already germinated, pale sprouts uncurling like worms.

I'm finishing the omelettes when Eliza comes into the kitchen. She pushes her IV pole with one hand, drags her oxygen concentrator with the other. As always, there's a relief in seeing her upright, still breathing. She pauses in the doorway, then circles the kitchen.

Every morning, Eliza and I make the same circuit of the room. We pause at the window first, looking out at the path leading to the house, the ghost gums beyond. Then around the table, and back to stand over the bloodstain on the floor, faded but never gone completely, no matter how much it was scrubbed.

The window was where Uncle Bryce was standing when he fell, dead from a heart attack a month into our isolation. It was also the place where, several months later, we saw the stranger approaching the house. Eliza and I were reading at the table, Mama in the kitchen making dinner, Annalee off on the farm. The stranger burst in, flung himself over the table and coughed once, right into Eliza's face. I will never forget the black stink of his breath: rotting blood, liquefying flesh.

In the kitchen, Mama fought off the stranger, a fight which ended with him running and her on the floor, the big chef's knife between her ribs. The knife vibrated with the rhythm of her heart, slowing and slowing, going still.

I buried Mama next to Bryce, both of them beneath the ghost gums. As I worked, black smoke plumed into the sky near the city, began creeping closer.

We knew the incubation period of the flu was seven to ten days. Eliza and I crossed off the days, watched the fire creep closer and closer to the farm. Annalee hid in her room the whole time, silent, waiting.

The fire came closer and closer, the sky filling with black and ash raining down on the farm. The wind changed, turning the flames away just short of the ghost gums. The incubation period passed, and none of us fell ill.

Her circuit complete, Eliza settles herself at the table, starts counting out pills for herself and Annalee.

"What happens when the medicine runs out?" Annalee asks from the next room. Some trick of air or architecture makes it sound as though her voice is coming from the space between the walls. "It won't last forever. And everything has an expiry date."

Mama scrounged extra prescriptions when she still could. Later, Bryce went out and ransacked houses and pharmacies, driving the car at first then switching to a horse and cart. Thanks to them, we have cartons of antibiotics, antifungals, antivirals, steroids and immunosuppressants. Case upon case of pancreatic enzymes, vitamins, sterile saline and syringes. Spare nebulisers, boxes and boxes of batteries. Mama catalogued everything in a small green notebook, kept records of every dose. Eliza keeps those records now.

Eliza finishes with the meds, updates the notebook, then fetches a jar of preserves from the pantry. Apricot, which she hates and Annalee loves. As she sits down again, her breath catches and she coughs hard.

She coughs and coughs, her ribs thrusting out against her shirt with every inhalation. It looks as though her bones are trying to press through her skin, break free. As her lungs fail, her ribcage expands more and more, her body doing everything it can to help her breathe.

I go to the pantry, get a can of Ensure. We've hoarded the supplement drink for emergencies, and I expect Eliza to argue with me about drinking it, but she just takes the can.

"An extra nebuliser after breakfast," I say. "And I'll do a longer therapy session after lunch. We can—"

I break off as the air raid siren sounds again.

For a moment, I think I am hallucinating, but then Annalee bursts into the room, the black phone in her hand.

"I couldn't get to it fast enough," she says. The phone buzzes, and her eyes go wide. "It was the hospital. There's a message."

She hands the phone to Eliza, who plays the message. A woman's calm tone fills the room, asking that Miss O'Grady attend the hospital as soon as possible, because the transplant centre has lungs for her.

I don't want to leave the farm, but we have no real choice. If there's the smallest chance that there are lungs for Eliza, we have to go.

We load the cart, make a nest of blankets in the back for Eliza among the hay for the horses. I hook up her oxygen concentrator to portable solar batteries. When the girls aren't looking, I fetch the chef's knife from the kitchen, slide it beneath the bench seat of the cart.

We stop at the graves beneath the ghost gums. I haven't been down here since I buried Mama, and last time I saw it there were only scraggly weeds and dust here. All of that has been cleared away. A well-tended carpet of flowers grows over both graves: poppies, daisies, lavender, alyssum.

This is Annalee's work; I know it. I turn to her, wanting to say something, but she looks away, plugs her ears with her earbuds.

I sigh and turn the horses towards the road.

"There's someone there," Eliza says.

We've been travelling for several hours through the fire-seared land, trading the reins between Annalee and myself so the other can rest or tend to Eliza. Though Annalee has done precious little of the latter, spending most of her time in the back of the cart sleeping. She's asleep again now, curled up, head on Eliza's lap.

Though it has been months since the fire, nothing has grown in the black. The ash is packed hard, and the air holds an odd, acrid scent. Even the asphalt of the road has changed, becoming something almost glassine and making a strange hollow sound beneath the horses' hooves.

Eliza points again at the side of the road. At first, I think it's a statue I see there, the girl is so still. Despite the heat, she's wearing an oversized jumper, thin legs bare beneath its ravelled hem. She has her arms tucked into the body of the garment, the jumper's empty arms trailing by her sides. Green shoots push up out of the ash at her feet. They are the first plant life I have seen since we entered the blackened land.

"Are you real?" the girl asks. There are heavy circles beneath her eyes, but she doesn't look sick as far as I can see, just tired and malnourished.

I slow the cart, but I don't stop, my hands tight on the reins.

Then the girl pulls down the neck of her jumper, and I stop the cart.

The girl has a baby strapped to her chest beneath the jumper. Curled in a sling, it is suckling at her breast, eyes half closed. Like her, it's too thin, but there's no sign of the flu.

"Ben left us," the girl says. "He took everything. The tent, the food, all..." Her hands clutch at the baby. It unlatches and makes a soft mewling sound, too weak to properly cry. "He said he was gonna look after us, but he lied, didn't he?"

I'd guess the girl is maybe fourteen, half Japanese. She has the kind of delicate face I always ached for, beautiful even when filthy and hungry. The twins have that kind of beauty, too, their gold hair and blue eyes just like Mama's. I'm all dull brown, my features too coarse, too masculine. Too much like Pa.

Eliza pulls a can of Ensure from a box, holds it out.

"Those are for emergencies," I say.

Eliza ignores me. "It tastes kind of gross warm, but it'll help." She glances at me. "The hospital will have more."

"The hospital?" the girl asks. "It's running again?"

"We're not sure," I say.

"It is," Eliza says, her voice as forceful as her failing lungs can manage.

"Can I...can I come with you?" the girl asks. "I think the baby might be sick."

"Sick how?" I ask. "The flu?"

The girl shakes her head. "She just keeps getting skinnier, no matter how much I feed her."

"You can come with us," Eliza says, shaking Annalee awake.

Annalee drags herself into the front of the cart. Her hair is tangled, sweat-damp, and she glances only blearily at the girl before curling up as best as she can on the bench seat and closing her eyes again.

"Eliza, we should—" I start.

"Georgie, it's a baby," Eliza says.

I've already lost this argument. I nod, and the girl climbs into the cart. Her eyes skate over my long sleeves and high collar, linger on the scars on my cheek, my always-bent right arm.

"It was an accident," Eliza says. "Georgie was trying to make tea on her own when she was little, and the kettle was too heavy. She spilled the boiling water over herself."

When I breathe in, I taste smoke and whiskey. My

scars itch, and my elbow aches. "Yes." The lie lingers on my tongue like chamomile tea steeped too long and gone to bitterness. "An accident."

As we move again, Eliza starts coughing.

The girl pulls her jumper down over the baby again. "Are you sick? Is it the flu?"

Annalee reaches into the cart and starts setting up Eliza's nebuliser. "It's cystic fibrosis. You can't catch it." She hands the nebuliser to Eliza. "I'm Annalee, and this is Eliza and our older sister Georgie."

"I'm Mari," the girl says. "The baby doesn't have a name. Just Baby. It didn't seem worth giving her a name, with the world the way it is."

We move out of the black and into the suburbs of Melbourne.

Everything is still and silent. Occasionally we pass houses gutted by fire, and once we pass a house that's tented entirely with red fabric. Most of the houses are intact, doors and windows closed, curtains pulled tight. Cars are parked carefully in driveways and garages. If not for the weed-choked gardens, I could almost believe that these were still real houses, not the tombs I know them to be.

We stop to rest in a place that had once been a park. The grass is long, browning in the sun. It crunches beneath my feet as I stomp down a flat space in the shade of a eucalypt. At the other end of the park, there's a swing set still standing. English ivy, escaped from a nearby garden, covers the slide. Despite the heat, the ivy leaves are glossy and green. I find myself hating that plant.

The twins eat and take their meds, and Mari drinks another Ensure. I tend to the horses while Annalee does Eliza's therapy. She pauses to rest often enough that I wonder if she's accomplishing anything, but Eliza doesn't complain. I sit down in the shade, sip water, press my unscarred cheek against the eucalypt's cool bark.

The horses crop placidly at their hay, seemingly unperturbed by the silence. When things were bad, you could always find Mama with the horses. I can almost see her with them now, stroking their manes and crooning to them.

The image twists, becomes Mama lying on the kitchen floor, the big knife between her ribs. Sour bile rises in my throat. Maybe Mari was right, not naming her daughter. What hope do any of us have for a real future in this world?

I lie back, gaze up at the tree and time my breath to the swaying of the branches. It always fascinates me, the way the forking limbs of a tree look like the air passages in lungs. From this angle, I can see that one branch of the tree is withered, the leaves all grey and twisted. Disease, I'd think, though the rest of the tree seems healthy.

The twins and Mari are lying in the shade, their eyes closed. The shifting light catches on the edge of the knife's handle, just visible beneath the bench seat. Three steps and I could have it in my hand. Three cuts for them, two for my wrists, one more for Baby. It would be almost painless. A relief. Easy.

I close my eyes and mind to those thoughts. Somehow I sleep, and the next thing I'm aware of is jerking awake. The twins are still sleeping, curled together, Eliza's oxygen concentrator humming. Mari and Baby are nowhere to be seen.

I look around, and finally see Mari emerge from a nearby house. Mari has tied her jumper around her waist, revealing a sleeveless dress. Baby is strapped to her chest, asleep. Mari holds a bunch of silk flowers. Red roses, faded at one side as though they have been too long standing in a window. She places them down next to the twins, then comes and sits beside me.

Her arms uncovered, I see the scars that ladder her from wrist to elbow. Some are thin, silvered with age, but others are angry-red and knotted, the scar tissue thick enough that the original cuts must have been savage and deep. There are marks in the crooks of both elbows, yellowing bruises centred on black pinpricks. Mari's upper arms are unscarred, but they are not unmarked. Someone—Mari, I think, judging by the crookedness of the design—has inked a pattern of red flowers. The flowers are not quite roses, the petals toothed and jagged.

Mari bumps a finger up the scars on her forearms. "I was sad a lot, before." She touches one of the bruised marks. "Ben said it would make things better. Make me forget about my family dying, all of it. There's lots of stuff lying around, if you know where to look."

"Did it? Make things better?"

Mari's eyes are far away. "It did, and then it didn't." She pulls at a thread dangling from her jumper's hem. "Ben always insisted on keeping everything. He was the one who showed me where to look, what to do. I siphoned off some when I could, kept it hidden. Not much, just enough that Baby and I could just go to sleep if things got too bad. I thought he didn't know, but I guess he did, because he took that when he left, too." The thread comes free, drifts to the ground. "Do you think that makes me a bad person, that I even thought of that? Of killing my daughter?"

I glance over at the twins, think of the knife in the cart. Fumble for a subject change. "Do you know why Ben left?"

Mari shrugs a shoulder, bones moving beneath flower-marked skin. "He always wanted to go north, but I didn't want to leave the city. I guess he got tired of waiting for me to change my mind." She pulls another thread from her jumper. "I had a cousin with cystic fibrosis. He lived in Japan, and I never met him. He died when he was sixteen, and my mother brought me to Japan for the funeral. I met my grandmother for the first time then, too. She was in Hiroshima when they dropped the bomb. The heat of the explosion burned the pattern of the kimono she'd been wearing onto her skin. Flowers, burned into her." She traces the flowers on her shoulder, red ink smudging beneath her finger. "They called her *hibakusha*, her and everyone who was there when the bomb fell. Said they were cursed." She traces the shape of petals on Baby's cheek; Baby doesn't wake. "Maybe we've been cursed, too."

One of Baby's hands has worked its way out of the sling as she sleeps. Her nails are tinged blue. She's not getting enough oxygen.

Something sparks in me. "This might sound weird, but have you ever tasted Baby's skin?"

Mari blinks. "She tastes salty. How did you know?"

"Salty skin is one of the ways CF was diagnosed before we knew about the genetics of it," I say. "You and Ben could both have been carriers, like my parents. Like me."

"You think Baby's sick like the twins? Like my cousin?" Mari's hands tighten on Baby. Baby's eyelids flutter, but she still doesn't wake. "You think she's going to die?"

"Even if she does have it, CF is treatable. People live a lot longer now, so long as they start treatment when they're babies." Mama's words in my mouth, things she had said to me over and over. "I was six when the twins were born, and I remember everything Mama did for them. Calorie supplements, enzymes, vitamins. The hospital will have everything we need." I try not to listen to the voice whispering in the back of my mind, reminding me that only a short while ago I was certain that there was nothing out there, that I was thinking that a handful of cuts would bring relief. "You got lucky finding us. Baby will be okay. I promise."

Mari relaxes slightly. "I wanted to be an artist, before. Took all these classes. Seems pathetic now. I bet you did something useful. Nursing, maybe. Teaching."

I look up at the tree above us. The light is catching in the withered branch. There are new shoots emerging from its tip, but the leaves are already blackening. "I did odd jobs. Mowing lawns, weeding, that kind of thing. I wanted to study agriculture, really. I wanted to learn about trees. How they breathed, how they grew."

"Why didn't you?"

"I got accepted at university, but I kept deferring. Mama and the twins needed me more. I thought that maybe after Eliza had a transplant, and they didn't need me as much, I'd go."

Mari is staring at my neck. I reach up, realise that my collar has shifted, exposing the place in the hollow of my collarbone where the scars are gnarled and thick as old wood.

"If you'd spilled the kettle on yourself, you wouldn't have scars there." Mari holds Baby close, her body tense again.

Baby's dark eyes open, fix on me. I need Mari to trust me if I'm to help them. "The twins were diagnosed with CF at birth. I guess Pa couldn't deal with it, because he left us. He'd walked out before, but Mama thought that it was for good this time. And it was hard for her, dealing with the twins on her own. I wanted to help. I was strong, and I always knew to lift the kettle with both hands." If I close my eyes, I can still see the pale blue Formica counter, Mama's favourite cup with the pink roses, the chamomile tea in the yellow box. Some part of me wonders why I'm telling a virtual stranger this story, when I've never told anyone, not even my sisters. Maybe it's because Mari has scars, too. Maybe it's simply because we might be the last people in the world. "I'd just boiled the kettle and poured water into Mama's cup when the door opened. It was Pa, drunk and reeking of smoke and whiskey. He didn't say anything, just picked up the kettle and poured the rest of the boiling water over me. He stared at me, then turned and left. I never saw him again." I touch the scar on my collarbone, feeling nothing but a faint pressure. "It didn't even start to hurt until after he'd left."

Mari relaxes slightly. She doesn't look shocked. She looks as though I've just confirmed something she's always suspected about the world. "Why did he do it?"

I shrug, the scars pulling. "I don't know. Maybe he was drunk and didn't know what he was doing. Maybe he just hated me."

There's a soft sound behind me. I turn and see that Eliza is awake. The look in her eyes tells me that she's heard everything.

*

Eliza insists that I lie in the back of the cart with her when we get moving again. I expect her to talk but she says nothing, just lies there looking up at the sky.

I turn away from her, watch Annalee teaching Mari how to steer the horses. I slide from wakefulness into sleep slowly, like sinking into a warm pool.

I dream of fighting my way through a labyrinth of roses. The plants are old, so tangled that I cannot tell where one ends and the next begins. There is no form to them, no branching symmetry, just a haphazard tangle that I tear at with my bare hands. Thorns tear at my clothing, strip away layers of fabric until I am naked, all of my scars exposed.

When I wake, the cart is still, the space next to me empty. I pull myself out, see Eliza and Annalee sitting together leaning against the side of the cart. Annalee has her earbuds in and her eyes closed, and Eliza is doing a nebuliser treatment. The horses are tethered to a nearby gate, shaded by a eucalypt. It is diseased like the tree in the park, except this eucalypt has two branches withering away. Mari is nowhere to be seen again.

"Why have we stopped?" I ask Eliza. "Are you okay?"

Eliza points. Beyond the nearby houses, the bulk of the hospital rises up against the sky. The sun is beginning to set, the thickening light reflecting off the windows, obscuring what is inside. The hospital looks intact, and relief washes through me. We made it. Everything will be okay, now.

"We should keep moving," I say. "What house did Mari go into?"

Eliza lowers her nebuliser. Her lips are blue, shining from the steam. "She said she couldn't stay." Her voice is breathy. Whatever infection she's fighting, it's eating her lung function fast. "She said she couldn't watch Baby die."

I step to the side, see that Baby is curled up between the twins, asleep in her sling. A single silk rose is clutched in her hand.

"I tried to stop her," Eliza says. "I couldn't stand up without getting dizzy."

I scan the buildings around us. Mari could be in any one of them, could be peering out at us through a crack in the curtains right now.

"Mari!" I call.

There is no answer. And I know suddenly that even if Mari is in one of these houses, she's not looking out at us. She said that there's lots of "stuff" lying around if you know where to look. I'm certain that she's found what she was looking for. That she's probably lying in some dusty room, the rest of the silk flowers in her hands. That she won't be coming back.

I should feel angry at her for abandoning Baby. But there's no anger, just a kind of grey numbness. Eliza is watching me, her breathing rapid and shallow.

"We should get you to the hospital," I say. "Get you on decent oxygen." I shake Annalee. "Wake up, Annalee. Time to get moving."

Annalee doesn't respond.

The anger comes now. Annalee was listening to her music while Mari was abandoning her child. Has been listening to her music while I work to keep her and Eliza alive, while her twin sister has been dying. While the world has been ending.

I yank the earbuds from Annalee's ears. Static spills from the tiny speakers. No music, just white noise that rises and falls like waves beating against rocks. Is this what she's been listening to all along?

Annalee still hasn't moved. I touch her forehead, and immediately snatch my hand away. Annalee has a fever, a high one, her skin dry and hot. Have I exposed her to some new sickness, taking her away from the farm?

There's something in Eliza's eyes that reminds me of the static still spilling from Annalee's earbuds.

I switch off Annalee's phone. The resulting silence feels heavy, a tangible weight on the back of my neck. "We need to get her to the hospital."

I help Eliza into the cart, then turn to Annalee. I brace myself to take her weight, but as I lift her, I almost tumble backwards. She's lost weight, a lot of it, her habit of wearing Bryce's baggy clothes hiding the loss. This is no sudden illness, but something that has burned beneath her skin for weeks, maybe months.

"How long has she been sick?" I ask, nestling Baby between the twins again. She's awake, though she doesn't react to anything until I try taking the flower out of her hand. Then, her fingers grip tight.

Eliza shrugs a shoulder. "I don't know."

"Has she been taking her meds?"

Eliza's eyes slide from mine.

I look up at the dying branches of the eucalypt above us. At the junction between healthy tree and diseased, the bark is swollen, bleeding oil. This isn't an infection. This is organ rejection.

"We only lowered the doses a little," Eliza says. "Just to make the meds last longer. I calculated everything. I thought we'd be okay."

It feels like something is falling inside of me. I trusted Eliza to manage the medication, treating her as though she were a doctor, not a sixteen-year-old girl. "You should have told me."

"You should have told us what Pa did," she throws back.

I hitch the horses to the cart, wrap the reins around my hands. Pull the leather tight enough to hurt. "You had enough to deal with."

"So did you."

The cart bumps as we start moving again, and Baby cries. The sound echoes and echoes around us, until it sounds as though the whole world is weeping.

I visualise what it's going to be like. The whole hospital might not be running. The emergency department, maybe one or two wards. The transplant unit.

The woman who called will be waiting for us. She will be blonde, I decide, with kind eyes and cool, soft hands.

Everything will be okay. Someone is going to look after us.

I almost believe it, too, until we turn the last corner and see the front of the hospital for the first time.

The angle of our approach gave the illusion that the building was intact, but from here, I can see that only that side of the hospital is whole. Everything else is gone, the bulk of the building replaced by a crater. The sides of the crater are smooth and black as obsidian. On the edge of the crater stands a eucalypt, all of its branches withering away. Everything smells bitter, the air I breathe in searing the back of my throat.

Beyond the hospital, as I look north, I can see other craters, whole suburbs reduced to black. It looks like half of the city is gone.

This isn't just the flu. Something else has happened. A war, maybe. I wish Bryce or Mama were here. They would know.

"This isn't how it's supposed to be," Eliza says. "Bryce always said the hospital would be up and running again by now. He *said*."

My scars are itching. I rub my arm, think of Mari's grandmother, of flowers burned into her skin. "The phone just glitched. That's all it was."

A pause. "No, it wasn't."

I turn to face Eliza. She's looking at Annalee, still sleeping—or unconscious—beside her.

"It was an old message," Eliza says. "I kept it. I made the phone ring that first time, too. It was the only way I could get you to leave the farm."

I stretch out my arm, pushing against contracted muscle and skin until it feels as though my flesh is tearing. The pain is good. It distracts me from being angry at Eliza, reminds me that she's sixteen years old, that she was only trying to save her sister.

"We'll go back to the farm," I say. "We can run steroids by IV for Annalee, and hopefully that will reverse the rejection."

Eliza touches the silk flower Baby still holds. "What about Baby?"

"We have powdered milk. For everything else, we'll have to make do."

I can hear Annalee's voice in my mind: *what do we do when the meds run out? Everything has an expiry date.*

Everything, including us. At least on the farm it's safe and familiar. And in the end, if it comes to it, there's always the knife.

"Can we rest?" Eliza asks. "Just for a while? I should do therapy."

I don't want to stay here, so close to the black crater, but I nod, turn the cart away from the hospital. Three streets away, we come to a house that had once been lovely: white with green trim, a garden full of roses. The windows of the house have been boarded up, nails weeping tears of rust down the wood. In the garden, there are no flowers left, just brittle leaves and spindly stems, thickets of thorns.

There, in that dead garden, Eliza starts an IV of steroids and fluids for Annalee. I manage to get Baby to take some water, then do Eliza's therapy.

After, Eliza sips on an Ensure, Baby sleeping in her lap. Twilight is descending, the sky deep violet. In the world before, it would have been an idyllic scene. Now, it just feels like an ending. Life, sliced through with a steel knife.

Eliza touches a rose leaf. Her fingers come away covered with powdery ash. "The roses are all gone. There's only thorns left now. Everything else is dead or dying."

The light shifts as the moon rises over the horizon. It's full, the silvery light bathing the small garden with a pure, clear light.

Two things happen at once.

The moonlight pierces deeper into the tangled roses than the fading sunlight had. By its light, I can see a tiny rosebud, its petals tightly furled. And then I see another, and another: a dozen of them, several opening to show white petals.

And the sound of an air raid siren breaks through the still of the evening.

Eliza's black phone is in the cart. By the time I find it, it's stopped ringing.

"That wasn't me," Eliza says. "Not this time."

I hand the phone to her. My scars are itching more, almost unbearable now.

"It's a Queensland number," Eliza says. "Someone else is out there."

I rub at the scars through my sleeves. It isn't enough; the itching feels as though it goes bone-deep. I breathe in, catch the scent of the new roses, breathe out slowly. Push my sleeves up to my elbows. It feels as though I am stripping away my skin, but the itching stops.

Eliza looks at my exposed scars, her fingers gripped tight around the black phone. "Are we still going back to the farm?"

I reach into the tangled roses, brush my fingers against the petals of a flower They're smooth and soft and warm, like unscarred skin. "No. No more waiting for someone to save us. In a minute, we'll call that number back. For now, just breathe."

Something in the Rain

Seanan McGuire

The end of the world was a misnomer. "The end of the age of humanity" would have been a better way of putting it, like the way we used to talk about "the end of the age of the dinosaurs." Or maybe "the end of the first age of humanity, you know, the one where they fucked everything up." We could still come back. The ballgame wasn't over yet, just the first nine innings, with the remains of the species clinging for dear life to the last few seconds of overtime. We could still pull it out, if we worked.

We weren't going to. I knew that. Everyone knew that. When the comet hit the dinosaurs, they were staring blankly at the sky, trying to figure out what that glowing light was. Humanity, we knew exactly what was coming. We'd seen it on the news and we'd read about it in the papers. Even my mum knew about it, and she was always Suzie Sunshine, refusing to admit that anything could ever be less than perfect. "They'll figure something out before it gets bad enough that we need to worry," she'd said. "They'll find a way to put things right, and then everything will be fine. You'll see. Now take your pills."

That was how she ended every sentence with me for years: "now take your pills." Even when it wasn't time for pills, even when I'd taken them hours ago, "now take your pills" was her solution and panacea for everything. Maybe she thought that once they built up in my system, I'd somehow be cured, and she could finally have the perfect little family she had always dreamed of. Mum always was one for magical thinking.

The planet didn't know that most of the mammals were gone—or maybe it *did* know, and it was happy about it. It didn't matter much. The world kept spinning and the sun kept rising, and while there were no clocks around worth trusting anymore, I had a copy of *The Farmer's Almanac*, and I had a window that faced east. Every day, the sunrise woke me, and I looked up the time. That kept things running steady. If I knew what time I started, I would know what time it *was* until I fell asleep and my clock reset itself again.

The last of the night rain lingered in the yard until 8:52 AM—four minutes longer than the day before, and six minutes longer than the day before that. Winter was coming, and stretching the bad weather out like a rubber band that wouldn't snap back until summer. I moved as close to the window as I dared, squinting up at the sky—the colour of a third-day bruise, all watery yellow and damaged apricot. Two morning rains today, then, one in an hour or so, a second right around noon. The first rain would be clean, or close enough to it. The first rain of the day always was. The bad stuff fell out during the night, and it took a little while for it to build up again. That didn't mean the rain was *safe*—clean didn't mean the same as safe anymore, if it ever had—but meant I could go out a little, if I was quick and careful.

Two raincoats, a roll of plastic wrap around my legs where they met my rain boots, and a pair of latex gloves later, I looked like something out of a low-budget horror movie, but I was as close to waterproof as it was possible to be. I clomped toward the door, where my umbrella and plastic kiddy-wagon awaited. The cat was there too. She yowled when she saw me unlocking the door. I pushed her back with my foot, offending her dignity so much that she went off to sulk in the kitchen, well away from any escape.

"Sorry, kitty, but you might be the last kitty in the whole world, and I don't want to lose you," I said. She couldn't understand me, of course, but I felt better for having said it out loud. I wasn't sure what I would do if I lost Kaylee. She was the last really good thing in the world, and she kept me from giving up on my eastward-facing room and my dwindling supply of pills in favour of sleeping someplace dark and swallowing only what I *wanted* inside my body, instead of what I needed. If I couldn't stay alive for her, who would I be staying alive for?

Me. And I knew I didn't deserve it. So I checked the tape sealing my gloves, and I checked the plastic wrapped around my legs, and I checked three times to be sure that the front door was locked. Old habits die harder than the human race, as it turns out.

A whole lot of things do.

Birds sang from the bushes as I walked down the street, heading for the big Target at the centre of the shopping district. I couldn't drive, and so I was engaged in emptying the place out one wagon-load at a time. I hadn't seen signs that anyone else was looting, in the shops or elsewhere, so I didn't feel like there was any urgency. Besides, as long as I did it a little bit every day, it didn't feel quite so much like stealing. I always had enough money on me to pay for what I'd taken. Even if the money never left my pocket, I *could* have paid, and that meant it was like I *had* paid. Sometimes the little workarounds were the best ones of all.

The shelves at Target were a pleasing cornucopia of survival. The rains had come so quickly, when they started coming at all, that most people hadn't even started to stockpile. It would be at least a year before I had to figure out how to talk myself into breaking into the homes of my neighbours. That was going to be a fun argument. I'd need to plan for three or four days where I didn't leave the house at all, just battled my own demons until one of us came out on top. For

Kaylee's sake, it would have to be the version of me that went outside and *did* things, not the version who hid in her room and refused to let her food touch.

Neither version of me was suited to surviving in this world alone. I couldn't afford to go off my medication and let the careful, compulsive, agonised me out of her cage, but I also couldn't afford to take the dose my mother had wanted me on—both for the sake of making the pills last, and because without my shadow-self, perfect and precise as she wanted the world to be, I would have died with everyone else.

When the scientists working up in the Arctic had started reporting mass die-offs of the whales and walruses, people had been sad—people were always sad when a whale died, even if they didn't care when it was another human being—but they hadn't done anything about it. The Arctic was very far away, after all, and sometimes things just died. That was the way the world worked. There was no reason to change the way we did things here at home because of something that happened far away. Even when the chemists and the biologists started anxiously saying that something was wrong, that some of the things coming out of the melting glaciers weren't supposed to *be* here anymore, that they were things from millions of years ago that didn't know how to play nicely with human bodies. Or anything mammalian, for that matter.

They told us those things were coming out of the ice. They told us those things were going into the water. They told us those things were getting more and more common, that soon there would be so many of them—or so much of them, I never really understood which word was correct, and Mum was always so afraid of scaring me that she wouldn't explain—that the ocean would change forever.

They told us, about a week before it happened, that there was a chance the things were small enough to change the way the rain worked. That the things could make the rain dangerous for humans. For anything mammalian, like the dog next door that always used to bark when I was trying to have my afternoon nap. Like the squirrels that used to play in the trees outside my window. Like Kaylee.

She used to get to go outside, before the people on TV started talking about the rain. I'd had a full-scale meltdown that day, what Dad used to call a nuclear tantrum, and Mum had agreed that I could keep Kaylee indoors. She'd warned me that the cat wouldn't be happy, and I hadn't cared. Better an unhappy cat than a dead one. Besides, this made it a lot easier to find Kaylee when I wanted to pet her or play with her. I should have asked for her to be an indoor cat years ago.

Mum didn't listen to the news the way I did. She didn't tape up her windows or start spending all her time inside. And it wasn't like they knew anything for *sure*. They didn't *know* that the little things that had come out of the ice would get sucked up into the clouds, or that they would travel all over the world. Or that they would start falling on the West Coast at 8:17 AM on a Wednesday morning in August. Or that they would be so very, very hungry, although I suppose the whales should have told us that part. And the scientists *definitely* didn't know that the little things would get sucked back into the clouds again and again, so they could just keep falling, forever.

It had been over a week since I'd seen another mammal. There were plenty of birds. The things in the clouds didn't like the taste of feathers, I guess. The crows were getting bold. There had always been too many of them around. They were scavengers, and people usually made a lot for them to scavenge from. With us mostly gone, no more garbage, no more roadkill, no more restaurant dumpsters, they were getting desperate.

Sometimes I thought about feeding them, putting out trays of dry dog food and luring them to my back porch. I could learn to interpret their croaks and caws, figure out how to tell them apart on sight. Maybe I could even love them a little, once they had become individuals to me, and not just a formless flock of black wings. They could keep me company in a world where all the other company was gone.

But the dog food would run out eventually. I would die eventually, even if I stayed away from the rain for another ten years. Where would the crows be then? This wasn't man's world anymore. It seemed selfish to keep forcing my sphere of influence outside the house

I shared with Kaylee. Better to loot what had been left behind and wait for the rain to find its way in. It would. I knew it would. It was inevitable.

It was 10:17 AM. I had time to get back to the house, rinse the wagon in bleach, and unload the day's acquisitions before I settled in to an afternoon of reading my books and petting my cat. I'd been doing home schooling for years. I was keeping up with my classes, as much out of habit as because I needed to have something to do with my time. If the remains of humanity ever figured out how umbrellas worked, I would be all caught up on my calculus.

A shadow moved under the trees. I ignored it and kept walking. Then the shadow stepped out onto the sidewalk, revealing itself as Cathy McCallen from my old school. She looked like hell. Her hair was scraggly and uncombed, and probably hadn't been washed in weeks. She was wearing jeans—bad call, one wrong step and those things would be wicking up rainwater like a sponge, trapping it against her skin—and three sweaters layered one over the other. She probably thought that would keep her safe. She was wrong, so, so wrong, but I wasn't going to tell her that, because she had a gun, and I knew better than to argue with people who had guns.

"Give me that wagon," she snapped, before her face softened in confusion, eyebrows rising and lips parting. It was a classic double-take. I wished I had my camera. I would have documented it. "Holly?"

"Yes," I said. "I would rather not give you the wagon, if you don't mind. I worked hard to fill it up. You could be working hard too, if you wanted to, instead of just threatening me with a gun."

"Oh my God, one other person survives the fucking apocalypse, and it has to be the moron," said Cathy. "I'm the one with the weapon. Now give me that wagon."

I thought about it. I thought about it hard. I thought about how much more difficult it would be for me to do my supply runs without the wagon, which was good plastic and wouldn't melt or rot or start to smell bad. I thought about how sad Kaylee would be if I got eaten by the things in the rain because I was slow walking home with her cat food. And I shook my head.

"No," I said. "This is my wagon. If you want a wagon, you should go and find one for yourself, and use that. If you want food, you should go and find some. And you shouldn't call me 'moron'. That's a mean word you use for someone who you think isn't as smart as you. I'm as smart as you. I'm probably even smarter. My grades are excellent."

"Then why did your mother pull you out of school, huh?"

I looked at her wearily. Then I looked at the sky, assessing the movement of the clouds, comparing their weight to the timetable I kept, ever-updating, in my mind. Finally, I looked back to her, and said, "Because of you. Because of your friends. Because of how you called me names and stole my books and told new kids that I always smelled like pee, even though it wasn't true and you knew it would upset me. Because you were a bully, and you *liked* being a bully, and no matter how much I begged you to stop, you wouldn't. Now you're still a bully. You're just a bully with a gun, and you can't have my wagon."

I started walking again, ducking my head down against my chest, so that if the rain came early, it wouldn't get into my eyes. That was what I was most afraid of: that my eyes would get eaten out of my head, and then the things in the rain would be full, and leave me stumbling blind through the melted world they'd created. Kaylee would starve. So would I, but that didn't matter as much. I was the people. I had promised to take care of her, and that was something I couldn't do with my eyes melted out of my head.

"Hey! Hey, where are you going?" There was a sharp note of desperation in Cathy's voice, like she didn't know how to deal with the reality of what was happening. I could sympathise with that. I frequently didn't know how to deal with the reality of the world around me. But I had to learn. Every day, I had to learn, and if I could do it, so could Cathy, who had waved her neurotypicality in my face like a red flag in front of a bull, claiming that it made her a better person than I could ever be.

"Home," I said. "If today's rainfall patterns follow yesterday's rainfall patterns, I have twenty-three minutes to get there, unload *my* wagon," stressing the possessive felt good, "and make sure everything is clean before I put it away. I don't have time to stand here and let you bully me. We're not in school anymore, Cathy. I don't have to take it just because you want to dish it out."

There was a seven-second silence, long enough for me to take five steps, before she said, in a small voice, "But what's going to happen to me?" The desperation was gone, replaced by something equally familiar. Fear. Cathy, the great bogeyman of my school days, was afraid.

That was amazing enough that I had to turn around and see it with my own eyes. She was still holding the gun, but she wasn't aiming it at me anymore; she was holding it so that it pointed at the ground. She looked…broken, almost, like the weight of the world had become too much for her to bear.

"You're going to go back to wherever you've been staying since the melt came, and you're going to close your windows, and you're going to hope," I said. "You have twenty-two minutes, now. Staying dry is the best way, but you probably know that. Did you know dry shampoo is a thing? You can stay clean even when the water isn't safe." Dry shampoo and baby wipes were doing a remarkable job of keeping me presentable, even with no one around to see but Kaylee. Now that I didn't have to deal with the fuss and disruption of the shower, I was doing better about keeping myself clean than I ever had before.

It was sort of sad. Even with a functional disorder

that meant people would always be looking for reasons to judge me, I had never been able to bring myself to shower on a regular basis. The ritual of it never appealed to me, and without the ritual, there was no point.

"You can't just leave me here," said Cathy.

I blinked slowly, trying to make sense of her words. "Yes, I can," I said finally. "It's easy. All I have to do is walk away from you, and I'll be leaving you here. My home is that way." I pointed. "Yours isn't. I would have noticed if you actually lived in my neighbourhood, and you would probably have tried to take my wagon away before now. Twenty-one minutes. I don't know how far away you live. You might want to get moving." I turned and resumed walking.

"Wait!" Cathy ran to catch up, trotting along beside me. "I can help you. I can pull your wagon."

"Then you'll have the gun *and* the wagon. No. It's mine. You can't have it."

"There aren't even bullets in this thing! I just wanted to scare you." Cathy sounded almost ashamed. "I'm hungry. I ran out of food in the house two days ago."

"Did you try breaking into the house next door?" I asked. "Houses next door are a well-established source of canned goods during the apocalypse." It sounded so reasonable when I said it like that, and yet here I was, still walking to Target every day, because I couldn't stand the thought of violating the property of my neighbours. They had always been kind to me. Their being dead was no excuse for me to be a bad kid all of a sudden.

Cathy looked down at the sidewalk. "I was scared," she said, in a small voice. "There was a skeleton in the living room of the house next door."

"Skeletons aren't scary," I said. "You have a skeleton. I have a skeleton. A skeleton is just the body with its clothes off."

From the way Cathy looked at me, I could tell she wasn't buying it. "You're still so weird," she said. She sounded almost disappointed, like the end of the human race had been intended to normalise me somehow. "Are you, like, medicated? Are you going to go schitzo and start peeing on yourself?" The word "again" followed the sentence, unspoken but there.

I glared at her through my goggles. "That happened once, in second grade, because my medication was wrong. I've been taking my pills. The pharmacy at Target is very well-stocked. And you shouldn't say 'schitzo.' It's a bad, mean word, and it has no place in your vocabulary."

"Oh, whatever." Cathy waved my criticism away. "What happens when the pills run out?"

"I don't think that's any of your business." I started walking a little faster. Nineteen minutes. Things moved so *quickly* whenever I was outside. It wasn't fair. A single hour could stretch into forever when it was just me and Kaylee, but when I needed time to go slow and treat me gently, it kept trundling along at the usual pace. "You're not my mother. No one is my mother anymore."

Mum and Dad had both been away from home when the rains fell. I'd tried to hold out hope, for a little while, but it hadn't been enough to change anything. I'd found Mum's car outside the Starbucks that shared the Target parking lot, one door open and the engine long since dead. I couldn't be *sure* that the skeleton sprawled beside it, wearing Mum's clothes and still clutching Mum's car keys, was her. It had been too many days since she'd been gone, and the hungry things in the rain had had too much time to eat. Still, I was sure enough.

"Sorry," said Cathy sullenly.

I kept walking, and didn't say anything.

"Can I—can I come over? Please? I'm scared to be alone anymore. And I'm hungry. Please?"

I kept walking, and didn't say anything—not to tell her to stay, or to ask her to go. As I had expected, Cathy interpreted that as permission. She followed me all the way home.

We made it inside four minutes and thirty-seven seconds ahead of schedule. The rain began two minutes and six seconds ahead of schedule. It was time to adjust the charts again.

Kaylee was waiting for me outside the garage door, her tail lashing and the fur on her haunches raised. "Mmmrow," she complained, before rubbing herself against my calves. She left a fine sheen of white and orange hairs behind, marking me as hers and hers alone. I leaned down to give her head a few pats with my free hand, and continued on toward the kitchen.

"Don't let the cat into the garage," I said. "It leaks there sometimes, and she doesn't know better than to drink the water."

"You have a cat?" Cathy sounded somewhere between disgusted and bemused, like she couldn't believe I had been able to keep something other than myself alive for this long. "I'm allergic."

"You can leave if you want," I said. "This is her house, not yours." I kept walking. I heard the door connecting the garage to the house shut, and Cathy's footsteps following me. I smiled.

It was sort of nice to have someone around to help me carry the groceries to the kitchen. Kaylee couldn't do it. Cats didn't have thumbs, and she'd never learned to follow commands anyway. With Cathy, I could get it all done in half the time.

Storing groceries in the kitchen probably didn't matter much now that the power was out and the fridge was just another set of shelves, but it was habit, and habits died hard. Like scrubbing the whole place down with bleach on Tuesdays, to keep the mould and the mice away. Maybe habits would also keep the things in the rain from finding a way inside, figuring out how to wheedle the delicious things out of the rigid wooden box that kept them safe and dry.

Cathy stopped in the kitchen doorway, looking

around the jumbled, box-filled kitchen with dismay. "How much food do you *have?*"

"I go shopping every day, except for Tuesdays, when I clean the kitchen," I said. "I move everything to the living room, throw away anything that's spoiled, and scrub the fixtures and the floor. Then I put it all back."

"Oh my God," said Cathy, and grabbed a bag of cookies, ripping it open and beginning to shovel pink and white circus animals into her mouth. Crumbs and flecks of frosting rained down on the floor. I grimaced, but didn't say anything. I could clean up once she was gone. Mum always said that I had to be polite to guests, no matter how awful they were to me. "Oh my *God.*"

"Please chew," I said, unable to fully contain my nervousness. "If you choke to death in my kitchen, I don't know what I'll do with your body." That was a lie. Her body would still be mammalian, still meat, and the things in the rain weren't picky: they didn't care if the things they devoured were alive or dead, only that they had the right balance of proteins and fats. I could throw her outside. She'd be a skeleton by morning, and I could close the blinds and ignore her.

Cathy swallowed hard, glaring at me the whole time. "I've been *starving*, you spaz, and you're in here with, like, an entire grocery store all to yourself. So you'll excuse me if I don't chew too good."

I wanted to tell her to stop calling me names. She wasn't even sticking with the right ones. I didn't have a muscular disorder; physically, there was nothing about me that deviated from what was considered "normal" for a seventeen-year-old girl. I had mild schizophrenia, for which I was medicated, and autism, for which I was not medicated, but that only changed the way I thought, not the way I moved. And since almost all the neurotypical people I knew had been summarily eaten by the things in the rain, I wasn't really seeing my "deviance" as a bad thing at the moment.

"Try not to throw up, and don't open any windows," I said finally. I turned, leaving her to raid my supplies, and went to check the seals on my house.

Keeping out the rain was a full time job. The house was sound and had never leaked, but the rain had been different before: it hadn't been filled with hungry things that bit and tore. I didn't *know* whether they could chew through wood, but I had no reason to believe that they couldn't, if they got hungry enough. I couldn't count on it. So every day, while the rain was falling, I would walk through the whole house with a roll of duct tape in my hand, looking for places that seemed damp. The tape seals around most of the windows were several inches thick by this point, and getting thicker by the day. It still wasn't enough. I still couldn't be *sure*. Better another strip of tape than a single drop of water.

By the time I finished my walkthrough, Cathy was passed out on the living room couch, snoring softly. She was still clutching the cookies in one hand, tightly as a teddy bear. I looked at her for a moment, considering my options, before turning away.

It was time to take my pills.

After pills, I played with Kaylee until the rain stopped—thirty-eight minutes today, three minutes longer than yesterday; the storms were getting more intense as we slipped down the slope toward winter. I needed to step up my scavenging expeditions, at least to make sure that we had enough bottled water and kitty litter and canned tuna to get us through to spring. Canned tuna was better than canned cat food, because we could *both* eat it if we had to. It wasn't the best thing for either of us, but it would keep us going, and that was what mattered.

Maybe by spring the hungry things in the rain would have all been flushed out, and it would be safe to go outside again. Or maybe by spring the roof would have sprung a leak and we would have been devoured in our sleep. Either way, spring would change things.

Once the rain had been over for fifteen minutes, I went back downstairs and shook Cathy by the shoulder. She lifted her head from one of Mum's best throw pillows, leaving a spot of drool behind, and blinked blearily at me. "Wha'?"

"Hello," I said. "The rain has stopped. Based on the time intervals of the last week, you have forty-seven minutes to get back to your house. Thank you for visiting. Goodbye now."

"Wait, what?" She sat bolt upright, instantly awake. "You can't kick me out."

I frowned. "Yes, I can. This is my house. I don't want you to be in it anymore. Please leave."

"No!" Cathy shrank back in the couch, looking alarmed. "There's no food. Please. I'm starving."

"I can pack you a lunch."

"I can help you."

"Help me with what? All you've done since you got here is eat my cookies and drool on my pillows. I have food and water for me and Kaylee to get through the winter. One person, one cat. Not two people."

"I can help, honest, I can."

"What about the cat? You said you were allergic."

"I can get Benadryl when I help you go to Target for more groceries."

I hesitated. I didn't want her in my house. She had never been nice to me before, and I knew full well that she was only being nice to me now because she wanted something. She wanted food and shelter and not to be alone.

I understood not wanting to be alone. I didn't want to be alone either. That was why I was so careful with Kaylee, who didn't understand that the world outside had turned against her while she was sleeping, curled into a ball of formless fluff, on the windowsill. Kaylee couldn't understand, so I had to understand for her. But with Cathy...

It would be nice to have someone to talk to. "This is my house," I said. "You have to follow my rules."

Cathy nodded enthusiastically. "Anything."

"No opening the doors unless I say it's safe. No opening windows *ever*. Don't waste food or water. We're going to have a hard time getting more after we finish emptying the Target. Don't tease Kaylee. And don't call me bad names anymore, ever."

"Sure," said Cathy. She was suddenly all smiles. That made me feel like I was making a mistake, but it was too late to take it back. Then her smile faded, replaced by a look of concern. "So hey, did you, like, take your pills?"

Over the course of the following three days, we fell into an uneasy sort of pattern. Uneasy because Cathy didn't understand my rituals, and had no respect for the fact that things needed to be done in a certain order. She was filthy, constantly eating, and when I suggested she take a sponge bath—a necessary waste of our precious bottled water—she sneered and said that I was one to talk, which didn't even make *sense*. Of course I was one to talk. I took a sponge bath every three days. Survival wouldn't do me any good if I got so dirty that I caught an infection from myself and died.

She was really only happy when we went outside to retrieve supplies. Then she seemed almost like her old self, except that this version of her old self was willing to talk to me without calling me names or asking whether I was supposed to be in an asylum. I could have liked Cathy, if she had been like this when we'd been at school together. Maybe we could even have been friends.

Sometimes she asked if I missed my parents. I looked at her blankly when she did that, until eventually she stopped asking. That was good. I had no idea how to answer her. Did I wish Mum and Dad were still around? Sure. But I had Kaylee to take care of, and plans to make, and there wasn't time to worry about them. Maybe someday. Not now.

It was 1:15 PM on the fourth day when I heard the front door slam. I came out of the kitchen, wiping my hands on a cloth and looking anxiously around for invaders or army men who had come to save us from the things in the rain. I didn't see either. I just saw Cathy, sucking on the side of her hand and glaring spitefully at the door.

"What happened?" I asked.

"That stupid cat *scratched* me," she said, taking her hand out of her mouth. "I was just trying to pet her, and she *scratched* me."

Kaylee wasn't in the hall, or in the front room, or in the kitchen. It was unlikely that she would have run up the stairs if she was scared. She would have run toward me, who had always protected her. And the front door had slammed.

"Where's my cat?" I asked.

Cathy stared at me. "Didn't you hear what I just said? She *scratched* me."

She didn't have the gun anymore. I had hidden it in the garage days ago. She didn't have anything, and when I rushed her, slamming her up against the hallway wall, she was unprepared. "Where is my *cat*? What did you *do*?" I demanded.

"You're hurting me, you retarded bitch!" she yelled.

I grabbed her by the hair and dragged her to the front door. Kaylee wasn't on the porch. I shoved Cathy outside, watching as she stumbled down the two low brick steps.

"What are you doing?" She tried to rush the door. I slammed it in her face. She began pounding. "Let me in!"

"Not until you find my cat!" It felt good to yell. "And don't think you can start breaking windows! You won't get past the plastic!"

Maybe that was true and maybe it wasn't, but Cathy was a bully and a coward, and she didn't know any better. She hit the door again.

"Eleven minutes to today's estimated rainfall," I called. "Better get looking."

"*Please*," she said.

"I told you, this is her house, not yours." I locked the door. Then I went back to the kitchen, and got the biggest knife I could find. It felt good in my hand. I sat down on the hallway floor, and waited.

Eleven minutes later, the rain began falling.

Twelve minutes later, I began to cry.

The rain lasted forty-three minutes and nineteen seconds. When it tapered off, I waited ten more minutes before unlocking the door.

The hungry little things in the rain had been very busy. Cathy had tried to run, but you can't outrun the rain. They had stripped her down to the bone in the middle of the street. I walked to her, clumsy in my waders, and used a stick to roll what remained of her body over. There were no smaller bones beneath her. She hadn't been holding Kaylee.

I left the front door open as I wandered the block. "Kaylee," I called. "Here, kitty, kitty. Nice kitty, kitty. Come home, please."

Ten minutes to the next estimated rainfall. I needed to turn back. I couldn't turn back.

"Here, kitty."

Kaylee meowed.

I turned to see her push her way out through a dog door. She walked to the edge of the porch and stopped, looking with disdain at the puddles on the path. I laughed and hurried to scoop her into my arms. She didn't even squirm as I carried her home. We made it inside five minutes before the rain came down again.

Maybe by spring the hungry things would be gone. Maybe by spring *we* would be gone. It didn't matter.

We had each other, and we had the time between now and then.

"Come on, kitty," I said, putting her down on the hallway floor. "It's time for my pills."

The end of the world was a misnomer. From where I was standing, the world was continuing just fine.

Did We Break the End of the World?

Tansy Rayner Roberts

They could do this with their eyes shut.

The house has been standing empty for a while—there's a smell that a house gets when no one's been living there for months or more, and Jin knows that smell better than he knows how to get the best operating life out of a zinc-air battery.

It's more than stale. It's dead.

The kitchen is the worst. It's rare to find abandoned houses with intact kitchens, because suburbia is the playground of the scavengers since the world ended. The cupboards have been stripped of anything resembling food. There's a lingering smell near the fridge-freezer that warns against opening the door.

No one associates fridge-freezers with edible supplies any more. Not since the Pulse that robbed the city—the world, probably—of a working power grid.

As for the rest of the house, it's barely been touched, because people are idiots. Okay, someone stripped the couch of cushions and a few cupboards have been smashed in. But the electronics have been left behind. Kids these days assume they're junk because you can't plug shit in any more.

Jin smiles.

He keeps a watch running, which is a luxury most people don't bother with—who needs to worry about appointments and school schedules any more? But he does it, and he keeps Aisha's running for her, too.

She refused it the first few times, crossing her arms and saying nothing, which is pretty much how she reacts to everything. Jin only convinced her that a watch was useful with the magic words: "It's for a challenge, all right?"

She went very still, her eyebrows raised.

"One hour. We get into a house, strip it, compare loot. Whoever wins…" and there, he ran out of steam.

[Next house] she signed. It saves batteries, being around Aisha. She never speaks, so he doesn't have to keep his aids switched on. They were together two months before Jin even figured out she knew enough Auslan for them to communicate in occasional words.

He doesn't know why she never speaks. It's not the kind of question you ask a girl who can kill you with a short length of cable.

It's been fifty minutes. Jin is prising tiny batteries out of an abandoned stash of dead phones from a bottom drawer when Aisha drops down in front of him, like some kind of giant freaking spider.

"Fuck," he says, too loud probably. "What the hell?"

[Done] she signs with a shit-eating grin. She's wearing new barrettes in her shiny black hair, with kitty skulls on them. There must be a teen bedroom somewhere in this suburban tomb.

"You've got ten minutes left," Jin grouses. "Can we even pretend this is a competition?" She's won every house challenge of the last two weeks, including the time he found a whole unopened box of AA batteries in someone's garage.

[Won] she signs.

"*I've* still got ten minutes, and I'm not done yet." Jin signs the filthiest words he knows at Aisha until she laughs and leaves him to it.

When his watch clicks over to the last minute of the hour, Jin takes his stash to the master bedroom. Aisha is lying on one side of the bed, her own loot spread out on the dusty doona cover. And yeah, she's won.

Jin blinks at the array of bottles—Nurofen, aspirin, anti-depressants, anti psychotics, heart meds, a few dodgy out of date antibiotics, not to mention condoms and lube.

Aisha jerks her right thumb against her left palm, which means [money]. She does it like three times and with a smirk that suggests she would be singing a song if she ever bothered to make a sound.

"Yep, untold wealth," Jin says sarcastically, joining her on the bed. "You could trade yourself a gold-plated backpack, maybe some diamond sneakers."

[Jealous] she replies, another of her favourite signs.

"I'm doing fine," he says, and unrolls the tea towel he used to bundle his own haul—batteries stripped from every abandoned device he could find. Oh, and a Raymond Chandler novel he found on a shelf downstairs, because he loves those things, and he hasn't read this one before.

Aisha pats him on the head. She prefers Harlequin novels, when she reads at all, and she never bothers to count them in her stash because they are plentiful in nearly every house in every suburb. Known fact about foster mothers: they loved their romance novels.

Jin and Aisha have many rules. Never stay more than two nights in any house. Never more than one house in the same street, unless you're sure there are no other scavenger packs around. One hour for the challenge, another full day to make sure you haven't missed anything useful and portable. They always sleep together, on the biggest bed they can find, with their backpacks and shoes between them in case anyone surprises them in the night.

Oh, and regular baths or showers in houses where the water is still on. That's Aisha's rule, and she doesn't have to use spoken words to let Jin know when he's due for a wash.

There's no real logic to the water thing. Some streets lost it in the Pulse—others kept on chugging for a while before breaking down. A few are still hooked up to a working system. Some houses have rainwater tanks, they're the best ones to head for, but other scavengers know that too.

Then again, other scavengers don't seem to care quite as much about regular showers as Aisha does.

Jin doesn't carry a weapon, unless you count the pocket knife in his sock. Aisha carries at least five weapons on her body, and more in her pack. She's taught him a few moves to get out of holds if he needs to, but nothing especially aggressive. That's what she's for.

Jin barely slept, the first six weeks after the world ended. It's better since he teamed up with Aisha. He's safe with her, and while he doesn't know what she gets out of this partnership of theirs, he trusts her to stick around.

Tonight, after stashing his new battery supplies in the various ziplock bags he keeps in his pack, Jin glances up to find Aisha looking at him. She does that a lot—waits for him to look at her instead of touching him to get his attention. It's considerate, but he actually wouldn't mind if she touched him more.

Not like that—he doesn't like girls that way, and even if he did, Aisha is far too terrifying. But he remembers a time when casual touch was a regular part of his life: hugs from his foster mother, tussles and fake punches from the foster sibs. There are days when he misses that old life so hard he can barely breathe.

He wonders sometimes what existed before then—before his foster family—but his memory brings up nothing.

[What?] Jin signs.

[Here] Aisha replies, a sign that's just her pointing at the floor.

Neither of them are expert enough at Auslan to manage complicated sentences—Jin was super lazy about learning more than a basic vocab back before the Pulse, and Aisha never uses three words when one will do. He hates her for it sometimes, because guessing wrong makes him feel stupid. If she would just goddamn speak, he could read her lips a little.

Aisha presses her fists together and pulls them apart, like she's breaking something.

"Smoko?" Jin asks, raising his eyebrows. He's fucking with her and she knows it.

The other kind of break. Yeah, that means something.

[Where?] he asks.

It's a teenager's room, the source of the kitty skull hair clips. Fresh words are sprayed across the ceiling. The same graffiti tag they've spotted across walls and dead trains, inside tunnels and alleys.

DID WE BREAK THE END OF THE WORLD?

He doesn't know what it means, but there's something about those words that always makes his stomach twist up.

He's been seeing it more frequently over the last few weeks.

Jin steals a pair of sleeping shorts from one of the drawers and changes into them because why the hell not? When he gets back to the master bedroom, Aisha has already changed into an enormous pair of flowery cotton pyjamas left behind by the foster family who lived here with their well-stocked medicine cabinet and their drawer of superseded mobile phones.

Before they let themselves sleep, Jin and Aisha ready their packs so they can run at a moment's notice, same as always.

Three houses later, DID WE BREAK THE END OF THE WORLD? is scrawled across the glass windows on the outside, as well as the kitchen ceiling and along a dingy corridor that smells of mould.

Jin wins the challenge in this one. The bathroom cabinet and the bedrooms were scavenged out months ago, by the looks of them, but there's a cupboard full of busted hair dryers and remote controlled cars and crap like that. The batteries are dead, but that doesn't mean they're useless.

The water is still on in this neighbourhood, which is a definite bonus.

Jin sets up his charger kit on the coffee table, hooking up the solar cell that he always hangs on the back of his pack to the lead acid battery that he traded with a seriously scary car-scavenging gang. It was worth the terror, because this baby allows him to renovate all kind of batteries, including his precious zinc-airs that run his hearing aids.

It won't work forever. But he's not thinking too hard about the future. Next week, next month, one foot in front of another.

There's no way they're going to sleep in any of those bedrooms tonight. Aisha joins him on the couch eventually, sulking over the single strip of aspirin she clawed out from behind a kitchen cupboard.

[Trade soon] she suggests, and he nods in response. They're getting low on food supplies, and Jin's backpack is heavy with the weight of the battery stash he's been building. According to the local graffiti, there's going to be a market next week two suburbs over. It makes sense for them to make for it.

That night, Jin wakes in the darkness with Aisha's hand on his leg. He scrabbles in his jeans pocket for his hearing aids. Nothing's worse than being deaf in the dark.

Her hand is flat and warm, near his knee. Every time she hears the sound that must have woken her, she taps against him. When his hearing aids come on, he mostly gets static and his own heartbeat, but by the third tap against his leg, he can hear the noise that goes along with it.

There's a scuffling sound beneath them. A possum? This is outer suburbia, with scrubby backyards and nearby bushland. So it's probably a native animal, or maybe even an abandoned pet: a dog or a cat.

But Jin can feel the tension in Aisha's fingertips. She doesn't think it's an animal.

Most houses in this area don't have basements, but Jin noticed a crawl space when they did their walk-around during daylight. There's an access door in the garage which produced nothing useful; garages are often a treasure trove for batteries and charging tech, but this one was empty except for several sets of bare metal shelves. Jin indicates the garage with a tap and a point and Aisha tracks the movement, nods.

Jin slides the pocket knife out of his sock, and the working torch that he saves for emergencies, before strapping on his pack and following her out to the garage. Aisha is wearing her pack, too. You don't leave the important shit behind, not even if you're only moving from one room to another.

She opens the connecting door, and steps out ahead of him on to the bare concrete. Then she lurches forward in the darkness and there's a crash that explodes loudly in Jin's head, his ears oversensitive after the day's silence.

He snaps on the torch, letting fierce yellow light blaze against the pile of tumbled metal shelves, and his friend, and the struggling figure beneath her. It's a kid, bigger and maybe a couple of years older than either of them, his face screwed up against the light.

"What the fuck?" the intruder roars, bucking against the tight hold Aisha has on his neck.

Jin's been there. It's distressing and uncomfortable. But if the kid is going to keep yelling, he's turning his hearing aids down. All this noise is giving him a headache.

"Be polite," he says, aware that his diction isn't great—he slurs when he's tired, or if he's spent too much time in silence, and this is the first time he's switched on his hearing aids all week. "She could kill you with her shoe."

The kid glares more fiercely at Jin, barely acknowledging Aisha despite the fact that she's on top of him. "What's *wrong* with you?"

"Deaf," Jin says, tipping up the torchlight to show one of the aids, then turning it back into the kid's face. "She doesn't speak. I wouldn't make a big deal about it—she's kinda mean if you piss her off."

"How do you—" said the kid, half choking now. "How do you have stuff that works? Nothing works any more!"

[Slow] Aisha suggests, sliding her free hand over the one still wrapped around the kid's neck. She uses that sign to mean "stupid" because the sign that actually means stupid is too blatant—any hearing person would recognise it, and Aisha's favourite thing about signing is that it's a secret code.

[Give him a break] Jin replies, the torch jerking as he makes the last sign, the one that means "smoko" and "rest" as well as "Did We Break the End of the World".

[Soft-heart] she replies. One of her favourite insults for him. It's literally a hand-squish movement, followed by pointing at his heart. She uses it more often than she uses his name.

"Yeah, yeah. You hungry?" Jin asks the intruder, lowering the torch so it's not in anyone's eyes.

Aisha releases her hold, and the intruder rubs at his neck as if it's painful. "I could eat," he mutters.

Jin puts the torch beside the couch so it works like a lamp. It's a stupid waste of batteries, but what are they going to do, lie down and sleep until daylight with this person they don't even know?

"This is Aisha," he says aloud, simultaneously making the name sign he gave her—a two-handed "A" followed by the gesture for "knife" because the first time they met, she totally tried to stab him. "I'm Jin." His own name sign reminds him of his family, and he hates that, but he demonstrates it anyway. Not that he expects this kid to pick up their fractured version of Auslan between now and whenever they ditch him, but there are certain polite habits Jin's foster mother taught him that even the end of the world hasn't erased.

Their intruder looks at them both, wary as hell. He has dark, lank hair falling into his eyes, wide shoulders under a filthy army jacket and he looks like he's been sleeping rough instead of house surfing. "Billy," he says after a long pause, blurting it out.

"What do you do, Billy?" Jin asks, handing over a muesli bar from his pack. He hasn't talked so much in ages, but it's not like Aisha is going to play party host.

Billy winces as if Jin is talking too loud, too aggressively, which he probably is—and he's okay with that. He and Aisha try to be decent allies to other kids when they can, but they have to be careful. Last time Jin was friendly to a cute boy who was nearly as freaked out as this one, he got himself sliced up by a razor blade.

Thank fuck for Aisha and her stash of antibacterials, or he might not have survived.

"What do you mean?" Billy asks defensively, shoving his hair out of his face like he's fed up with them already. "Does anyone do anything these days?"

Oh, shit, Jin didn't see that coming. This kid is grimy, angry at the world, and probably going to try to kill them at some point, but he also has the prettiest eyes Jin has seen in a long time.

Enough of that. Better to focus on Billy's mouth instead. Jin needs to learn how he shapes words, while the aids are switched on. It will help later.

"Scavenging is easier if you specialise," Jin explains. "That's how we survive. Food and weapons are what gets stripped out of a house first, and it's hard to compete with the alpha kids, the bully gangs. But if you scavenge something special, something maybe no one else thought to collect, it's easier to trade for what you need."

Billy's chin goes up. "So you want me to trade for this?" He hasn't opened the muesli bar, but he's squeezing it between his fingers like you'd have to kill him to get it back.

Aisha laughs. It's a jolt of a sound—Jin forgets sometimes that she is perfectly capable of making noise.

"Nah," says Jin. "We're not arseholes. Eat the damn bar."

Aisha and Jin sleep in shifts. They don't trust this kid yet, and they've got too much to lose. Jin lets the torch go out, but keeps his aids on while he takes watch. His ears are aching already. Aisha curls up practically under him, using her pack as a pillow.

He's pretty sure that Billy doesn't sleep at all. They slouch in the darkness, keeping each other company from opposite sides of the room.

When it's Jin's turn to sleep, Aisha climbs on top of him, like he's more comfortable than the damned couch, and he finally takes the aids out and tucks them away in his pack.

Enough talking. Enough noise. Jin sacks out until daylight.

When he wakes up, he stares at the ceiling and reads the words DID WE BREAK THE END OF THE

WORLD scrawled across the ceiling. They weren't there before. The air smells of freshly sprayed paint.

Aisha is asleep, damn her, sprawled on top of Jin like a cat. Jin pushes her off, dodging her half-hearted attempt to pull a knife on him. She's never at her best in the mornings.

Billy is in the kitchen, going through the drawers. He glances up at Jin and mutters something half into his chest, so no chance of lip reading.

Jin touches his ears and makes a flicking motion, to show he's running on silence.

Billy holds up a wadded handful of plastic bags, with a questioning expression.

"Not bad," says Jin aloud. He can't control the volume when he talks, but it's not like he's trying to impress anyone. "Plastic's useful, and lightweight. You're better off taking them than leaving them behind."

What he doesn't say—the really good scavengers, like he and Aisha, they care about their specialty. They know it inside out. They're romantic about it—it becomes part of their identity, and it certainly helps build a reputation with the other traders. No one ever falls in love with plastic bags.

Billy nods and keeps digging.

"So you're an artist," says Jin, and takes some satisfaction from the way Billy rockets back on his heels, practically slamming his head on the underside of the sink. "The words." And he makes the sign [break] though Billy won't know what he means. "Did we break the end of the world?"

Billy just stares at him, crouched there on the floor of the wrecked kitchen like he's expecting to be hit, or laughed at.

Aisha interrupts their moment, stomping in with a musty towel from one of the cupboards. She hurls it at Billy's head, then follows it up with a bar of soap from her personal collection.

Billy gapes as Aisha turns around and leaves the room again.

"She must like you," Jin observes. "She's not usually that subtle."

Picking which house is the right one to scavenge— that's a kind of magic. Aisha has a feel for these things, so Jin usually lets her take point.

They're getting close to the new market site, so it's likely they're going to run into other scavengers over the next few days—gangs or trading teams or indies or all of the above. This is a small cul-de-sac, with no sign of life, but that doesn't mean it's safe.

Aisha doesn't make a move. She looks straight at Billy, waiting for *him* to pick a house for them. Billy isn't confident, but he points and Aisha strides towards the weatherboard with its peeling gum-green roof like she's the one who chose it.

They do a walk-around, noting exits and potential hazards, then Aisha approaches the back door. It's locked, which hasn't happened in weeks—either no one who ever turned the place over used this door, or this is that rarest of commodities, a house no one has broken into since the Pulse.

Aisha employs her rarely-needed lock-picking skills to get them inside.

There's something wrong. Jin knows it before they've even got past the small laundry at the back. When he sees what's in the kitchen, his limbs go all numb and prickly in shock.

It's a foster mother. He hasn't seen one in months. Usually when they turn up it's in scrap heaps or lying naked out on front lawns like so much refuse. Not like this. Not perfectly made up and dressed, frozen in the act of making a cup of coffee.

There's a fruit bowl full of gross mush on the counter, and the remains of a sandwich after mice and ants got to it. She's standing right there like that's what she was doing when the world ended.

Billy's mouth shapes the words "Oh wow." Aisha leans in, fascinated by the still figure.

Jin can't stay here. He can't be in this house, not with her standing there, perfect and lifeless like all it would take is a fucking battery to get her moving again. He shoves his way out blindly, collapses on the back steps and sucks in slow breaths until he can feel his heartbeat settling back to something like normal.

She reminds him of Greta, Jin's own foster mother. The hippy chic clothes and the thick-rimmed glasses, that's how she used to dress. It's like someone assembled a new Greta from a vague description, and placed her in that kitchen for Jin to find.

Everyone acts like it was always this way, a world full of suburbs to scavenge and teenage gangs and trading. But Jin's thoughts are never far from the world of ten months ago: the world of foster mothers and school and computers and TV and hearing aid batteries you don't have to fucking ration because you can buy new ones from the shop any time you like.

Jin wants that world back, and he feels stupid and weak even for admitting it to himself.

He's been doing fine. He's great at end of the world shit. He's a top rate scavenger: he and Aisha are the best indie team in the business. But the memory of having Greta to look after him, to make dinner or nag him about his homework or drive him to the doctor— it's too much. It's a hurting hole in his chest.

It's a long time before Aisha and Billy come out to find him. They sit on the steps, one on either side of Jin, shoulders jostling against his. It's nice. As close to family as he's ever going to get, and is it weird how quickly Billy got included in that?

Aisha cradles her palm around her fist to make a ball that means [precious] but is also the name sign that Greta gave him on the first day he was assigned to her as a foster kid. It's Jin's earliest memory.

Aisha lays her head on his shoulder, and nudges him to look towards Billy, who makes an awkward attempt at his own signs:

[We] [Move] [Woman]

He looks awkward about the last sign choice, but Jin is glad he didn't go for "mother" instead. Or rather, that Aisha didn't, because there's no way Billy knew those signs off the top of his head. She must have spent more time teaching him those signs than shoving the foster mother into a cupboard, or whatever they did to get her out of sight.

Jin signs [Okay] back to them both and then they sit there together for a while longer.

Finally Billy says [challenge], raising his eyebrows to show it's a question, and Jin can't help smiling.

He's pleased that their new teammate has gone to the trouble of learning how to sign. That must be why he feels warm all over. It's in no way because Aisha's insistence on bathing and clean clothes has revealed that Billy is pretty damned hot.

Still, Jin doesn't feel like scavenging, not with that foster mother and her inert plastic body hidden somewhere in the house. "You go ahead," he says aloud, and tries not to be too hurt that Billy and Aisha jump to their feet, ready to get started without him.

Billy pretends he's not specialising. This is the third house they've done since he joined them, and he always grabs a few practical, general items like tools or plastic. Still, Jin and Aisha both know that his eye is on art supplies. It's ridiculous to have a specialty that isn't about basic survival needs, but neither of them are going to tell him that. Not when the sight of a packet of permanent markers or a spray can of paint makes him so fucking happy.

It's a long hour for Jin, sitting out on the steps alone while his team does their thing without him. Leaning against the back door, his pack at his feet so the solar cell can drink up rays, he feels the occasional vibration of a door slamming, or cupboards and drawers being shoved open. It's a nice afternoon. The backyard is full of birds and sunshine, and hey, why not take the day off? He's earned it.

Some time later, he's jolted awake when Aisha throws the back door open behind him. [Cook] she signs impatiently. When Jin frowns at her in confusion, she points at his pack before signing it again. Oh, not cook. [Stove]. One of the heaviest and most useful things he owns, other than the lead acid car battery, is a battery-powered camping stove they found buried at the back of a shed a few months back.

"Nothing to cook," he says aloud, because what the hell is she on about? They ran out of anything but dry rations and power bars a month ago.

Aisha raises one eyebrow and smirks. Okay. For real food, he's going to put up with the creepy foster mother house.

In the kitchen, Jin and Aisha find Billy unpacking a larder full of honest-to-god canned goods, like the foster family of this house were preparing for, well, the end of the world.

"Holy fuck," says Jin. Billy turns around and gives him the most beautiful grin he's ever seen in his life. Oh, great. Food and a heart attack. Just what he needs.

[Kiss the cook], Aisha signs with a mischievous look on her face, and just about kills herself laughing when Jin gives her the world's most mortified expression.

They sleep in the master bedroom that night. Billy lies next to Jin, because Aisha hates being in the middle, though Jin's now wondering if she insisted on that configuration out of a matchmaking impulse. Bedtime is still awkward, between the three of them. Billy always hesitates, like he thinks he's intruding. Jin pretends to ignore his hesitation. Aisha judges them both silently. It's a whole thing they do.

Once they're settled, in the darkness, Jin admits to himself how nice it is to feel the warmth of a person on both sides. Three feels safer than two, and Jin no longer assumes that he and Aisha are going to ditch Billy any minute.

Tonight, he can't stop thinking about the food, so many cans and bags of dried stuff down in that larder. Bottled water, how stupidly luxurious it is to drink water from a sealed container instead of their usual

Russian roulette with whatever comes out of the tanks or the taps.

Jin's still thinking about it at breakfast, which is tinned casserole mixed with a can of soup that Billy puts together, followed by actual goddamned peaches in syrup.

"We should skip the trade market," Jin says. He's put in his aids for this conversation, prepared for an argument.

Aisha makes one of those double hand gestures that has nothing to do with Auslan. She makes them up on her own, usually when she's pissed off, and they almost all translate to "Are you fucking kidding me?" At least, that's what Jin assumes from context.

"I mean it," he says patiently. "We've got food, Aish. Enough for a month or more, maybe two if we're careful. Why risk the market?"

She looks at him like he's crazy, then waves imperiously at Billy, who hands over his pack, already well trained on the pecking order around here. Aisha rummages through Billy's stuff—markers and paint and spare clothes. She comes up with a small, colourful package and Jin rolls his eyes when he realises that it's a pack of fluorescent pink Post-Its.

Billy makes grabby hands, but Aisha keeps him at arm's length long enough to steal one of his pens and scribble the words Battery Specialist on one, which she rips off and sticks to Jin's chest. The next note is Artist, which she sticks to Billy. On her own, she writes The

Pharmacist, glares at them both, and attaches the note to herself with pride, her chin in the air.

"I'm not having an identity crisis," Jin mutters. "I just don't see the point in going to the trade market when we just scored a shitload of canned food. What are we trading for?"

They stay one more night at the creepy foster mother house, to pack up all the cans and sealed packets and jars into garbage bags. As dusk draws in, they bury the stash in a soft flower bed, then scatter a bunch of old cardboard boxes and other refuse over the spot so it isn't obvious that the earth has been recently turned over.

Jin's hands are sore afterwards, from all the digging. He didn't notice he was giving himself blisters at the time, too fascinated by the discovery that Billy is hiding some serious muscle under that over-sized army jacket of his.

Aisha patches Jin up afterwards, with Band-Aids and stinging antibacterial gel and doesn't even tease him about his obvious crush.

The trade market is held at what used to be a school, before the Pulse. The doors and windows hang wide open, and most of the serious traders have already set up in the gym.

Aisha lays down her blanket outside the doors, in a spot with decent line of sight to the school gate, and a couple of other easy exit points. Jin sets up next to her. There have been too many incidents of traders being knifed or threatened for their stash for him to risk being too far away from Aisha—not just because she will kill anyone who tries to hurt him, but her badass reputation means it's unlikely anyone will even try.

Billy disappears, and it occurs to Jin that maybe he isn't here to trade at all, or that he doesn't want to do it in front of them.

The Batteries Specialist Post-It note is still attached to Jin's shirt. Aisha doesn't wear hers, which means that half of Jin's customers come to him only to mouth, "Is that the Pharmacist?"

Jin's not wearing his hearing aids because a crowd like this makes too much messy noise from every direction, and his wares aren't for casual trading. He prefers to deal with people he knows, those who have bothered to learn a few signs in order to communicate with him.

Most kids think the way Billy did when they first met him—nothing works since the Pulse took out the power grid, and who the hell hangs on to anything battery-powered, when they're all living hand to mouth?

It's scary, how many kids haven't got the memo that they have to be the adults now. So many gangs survive by sheer luck and balls, never thinking further than their next meal or their next score.

Jin has enough diehard customers to make the trade market worthwhile, even if it's a fraction of the number who go to Aisha for their pharmaceutical needs. There will always be those who aren't willing to lose access to one particular device. They want to be able to cook hot food, or run a tattoo gun or a nebuliser or even something simple like a torch or a kettle. They know he's the man to provide what they need.

Jin is stingy about the zinc-airs, the batteries that he uses for his hearing aids. He'll reluctantly trade them to other hard-of-hearing kids, but only if they can prove they know how to take care of their aids, and they promise to bring back any dead batteries to him for recharging, no one else.

With the knowledge of their buried stash, Jin finds himself inquiring about luxuries and fresh fruit instead of the usual long-lasting power bars and tinned shit. He takes payment in dead batteries too, and charges others while customers wait.

Billy returns after a few hours, with hot coffee and an actual goddamned souvlaki to split three ways between them, and it's all Jin can do not to kiss him on the mouth.

Any excuse, right?

Aisha heads off for a while, to do some quiet deals in an alley. She wouldn't normally abandon Jin during trading, but it's obvious she trusts Billy to protect him. So Billy sprawls over her blanket and watches Jin trade recently charged AAs for chocolate and that spicy tea Aisha likes, a bag of squishy pears and one of his beloved vintage detective novels.

The one time a couple of skinheads come over acting like they might kick over Jin's display, Billy takes on a threatening stance that makes them think better of it.

It might save time if Jin just counts the moments when he doesn't want to kiss Billy on the mouth.

When Aisha returns, she shoos Jin away to stretch his legs. Billy slides over to take Jin's place at his battery display and gives him one of those beautiful, brain-melting grins.

Jin takes off the Batteries Specialist Post-It and sticks it to Billy's forehead, which is the closest he's ever got to flirting.

He does the rounds of the hot food vendors, checking if any of his regulars who haven't been by the stall yet need new batteries for their equipment, and noting down requests for the next market.

He finds Billy's latest work on the far side of the school—a wall with the words DID WE BREAK THE END OF THE WORLD? scrawled in massive letters. Billy must have used two cans.

There's more, as Jin steps closer to the drying paint. Small but distinct lettering underneath the usual slogan.

One Night Only
State Stadium
New Year's Eve

That's two months from now. New Year's Eve. The first anniversary of the day the world ended.

Jin leans against the opposite wall. Other kids come by, in twos and threes, to check out the message. After a while, Jin puts his aids in, because there aren't so many voices back here for him to get overwhelmed, and he wants to hear what people are saying. There is plenty of speculation about what the sign means.

"…it's a rock band, I heard."

"Like, the best album ever."

"He's a travelling philosopher who's gonna explain the meaning of life since the Pulse."

"It's punk art. It's not supposed to mean anything."

"A government conspiracy…"

"…aliens."

"…trap."

"…hoax."

"…There's this church that reckons we've been doing it all wrong, since the Pulse, that we were supposed to…"

Jin has heard enough. Surrounded by strangers and their chatter after the last week hanging out with Aisha and Billy, he feels desperately lonely. All he wants is to sit between the two of them and share their warmth.

But when he turns the corner, in sight of the gym doors, he sees immediately that they're gone.

It's all gone. Jin's pack (you don't leave anything behind), his display of batteries, his charging kit, Aisha's blanket. Like they were never there.

His feet are too damned heavy to move at first, because there has to be a reason...

There's a piece of bright pink paper fluttering in the breeze on the concrete. Jin doesn't have to look closer to know it's his Batteries Specialist Post-It.

Jin makes it as far as the school gate before things get weirder, because they're right there, Aisha and Billy together, packs slung on their backs (Jin's own pack resting against Aisha's feet like she's waiting for him, like this is normal). They're talking to each other with mouths and hands—not signing, but angry hand-gestures that people who know each other well use when they're arguing.

That's when Jin realises how stupid he's been. Of course they know each other. Since when do they take on a third teammate for more than a day or two? Since when does Aisha trust a new person to share their room at night, to share a bed?

That first night, she fell asleep when she was supposed to be on watch. She has never seen Billy as a threat.

The painful wash of noise from the market overloads Jin's ears as he stares at them both. They catch sight of him at the same time. Billy grins uncertainly, but Aisha's face shows something else altogether.

Caught out. Because yeah, turns out Aisha can talk just fine. That's the biggest betrayal of all. Why would she pretend otherwise? Jin has hearing aids, he can lip read, they could have had actual conversations, not long days of silence punctuated by their limited Auslan.

That's two secrets she's been keeping from him. Two massive, unnecessary secrets. He trusts her with everything, has done ever since they fell into each other's lives. She never trusted him at all.

"Jin," says Billy as Jin marches up to them both, grabbing his pack because he's damned if he's going to try to make it on his own without his gear. "Everything Okay?"

Aisha starts to make the signs, translating for Billy, but Jin shrugs and taps his ears. "I can hear fine. I just don't want to talk to you."

He turns and walks back through the market, away from them. He doesn't want them to follow, but it really hurts when they don't.

It takes only a couple of hours of wandering through the local suburban wasteland before Jin accepts that he's going to spend another night at the creepy foster mother house. He's going to need some of those buried supplies to make it to the next market, now that he's flying solo.

The sky is still bright when Jin lets himself into the back garden. The days are getting longer, as they head into summer.

Only, there isn't a 'they' any more.

Only.

There's a hunched figure sitting on the heap of squashed cardboard boxes over their food bank, and

Jin shouldn't be surprised. Of course the others would come back here. They need supplies as much as he does.

Billy jumps to his feet and starts talking at Jin, too fast, the words spilling out of his mouth and into the air. It's fascinating to watch, except that Jin can't make head nor tail of the frantic gabble.

Jin pinches at his ears, to show he's running on silence.

Billy mimes putting the aids back in, pissed off and impatient. Then he shoves a pink Post-It at Jin for him to read.

We're waiting by the gate. Get a move on.

Jin reads it through and then gropes for the aids. Okay. So they left him a note. He should have stopped to read it. That doesn't mean he can't be pissed off about the other stuff.

Once his aids are in and turned on, Billy's staring at him like he doesn't know how to start talking.

"You had plenty to say a minute ago," Jin grumbles.

Billy nods, runs his hands through his tangled dark hair, awkward as hell. Then he leans in, and oh. Apparently they're doing this without words.

He tastes of stale coffee and fresh strawberries—when did Aisha trade for those—and one kiss isn't enough for Jin, so he slides one hand into the front pocket of Billy's ragged jeans and curls the other arm up around his neck so they can press up against each other, kissing fiercely with teeth and tongue and a whole lot of heat.

He's angry, still so angry, but apparently that doesn't get in the way of kissing, not at all.

Finally they lean against each other, catching their breaths.

"So, we have to talk," says Billy in a low rumble. "Not about this—well, maybe about this, but not first—"

Jin pulls back, to see Billy's lips more easily. Even with the aids, lip reading helps to make better sense of the sounds.

Also, he likes looking at Billy's mouth.

"Did we break the end of the world? One night only, State Stadium—New Year's Eve?" Jin repeats the words he saw scrawled on the wall behind the school. He feels stupidly kiss-drunk, and maybe if Billy feels the same way, this is his one chance to get answers.

Billy nods carefully, and then looks beyond Jin to the back door of the house. Aisha is standing there, waiting for them. "We have a lot to tell you," she says. "If you boys can take time from your vital make out session?"

"Oh," says Jin. "So *now* you want to talk?"

Aisha raises her eyebrows, unimpressed.

They could have stood there all day, outstaring each other, but Billy threads his fingers into Jin's, and it's so hard to be angry when things like that keep happening.

"Okay," Jin relents. "Talk."

He shouldn't give them another chance, he knows that, and yet…he doesn't want to lose this. Not unless he's sure there's nothing left here to save.

*

They convene in the foster mother's floral living room, with Aisha and Billy perching on one couch, and Jin on the other. He knows they did it so he can see their lips but it still feels like they are the team now, with him as the outsider.

"So you know each other," he starts out. "From before?"

Aisha and Billy exchange glances. "We were in the same foster home," she admits. "Until—you know."

Until the Pulse took out all the power, leaving a generation of teenagers without communications, electricity, or functional foster parents.

"You were family," Jin says, a little bitterly because Aisha has been *his* only family for the last eight and a half months. He doesn't know which of them he's most jealous of right now.

Billy blows out a breath. "Jin," he says calmly. "Do you ever think that there's something really weird about all this?"

"What, you mean living in a post-apocalyptic suburban wasteland with only teen scavengers for company?" Jin drawls. If there's going to be any more kissing in their future, it's probably for the best that Billy knows up front about his tendency towards sarcasm.

Based on the impatient eye-roll he receives from Billy, that probably isn't going to be an issue.

"Yes," says Billy. "But I mean our life before the world ended. Does it make sense no one's ever been outside the bounds of this city? That our world was populated by suburbs full of Australian teenagers, and robot foster parents? Does it make sense that none of us have ever met a kid under twelve, or that we don't know anyone human over the age of eighteen? That no one remembers life before they joined their foster family?"

Jin has honestly never thought about it before because, yeah, that was how life worked before the Pulse. It was how life worked in TV shows and books—except the really old books, like the detective novels he loves, and he always assumed they were pure fantasy.

Now, he looks at the thin line of Aisha's mouth, and he realises that for her at least, this isn't a new idea.

"Yeah," she says softly. Her voice is nicer than he'd ever imagined—musical and sweet, unlike the rest of her. "I know you're wondering why I didn't talk. I needed the silence. Needed space to get my head together. I walked out on him, on what was left of our family…the only reason I could stand to be around *you* was because you didn't expect me to speak. I wasn't ready to deal with what happened the night it all ended."

"Whatever it is, please, tell me now." Jin means it. He does. Even if he's pretty sure he will feel worse once he knows.

"You're the one who likes to talk," said Aisha, kicking Billy lightly on the foot.

Billy gives her a friendly shove, and she doesn't even draw a knife on him. Yeah, Jin is an idiot for not spotting before that they are sibs.

"We're a failed experiment," Billy tells Jin. "At least—I don't know. Maybe not failed, but they were done with us either way. We're an artificially created generation, that's why no little kids and no adults. Our whole world—there's only the city centre and eight suburbs. They faked it all."

"I think they ran out of funding," says Aisha. "Or maybe we were wildly successful and they always meant to do this. Always meant to set the Pulse on us on their way out, like the world's shittiest mic drop."

"But how do you know all this?" Jin blurts out. "How do you even—"

"We found the scientists," says Billy. "Didn't even mean to, not really. I wandered off once, when we were at State Stadium for a soccer game."

"You mean you were looking for a clean wall to tag," Aisha scoffs.

"I found this whole...lab, I guess, set up behind the stadium wall. They had cameras looking into the homes, a bunch of other creepy stuff, but only monitoring the houses with foster families."

"The ones with humans," Aisha adds. "The kids like us."

"Aish and I sneaked in a few times after that, trying to figure out what they were up to. We didn't even know they were robots like the foster mothers, not then. Not until after."

"We were there that night," Aisha says flatly. "They were uploading the last of their data. They even talked about setting off the Pulse, but we didn't know what it meant, didn't know..."

"Disposable adults," says Billy, biting off the words. "One big fucking self destruct button. We were halfway home when the Pulse hit. The world ended because they meant it to end." His grin is savage. For the first time, he looks as dangerous as Aisha. "Only we fucked it up for them. All of us. The whole—" he waves an arm around to indicate the world around us. "They left us without foster parents or power or rations, and I guess they expected us to die off here in their little fake suburbia. The first winter should have taken the last of us out. But instead we adapted this whole teen scavenger mobster shithole economy that makes no real sense to me. All I know is, you and Aish are rock stars at it."

"Good thing we're not all dedicated to the starving artist mentality," says Aisha primly.

Jin nods slowly, taking it in. "Did we break the end of the world?" he says aloud and is rewarded by one of those amazing smiles that reminds him all over again how goddamned beautiful Billy is.

"It was supposed to end, and it didn't. We wouldn't let it," says Billy.

"It's not the miracle you think it is," Aisha groans. "It's just humans surviving. It's what people do."

"But they didn't think we were people," Billy says, sounding almost too excited by the idea. He doesn't see what Jin does—the look of stiff discomfort crossing Aisha's face. *They didn't think we were people.*

"So what's happening New Year's Eve?" Jin asks, to push the conversation past the awkwardness.

Billy leans forward, brimming with energy. "It's all still there—the lab behind the stadium. Full of deactivated scientist robot bodies, but full of other stuff too. Tech that we need. If there's any chance of getting the power back on—of fixing this fucking mess, then it's in there, waiting for us. I haven't been able to get in—something about the Pulse jammed all the electronic locks, but I reckon Aisha can do it."

"And we become heroes of the apocalypse," Aisha drawls.

Billy turns on her, impatient. "Sorry, am I getting in the way of your drug dealing empire? Do you seriously have something *better* to do?"

"I'm not the one kidding himself he can rebuild society from the ground up!"

"We can try! Maybe we can do better. Maybe we can have hot showers again, I'd settle for that. We can aim higher than survival, Aish. Can't we?"

"Maybe we should have stopped them killing us in the first place," she snaps back, shaking with fury and…what, guilt? "We were there, that night. If we'd put the pieces together better, if we hadn't been so scared…maybe we could have stopped them."

Jin is used to Aisha being amazing at everything, all super confident and capable. Turns out she has been nursing a huge guilt complex because she couldn't prevent the end of the world. He wants to hug her, but they don't do that. Instead, he says, "Can you get me into this lab to look around?"

Billy grins at him. "Thought you'd never ask, babe." At Aisha's scoffing sound he adds, "What you think I didn't notice you teamed up with someone who knows how electrical shit works? You haven't given up on fixing the world, Aish, so let's get on with it." He turns back to Jin, words spilling out of him in excitement again. "There are other kids like you, right? Who know about tech or engineering, so we can put a team together—"

"I know a few people. We can track them down through the trade markets, and maybe your wall messages—"

"I figured you would, you and Aish are practically famous, everyone at that market knew who you were—"

"You've already picked New Year's Eve as our deadline—"

"It was all I could think of, to get enough kids in one place, amped up to pool our skills. We have to stop acting like it's all teams and gangs, start thinking like a community."

"If we can get the power back on, even in a small way, something to give them all hope—"

"And start organising—we need to get some fucking crops happening before the next winter, make the most of the back gardens we've been left with..."

"OH MY GOD!" says Aisha loudly, jumping to her feet. "It was bad enough when there was just one of you." She glares at them both. "I'm going to take a bath and eat some of that chocolate Jin scored today, maybe take a Valium, while you two indulge in this—annoying world-saving shared brain strategy session. When you come up with a plan that involves me hitting, stabbing or drugging someone, let me know."

She slams her way out of the room, only to return three seconds later to add: "And you'd better get all the kissing out of your system during daylight hours, because if you don't keep your hands to yourselves when we're sharing a bed, I'm going to cut your fingers off." The last sentence is accompanied by viciously accurate hand-signs for [cut] and [fingers] before the door bangs behind her again.

The boys sit there in a haze of shared embarrassment, until they hear the bath upstairs starting to fill.

"I preferred it when she didn't want to talk to me," Jin whispers. They crack up, laughing quietly, because they don't want to risk her yelling at them again.

"So, saving the world?" Billy says. "You in?"

[Yes], Jin signs, and rockets off the floral couch to throw himself into Billy's lap. "Only I'm thinking—"

"Thinking is good." Billy's hand traces up his spine, over the top of Jin's T-shirt.

"I'm thinking we should start tomorrow," Jin says breathlessly, taking out his hearing aids and shoving them into his pocket.

Billy smirks at him, and signs [Sounds good, Jin]. With his hands still wrapped around each other in the sign for [precious] that also means [Jin], he hooks his wrists around Jin's neck, and reels him in for another kiss.

They've already broken the end of the world. Surely there's time for a little making out, before they start building a new one.

In the Sky with Diamonds
Elinor Caiman Sands

The moondust gets everywhere. It always did but there's more stirred up tonight. The gunpowder stink of it is here, in my spacesuit, in my orbiting capsule, as much as I've tried to keep it out.

Below, Earth's only satellite stretches grey and cratered, while in the distance the alien destroyers finish their job of smashing up the lunar colony. I'm lucky I escaped. Plumes of glittering rock scatter into the vacuum, alongside sparkling bits of twisted metal, cracked bottles, a golf club, a child's shoe.

I should be fleeing with the giant Earth-Moon shuttle *Tangerine Sky*, Lucy's ship, *my sister's ship*, but I'm too slow for that. It brims with human passengers—miners, builders, tourists. It flees with all the little ships, all that escaped in time, all those with crews who can steer their craft so much better than me. But for once I'm content to be left behind, with the eternal camera behind my eyes. Left behind with a chance to make a difference protecting Lucy and those other ships, now that I'm stranded here anyway. Lucy who cared for me, her older sister, when she was only a child herself.

Jennifer, tell me we can get between the Tangerine Sky *and the alien vessel.*

Perhaps we can, whispers the accessibility device in my head. *I'm not sure why you want to, Megan, but our ship is fast enough.*

I know what she's thinking. When fighting the alien jellyships, speed and agility is everything. We learned this quickly. The aliens can hit big dumb rocks like the Earth and Moon but not a fighter jet. Yet dexterity is the one thing I lack. My brain was damaged at birth and my body does its own thing, independent of instruction. My speech is an unintelligible slur. I have cerebral palsy. Some call me spastic, though if they do they're likely to get a kick in the groin. *Oh, I'm sorry, must have been a leg spasm.*

Jennifer, you have no sense of urgency. My AI is my friend but sometimes her timidity is frustrating. *Give me a neural link to the guidance controls. And get the* Tangerine Sky's *flight plan. Draft a tentative schedule and checklist for us.*

Working, says Jennifer. I can feel her processing. There's a faint warm buzz where she lives at the crown of my skull. She's been here reading my fractured mind for a long time, since she was implanted when I was six years old. She spoke to me then and showed me how to say my first word: "Mamma." I remember the tear that rolled down my mother's cheek; she hugged me and told me how clever I was.

Mother died years ago. It's just my sister left now, out there.

We're ready, says Jennifer. Thankfully she doesn't question my lack of piloting experience. Normally these lunar capsules will fly by themselves; their on-board computers programmed to orbit and de-orbit from lunar space. Usually my wayward limbs don't have to touch the controls at all, but if you want to do anything more complex or untoward you have to manage it yourself. The arrays of buttons and displays in the glass cockpit make no sense. But maybe Jennifer knows it's pointless to nag when I've set my sights on the marshmallow pie beyond the next crater.

She gives the first set of figures and I think the command to fire the attitude control thrusters, followed by a brief burn. The hydrazine monopropellant rocket gets us moving towards the alien vessel.

The spacecraft shakes and vibrates. Then it falls silent. Gradually, the aliens' curious craft grows larger.

Up close the ship reflects a kaleidoscope of colours. It's translucent through my spacecraft's spyhole window. There are stars and gemstones in it. The fact that it's beautiful only makes it seem more alarming. Something that deadly shouldn't look that pretty. It should be ugly, vulgar, with hideous slime-green monsters inside.

Do you have a plan, Megan? asks Jennifer.

To distract them, I say. *To draw them away, and not get hit. Make sure you record it. If we pull this off, it'll make one hell of a story.*

That it will, she says, though Jennifer doesn't really know. She could never understand why I've wanted to be a war reporter all my life. It's not that the work of a desk-bound industrial hack is without value. For three years I've reported company profits and boardroom takeovers. Someone has to do it, but my war correspondent father was a hero. He died on Earth, killed by a landmine before I was born. It's people like him who make a difference in the world.

I get Jennifer to bring us about in front of the aliens. We're blocking their flight path towards the *Tangerine Sky*.

Come on you monsters. Look at me.

They must have seen us.

A small meteoroid barrels towards us on a collision course.

Megan, look out! I swear there's blind panic in Jennifer's ice-cold circuits.

End over end the space rock hurtles towards us. My stomach somersaults. I clench my fists. My nails cut my palms.

The aliens don't need missiles; they just capture our local debris and fling it at us, as if we're not worth the expense of real ammunition. Big stuff they throw at the Earth or Moon, small stuff at our spacecraft. The merest speck, if thrown fast enough, will punch a hole in my ship.

Damnit, roll us forty-five degrees, engine start, two second burn, I say.

One set of thrusters fires. The main engine powers us away, clear of the near-death experience. But what looks like a lump of iron pops from the gelatinous mass of the alien craft, closely followed by a stony planetoid.

So the aliens intend to give me no time to contemplate fresh manoeuvres.

Both missiles speed toward us. I swallow hard. I don't intend to end my days as orbiting space junk.

Pitching, says Jennifer, as she does just that. We yaw too, at my command. I order more burns, the propulsion systems work overtime as another rock follows, part stone, part ice. Sweat trickles into my eyes.

But the alien craft is slowing. The translucent mass takes time to launch each attack, and the *Tangerine Sky* is getting away. The shuttle is a tiny grey pillbox in the distant black, and beyond it the blue-marble Earth shines, a swirling sapphire in the night.

Megan, fuel is running low. Jennifer's statement draws my eyes to the displays, in search of the propulsion meter.

How low? I ask Jennifer.

Thirty seconds of main engine thrust remain.

Just thirty seconds. It'll take minutes for the *Tangerine Sky* to reach maximum velocity and have a hope of escape. They're not going to survive unless I do something radical.

The thrusters shoot us sideways. A small rock misses my capsule by inches.

Megan, we should leave.

Don't even think about it, I tell her. Does Jennifer have inbuilt safety features? That would be too bad. *Do we have reserve fuel on board?*

Jennifer doesn't reply. Jennifer always replies. *Jennifer?* If she's having a system crash she's picked one hell of a time. She can't be having a meltdown, I can't be that unlucky. *Say something you mouldy hunk of silicon.*

Xe ere, she says. *Dimo giv.*

A cold chill runs through me.

Dimond giv else die.

My muscles tense and spasm. That's not Jennifer. It's them, it must be. They're not known for being chatty but it's the only explanation; they've hacked into Jennifer.

My mouth is dry. What can I say to hostile ETs that have already caused so much fear and devastation? I feel my own precious diamond tight on its chain around my neck. Their harvesters have ravaged Earth, emptied every jeweller's shop and bank vault without explanation. Maybe they use the jewels in industry, or as currency. Nobody knows. We only know that diamonds are what they are here for. We don't know why Earthly diamonds. There are diamonds elsewhere in the universe. We don't know what's so special about ours.

If I could get answers to these questions, it would be the news story of my career. Besides, if they're going to murder us all, I'd at least like to know why. Whatever their reasons, they're ruthless plunderers. Rings and stones have been willingly surrendered by terrified populations, collected by governments and received by the aliens. Some called it appeasement. Protest groups marched and called the strangers Nazis. Some cities resisted and hid their diamonds ... until the asteroid flattened Amsterdam.

The holders of memorial diamonds hide them too and mine is one of those. My diamond is my father. When he died, Mother took his ashes to a jeweller's shop, which cooked them and pressurised them, extracting the carbon to form this sparkling gem. And since I inherited it, he's always been with me.

So I can't give it up. Using it to lure the aliens away is Lucy's only hope. As well as being all I have left of him.

No. The diamond is mine, I tell them. *Go to hell.*

Their response is swift: another rock comes flying. I give the command to fire the thrusters, to take us out even further from the *Tangerine Sky*. I remember too late that Jennifer might not be alive to execute my order.

Forgive me, Megan. It's Jennifer! I would hug her if she weren't in my head. Perhaps her timing isn't so bad after all.

Though I have an instinctive sense: Jennifer might be back but something is still awry in my head. I clutch the sides of my pilot's chair, though I know that won't save me.

Jennifer! No! I gasp as my plans unravel and Jennifer fires the wrong rocket.

The engines roar and we surge ahead, towards my sister's shuttle when we should be moving away.

Jennifer's behaving with almost irrational human emotion. Whether she's trying to save herself, or me, or both of us together hardly matters. If she keeps this up we'll have no fuel left to perform docking manoeuvres with the shuttle even if we reach it.

I knew I should have been more careful of her programming. I might have guessed she'd do this. But she's never disobeyed me before, not in two decades. Her betrayal hurts. I have no time for this. There's only one thing I can do, something I've never done before: I put her into safe mode.

This effectively shuts her down. Her intelligence, her personality, all that makes her what she is. *Goodnight, Jennifer*, I say, though she's already beyond hearing. Now I'm really alone out here, in the vacuum of space. The capsule shakes and vibrates as the thrusters fire; in front of me the burn button is lit up like a supernova— it has to be pressed to shut the propulsion system down. Shakily I extend my right arm. I bite my lip, too hard, and taste blood.

My accuracy would be better if I were calmer but I can't waste time generating dexterity strategies. Instead I go ahead and punch the glass cockpit controls, blindly. Pain sears through my knuckles but by some miracle I stop the burn.

The spacecraft falls silent; it drifts on through the nothingness.

But I know, even without looking at the displays, that the fuel tank must be almost empty; even if I could control my ship manually, I couldn't correct its course for long.

Inertia carries treacherous Jennifer and me straight onwards towards the *Tangerine Sky*, with the alien monsters on our tail. It's not Jennifer's fault, though part of me curses her. Slowly, inevitably, the *Tangerine Sky* grows.

I can't control my ship without Jennifer, but maybe I don't need to. Perhaps there's another way.

I twist my body around this way and that, so I can see behind me and to each side through my helmet faceplate. On the left-hand wall rests a SAFER unit, bolted to the metal. Its controls are substantial, designed for gloved and pressurised hands. I fancy even I could operate them.

I watch the *Tangerine Sky* through the capsule window. It looks so shiny and inviting, but that's an illusion. It won't reach Earth at all without my help.

I have no choice, I must venture out into the darkness. I swallow a Valium through my medication tube and try not to choke. I hate the blasted stuff but the situation demands it. The prescription is meant for emergencies, to calm me enough to control my shakes a little. And if this isn't an emergency then my name is Neil Armstrong. I hope it doesn't make me woozy. I need to be strong, not wobbly; strong like my father.

I check all systems on my suit: pressure, cooling and most important: the SAFER unit. Then slowly, clumsily, I unbuckle my seat belt and float free.

I try to relax. This isn't going to be easy, even with the Valium.

When my bosses sent me to the Moon, I think they thought low gravity would be good for me, but what fools they were. Where the smallest uncontrolled movement or the lightest touch sends things flying through space, my body contrives to propel me or my stuff into infinity with each leg spasm.

I get my arms through the SAFER unit and strap it to my back.

I'm ready to depressurise and open the hatch.

My capsule's too small to have an airlock so I need to hit more buttons to let the air out manually. I hold my breath and stab into the dark. One. Two. Three, the last one. Victory.

As I exhale I can hear the hiss of escaping air. Eventually I'm ready to open the door.

Clumsily, I seize the ratchet handle and push. Nothing happens. This ought to be the easy bit.

Cursing, I brace my legs against the pilot's seat and put my shoulder to the hatch. I push and push but it won't budge. I'm sweating now but it's only a door, it has to open. I grab the screwdriver strapped to the leg of my suit and try to wedge it in the crack. It still won't open. My hands wobble at the behest of their own personal puppet master. My mixed up brain won't persuade them to fix the metal tool in place. If my sister were here, or my mother, *or my father,* we'd be out of here in seconds. I yell in frustration, incomprehensibly, and then, in fury, smash the door with the screwdriver. The whole ship vibrates but the door stays firmly shut while I swear at it like a demon.

After a while, I rest and take some deep breaths. I'm starting to relax.

I try once more and the screwdriver slips into place. I lean on it until it bends and now I worry it'll snap before the wretched door moves. But then it pops open, swinging wide onto space and stars and I float into the sunlit emptiness.

My first EVA. It's beautiful out here, just me and the stars. I wonder idly which one the aliens came from.

Grasping the door with both hands, I manoeuvre myself with some difficulty so my feet are flat on the outside of the capsule. Now the drugs have kicked in, my head is swimming, my eyes are blurry but my limbs are steady.

On a count of three, I lift my helmeted head to the blackness and push away from the spacecraft. Let it follow the *Tangerine Sky* without me in it.

Will my ploy work? I wonder. It's the diamond they want after all, not my ship, not even me. I watch the shimmering alien mass as I recede into the nothingness. Then slowly, surely, the jellyship shifts and swings about slow as a lunar day. It drifts closer. If I felt like bait before, now I come with added sugar.

Wait you.

I don't think I shall. Catch me if you can. I laugh at them, a hideous gurgling sound. What will get me first, the vacuum of space or the ghostly invaders? Neither, I hope.

Unfortunately, the invaders have plenty of speed. It's only manoeuvrability they lack. Soon they're a pale and shimmering horror through my visor. Then the missiles come. My muscles tighten—perhaps they're playing cosmic billiards, with me as the eight ball. I wonder why they have so much trouble snaring small but moving targets. Maybe they're as fragile as they look, maybe they dare not approach. We know they have remarkable deflection technology; they've used it to repel every missile and weapon we've aimed at them, yet maybe they're not invulnerable.

Still, it seems too much to hope that I could just punch them between the eyes.

I have my hands clamped on the SAFER control box. At least I don't have to manoeuvre the entire spacecraft this time, just myself in the vacuum. I try to relax, then move the joystick. My movement is as smooth as it ever is, and that's smooth enough. The little nitrogen-jet thrusters fire and navigate me away from the alien vessel.

Stop you.

No. *What is so special about Earth's diamonds anyway?* I don't expect a reply, but I'm a journalist, I have a pathological need to investigate.

They surprise me.

Diamond perfect carbon structure reflection of god.

I stare at the alien vessel as shifting shadows move within. It almost sounds like the ETs worship the sparkly gems. Strange. Or maybe not, considering how we ourselves hoard them.

Humanity worships diamonds too, in a way, I tell the invaders. Perhaps we worship them too much.

No you unearth you lacerate perfect carbon structures.

Lacerate. There's a word you don't hear every day in relation to diamonds. But surely this is it, the answer to the great puzzle at the heart of the invasion. They're trying to protect the diamonds from us, not merely harvest them. Because we cut them, and sometimes destroy them, as we destroy so much.

So the invaders are moral beings, not just killing machines.

Still. *We do genuinely cherish them.*

You do not you are nothing.

And here was me thinking I'd found a new friend. My jaw tightens, I'm achieving nothing. As if to prove my point, another rock comes tumbling. Cursing, I activate the SAFER unit and blast myself aside.

I have limited propellant in the SAFER unit too. Maybe I've miscalculated. Even if I go on until they inevitably catch me, it might not be enough. Maybe the alien ship will still catch my sister's shuttle. After all, would they really bother coming after me if they doubted they could catch the larger ship? I know for a fact there are diamonds on board, and the aliens have some unknown means of sniffing them out. They are the evil scientists; I'm the mouse in a maze. And yet, even the tiniest mouse has pretty big teeth.

Another asteroid, a really big one this time, comes hurtling towards me. All thoughts fly from my head as I struggle to avoid it but at least the SAFER unit is holding up. My sweat-soaked hair is sticky against my forehead. I wonder if the suit cooling system is working as it should.

Listen. What if I told you the stone around my neck was once a human being? Maybe it's time I tried a different tack, more than cat and mouse, now we're communicating. *Humans are made of carbon, the same stuff as diamonds. We don't just destroy diamonds, we manufacture them too—sometimes from our mortal remains. If you kill us, you'll be killing future diamonds and those who make them.*

Silence. They're probably not even listening anymore. Maybe they're just waiting for me to run out of fuel or air. And even if they're listening, when does faith consider reason? I've never been one for believing in deities. Jennifer took the place of all such imaginary friends when I was six. Although right now a friendly god might have been useful to have around. The mirror on my wrist reflects the displays on my chest and those show all my supplies are running low: air, propellant, cooling water, all of it. I have a little drinking water left, though, so I take a sip, clenching my teeth on the plastic tube. A tepid dribble drips into my mouth, tasting of moondust.

And still they don't respond. Though at least they haven't thrown any more rocks.

The alien ship accelerates as I take a second swallow. It wobbles for a moment, goes extra blurry then hurtles away faster than I've ever seen. And it's not going towards the shuttle, or Earth, or the Moon. It's heading far out into deep space.

More of the jellyships appear from their stations about the Earth and pass before the Sun before vanishing into distant constellations.

Is that it? Have I done it, just like that? After terrorising humanity for five months, are they leaving without so much as a thanks for all the fish?

It seems hard to believe. Nothing has changed for me, I'm still floating here, hours from death.

But even if I'm doomed, the Earth will go on. And Lucy. I smile despite my predicament. Mother would have been pleased. Lucy was born through IVF when Mamma failed to accept the death of our father. People sometimes call me special but really they've got it all wrong, it's my sister who is the special one.

I close my eyes and remember how she cared for me when we were only kids, including that time she beat Sean Walker to a pulp in Grade Three for calling me a moron and putting beetles in my chicken tikka masala. Now at last I've returned the favour.

I think my air is failing. My thoughts are getting fuzzy and I'm turning sentimental. I could wake up Jennifer. Then I won't die alone. But I dismiss that idea. No doubt she would be full of remorse. I'll let her rest in peace; she'll never know how much she disappointed me. I'll just float here with my eyes shut and see what happens. Maybe I'll just doze. I'm so sleepy.

I open my eyes with a gasp. I don't see stars anymore, or Earth, or the Sun. I'm back in my capsule with the hatch shut and the cabin pressurised. My helmet is off too but that's okay as there's plenty of air in here.

I look through the window, and there's the alien jellyship, hazy against the Milky Way. There's the *Tangerine Sky*, too, whole and safe, within easy docking distance.

I stare at the jellyship. Did they come back to save me? They must have had a hasty conference and decided humans weren't so bad after all.

I feel like the mass of a neutron star has been lifted from my back. I'm going to live, though I'm not sure why. Am I really that persuasive? A moment ago the aliens were acting like monstrous psychopaths, now they're carrying out roadside rescues.

You please not lacerate diamonds.

I can arrange that. I promise. Perhaps it's presumptive of me to promise on behalf of everyone but surely people aren't so silly they'd refuse. It would mean the loss of an industry, but the survival of our species.

All humans keep yourselves safe.

Yes. We will. We certainly will.

We made error.

Oh really?

You easy to understand unlike others.

Well, that's a laugh. Maybe I should go into the peace envoy business. And I laugh even more at the thought. It's easy to communicate with them too, as scary as that is. Speaking with them is direct, immediate, like they have a hotline to my Wernicke's area. I don't have to rely on Jennifer's AI, which perhaps was never truly a part of me. I guess I'm more different than I thought.

I ask them for a formal interview. An interview with an alien. Wouldn't that be the scoop of the millennium? It would surely get me a raise. Several raises.

Perhaps, they reply.

With that they disappear into the blackness and I'm left to wonder what might come next.

Two Somebodies Go Hunting
Rivqa Rafael

Mum pushed them out the door, pretty much. It didn't occur to either sibling that their mother might have done better if she'd gone hunting herself. But no, little Jackie had an ominous rattle in her chest and no one had heard from Dad for months, so it had to be them.

"She picked out two somebodies, Sally and me," Jeff chanted gleefully.

Mum smiled. Lex scowled. "Mum, is he going to do that the whole time?"

"Probably."

"It's already not funny, Jeff."

Jeff repeated the line.

"I think he disagrees," Mum said. "Jeff, you need to look after Lexi, okay?"

Lex snorted, and Jeff nodded. "Yes, Mum."

"And you need to look after Jeff, Lexi."

Lex put on her big hat, Velcroing the brim out of the way for the time being. "Always do."

Mum's voice was tight. "I mean it. Be careful. Keep your high-vis vests on *all* the time, no matter how hot it gets. There might be other hunters." There might be lawless scavengers who killed on sight, but Mum didn't need to mention those. They could be anywhere; everyone knew that. You just had to hope they weren't near you.

Mum scooped Lex and Jeff in for a hug. "Just stay safe; that's the most important thing. And stay together. And stay clean."

Lex kissed her mother's cheek quickly and squirmed away. Mum looked at her quietly for a long moment and guided Jeff by the shoulder, out of the dugout to the quad bike. Following a couple of steps behind, Lex tried not to favour her right leg; shorter and misshapen as it was, it was hard to keep her gait even.

Jeff scrolled through the maps on his GPS with an intent expression, while Lex squatted down to help Mum check the supplies one last time.

A little gasp escaped Lex as she stood up. The chill of dawn was pleasant on her skin, but it wasn't kind to her bones. The muscles around that old fracture twinged and pulsed with a deep ache.

"Next time, I'll do that," Jeff said.

"I'm *fine*," Lex said. "You keep playing with your toy."

"It's not a toy. It's going to get us there and back again, you know."

Mum nodded. "Once you're out there in the desert, it's hard to tell which way is which. Got your compass just in case, Jeff?"

Nodding, he pulled it out from under his T-shirt to show her. "And the paper maps."

"I think that's everything." Lex turned the bike to face the wattle orchard that surrounded their property, away from the town. It was far enough away that they weren't likely to be spotted by its sparse population, but Lex would still be glad when they were really in the desert. It wasn't often they had any sort of head start on a hunt.

Mum sighed, every line on her forehead visible. "You'd best get going then, before it gets too hot."

Forcing a smile, Lex nodded.

Jeff tackle-hugged Mum and jumped on the quad bike.

"Jeff, I need to get on first. Get off." Lex glared at her brother's enthusiastic expression.

"O-*kay*, Sally."

"Don't call me that. Do you see any snow here? Or stupid cats in hats? Grow up, Jeff." She gripped the handlebars tightly and threw her weaker leg over the seat.

Mum made a disapproving noise as Jeff clambered on behind Lex. She'd warned Lex time and again not to make fun of Jeff's love of Dr Seuss, and not just because it meant he'd read to Jackie.

She ducked her head. "Ow, you're pressing my leg."

"Sorry, Lexi."

Grunting an acceptance, she turned the bike on. "See you soon, Mum."

"Yes." Mum's jaw was set straight, along with her shoulders. "Good hunting, kids."

Lex could feel Jeff waving. "Bye, Mum! Love you!"

As Lexi drove them away, Jeff watched Mum over his shoulder, heading back into the house looking all droopy. "Do you think she'll be okay?" he asked. He cuddled into his sister lopsidedly, trying to avoid her sore leg. Lexi was nice and squishy to cuddle, when she let him. Mum always cuddled him when he needed it, but she was bony in more places.

"She'll worry about us, but she'll be okay. We just have to do what she said, stay safe, so we can get back to her. Even if we don't get the roo." Lex's tone was light, but there was a hard edge to it that made Jeff worry. There were lots of things that could go wrong, enough that he didn't feel like joking around anymore. There might not have been any cats in hats around to cause trouble, but there weren't any to magically solve their problems either.

He nodded, even though Lex wouldn't be able to see. The sun was still rising behind them, bathing the desert ahead in pinky-orange light. He almost asked another question, "What about Jackie?" but instead just mouthed the words so that Lexi wouldn't hear. He didn't want to hear her answer. It wasn't like he didn't know, anyway, what it might be. Everyone did. Instead he looked down at the ground. The dirt was still brown here, still okay for growing things, but full of bugs too. *Burkholderia. Clostridium. Sporothrix.* Nasty bugs. He glared at them, then looked up because it made him nauseous.

Lex was asking him something. "…long will it take to get to the area?"

He started pulling the GPS out of his pocket, even though he didn't need it to answer her question. "About five or six hours, depending on the wind in the dunes and that. Then we need to try and track him."

"I know *that*."

He put the GPS away, still switched off. "It's a long shot, isn't it?"

"Yeah. Dunno why he's on his own, either." Lex shrugged. "Maybe he's a reject. Lost a fight."

"Maybe he *smells*." Jeff giggled.

"As long as he tastes good, I don't care. I can't remember the last time I tasted meat."

Bush gave way to red soil with the occasional scrubby plant. "Do you remember what chicken tasted like?"

She snorted. "I'm only two years older than you, Jeff. Chicken was banned when I was a baby. Bloody bird flu."

"And MRSA. And VRE. And mad cow disease." Jeff was glad he hadn't been born yet. Mum had told him not to look at the pictures of all the dead animals, burned up so they couldn't kill any more people. She said it was too gruesome for him. He knew it would upset him, so he listened to her, but sometimes he thought about looking.

"Well yeah, fuck that shit. Placentals, why'd they have to be so related to humans?"

Jeff couldn't help himself; he gasped. "Don't swear, Lexi. Mum doesn't like it."

"Mum's not here."

He whimpered.

"*Fine*. Don't freak out on me, 'kay?"

"I'm not freaking out." He reached for the magnetic beads in his pocket, just in case. "I just want Mum to be proud of us."

"She's always proud of you. Don't worry, Jeff."

He'd meant us when he said it, but he let it drop. They drove in silence, any sounds that the desert might make covered by the scratch of the tyres against the sand. The wind wasn't strong that day, not yet anyway, so everything was calm, just how Jeff liked it. It made the desert seem empty, which it wasn't, not really. There were insects and lizards and tiny hopping mice and other marsupials, all creatures that were slowly regaining a foothold since so many humans had died. But the bike made enough noise to scare them off when it got close. A hopping mouse would make a nice pet, Jeff thought, even if Lexi would rather eat it as a snack, and Mum would look at him sadly and say it wasn't practical. He'd seen mice a couple of times, and they had faces that looked like friends.

"Lexi?" Jeff rubbed his fingers together in careful circles. "Do you think it's wrong to eat animals?"

"Nope. I think it's *delicious*." She chuckled at her own joke.

"North a bit now, Lexi." An abandoned mining post lay a few kays ahead, and nasty scavengers might have claimed it. A rusting, crumbling poppet-head was just visible in the shimmering light. It might have been imposing once, or a good lookout, but now it was just a hazard, rubbish too big and unimportant to ever be cleaned up. "I know we need everything we can get. But what if we didn't?"

She turned the bike to circumvent the danger. "Dunno. I'd probably still eat them, if I could. I mean, some of them would eat us."

Jeff wasn't sure if he'd seen people rise out of the shadows of the old tower, or just imagined them. He breathed out loudly as they zipped away. "Not in Australia, though, not anymore. What if that kangaroo's an endangered species?"

They were clear of the mine. Lex actually turned to look at him quickly. "*We're* an endangered species. Seriously, Jeff, if you're going to do something stupid when we see this roo, try and stop me shooting it or something, I will turn this bike around right now. I'll go by myself, no matter what Mum says."

Pulling back from his sister as much as he could, Jeff shook his head. "I know we need it, all of us. But still…"

She exhaled loudly. "If wishes were horses, I wouldn't have to share this bike with you. Come on, let's take a break. I need to pee, and we should put some zinc on."

It got hotter. Their skin had been burnt dark from years in the harsh sun, but Lex and Jeff were used to staying in the shade in the middle of the day. Sweat mingled with the stripe of green zinc over Lex's eyebrows and threatened to drip in her eyes, but dried too fast to get there. Which was lucky, because Lex couldn't think of much worse than sand-studded zinc in her eyes. The heat lessened the ache in her leg, but feeling like a dried-up piece of leather did nothing for her overall comfort. "How close are we to the place the drone spotted him?"

Jeff showed her the GPS. His skinny body seemed to cope better with the relentless heat. The yellow zinc over his eyebrows and under his eyes was still in place, also frosted with sand, and his expression was cheerful as always. Infuriatingly cheerful. "Here's the marker, and we're here. Looks like the dunes have moved around a fair bit. We'll have to go up this way."

Dragging herself off the bike to study the incline, Lex clicked her tongue. "I don't think the bike can manage that slope."

"We'll have to walk."

"No way I can make it up. And we can't leave the bike so far off, anyway. What if we can't find it again? What if someone nicks it?" She leaned on the bike, gripping a handlebar tightly.

"I could climb up and try to get a better view."

Crossing her arms over her chest, Lex huffed at him. "Mum said no splitting up."

Jeff smiled. "I wouldn't go far. Just enough to have a look."

"Mum wouldn't like it." What if something happened to him, all the way up a dune she couldn't climb?

Jeff lifted his shoulders and let them fall again. "I don't want to disappoint Mum."

Relieved that her tactic had worked, Lex said, "We'll have to try and go around, then. See if we can find a waterhole."

He whipped the GPS out of his pocket again and consulted it. "The closest water source is here…about five kays away."

Snorting, Lex scanned the area. Rock formations, the occasional patch of scrub, and endless sand were all she could see, until… "There. See that dark patch?"

"There's nothing on the map," he said, scrolling frantically.

"Use your eyes, Jeff."

"I am!"

Lex grabbed the hand holding the GPS and yanked it up. "If you just—"

Jeff shrieked and snatched it away from her. "Don't touch it!"

Rolling her eyes, Lex threw her hands up in mock surrender. "I'm not touching your stupid toy. I just want you to look up for once."

"It's not stupid. It's not a toy." He cradled it to his chest for a minute before putting it back into his pocket with a reverent pat. He huffed at her while he Velcroed the pocket closed again with maddening slowness. "Be hard to get home without it."

"Well, fine, but they don't exactly update the maps out here all that often, do they? The dunes move around like you said, and an old soakage might be uncovered, and that's exactly where we might see the big red. Honestly, Jeff, you didn't think the GPS was going to lead you right to it, did you?"

"I thought maybe the drone…"

"Maybe. It's probably moved back east, though. It's not *our* drone. Just because it guided our air drop." She ground her teeth and waited. Jeff was wasting time, but he hated being told that. Like Mum always said, the more you hurried him, the longer he took. It was an effort to remember, so Lex repeated Mum's words in her head while she waited. Her leg was throbbing again. She shifted in place, trying to take the weight off.

Jeff looked at her for what seemed like forever, then spoke at last. "Okay, let's go that way and look around. We've got a while until dusk, anyway."

Limping back to the quad bike, Lex glared at Jeff's back. "Are you just feeling sorry for me." It wasn't really a question.

"No."

"Good."

"But you could take some of your medication if you needed to," he suggested.

She growled, a low rumble in her throat.

"You don't have to."

If her eyes were lasers, there would have been holes in his back by now. He'd reached the quad bike a few steps ahead of her, and he turned to smile at her. It flickered a bit when he saw the expression on her face. "Why are you angry, Lex?"

"I'm not."

"You look angry."

"I'm. Not." With some difficulty, Lex got herself back on the bike. Not making eye contact with Jeff, she opened her tube of pills after a brief struggle with the child safety lock. She knocked back a couple of tablets and chased them down with a gulp of water.

Jeff waited until she'd put the pills away again, then slid on behind her, moving slowly, almost gingerly. He had done something to upset Lex but he wasn't quite sure what. Why didn't she want to take her medication if it made her feel better? He didn't want to hold onto her, but he had to, so he wrapped his arms around her loosely. Staying quiet was best for now; maybe Lex would cool down on her own.

The drive was a few minutes of tense silence. Lex parked the quad bike in a sunny spot so that the solar panels would keep charging. Then she stomped off to a patch of shade offered by an overhanging rock formation, leaving Jeff to explore.

It wasn't much of a waterhole. More of a dirty little puddle that even Jackie would've had enough sense not to touch. *Giardia* and *Cryptosporidium* might be lurking there, or any number of bacteria. Jeff wasn't clear on how animals managed to survive invasions of bugs that humans couldn't cope with. They didn't always, of course; plagues of viruses and deadly bacteria had decimated plenty of native species along with the humans of Australia, but somehow the wildlife clung on.

Unable to sit still, Jeff prowled around, keeping close so that Lexi wouldn't worry about him. "I don't see any roo poo. Or any poo, or anything," he reported after a few minutes.

"Maybe it hasn't got here yet," Lex said.

Jeff walked in the opposite direction and suddenly the unremarkable waterhole felt different. He'd found the remains of a campsite. There wasn't much to be seen; the desert was quick to reclaim its own. Just a couple of empty jerry cans and a torn polar fleece blanket, already mostly covered with sand. "Uh oh."

She scrambled to her feet, wincing. "What's—oh."

Jeff squatted down to look at the blanket, carefully not touching it in case it was infected with something. "Hard to tell how recent it is," he said.

Lex scanned the area again. Seeing nothing, she settled back in her shady spot. "We shouldn't stay long… I just need a couple more minutes." The drugs still hadn't kicked in properly. They wouldn't get rid of the pain, of course. They took the edge off, made it seem a little further away. But anything, anything was better than the constant ache in her leg that made concentrating on a thought for longer than a second really difficult and being kind somehow impossible and it just really. Fucking. Hurt.

Jeff sat down at last, a pace or so away from Lex, and studied his GPS. Lex alternated watching him idly with staring out into the desert.

She was starting to feel almost normal when there it was; the red kangaroo bounding over the dunes, over the very rise where the drone Jeff had hacked had caught it on camera. The footage hadn't misled them. Even from that distance, it was huge, surely as big as they could get. It was majestic, stoic, focused on some goal that had nothing to do with becoming anyone's dinner, whether theirs or anyone else's.

Still immersed in his device, Jeff said, "I just can't really—"

Lex interrupted him by jumping up awkwardly and tugging on his arm. The GPS tumbled from his grasp into the sand and Jeff howled, the sound ending with a deafening shriek.

"Fuck's sake, Jeff, it's *fine*, just *look*."

He wouldn't, though, until the GPS was back in his hands and he'd verified that it still worked. At best, Jeff might have seen that strong tail, balancing the hopping motion as it bounded away.

But Lex had seen it all. There was no time to lose. Hobbling to the quad bike, she slung the shotgun over her shoulder and got herself on as fast as she could. She started the engine. "Come *on*, Jeff," she called. Grumbling, Lex steered the bike right next to him. "We can still catch it, maybe, if we go now."

Making no move to get on, Jeff carefully brushed sand off the GPS. He was crying. "What if you got us lost, Lex? What if we couldn't find our way home?"

Frustration punctured Lex's bubble of optimism and pain relief. "And what if your little tantrum made us lose the roo? Because that's what's happening right now."

"You're not allowed to grab me like that and you always do."

"Sorry. Now get on and let's go."

Tucking the GPS deep in his pocket, Jeff reached for his magnetic beads, working them frantically. He dug his feet into the sand. "You're not sorry."

His accusation ripped her open and all the words tumbled out of her, all the things she knew better than to say out loud. "No, I'm not, because we're never going to catch the roo, and what are the odds another one will come close enough ever again?" She regretted each word as she said it, and not just because yelling made her throat sore. But still they kept coming. "And we're all going to starve, and you're ruining everything, and you're so annoying, and it's your fault that, that…" She ground her teeth together, stopping herself before she said something she'd *really* wish she hadn't.

Jeff had collapsed onto the ground, whimpering. He looked so small; he always did, but now more than ever. Lex pushed away memories of when they were little. Nothing had changed, really, he was still so aggravating and still made her feel guilty, and that just made her angrier.

Lex looked over her shoulder. The roo was long gone, but she could still picture it hopping away, over and over, bounding higher and faster and further with each replay. Stifling a scream or a sob, she wasn't sure which, she ripped open the packet of an emergency blanket with angry teeth and let it unfurl. She wrapped it around Jeff's shoulders as roughly as she could; which is to say, not very. Jeff closed his eyes and let out a little whisper. "It's scratchy," he said.

"It's the best we've got right now. The sleeping bags are underneath the tent." Lex pulled him in close for a hug, the way Mum did. She said, like Mum always did, "Just try it for a minute?"

*

Gulping big breaths of air, he nodded. The blanket itched at his skin even through his clothes, but it was good to feel something solid around him. He closed his eyes and drew circles on his thumbs with his index fingers. Both at the same time. Round and round.

Lex disappeared for a second and he drew the circles faster, but she was only gone a minute and soon returned with a polar fleece jumper. She worked the jumper over his head and helped him get his arms into it, under the blanket, as though he was a little kid. It felt good; soft was good, even though it was so hot. He opened his eyes. There were damp streaks on Lex's cheeks, and her lips were frowning, and for once she didn't look cross with him, just sad.

"I really am sorry," she said.

Wrapping the blanket around her shoulders as well, Jeff cuddled into her. "I know you are. It's okay."

They sat in silence together. The roo was still hopping away, but it didn't matter anymore.

The sun began to set. Still quiet, they set up the tent, doused their hands with alcohol gel and made tea and wattle seed damper on the metho-fuelled camping stove. Somehow, Lex wasn't very hungry, but Jeff ate her leftovers after asking multiple times if it was okay.

Jeff insisted that Lex let him set up the tent by himself. As the light faded, they got in and cocooned themselves in sleeping bags that felt too hot, but would be essential to survive the night. When they were settled, Jeff asked, "What was my fault, Lex?"

Lex crossed her arms over her chest. Lying down, they felt heavy. "Mum said I was never allowed to tell you. That she'd tell you when you were ready."

There was a long silence. "Tell me. Please."

At this point, Lex was in trouble with Mum no matter what. She sighed and pushed the words out. "My leg. I broke it when I was four and you were two. You were playing in the creek bed—it was dry then, like always. You slipped and I jumped and caught you, but I landed wrong and…yeah."

Jeff shrunk away from her, as if trying to make his body as small as possible. "I'm sorry."

"It wasn't your fault, Jeff. You were just a baby and it was just bad luck and *I'm* sorry. It was wrong to say that. Or think it."

"But it was a bad break. Mum said you should've had surgery on it. If they still did that kind of operation."

"Still not your fault." The more she said it, the truer it felt. "Unless you did it on purpose?"

Moving closer again, Jeff rested a head on Lex's shoulder. "Of course not. I was just a baby."

"Well, then." She ruffled his hair quickly and exhaled the last vestiges of the secret.

In the silence and darkness of the desert, they slept.

*

They woke to a soft pattering sound.

"What *is* that?" Shivering, Lex sat up. Faint light shone through the walls of the tent.

"Rain! It's rain!" He grinned, his hair standing up on end as he crawled out of his sleeping bag.

"Shit. Come on. We need to pack up."

After packaging his GPS carefully in its waterproof sachet, Jeff helped Lex bundle up their belongings and pack the tent. Sand and water resistant it might be, but torrential rain was another story. Only once everything was stowed and they were garbed in their rather useless plastic ponchos did they stop to survey their surroundings. Lex could remember seeing rain once. Her leg had mended, but not quite right, and their parents were still anxious about whether she'd ever walk again. She'd watched it from her window, marvelling at the strange colour of the sky and the multitude of containers filling with water spread around the property. But she'd never stood in it, never felt the rush of warmth that quickly turned cold.

Tipping his head up, Jeff let the water fall on his face. "Wow," he said. He stuck his tongue out. "It tastes so clean."

"First rain of the decade," Lex said, even though he surely knew. "We should go. Mum will worry about us catching our deaths or drowning or something." Despite her words, she didn't move straight away. But after a few more moments, they dragged themselves away and got on the bike.

"I feel like I peed myself," Jeff said.

"You better not have."

"I didn't! The back of the seat was wet. Gross."

"Good." Lex started the bike up. "It's charging pretty slowly. Let's hope we can get home."

"I'll navigate!" Jeff studied the topology on the GPS, and pointed. "That way."

They travelled mostly in silence, exchanging small talk every so often. The rain continued without break, making the terrain muddy and treacherous. By unspoken agreement, neither sibling speculated aloud on what Mum would think about their journey. As much as Lex would prefer to keep some of it secret, Jeff wouldn't be able to, and Mum always seemed to be able to mind read, anyway. She'd see something different. She'd know.

The quad bike got them pretty close to home, but they were still a few kays away when the main and spare batteries both declared themselves dead.

Grumbling, Lex put the bike in neutral and they started pushing. "You did good navigating, Jeff," she admitted. "Could've been much worse if we'd got lost in the dunes."

"Told you it wasn't a toy."

Looking across at him, Lex scowled, but her expression changed when she saw a twinkle in his eye. "Are you...teasing?"

He grinned. "Yes! Did I do good teasing?"

She laughed, a real laugh that made her eyes crinkle, although it was short-lived. "Yes. But...ow. Let's just push."

They reached the creek bed...the creek, Lex amended, staring at the rushing water in awe.

"I want to see," Jeff said. He left Lex with the quad bike to meander closer.

"Jeff..." Lex was too defeated to whinge. "If you hurt yourself, Mum will kill me. Just...stay away from the edge. Please?"

"There's fish. In the creek. The rain must've brought them down."

Lex dragged the bike off the track and left it behind a tree.

Jeff was lying on his belly, right on the bank. He looked up at Lex when she got close. "Look how big they are!"

Almost as long as Lex's arm, they looked pretty fat for fish living in the struggling river system. They nosed around the bottom of the creek, swimming lazily. She had to swallow down the saliva that formed in her mouth at the thought of them grilling in Mum's frying pan. She could almost smell it. Protein for Jackie. And omega-3, even better.

"Reckon we could make a fishing rod with something?"

Lex grinned. "I reckon."

Given Sufficient Desperation

Bogi Takács

An ice cream cone.

A ceramic mug—brown with a single green stripe around the rim.

A smartphone—I don't recognise the brand. It's been a while.

Two sheaves of corn.

A plush caterpillar toy from some cartoon.

A table—rather worn, I'd say Danish Modern, but I'm not sure.

I need a break.

Looking at objects for hours upon hours wears me down, even though I'm not supposed to do anything with them. I remove the helmet that records my responses to the images and wave my hands around my chair to find my forearm crutches. My eyes are still adjusting to the different stream of sensory input. I grasp one crutch; the other falls to the floor with a loud clang. I wince.

Small Purple Circle comes up to me, twines two of his tentacles around the crutch and hands it to me. I frown at him and rub my eyes with my free hand. "Thanks," I mutter. His colouring seems to be more faded than usual, more pink than purple.

"How are you doing? Are you all right?" he says in the voice of Oszkár Gáti—the Hungarian dubbing actor of both Arnold Schwarzenegger and Sylvester Stallone. Before the invasion.

I just groan in response. My ankle sprain will heal, but there will surely be another injury after that, and another. The aliens don't really understand that my motor coordination issues get worse if I don't get enough sleep, and they think eight hours of sleep should be enough for a standard human.

"Tell me about Danish Modern sometime," Stallone adds.

I stream past other workers in the narrow corridor while they stare. I don't hobble on crutches, I whoosh. I'm very, very good at it. Of course my shoulders will protest, but frankly, I'm faster on crutches than on my undamaged feet. Not that they're often undamaged these days.

"Vera," somebody yells after me. I turn rapidly, slip, crash into a stranger. I'm still trying to extricate my limbs from his and muttering apologies when Kati catches up to me, her two thick dark braids slapping at her shoulders.

"What's up?" Kati asks. "This is not your regular break."

"I earned twenty-three minutes off. And I felt like I really needed it," I say. "Let's go up to the roof?"

We walk. The slower I go, the more my shoulders hurt.

I lean against the parapet. In the distance, the ruins of Pannonhalma Abbey are still smouldering. How is that possible? It has been such a long time since the attack. I point, ask Kati if she knows.

"There's a group squatting up there on top of the hill. The pacifist anarchist kind, like the Two-Tailed Dog or something, but a different name. I haven't heard of them before."

I nod. The aliens only seem to care about the militant ones. I consider if I should just walk out of the compound, join the group. We haven't seen people passing by lately; I was wondering if there were any groups of stragglers still out there.

"It's not worth it," Kati says. She can guess what I'm thinking—she always says my emotions are written plainly on my face.

I know it's not worth it. For one thing, it's a lot harder to use my crutches on an uneven surface. And that's before I consider the painkillers and the occasional brace. Though at least I haven't needed a plaster cast in a while. How do I find any of that in the wilderness?

If not for dyspraxia, I would have long since run away. I'm still considering it.

I swear under my breath. We go back to our workrooms in silence.

A picture book, in Swedish.
A ballpoint pen.
A succulent of some sort, planted in a glass jar.
An axe with a red handle.
A flatscreen TV, looks like Samsung.
A large crucifix, made of silver, I assume.

I'm done for today; I take off the helmet, clock out, go back to my dorm room in the same building. Ten of us for each, white walls, white plastic crates for storage.

There are no wardrobes; we wear what we are assigned each morning. Usually something grey with tiny blue speckles. The aliens love the colour grey with tiny blue speckles.

Large Blue Triangle admonishes me, in the Hungarian voice of Will Smith, to move more cautiously lest I injure myself again. I saw the actor, Artúr Kálid, in a play back before the invasion. I wonder if he's still alive, and if he ever meets an alien talking in his voice, using his words.

*

I fall asleep every day like a rock. I try to force myself to stay awake just for a few minutes, just to give myself time for my own thoughts. The aliens drive us mercilessly while they gloat that we are all voluntary workers. Human-aided categorisation. Their algorithms have no clue what our everyday objects are.

Why is Stallone interested in Danish Modern?

A bag of Chio chips, peanut flavour.
A small spoon—teaspoon, I think.
A pair of yellow candlesticks.
A small whiteboard.

I hoard off-time. I want to go for a walk.
Days run together.

A macramé wall hanging.
A pocket knife.
A brown paper bag.
A pair of scissors.
A bin liner.
A fork.

*

Accumulated off-time: three hours forty-three minutes. My ankle is better and I can walk without crutches. It will have to be enough. I am sleepy. Uneven ground.

I walk.

We are not, technically, restricted to the compound. There's just nothing worth leaving for. We are not, technically, forced labourers. There's just nothing else to do.

I walk.

A large oak tree.

An overgrown drainage ditch.

Clouds.

My brain is stuck in object-labelling mode. I wonder if it's permanent.

We all do what we can to survive. I just want to know what these others do to survive. I should've brought my crutches with me—what if I wanted to stay?

A road uphill.

Burned-out houses.

Off to one side: remains of the botanical gardens.

Lavender growing wild.

Pannonhalma Abbey, razed to the ground.

Pannonhalma Abbey.

An abandoned camp.

Hastily assembled tents.

A tuna fish can now holding cigarette butts.
Fires burned down to ash.
Far-off voices carried on the wind.

I turn around and in the distance I can see the alien compound, smouldering. My mind can only label, not understand. I hobble into a tent.

Comforting semi-darkness.
Rusty-framed cots.
Sleep.

"You from the compound? Down there on the plains?" A soot-smeared face. A teenage boy.

I murmur something.

"I didn't realise there were any survivors," he says. "I'll let you sleep."

By next morning my brain works better, the forced frame of object-labelling faded into the background. I sit on the boy's cot, sipping hot nettle tea. His name is Brúnó and he has cinnamon-brown curls. He describes what has been going on: the pacifist stance was all an act, a charade while the militants smuggled in weapons, brought a small army up the hill one by one, occupied the wine-cellars dug into the hillside below the abbey hundreds of years ago.

"So what were you doing down there?" he asks.

"Labelling objects for the aliens. You sit and the computer shows you things and they record the responses your brain makes. Something like that."

"What's the point?"

"They always told us they wanted to rebuild."

That's when it hits me—and I'm still too exhausted to even cry, and I didn't know anyone in the compound besides Kati, socialising was *not* encouraged—but I did know Kati, and I can barely believe I should start mourning.

I can't; I just can't. I save it for later, provided there will be a later. I've lost so much. I refuse to think of my family—I think they are still alive somewhere, in a different compound, in a different corner of Hungary, tucked away safely. I refuse to think of my friends. I refuse to think of my life. My former life. I refuse to think of hot chocolate and video games and ranting at my friends on chat and imagining that one day I will be Internet famous. I refuse—what am I even thinking?

I turn away from Brúnó, stare at the mushy afternoon sky. Is it spring or autumn? Everything has become indeterminate.

The next day I drag Brúnó off the hill, or rather he drags me, my ankle still painful. Downhill is worse than uphill; I'm never sure why. He drags me and I urge him, while he's attempting what innumerable compound-dwellers have tried and failed: to puzzle out the aliens' motives.

Raze, then rebuild? "Maybe it's a different faction," he suggests, and he has a point—why would the aliens form one homogenous group? But there was nothing I'd seen during my time of work to suggest any kind of difference between one movie star voice and another. I tell him so.

"But how do you know these aliens are the same aliens who bombed us back to the Stone Age?"

I shrug. We're almost back to the compound.

I wanted to have smouldering ruins, and I got them. As I slip and slide among rocks, half-melted pieces of plastic with jagged edges and undefinable heaps, I realise I'm not going to find Kati here.

We trundle back to camp and I find her on top of the hill.

This is too much disruption. I'm glad to see Kati, but this is too much. We stare at each other. Her left ankle is immobilised between two thick tree-branches and wrappings of dirty gauze.

"You're the expert," she says with a lopsided, pained smile.

"I left my crutches back in the compound," I respond; they must've melted into slag.

"I wanted to catch up to you when I saw you walk out, I tripped and fell. I stepped into a hole or something. It took me a day to get up the hill and find help," she says. The militants helped her. Maybe they would help me? Maybe it would be all right?

The people sing marching songs—I vaguely recognise old Communist melodies, with new lyrics. I wonder if someone is passing them off as originals. I only know them because it was a hobby of mine to collect those recordings, post them on YouTube. I will not think of the loss. I will not think of anything missing from the world, bits and bytes forever scattered. I will not—

"Tomorrow, we go," trills Brúnó at me, and before he can dash off, I grab his shoulder.

"We go, where?"

"To the next station, the next fight!" He shakes my hand off, runs away.

I don't want to fight. I just want to be left alone on a cosy sofa with a laptop, watching random crap on the Internet. What, maybe five aliens were killed—and how many dozen workers? Other people can do this, and be cheerful about it, for all I care.

At least Kati doesn't seem to be enthusiastic either, sitting on a half-rotted pillow with her back to a bag filled with straw. "I'm not going to march *any*where," she declares to Brúnó, who's busy running back and forth. He shrugs and responds with, "Then we'll just leave you here. No dead-weight."

I slap him on the top of the head with an open palm, but he laughs it off, thinks I was just joking, horsing around. Not recognising his own cruelty.

I lie down on a spare cot, busy myself with recalling the stream of images before sleep. It gives me an odd, uncanny kind of peace. Now that I can do anything I want, I'm surprised that I want this. Routines can be comforting.

A head of cabbage, sliced in half.

An empty windowpane made of wood.

A sack of potatoes, about five kilograms, give or take.

If they want to know what these things are, why don't they just ask us?

Up above, I hear the rumble of their aircraft. So much for flying saucers being silent. None of them have landed near the destroyed compound, no one came to look for survivors. But maybe now?

I wish I had Small Purple Circle at hand. I'd tie him to a chair and interrogate him. He'd creak in the voice of Arnie and I'd hit him with the butt of a gun like Sam Fisher in *Splinter Cell*. Not with my bare hand which even Brúnó can shake off and laugh. I would hit them both. My ferocity surprises me; I draw back from my own thoughts.

In this moment, I hate everything and everyone with pure, hundred-proof hatred. And I also know that I will go back, to the aliens, to another work compound. If nothing else, I will pretend to myself I am an infiltrator, seeking to bring down the heartless taskmaster aliens and the crude, brute-force humans alike. Winning with cunning, not overwhelming power.

It doesn't last—power fantasies never do. When I put the console into sleep mode, it's always over. When did I last play a video game?

As I contemplate this, sleep claims me and I don't wake until the next morning—restless, but well-rested.

The march-column is leaving, and all the accommodation the two of us got was that we didn't have to strap a full-size army surplus backpack to our shoulders. Brúnó is also supposed to help us, but I send him forward to carry some made-up, inconsequential message to our section march-leader, while Kati and I hobble in the opposite direction, towards where we can see a flying saucer landing, behind the hill. We do not want to stay with the militants, and we don't think we can survive on our own. This is the alternative we have.

The militants don't care. Which is good because our two-girl march is slow-going, loud with all the assorted obscenities we can produce.

I will not think of my gaming stream, I will not think of my gaming stream, I will not think of how I miss my gaming stream and all the cuss-worthy moments and all the glorious ridiculousness of it.

I will only think of Sam Fisher, infiltrating the enemy compound. I will think of Arnold Schwarzenegger, late governor of California, epic action-hero of the previous generation.

I will rip the aliens' heads off.

"Welcome back, Earthlings," Will Smith says, and I don't know if it's the same alien, Large Blue Triangle, or a different one. His colouring is different and his texture is all puckered up, but for all I know they can change those on demand, like cephalopods. They don't do it in front of us.

I stare at the images and my gaze could burn a hole in the world.

A flagpole, ideal for stabbing people in the stomach.

An empty glass Coke bottle, ideal for making Molotov cocktails.

An egg cup, ideal for jamming down people's throats.

I sigh, try to look away, but the images keep on coming, direct through the helmet to my visual cortex.

A candle-holder, ideal for bashing in people's heads.

A pink flowerpot, ideal for bashing in people's heads.

An old gramophone, ideal for bashing in people's heads.

"No, no, no," Keanu Reeves says—this is a new alien; I don't remember the voice actor's name. "This is not good. You're messing up the data! All the affordances!"

He tears the helmet off my head and I stand. We face-off, the heat of anger rising from me while he puckers up and deflates in cycles.

"All the what?" I glare at him.

"Did you figure it out?" He seethes.

Everyone else in the room is still under their helmets, but the work doesn't involve the auditory cortex. They can potentially hear us. Keanu Reeves—Soft Green Oval—ushers me outside, then into some kind of closet.

He mutters something unintelligible. Is he swearing? Then: "I always thought someone would figure it out under my watch. It has to be my watch; it has to be. What am I supposed to do with you?"

I'm shaking with barely repressed fury. "Am I supposed to tell *you* what to do with me? How about a nice comfy sofa and a jar of sweets?"

"Th-that can be arranged," he mutters and I realise he thought I was serious. Oops.

He starts trembling, inflating and deflating at an alarmingly rapid pace. We shiver in unison, but for very different reasons. "I can't just kill you," he says, whining. "Besides, the recordings have already been transmitted to Centerpoint."

"Explain," I grimace at him. "Explain before I throttle you." Do I really have the upper hand?

Maybe I do, because he explains. "It's not really about identifying objects. It's about their affordances, meaning what can be done with them. We're recording immediate, implicit reactions. Specifically, we're trying to identify which objects can potentially be used as weapons. There is a marker…"

"And?" I don't see where this is heading.

He spreads his tentacles in a gesture I'm sure he learned from his workers—a display of helplessness. "I saw your data. Everything can be a weapon. Everything can be seen as a weapon."

I stare at him. I realise I've been clenching my hands and I slowly unclench my fingers. If this were a movie, blood would be dripping from my palms at a bare minimum.

Have I just condemned the human species?

We can use everything as weapons.

I look away, disgusted with him, me, the entire world. But something doesn't make sense.

I look back. "You bombed us to smithereens. Why would you need to know about our weapons?"

He doesn't respond. His motions halt. Is he even breathing? And at that moment I understand—Brúnó was right. These are not the aliens that destroyed civilisation. They are not. They are opportunists, bottom-feeders, here to fill a suddenly empty niche. Maybe the ones who attacked us didn't care anymore, once we were no longer a threat.

Maybe. It makes sense.

I hiss. "This is why the militants could take your compound so easily. You are weaklings."

He doesn't say anything. His skin slowly undulates. Is he afraid of me? If they are weaklings, what does that make us—what does that make me, with my boundless display of rage? I feel suddenly raw, exposed, my anger evaporating and giving way to pure existential dread.

"So what happens now?" I whisper.

Keanu turns away. Is he more disgusted than afraid? He speaks softly, almost gently. "The data has been transmitted. Centerpoint will decide."

I walk back to our dorm room, built to the same specifications as the previous one, every compound an almost exact duplicate.

I want to cease to exist. I can't even cry.

Was I really the first human to get so angry, so desperate, so furious? Surely there had to have been others, people with their families murdered, their entire way of life destroyed. Surely it couldn't have been me. Then again, in the compounds, people are volunteers. Collaborators. People who play by the rules.

I half sit, half crash down on my bed, turn to Kati and try to haltingly explain. I break into tears halfway through, remembering the egg-cup, the most innocuous of all household objects.

The evacuation signal sounds exactly then, and as we run out to the courtyard—Kati half-jumping on one leg, holding on to me—the saucers are already overhead, streaming toward space, away from Earth. The aliens are leaving. Fleeing? Escaping?

They don't want to have anything to do with us any more.

I think of Danish Modern, hug Kati and endlessly, endlessly weep.

Endnote:

The science in the story was extrapolated from Shenoy P, Tan DS (2008): Human-aided computing: utilising implicit human processing to classify images. Proceedings of the SIGCHI Conference on Human Factors in Computing Systems: 845-854.

Selected Afterimages of the Fading

John Chu

A row of dumbbells sorted by weight, ranging from pointless to respectable, sits in a rack against one wall. A squat rack and the tree of plates next to it stands against the opposite wall. Assorted benches, flat, incline, decline, lie scattered on the rubber matted floor. All of the equipment looks sharp and opaque. You're easily the blurriest presence in the room. The blue rubber floor mats are just noticeable through your arms. The hotel undoubtedly has super-perceivers who sweep through and lavish their attention on everything when things start to fade, go blurry and translucent. No one wants anything to fade out of existence, much less while they're hosting a conference of researchers trying to understand or mitigate the fading.

For a hotel, this is actually a pretty decent weight room. When you realise you can have an okay work out here, you relax. Your heart stops pounding out of your chest. Your breathing slows. That feeling that your stomach is falling into an infinite abyss goes away.

You're not going to make any gains here, but you probably won't shrivel. Probably.

Except one of the one hundred pound dumbbells is missing. One sits at the respectable end of the rack where it's supposed to, but there's an empty slot where the other is supposed to be. It's wedged behind the weight tree. You didn't see it the first five times you checked there because it barely exists. That the wall seems a little greyer and a little warped are the only signs that the dumbbell is there. Another few hours and it might have disappeared forever. You heft it with one hand, then pay some attention to it. The dumbbell's handle grows rough. It starts to dig into your hand. The shadow it casts on the floor shrinks and darkens. As the dumbbell grows sharp and opaque, the other person who would lift at a hotel gym at five in the morning shows up.

He stares at you, his jaw slack. You don't know his name, but his lab is the floor above yours. You've never worked up the nerve to introduce yourself to him, and you've both travelled hundreds of miles to bump into each other at a hotel gym.

He's tall and lanky. You come up to his chest. Broad shoulders and a wide back make him present like a beautiful giant. He doesn't need thick, bulging muscles to hit you like a ton of bricks, but you see hints of them beneath his shirt. Or at least muscles thick and bulging compared to yours. Maybe it's just the lighting. Perfect lighting follows him wherever he goes.

It points up the planes of his face and structure of his body. Rationally, you know that he's not constantly bathed in lighting that always hits him just so. He's just absurdly good looking. Still, in a world where whatever doesn't receive enough attention disappears, you want to stick him in a dark room to see whether he glows or just blends into the dark.

"I know you." He stabs his finger at you. "You're Caleb Chan, the muscle-bound guy with the tight T-shirts. You run the digital archive lab."

You make some sort of non-committal noise. Tight T-shirts make people pay attention to you. It keeps you opaque, or at least it did. The fading is happening faster and faster.

"How is it that a super-perceiver... No, not just a super-perceiver, a *high-capacity* super-perceiver lets himself become blurred and translucent?" His gaze is stern. "You of all people should understand casual self-attention."

Your heart sinks. This is not the first meeting you'd once let yourself imagine.

"I'm not high-capacity." The words are muttered. He's wearing boots, not sneakers. They can stomp someone into a bloody pancake.

You get the other hundred pound dumbbell and walk them both to a flat bench. It doesn't hit you until after you set them down that you've proven him right about high-capacity.

He rolls his eyes. "Rescuing that dumbbell from oblivion didn't even wind you. Besides, look at those arms." He points to you as he closes. "Look at that chest."

The rest of the Sondheim reference tumbles out of you. "Not to mention—"

"You're like the opposite of a Miles Gloriosus," he says, acknowledging Sondheim's reference to Plautus. "You haven't kept yourself opaque despite being high-capacity." His gaze narrows and he nods as though he, The Great Detective, has cracked the mystery. "You can't keep yourself opaque. Muscle dysmorphia?"

You nod and brace for the wise-crack. A body image disorder where you can't see yourself as anything but small and weak never engenders any sympathy. It forces you to strive for bulging muscle and, if you're at all successful, you don't look like you have a problem. Of course, it also forces you to work out injured and shut people out because they get in the way of your diet.

What you know is what your therapist has told you and that your lab mates call you "The Great Wall of China". The latter is either vaguely complimentary or vaguely racist, probably both. When you look in the mirror, you see someone simultaneously too scrawny and too fat. To your eyes, everyone else in the world rocks their body shape, but not you. You can't perceive yourself as you actually are.

"Self-attention doesn't work for you." He smiles sympathetically. "I dated a guy with muscle dysmorphia once. Not a super-perceiver though. Not as buff and jacked as you. Convinced he was puny compared to me."

"Maybe he wasn't, but I am." You wince. Intellectually, you get that it's stupid to be honest to people about how you see yourself, just never in time. "I've been the boyfriend. It never goes well, does it…"

"Call me Latch." He grabs your waist. Someone akin to a granite cliff surrounds you. "Hold still. I am a super-perceiver too, just not high-capacity. You're not so far gone that I can't bring you all the way back."

His hand grasps your forearm and the feeling is literally electric. The shock rushes up your arms then spreads across your body. His face grows stern. You grow opaque under his gaze.

When he lets go, his legs buckle. You reach out to catch him but he saves himself. His legs bent, he flops over, breaking at the waist. One hand braces him at his knee. He raises the other hand, gesturing with his palm as if to say, "I'm okay."

His chest pumps. It doesn't seem like air has had enough time to get into his lungs before it rushes back out again.

You mutter your awkward thanks, then start the warm up set of push ups you do before you bench press. Nothing you can do for Latch. He'll catch his breath eventually.

Eight reps into your first set of bench presses, Latch looms over you. It's a friendly loom but there's still an avalanche-like quality to it. He waits for you to squeeze out another seven reps, for the dumbbells to hit the mat, before he speaks.

"You're a high-capacity super-perceiver who isn't already burning up that capacity rescuing things in the private sector, so I have to ask..." He rubs his hands together. "Practice is running ahead of theory with the fading, of course. We think we have a way to perceive at a distance and over an area. We're going to need something like that soon unless we want farmland to disappear. However, we're gonna need someone with a lot of capacity to spare to test our current prototype out."

This shard of virtual sunlight hovers over you, still lying on the bench. Warm browns outshine the lights on the ceiling but still strangle you in their shadow. Words abandoned you when he started looming. Thoughts of being small and weak compared to this god who stands before you crowd everything else out of your mind. At first, all you can do is look at him quizzically before a glint of realization pierces you.

"Oh, you want *me* as a test subject." Words go away again and you babble for a few seconds before you make another stab at coherence. "I'm sorry. Can't think right now. I need to lift."

"Okay. If you change your mind, you know where to find me." His disappointment almost makes him mortal. Almost. "See you later."

"Not gonna work out?"

"I was but not any more. I'm beat." He yawns. "After making you opaque, I'm going to be useless for a few hours."

With that, he turns to leave. His stride is languid. When he's gone, you realise that you probably carry more muscle than him. It didn't feel like that when he was here though.

The gym down the block from your lab, like most everywhere else in the world these days, is one step out of focus. Massed casual attention can still keep a place solid, but it can't make any place as sharp as it once was, not any more. Forty-five pound plates are black smears that rest on the long, silver smudge that is the barbell on your squat rack. The bar gives a little when you grip it and set it on the back of your neck, as though it were covered with a thin layer of foam. A buzzing sensation crawls through your elbow to your fingers as your arm slowly goes numb. You must have strained something a workout or two ago, but you're not sure what. A sensible person would stop. You can't. You keep going. Squats don't actually work your arms, you rationalise to yourself. Besides, after a week at a conference, without a real workout soon, you'll be useless.

Exercise after exercise, rep after rep, blood swells your muscles. Your shirt stretches across your chest and back more than it does outside of the gym. Your arms bulge harder against your sleeves. The gym is this fantasyland where you look in the mirror and you can almost puzzle out how others see you. A couple of hours in the gym clears out the thoughts of being small and weak for long enough. It makes room for other things, like your day job: how to archive the world into dense and easy to perceive media so that everything can be restored again once scientists understand the fading. You'd lift every day, except you've learned the hard way you'd destroy your body if you did. When you're seriously injured, you can't lift. The ensuing anxiety and fear that you'll lose what little hard-earned muscle you have makes you useless until you heal.

Your lab, unlike the gym, is crisp and opaque. Racks of motherboards and disk arrays fill the room. Rust dots their tall square storage cases, which line the walls, leaving room for a lab bench and some chairs. A black box sits on either end of the bench, connected to a computer in the middle. Dried protein shake stains cover the keyboard. Sticky bits of clear juice are scattered across the display from all the times you've peeled grapefruit at the computer.

Your legs still ache a little from all those squats. Your shirt hugs your body. Those things keep your mind clear for the mathematical transformations that render an object as data then reify them back into an object again. Your fingers glide over the keyboard. You translate the latest versions of those transformations into code on the screen. In theory, you've licked this problem. Things no one has the attention to spare for can be stored on disk. Once the scientists and engineers trying to understand the fading do so, you can retrieve those things again. In practice, you haven't. Not yet anyway. You're just trying to stomp out the bugs you found during the previous trial.

It takes an hour of build-fail-retry for the new code to compile cleanly. With a deep breath, you start the next trial.

Your stock of tiny iron cubes sits in a lab bench drawer. You take one and lavish some attention on it, letting it grow colder and harder in your hand. Its molecular structure needs to be as easy to detect as possible.

The iron cube goes into the scanner, the black box to your left. A soft, low-pitched thrum fills the room. The scanning process destroys the object. For now, you're capturing the energy that scanning releases to power the reconstructor, the black box on your right. If governments, museums, or even private citizens ever scan things to archive, you have no idea where they will find the energy to reconstruct those things. Maybe they can store the energy released during scanning in some ultra-dense battery that, like the archive, will also need to be kept solid. That's not your problem yet.

The lingering effects of your workout haven't dissipated yet. Your mind can still focus. Your body will always be inadequate but it should be hours before your constant internal reminders can debilitate you. It'll be a while before the trial has produced any result you can check. This is the right time to engage the broad, black-haired, bronze god upstairs. If you can't hold yourself together around him right now, you may never be able to.

The door to Latch's lab is open when you get there. His surprised expression when he notices you matches your own. He's still tall and he's still broad. Perfect lighting still seems to set him up just so. However, he's no longer an avalanche, a ton of bricks or a god masquerading as a shard of sunlight. His arms seem a little thin for a hulking man his height. Even your arms may be nearly as big as his. This may be as close as you'll ever come to getting your relative sizes right. You still think he dwarfs you, however, and you're still wrong.

"Caleb." One word with a bright smile and you want to run back downstairs. "Change your mind?"

"Yeah." You stuff your hands into your pockets. "I was too distracted to decide when we spoke at the conference."

"Great." He comes to the door and shakes your hand. "The lab isn't ready for the trial yet, but why don't we have lunch together tomorrow? Just to make sure you're fully informed first."

"Sure." You draw the word out as your mind races. The endless rearranging of meals like pieces in a jigsaw puzzle and the attempt to make lunch with him a piece that fits crowd everything else out of your head. The need to hit your required levels of macronutrients every day once meant you never ate with anyone. The fear that if you didn't get just the right amount of protein every two hours, you'd shrink down to nothing made you refuse anyone who asked. Now, your heart just pounds way too fast and hard.

"You usually bring lunch, right?" He doesn't wait for a response. He's seen you eat. "Why don't I just meet you in the cafeteria tomorrow at noon?"

"Okay, thanks." Your heartbeat slows. Your fists unclench, which is when you realise you'd squeezed your hands into fists in the first place. "See you tomorrow."

You retreat back into your own lab. The status of your trial fills your computer's display. It's done with no errors flagged. Hope does not well up in your heart. The reconstruction phase has failed too many times.

You open the black box on the right. Instead of a reconstructed small cube of iron, what sits inside is slush, not metallic, and the consistency of oatmeal. You collect it into a vial for analysis so that you can guess at what went wrong. Another day, another pile of bugs.

Two lab benches sitting on their side, one lashed on top of the other, form a wall that splits Latch's lab in half. In preparation for this trial, he's left the other side unattended for weeks. Whatever is on the other side is undoubtedly translucent and indistinct by now.

Latch is futzing with a short server rack he's wheeled next to the wall. Tendrils of black cable stretch away from it in two directions. Some are entwined around the legs of the lab benches. Others end at a harness next to him.

After several weeks of lunches and conversations about musicals, football, and Nabokov, among other things, you're starting to crack the code of how Latch presents. He's an avid rock-climber and his body has moulded itself to the sport. A broad back with thick thighs and calves that poke out from his jeans make him present bigger and taller than he actually is. Climbing isn't about the biceps, triceps or the pecs though. You keep reminding yourself that you both wear the same size shirts but his leave plenty of room for his chest and are loose around his arms. You keep reminding yourself that he's not as overwhelmingly buff and powerful as you can't help thinking.

Latch turns towards you. He assesses the way you're staring at him. "You didn't lift today."

"No." You shift your gaze away. "It's a rest day."

"I can't get you to take off your shirt?" He approaches you with the harness. "It'll make better contact if you do."

"No, shirt stays on." You wave your hands in front of you. "Gotta create the illusion of size somehow. Otherwise, you'll realise how puny I actually am."

He rolls his eyes at you as he wraps the harness around your head. Sensors stick to your temples. Ribs of elastic cable stretch across the back of your head. He unfolds the harness down your torso. It stretches tight against your shirt and binds your forearms.

"Ready?" His gaze sweeps up and down your body. He prods and stretches the harness.

You take a deep breath. No one knows exactly what will happen when Latch turns on the machine in his server rack.

"Just do it."

Latch backs away from you. He reaches inside the short server rack then flips a few switches. They click and the sound bounces around the room.

Almost immediately, a sharp pain cracks your head. It stabs like twin awls through your eyes. What had been ribs of elastic cable are now cold, hard curves of rusty dulled steel. They bite into you and tear at your flesh, but there are no wounds and there is no blood. Ghosts of scattered computer gear and office furniture on the other side of the wall clutter your mind. It hijacks your gaze. You can see benches and chairs slowly resolve into focus when your legs buckle and you lose consciousness.

When you wake, you are lying on the floor. The harness sits in a shredded heap next to you. Latch, crouched by your side, looms. His shoulders never seemed so broad. His thighs balloon against his jeans. You feel weak. Your shirt feels loose. It droops off your arms and pools around your torso. Latch, however, looks ready, not merely to climb a mountain, but toss it on his broad back and march it around the world. It's as though what muscle you've gained over the decades has been stolen from you and packed onto his mighty and beautiful body.

You scuttle away from Latch. He reaches for you but you're somehow fast enough to evade his grasp. You struggle to get your feet under you.

"Caleb, don't panic." He's barely touched you, but you rocket to a stand. His strength must be superhuman. "You're just tapped out and, knowing you, massively misperceiving our relative sizes. That's all. You'll be yourself in a couple of hours."

He wraps his arms around you. They feel like a vice around your chest but they look relaxed and thin, not the massive tree trunks they must be when he flexes them.

"Seriously? I can see you just fine." You break away too easily. Maybe he let go. "I can't be here with you."

"I don't think you should be alone right now." He takes a step towards you. The perfect light that follows him highlights every muscle on his body.

"I'm fine. It's not always about muscle dysmorphia." You back your way out the door. "I just need to be alone for a while."

The shame of being so small and weak can be hard to deal with. Right now, you don't want to be seen by anyone. You scramble out the door.

"Call me. Anytime you want. If you need anything. Please, just call." Latch's words are echoes from down the hall.

You huddle in a seat at the end of a subway car. Everyone seems to have their moment staring at you with a sneer before looking away with revulsion. It's a relief when you barricade yourself in your apartment.

Despair pins you in bed. Not even the automatic urge to lift can get you out of bed, much less the apartment. It's a couple of days before you remember again that shirts stretch and relax. Even the ones that feel unconscionably tight in the morning develop a little play in the sleeves by the afternoon.

This is hardly your first meltdown. They always take a couple of days before the fear of shrivelling even further overtakes the despair of being weak and small. However, the fading is getting quicker and quicker. This time, when you turn on the bedroom light for the first time in three days, the room is blurry, but you're barely here. You cast no shadow and your gaze solidifies your chest of drawers through your forearms.

Your indistinct blob of a phone slips through your hands at first. However, it becomes substantial under your gaze and you call the only person you can think of.

"Um… Latch?" Words dribble out of you. After your meltdown in front of him, you're not sure he will ever want to talk to you again. "I need…can you…"

"I'll be right over."

"No, um—" Latch hangs up before you can get anything else out.

Your apartment is a blurry mess. The idea Latch

will see this sends you into a tidying frenzy. You take off the shirt you've worn for days and put on a clean shirt you make opaque and crisp. Unaccountably, it strangles you even though it's been whole days since you've even seen a weight or eaten. Despite everything that's happened, the shirt squeezes your shoulders and stretches across your chest, back and arms.

By the time the doorbell rings, your clothes have all been stowed in a laundry hamper or a closet. Dishes have been washed. Bottles of protein powder have been hidden in the pantry. Your living room has never been so tidy. Books sit in the bookshelves not on the floor. Sofa cushions rest exactly in their proper places. For the first time in months, you can see the surface of the coffee table. Your apartment looks as sharp and as opaque as it did before the fading became a thing.

You open the door. Latch's eyes widen. His words catch in his throat, leaving his jaw hanging. Like you, he's too dark to actually pale but, as blood drains from his face, his attempt is heroic.

He grabs your forearms. His stare sweeps up and down your body. Your jeans grow distinct, but you don't.

"Can't do it." Latch is out of breath. "You're so far gone. Need to see more of you to have a chance."

You shake your head as you back up. He follows you into your apartment then closes the door behind him.

"Oh." You sit on the sofa, and run your hands over your scalp. It's past time to shave. Might as well go to oblivion clean shaven. "I'm sorry I called you over for nothing."

"Caleb." If only the incredulity in Latch's voice could bring you back. "Even if your body were something to be ashamed of—which it's not—plenty of guys see you without a shirt on in the locker room, right?"

"Sure, but I don't care about them." You shrug. "You, on the other hand... Maybe there's nothing to me besides the illusion generated by a tight T-shirt. If I take my shirt off, you'll see what a fraud I am."

"OhGodOhGodOhGod." Again and again, he taps the palm of one hand with the back of the other. His eyes shut and he swallows hard before he opens them again. "This is so not the time for a conversation about our relationship."

"Relationship?" You furrow your brow. "We don't have a relationship."

"Not if you don't take off your shirt, we don't, because you'll be dead." He leans into you. "I'm not even going to try to convince you that how you look in a T-shirt isn't an illusion, Caleb, but I'd really like the relationship conversation with you. Please, Caleb, just do this for me. How you look is the least interesting thing about you."

You peer up at him. He stands over you, but he's not overwhelming. Latch does not have a chest that needs its own time zone and, as much as he loves watching football, he doesn't play. As you settle into the calm of your impending death, you get that his skeleton is large enough that he can't pack on enough muscle mass to be a bulging powerhouse. That's just what you keep creating in your mind from a set of broad shoulders, a trim waist, and oddly perfect lighting.

His face looks concerned. The calculation of whether he can force the T-shirt off you grinds behind his eyes. Whatever the answer, though, he simply waits for you to do something. He's talked you into his experiment and, even if it went disastrously, he's still the first person you called. You'd like that conversation with him. That means, though, your T-shirt has to come off. You have to show him what you actually look like, and it's not the illusion a tight T-shirt implies.

The T-shirt fights back at first. Crossing your arms to grab the hem flares your lats. The shirt you'd expected to be loose was already snug to begin with. This just makes it dig into you as you pull it over your head. You're sure you look ridiculous as you stand then wriggle and twist for the minute it takes to get the shirt off, but Latch doesn't laugh.

The shirt is still in your hand when his gaze lacerates you. His arms nestle your waist. The two of you stand motionless, staring at each other, for what seems like days. When you are opaque again, when the shadow you cast on the floor is as sharp and defined as the coffee table, he shakes his head and blinks a few times.

"Nothing wrong with that." He makes an appraising gaze of your torso, his arms now folded across his chest. "I wouldn't mind seeing that again."

"Thank you. I—"

"Catch me—"

Latch collapses and you catch him before he hits the coffee table. You shift your grip so that he lies across your arms then, gingerly, you lower him onto the sofa. He takes up most of its length. He's lighter than you expected. Then again, you're always surprised when the strength you seem to show in the fantasyland that is the gym crosses over into real life.

You sit on the coffee table, watching the slow rise and fall of his chest. Even now, the lighting in the room seems to have shifted to accommodate his new position.

Even though you both know better, he asks you out to the theatre and you accept. It's a production of *The Human Comedy*, after all. It's pretty much never produced and you've wanted to see this on stage since you were a kid. This is a production that fulfils the promise you heard in the show's cast album. The audience laughs and applauds at all the right places. Their massed attention keeps the sets and actors solid and opaque. Before, during, and after the show, you are both perfect gentlemen with each other. Even in bed.

Your experiments are going better, you suppose. At least iron cubes now reconstruct as something metallic, if not cubic. The result still kind of looks like breakfast. Latch's work shows more promise which is why, you tell yourself, you find yourself back in Latch's lab, caged again in the contraption that, weeks ago, convinced you that you had the body of a spindly teenager too weak to bench even an empty bar.

Latch flicks the switch and you brace. Outlines of ghostly lab benches and computers from the other side of the wall overlay the solid lab benches and computers here.

"How do you feel?" The expression on his face smacks of fear.

"A little weak. A little small." You hold up a hand to stop him when he reaches to unstrap you from the harness. "But I've been more intimidated by you before."

It's not a good idea for you two to date each other. Eventually, he'll become too annoyed at how you constantly misperceive yourself to deal with you. Maybe, one day, his mere existence will cow you so much that the despair will finally get to you. However, he's sweet and smart and you two have far too much in common.

Besides, the rate of the fading is increasing every day. Unless someone figures out what's going on, one day, super-perceivers won't be enough to keep the world in existence. You don't want to be alone when the world fades away, and you don't think he does either.

"Latch." You can't look at him. "There's a production of *The Golden Apple* coming up."

Again, another lost gem you thought you'd never see in your lifetime. Something about the end of the world makes artistic directors program shows that only diehards can love.

"Really? Where? I saw a concert version once."

"The Berkshires."

"Well, we gotta plan a weekend trip or something."

You were planning to see it anyway. It might as well be with the one other person who will appreciate it.

Slowly, what's on the other side of the wall gains heft and solidity. The visual contradiction of what's there overlapping with what's here becomes a bit much for you and you squeeze your eyes shut. Computers and benches from the other side, though, remain in your gaze. Whatever Latch's contraption is doing, it doesn't just spread your attention over an area, but one physically isolated from you. There seems to be a lot of attenuation even over the few feet to the wall, though, given how slowly things are returning. It's still a step towards making sure farmland doesn't disappear overnight.

Minutes pass and your legs start to shake. A chill passes through your body. You're not infinite capacity. No one is, but you're higher than many, if not most. You're nowhere near tapped out and you know that, but you know what you're like when you are. What courses through you is more fear than exhaustion.

"Say the word, Caleb, and I'll pull the plug on the trial."

It's hard to shake your head in the harness but you do anyway. "No, keep going. I'm fine."

"Thank you, Caleb."

A large hand with slim fingers works its way into your grasp. Its warmth seems to spread up your arm and through the rest of your body. The fear racing through you ebbs. Your mind clears a little and, in this age where attention has become important, you can see your way to using more of your capacity.

The hand grips yours firmly, but not too firmly. You can let go anytime you want, but you don't.

Five Thousand Squares

Maree Kimberley

It started with a crack. I suppose that's why no one heard it, except for Micha. She was always awake at 4 AM, her "pain prime time".

Soft pings from my connector finally woke me at 5.30 AM. I rolled onto my side and battled my fatigue-clogged brain to see a scroll of Micha's messages flowing down my wallscreen.

Are you awake?
I can feel rumbles.
Water's coming.
Wake up, Kaye!
Pack food, clothes etc and get over here now.
Bring all your meds!!

I winced as I dragged my body into a semi-upright position and scowled at the wallscreen. *Water? Why is she going on about water? The rain stopped yesterday.*

The first glimmer of dawn filtered through the window. I slumped back onto the bed and pressed my palms into my face to muffle my morning groans. I didn't like the sound of them to disturb the morning quiet.

The peace.

The silence.

Too much silence.

I lifted my palms from my face, and listened.

No birds.

No magpie warble, no mynah bird squabble, no cockatoo screech. No raucous caw from the scavenging crows feasting on my back neighbour's overflowing bin. Not a single kookaburra laugh.

Nothing, except a faint gurgle, like the last swirl of dishwater vanishing down a plughole. I scrolled back through Micha's messages, to the first one sent at 4:06.

Are you awake? My hip's telling me something is up. My knee agrees.

Micha's body spoke to her in throbs and stabs. My body had its own tricky methods: a gripping fatigue that pinned me to the bed. As I scrolled through the messages, I fought the tight bands of exhaustion that wound around the inside of my skull and pressed into the soft folds of my brain.

I had to get up.

Rouse Tilda and Ren.

Pack the bags.

Get us all in the sola-bub and get to Micha's before the deluge she sensed was coming meant there'd be no way out at all.

Adrenalin failed to kick in so I had to go through the usual rigmarole of rotating ankle joints and bending knees and clenching and unclenching my fists to rid my body of stiffness.

"Tilda…" I croaked.

I cleared my throat and tried again. "Tilda! Ren! Get here now!"

No response, of course. They automatically screened out any Mum-pings from their connectors. And pings from their friends were, I assumed, non-existent. The apocalypse itself could not raise teenagers out of bed at this hour. My body protested, too, no matter how much I tried to kid it into thinking that *now* really was a good time to get up.

I grimaced and grabbed the sheets to get some purchase while I pushed my head up off the bed. "Tilda! Ren!"

The silence sat in my ears, cavernous and unearthly.

Just get up, just get up. I repeated the mantra in my head as I rolled onto my side, pressed my fist into the mattress to steady myself and pushed my body upright. My feet rested on the timber floorboards. When I stood, razor blades of pain sliced through the balls of my feet. I gritted my teeth and hobbled to the toilet. Two minutes to rid my body of waste and recollect the details of the plan Micha and I had constructed, dissected and perfected over the years. Two minutes to review the angles considered, the threats posed and dismissed, the hours spent going over all contingencies. We were a couple of women aged before our time by an unwelcome disease that attacked our joints, swelled our limbs and twisted our bones. But, fuck it, we were nothing if not survivors.

I washed my hands and looked at my reflection. A too-goddamned-early glaze dulled my eyes.

"Well, woman—" I ran my fingers through my hair and flicked the greys that came out onto the floor. "This is it."

The important thing was to pace myself, not an easy task when Micha's pings flowed with increasing urgency.

Are you on your way?

Did you remember the spare chargers?

Double-check the list!

These bloody kids won't listen to a word I say.

*Should I send them down to the street to see what happens? *jokes**

No, really.

Jesus, Kaye are you on your way?

I pinged back. *Yep, don't stress. Getting organised.*

We'd run a drill last week, so at least everything was in the right place. I dressed as fast as I could and sat on the edge of the bed to lace up my boots, then headed to the kitchen to pack boxes into the wheeled market bags. The old tartan vinyl had seen better days but it was more or less waterproof.

Clothes.

Lenses.

Meds.

Hypos.

Batteries. (They took some tracking down, but I'd found them at a warehouse rummage. Those old-time survivalists knew a thing or two.)

Another ping.

You got about thirty minutes. Hope your arses are just about out that door.

I stretched my arms up, spread my palms, slowed the breathing I realised was gathering pace into hyperventilation territory.

"Do. Not. Fucking. Panic."

Going as fast as I can. I pinged back. *Be on our way soon.*

I relaxed my shoulders and stamped my boots as loud as I could down the timber-floored hallway. I flung open Tilda's door then Ren's. The doors whacked against the walls, a one-two punch combo.

"Ren!" I dragged the doona off and flung it to the floor. "This is not a drill."

He blinked up at me. When he read the expression on my face, his lip quivered.

"You got three minutes to dress and grab anything you can't live without." I hurried across the hallway to Tilda's room but she was already out of bed pulling on jeans and boots.

"You heard?"

She nodded.

"Front door in four minutes."

I wheeled the packed bags to the end of the hall. The sun's early rays filtered through the coloured glass panels on either side of the door, staining my bare skin in streaks of rose pink and lemon yellow. The misshapen knuckles on my left hand—a legacy of the six month period when my meds had been out of financial reach—loomed like desert hills. Fortunately, more recent governments had taken a big-picture view of health, ensuring I had a good supply of meds stocked up. Better meds meant healthier citizens working more and paying more tax. Less fortunately, the current government stuck to an "optimistic" view of disaster readiness, having convinced much of the nation's population that technology had successfully negated all threats of natural and human-made disasters. The nation's satie-cities, the government assured us, were technological and engineering marvels built to withstand any climactic conditions. Many people believed them.

Micha and I did not.

"Ren. Tilda," I yelled. "Two minutes."

Inside the hallway cupboard door I fiddled with the latch my ex-husband had installed in a location that was awkward for me to reach. My shoulder muscles crabbed with pain as I twisted into position and forced my fingers to defeat the latch. Finally, it sprung open. I slid the panel across and pulled out the sola-bub. It wasn't the prettiest but in light traffic it could get us to Micha's in fifteen minutes flat.

"Ren! Tilda! Thirty seconds."

Boots shuffled and god-knows-what thumped and slammed while I opened the front door and dragged the sola-bub out onto the verandah. At one time sola-bubs had been a compulsory household safety item but since the end of the Regional Wars most people considered them a waste of space, or, at best, a quaint conversation piece. They'd been chucked out by the thousands. Ours was an old model that had outlived its self-assembly modules by at least a decade. I cursed the fiddly bloody thing as my morning-stiff fingers struggled with the manual buckles and clips until it was ready to roll, or float, whichever was necessary.

With a final blurping-hiss the sola-bub flapped open on the verandah like a gulping fish. I turned to yell one more time as Ren and Tilda tumbled out of the door one after the other.

"Ready?"

They nodded, faces pale and lips pressed thin.

I pinged Micha.

We're on our way.

That was the last ping that got through.

Micha and I met at an arthritis support group. We sat on opposite sides of the room until drawn together by a fierce need to avoid the serial whingers and the over-seventies. (The over-seventies were really very nice but couldn't comprehend the intricacies of having to deal with a debilitating chronic disease while raising kids.) It didn't take us long to realise we shared the same disdain for bad coffee and self-entitlement, and although our politics were eons apart we mostly agreed to disagree.

"You've got a socialist in there just screaming to get out," I teased her as she railed against her own party's refusal to tax the tech-giants who were doing their best to gene-patent people like us out of existence.

"And you have the heart of an economic rationalist," she countered.

When our respective parties were booted out at the last national election by the upstart Triparates we were both shocked. For weeks we bitched over coffee and no-flour brownies about how the Tri-ers had pushed their laissez-faire approach to the running of local satie-city security precincts into the realm of absurdity.

"Look," said Micha, "I don't have a problem with them disbanding street safety officers. Goddess knows those bumblers were more of a danger than a public service."

"That pile up at the Whitlam Day celebrations did them no favours." I nodded. "And the random safety equipment checks were nothing more than a chance to sticky beak inside peoples' houses."

"But"—Micha poked her quilting needle in the air for emphasis—"de-funding the emergency response group? That makes no sense at all." She smoothed the squares of fabric she'd stitched together out on the table. "Like it?"

"Nice colour combo." I nodded. "At least we'll be warm and stylish in an apocalypse. But what about the cuts to the community recovery teams?" I counted off on my fingers. "And to pick up services, clean-up services, maintenance services, emergency shelters. It's all gone."

"Which leaves us where, exactly?"

"Same place as our gene pool rankings." I sighed. "Up shit creek without a paddle."

"Not good enough." Micha pursed her lips. "I don't intend to be left floundering in chaos the next time weather-net gets its nano-wires crossed, or worse." She raised her eyebrows. "When the satie-cities' chief engineer decides to permanently leave the country, it's time to make a plan."

We drew up our first list that day. Turned out it wasn't as difficult as we'd thought to source the stuff we needed. In the fifteen years since the wars ended people had become complacent, and the Tri-ers' constant bombardment of messages declaring a *New Age of Reliability* lulled the population into an ever greater sense of security. Sellers who believed we were all safe and sound in our disaster-proof satie-cities couldn't get rid of items fast enough, and we soon learned we could be choosy in what we decided to buy.

Our kids thought we were nuts. So did my ex. Most of the time Micha's husband Keelan kept his opinions to himself about what he termed our "weird little hobby" though he did protest at the stockpiling of sealed packages of lentils. Micha said that was because Keelan's mother had fed him nothing but lentil soup for months on end during the third wave financial crisis. I understood how he felt. It was the same for me with canned tuna. But tinned fish of all kinds went into the stockpile along with kidney beans, rice, pasta, oats, brown sugar, honey, salt and whatever other long-term survival food we could get our hands on. Before long, Micha's sewing room had become a store packed to the brim with enough supplies to see us through a few years. She complained sometimes of having to battle through an ever-decreasing corridor of space to get to her machine, but although we had plenty of room at my place, we also knew that its location was too risky. Micha was safe and sound in solid packed terr-forma blocks on top of a hill. If her place went under, so did our whole satie-city.

We were five blocks away from Micha's when the roar of water swelled behind us. Tilda looked over her shoulder and screamed. Ren whimpered, his eyes wide with fear.

"Hold on kids." I retracted the wheels and inflated the buoys. "It'll get bumpy but we'll be okay." The water hadn't begun to fill the streets when we'd left home and people in our neighbourhood had regarded our little sola-bub with either amusement or disdain.

They were not long for this world.

When the wall of water hit us, my breath caught in my throat. The wallop lurched us forward, bruising our chests against the seat restraints. Pain ripped through my shoulders, my ribs. My teeth snapped into my tongue and blood filled my mouth.

Tilda and Ren's wails tore through my heart.

"Hold on!"

The brown water tossed the egg-shaped sola-bub over and around, a puny piece of flotsam in its cavernous maw. My stomach lurched as we somersaulted over. Ren's vomit hit the back of my neck as my head rocketed towards the ceiling. Tilda's fingernails scratched at my arm as she tried to grip hold of me. The water howled, a voracious demon, and the whole world was a turgid brown liquid mess. I must have blacked out for a few moments because next thing I knew we'd come to a stop. The kids' sobbing filled my ears while below us water still roared. The sola-bub had wedged itself in the remains of a front verandah. I closed my eyes for half a minute and waited for my breathing to slow from high panic to wary.

A rapid tap-tap-tap clattered against the sola-bub's biospex window beside my head. My heart thumped fast three times. I half-opened my left eye, not sure if I wanted to see what was making the tapping sound.

"Mum, it's a kid," said Ren. "A little kid."

I leaned forward, grimacing at the stab of pain between my shoulder blades, and turned my head towards the window.

The child pressed its nose against the biospex. Small spots of condensation waxed and waned with each breath it took.

"Are you guys okay?" I asked. "Any broken bones?"

"I'm fine, I think," said Tilda.

"I bit my lip," said Ren. "But that's all."

"Don't move yet." I leaned as far forward as the seat restraints would let me and gauged our position. The floodwaters continued their swirling rage about a metre below us. To my left, a tree branch had wedged itself between the verandah's broken edge and the underside of the sola-bub. Our position appeared to be stable but the waters were unpredictable. A wave could swell and carry us off at any moment.

The child resumed its tapping, its small fingernails scraping against the sola-bub's sturdy exterior.

"Mum." Ren's voice held the hint of a whine. "We have to let him in."

"It's a girl, not a boy," said Tilda.

I gazed at the child's small face. Girl, boy, I couldn't tell. I craned my neck the few centimetres I could move it. There was no one else around that I could see. No adult hands clutching the child. No larger fists coming to bang on the sola-bub and demand entry.

My conscience spat rapid-fire accusations.

What? You're going to abandon this kid? Seriously? Is that what you've come to?

"It's not that simple," I muttered.

"What's not simple?" Ren reached for my upper arm. "Mum?"

"I can't just fling open the roof hatch and grab the child. I'm not sure how stable we are here."

"But we can't leave her here," Tilda's voice pitched up towards a squeal.

"Quiet. I need to think."

I loosened my seat restraint and wiggled forward, centimetre by centimetre. The water below us thrashed and gurgled. It appeared to be rising but I couldn't be sure.

"Tilda, see that broken timber rail to your left?"

"Yes."

"Keep an eye on it, and watch to see if the water is coming up to that level or not."

"Okay."

"Ren, you keep watch out the back. Let me know the second you see any change in the water, any object coming towards us, anything at all."

"Yes, Mum."

"And don't move a muscle. Got it?"

I pressed my fingers against the biospex and held them there. The child pressed its fingers towards mine. I breathed deep into my lungs. I forced a smile.

"Okay," I whispered. "Okay."

I flicked the release button on my seat restraint, leaned to the left side and stretched out my arms until my hands pushed against the sola-bub's inside walls. Beneath us, the verandah groaned.

Ren and Tilda yelped.

"Stay calm!" I snapped. "Watch what's happening outside."

My shoulders ached with the effort of stretching and pushing as I raised my bum off the seat. I gritted my teeth against the pain shooting down my upper arms, through my elbows, forearms, wrists. I flexed my fused left wrist as far is it could go to give myself leverage.

"Ugh!" I breathed in short gasps. "Ah! Ah!" Tears sprang to my eyes as I pushed myself up. "Ugh!"

I planted my feet to keep myself steady. The sola-bub shuddered. It listed to the right.

"Mum?" Ren squeaked.

"Is something coming?

"N-no...but—"

"Mum, I think the water's rising," Tilda whispered.

"How much?"

"A couple of centimetres."

"Okay. I'll be quick."

I relaxed my arms for a moment's respite, and took in a deep breath.

I've given birth. Twice. No drugs. I can do this.

I raised my arms again and pushed through the ache that crushed my bones. My fingers fumbled with the latch.

"Mum?" Tilda choked back a sob. "It's rising. The water's rising."

"Nearly there."

I grunted as my fingers pushed and pulled at the latch. It sprang free. I shoved my palms against the roof hatch and screeched as pain cracked through my left wrist.

The hatch sprang open.

The sola-bub lurched forward.

"Mum!" Ren and Tilda screamed.

Somehow I twisted my body up and around. My hands grabbed the kid's elbow. I snatched at it, dragged the small body in as the sola-bub slid forward half a metre.

"Mum!" The kids screamed.

Outside the water roared.

The child fell to the floor.

I punched my hand up, snatched at the manual rope pulley and slammed the hatch shut. A wave of water swelled beneath us. The sola-bub whined as the verandah split away. Something slammed into the side and tossed me backwards. I scrambled to grab the child as its body flung towards the windscreen. Something popped in my neck. I wrapped my arms around the child, pulled it to me.

"Hold onto me!"

The child's face pushed into my chest as I scrabbled for the seat restraint. I locked it in. We were thrown forward. The sola-bub tipped and swayed. It dropped two metres into the water. A dead weight dragged at my body, pressed in against my head, twisted my guts as the sola-bub rolled in the water and popped up again, spat out like poison.

The children sobbed and wailed.

"Hold on. Just hold on!"

We shot through the water, tossed across the yellow flood scum while outside the world tilted and spun to Mother Earth's wild rhythms. I held the unknown child against my chest and hummed quietly into its ear. It clung to me, silent except for the short breaths snuffling through its snotty nose. I closed my eyes against the chaotic world and wondered if this ride would stop.

My hips and knees cracked as I stood, unsteady in the still floating sola-bub, and pushed the roof hatch open. The water had been still for around thirty minutes and silence had replaced the deafening roar of the deluge. I poked my head out of the hatch, hoping to catch some fresh air. The smell outside was a little less putrid than the acrid vomit stench inside the sola-bub, but only just. The blue sky was clear, an innocent witness to the broken lives scattered below. Houses crushed together, a clutter of itinerant poly-crete and metal scraps in search of somewhere to belong. The flotsam and jetsam of domestic items floundered in huddles, too. A clutch of sodden mattresses. A tumble of chairs. Assorted sofas. When a body floated by I pretended I didn't see it and looked instead for landmarks.

Tilda's head popped up beside me. She tugged at my T-shirt sleeve.

"Mum, it's that way." She steered me one-eighty degrees towards the hill that rose up from the brown floodwaters. A mess of torn-off roofs, collapsing walls and shredded trees loomed around us.

But I could see the white painted terr-forma blocks of Micha's place squatting on the hilltop about eight hundred metres away, across an expanse of brown floodwaters. I hoped the sola-bub's panels had been able to absorb enough power to get us there.

I lowered myself back down into the driver's seat.

"It's a boy, Mum," said Ren. "His name's Sacha."

"He talked to you?"

"No, I checked the tag on his T-shirt. It said Sacha."

"Sacha is a girl's name, too." Tilda rolled her eyes. "And that doesn't mean *her* name is Sacha."

"It'll do for now," I said. "Give Sacha a packet of dried fruit. Have one yourselves if you want it. Then strap yourselves in. Not sure how well this thing will go now."

I pumped my foot onto the power pedal.

Nothing.

"What's wrong, Mum?" Tilda poked her head forward.

"Nothing." I forced an even tone. "It'll be fine."

I pumped my foot a few more times, then a few more.

Still nothing.

"Is it broken?" Ren stuck his head next to his sister's.

"Just look after Sacha and let me worry about this, okay?" I snapped.

Hold it together, my inner voice berated. *You're the parent.*

I breathed in and tried again, pumping the pedal in a steady beat. The sola-bub was a simple craft, designed to withstand rough treatment. In theory, wild floodwaters shouldn't affect the engine, or steering mechanism, or any other vital moving parts. But it had been stored, unused and untested, for years. Maybe, the short spurt it had used up when we'd first left the house was all it was good for.

I pumped harder. Pain scored up my leg, a burning sensation like a tattooist's needle going over the same piece of flesh again and again, but I kept up the rhythm.

"Start you bastard," I hissed between clenched teeth. "You clapped out piece of junk, start!" My muscles burned. The bones in my feet crunched as if gripped in a vice. Tears smarted in my eyes. I pushed my chest into the steering wheel, desperate for leverage, and slammed my foot down again and again. A faint whirring sound filtered from the engine at the back of the sola-bub.

"Keep going, Mum." Tilda's hand rubbed the small of my back. "Nearly there, keep going."

The engine spluttered and choked. I pumped, desperate, my whole right side burning and aching. The engine clicked. It purred and hummed. It lurched us forward.

"Mum!" Tilda pointed at a piece of flood-junk looming towards us, big as the side of a house. A few hours before, it probably had been the side of a house. I wrenched the steering wheel to miss it. Pain ripped through my shoulders. The right one was seizing up. The house slammed us sideways but the sola-bub sprang back up without missing a beat, and kept going.

I wrapped my forearms around the wheel and eased my foot off the pedal. The pain level in my body scaled down from unbearable to excruciating while the sola-bub chugged along, easy as a Sunday afternoon on the lake. Ren started up a round of *The wheels on the bus*. Sacha clapped his hands. Tilda joined in.

"Come on, Mum," Ren said.

"The mums on the bus go shush, shush, shush," I sang.

Micha's house was straight ahead, less than ten minutes away if our luck held. About forty verses of *The wheels on the bus*.

The sola-bub chugged forward, and we kept singing.

As the water ebbed into the shallows at the base of the hill I set the sola-bub's wheels to re-inflate. But it was soon clear that the climb up the hill to Micha's was too steep for the tiny engine. My guts clenched as the engine whined.

"Mum?" Tilda's face was centimetres away from mine. "Want me to get out and have a look around?"

"Hang on." I veered left towards a flat section and pulled on the brake. "Push the hatch open for me, love."

While the engine idled I forced my aching legs to stand, and peered out of the top. A metre thick line of debris coated in grey scum circled the base of the hill. Further up, fallen trees slumped like 5 AM drunks. Gangs of flies, dizzy with choice, buzzed above bloated animal bodies. Everywhere I looked, the ground was a putrid cocktail of the clutter that had filled peoples' lives. There was no clear track to Micha's house. Even if the sola-bub's tyres survived the hazards of scattered debris, the risk of it slipping on the unpredictable surface and tumbling back down the hill was too great.

We were going to have to unload and walk.

My exhaustion was a tangle of worms burrowing between skin and muscle, down my back, my thighs, my calves, dragging at my body. Inflammation gripped my shoulders in a vice so tight I could barely raise my arms above my waist. All I wanted to do was sink on my rubbery legs, fold into the corner of the sola-bub and sleep.

"Mum?" Tilda tugged at my T-shirt.

I sighed, and lowered my body into the driver's seat.

"Okay, kids. This is how it is." I switched off the sola-bub's engine and turned to face them. "We have to walk, carry as much stuff as we can. It's not far but the ground is muddy and covered in debris."

I checked Sacha's feet. At least the child had closed-in shoes.

"Ren, you'll need to hold Sacha's hand." I closed my eyes for a moment, and took in a deep breath. "There are dead things lying around. Try not to look at them."

"Dead animals?" Ren's voice trembled.

"Yes, and…" I trailed off. I forced an energy I didn't feel into my voice. "It's important not to step on anything. We'll have to take it slow but that's okay. At least we're safe here from the water. I'm going to open the main doors now. It's going to stink. You'll get used to it."

I moved my body forward and pressed the release button. The sola-bub's doors retracted, opening up each side of the capsule.

Sacha darted out and ran.

"Grab him!" I yelled.

Ren jumped out. He reached the child in four quick strides and wrapped his arms around him.

Sacha screamed. His cry ripped through the silence. Shocked, Ren let him go. Sacha ran again. Ren lunged for him. He tripped and fell onto hands and knees.

"Jesus." I forced my body to move but Tilda had already scrambled out and sprinted towards the child. She grabbed hold of him and didn't let go.

"You okay, Ren?" I moved towards him on stiff, unsteady legs, fighting the fog that clawed at the inside of my skull.

"Kaye! Kaye!"

"Mum, it's Keelan!" Tilda hugged Sacha to her and jumped up and down. "Keelan and Micha!"

Thank fuck. A sigh released from deep in my belly. My shoulders dropped tension I didn't know I was holding.

"Kaye! Don't move," Micha yelled. "The ground's unstable down there." She pointed to a house roof about ten metres away from where Tilda clung onto Sacha. "That house was standing fifteen minutes ago."

"Holy shit," I muttered. "Tilda, Ren walk back down here to me. Slowly." Throbs of pain gripped my shoulders again. I gritted my teeth and ignored them. Nothing was going to stop me getting my kids to safety. I'd scream with pain with every movement if I had to, as long as I got us through.

A low rumble shuddered below my boots. A corner gutter on the sunken roof lurched deeper into the ground. Tilda and Ren flung themselves at me, clung to me, Sacha squashed between them.

"Slow," I hissed. There were five metres between us and the sola-bub. "One step at a time." We moved towards it together, crossing the space with held breath. "Now, get back in. Gentle movements."

I eased my throbbing joints into the driver's seat and stared up towards Micha and Keelan. The kids climbed in behind me.

What now?

Ren snuffled, and stifled a sob. Tilda held Sacha on her lap and crooned a melody into his ear. Up on the hill, Micha waved her arm. She opened and shut her hand to signal "ten". Ten of what? It wasn't clear. In all our preparations Micha's house had been the safe place, the place that could shelter both our families and a few others as well. We hadn't counted on subsidence on her hill. Even in our worst-case scenarios, we hadn't imagined this level of devastation could manifest so fast.

Another rumble shuddered the ground below us, and the sola-bub slid a few more centimetres towards the floodwater line.

"Strap in, kids."

"Where are we going?"

"Nowhere, yet."

Micha had disappeared back inside her house. I watched an ibis alight from her roof and circle down towards an upended yellow sofa that stuck out of the ground like a fang. The ibis landed on the sofa's arm, spread its wings and dropped a massive, runny crap that slopped down the side.

"Mum." Tilda sniffed hard. "I think Sacha has had an accident."

"Well, Tilda, where there is life, there is shit."

"Mum!"

"There's going to be a lot of it, kids, both physical and metaphorical. Better get used to it."

A roar, shrill as a chainsaw, screeched at the top of the hill. I pressed my hand to my neck to support the muscles as I craned my head around in the direction of the sound. It eased off from a demonic screech into a loud hiss.

"Holy crapoly. What is that thing?" Ren clambered off his seat. "A jumping castle?"

The sola-bub shifted another half metre.

"Ren!" I screamed.

"Sorry!"

From behind Micha and Keelan's house a huge swathe of fabric rippled and mushroomed outwards.

"Oh my god!" I laughed. "Oh my god. I don't believe she actually did it."

"What is it, Mum?"

I shook my head. "The woman is a genius."

"What'd she do, Mum?"

"You'll work it out. Just watch."

As the minutes passed, the fabric filled with air, thousands of pieces of coloured silk stitched together, riotous as a spring garden, flapping, rolling, billowing into the sky. The flame hissed and the balloon rose up above the roof of the house, a large basket dangling below it.

The balloon drifted across the fifty metres that separated our families. As it drew closer Micha leaned over the wicker.

"Five thousand friggin' squares of fabric," she yelled. "Finished it two days ago. My hands are swollen as an Arts Minister's belly."

"Woman," I yelled back, "you are an absolute fucking legend."

*

Turned out Sacha was a girl. We listed her on the lost and missing register but heard nothing back. She seems happy enough with us, and Ren is good with her, so as long as she's happy, she'll stay.

It's not a bad life out here on the farm but it gets lonely sometimes being hidden away, miles from anywhere. Every now and then Keelan or his father will take the few-day trek to the nearest ration centre to barter a few crates of their homebrew for some contraband and gossip. When they come back with the latest rumour from the Commission of Capital Inquiry into Infrastructure Failure—about intra-region terrorism or power plays within the ruling party or a media-baron plot to destabilise the national government and expose its weaknesses—we all have a sad laugh. We suspect the truth is more simple.

Massive new satie-cities to house populations no longer able to live in sea-inundated coastal areas, rushed through planning and surrounded by walls that stopped waterways running their natural course: in the past few years they'd popped up all around the country's inland fringe. Technological marvels, the government had spruiked, made possible by a new era of national cooperation. They ignored the sinkholes that sprung up outside city perimeters, even when they'd started to number in the hundreds. Soon everyone else ignored the sinkholes, too.

But the weeks of torrential rain that broke years of drought sealed the disaster deal. From west to east and north to south, the deluge pressed in behind the satie-cities' walls so that even when the rain stopped the water's force continued to build.

The walls cracked.

Water burst through.

Thousands of megalitres gushed out in dozens of uncontrollable inland tsunamis. Entire satie-cities wiped out across the country. Decimated. Hundreds of thousands, perhaps millions, of people dead. Lives cut short, families torn apart. Comfortable and uncomfortable lives shredded like paper in a hamster cage. It's what happens when too many humans crowd together and a few dickheads think the laws of physics are mere suggestions.

Micha and I still argue about politics sometimes, but not often. It's a hollow game when your worst fears have been realised. But when we do, I never point out that we're all living together on Keelan's dad's farm like hippy socialists. And she never mentions how I guard our precious stores with the puritanic zeal of a heartless economic rationalist.

Portobello Blind

Octavia Cade

The worst part of the apocalypse was the sheer bloody *boredom* of it.

Anna had never expected to be the—apparently— sole survivor of a quick and dirty plague, but if she had, her expectations would have been different. All the apocalypse stories she knew had conflict and danger and high stakes, arenas and journeys and great symphonic soundtracks.

Anna spent hers fishing.

She had to do it, had to eat. She was stuck out of the way at the marine lab at Portobello, the most distant part of the university, and there was nothing left in the break room cupboards. If anyone had hidden a stash somewhere else she hadn't been able to find it, though she didn't know all the lab secrets anyway, built on multiple levels as it was. That alone was a difficulty, and one best suited for sighted people.

"Don't use the lift while I'm gone," her father told her. "There's no telling what'll happen if the power goes out." And that was the last thing she needed, to be stuck between floors with no food and no toilet.

"I'll be back soon," he said. "We should be isolated enough here. But we need to stock up." Not just with food, but the asthma medication he needed.

He hadn't come back. Anna didn't know why, but she was certain he was dead. Her father wasn't the type of man to abandon anyone, let alone his blind fourteen-year-old daughter.

Anna grieved, but she could only cry so much. It was so *lonely* without him, without anyone. All there was to do was gather food, and with the best will in the world Anna wasn't so incompetent that feeding herself took all day.

On the beach, Anna called out, "Can you hear me? Is anybody there?"

"Please," she cried. "Please."

There wasn't a hint of breeze. The air was so still that her voice carried across water, echoed up and down the coast. "Is anybody there?"

Maybe she'd echo to the small settlement at Portobello. Maybe someone would hear her across the harbour.

There were life jackets in the shed. She put one on and it smelled of salt and rubber, of plastic. The life jacket had a whistle attached: a sharp, high sound like a gull. It was designed to carry over long distances, but if there was anyone around to hear her screaming through it, they never, ever came.

It helped that she was relatively familiar with the lab. Her father had worked there for years, and she'd spent many afternoons in the break room, doing homework, while he did experiments in rooms that smelled of chemicals.

Because she was familiar with it, she knew that there was a fishing kit in one corner of the break room. Some experiments ran long; some had to be monitored only periodically. She remembered that more than one of the scientists had taken advantage of this and had gone to the jetty for an hour or two of fishing when they had the chance.

Anna had never fished before but she had been out to the jetty, when she'd been taken on boat rides, through the harbour and out past Taiaroa Heads where the albatross colony was. She could find her way out there with her cane all right, if she was careful about the rocks and slipping—and fishing couldn't be that hard.

"Rod, line, hook," she said. "And I've got bread." There'd been some left over in the break room fridge. She thought it was going bad—there was a powdery residue on some of the slices and it smelled off. "Good enough for fish," she said.

Before she sat down on the edge of the wharf, Anna circled it carefully, taking single steps and then stopping, waving her cane over the water. She'd hoped one of the research boats would be tied up there. If nothing else, there'd be a comfortable place to sleep: a bunk and a small enclosed space, something she could learn to nest in. Disappointingly, none were present. "But that means they might come back," said Anna. "Maybe some of them are still out there, on the ocean." Safe, and uninfected by plague. Anna had rung everyone she knew, rung emergency services and there was never an answer. She even started random dialling, hoping that someone would pick up but they never did. She knew how to use the satellite radio— *"No child of mine is spending time on a boat without knowing that"*—but no matter how often she called her mayday there was never a response.

Not yet anyway, but the empty berths gave her hope. It made it easier for her to reframe "apocalypse" in her mind, to cast it in the shadows of "vacation".

"I'm on a deserted island," she said. Not tropical, because Dunedin would never be that, but she pushed the fantasy as far as climate would allow. "A deserted island. Soon it'll be time to go home. Soon a boat will come for me, and they'll want to know all about my fishing while they take me home to shore."

She baited the hook. It left her fingers bloody, but, "Maybe that'll attract more fish," she said. "Maybe I won't even have time to finish my piña colada before they bite." Not that she'd ever had a piña colada, but it sounded recreational. Like it came in a fancy glass with a little umbrella.

It took a long time for a fish to bite, but she didn't have anything better to do. When Anna hauled it up, however, she realised she'd forgotten to consider actually killing the thing. All her previous experience of fish said they came with batter and some nicely vinegared chips. "Shit," she said, trying to grab hold of a flapping body that she couldn't see, trying to grip slippery scales and bash the head against the planks.

The fish squirted out of her hands. Anna made a grab for it and overbalanced. She fell from the jetty and into the water. The splash of fish beside her was something to be ignored as she flailed and caught until she was clamped to one of the jetty posts. She wrapped her arms and legs around, slicing them open on the sharp edges of baby shellfish, of little mussels.

When she got her breathing under control, when she managed to stop weeping against the wet wood, Anna listened for the waves that spoke of shoreline and swam in that direction. Letting go of the wharf was the bravest thing she'd done in her life.

When she reached the rocks, she clambered over them and crawled up the path, crawled back to the lab with her skin all scraped off.

She went hungry for three days before trying again. Part of that was fear, and part of it was anger and punishment. "Why didn't you wear the life jacket?" she said. "Stupid, stupid. Anyone would think you *wanted* to drown."

If she drowned she'd never know if anyone else was out there.

(If she drowned she'd never care.)

The temptation was to attach herself to the radio and scream over airwaves. It couldn't be true that she was the only survivor. It couldn't be...but Anna woke in the nights anyway, shrieking, running for the radio. She woke in the mornings with new bruises from crashing into walls and her neck ached from untenable positions, bent over and straining for sound.

She was careful with the battery. One day the power could go out and her calling would wind down. She'd have to ration her reaching out, preserve the power that was left.

(One day even the battery would die, and the only creatures to hear her screaming then would be albatrosses.)

The satellite radio had cables that she followed to the wall, a double socket where only one was used. Anna plugged the kettle from the break room into the second socket. When it was filled with water, she could hear the boiling and that told her the marine lab still had power.

She sat before the radio most nights, when the windows turned cold, weeping with condensation. Boiled water and called, boiled water again to check that it wasn't the battery that was running down.

"Is anybody out there?" she called. "Please, can anybody hear me?"

"Please."

It was the bleating that did her in, that really provoked her to action. She'd come to terms with the fact that she couldn't help anyone. That she couldn't help anything—that even the fish tanks and the aquarium, next door to the lab, were beyond her capabilities. "I don't even know where the controls are," she wept. "And I wouldn't know how to work them if I did. I'm so sorry." She'd shut the aquarium door behind her and resolved herself to insularity, to hard-heartedness. At least until she heard the constant pathetic sounds of abandonment, the sad vacant cries of a dozen hungry sheep.

"What do you expect me to do about it?" Anna shouted, standing in the front door of the lab. The car park was before her, she knew that much—but the lab was out on the peninsula, and after visitors left the coastal road there was a ten minute drive over a twisty unsealed farm track. *Lots of sheep here. And geese.*

She heard the geese but she wasn't worried about them. "You've got wings, you can fly," she said. But the sheep, trapped in paddocks, could eat everything down to the ground and they'd do nothing but starve then.

"They're only sheep," Anna said. "There's nothing I can do for them." She knew even less about sheep than she did about plague. Even less than fish, and she hadn't been able to save the aquarium. For all she knew the sheep were carriers…but when the plaintive bleats were punctuated by the tiny high cries of lambs, Anna knew she couldn't take it any longer.

"This is going to be a nightmare," she grumbled, lacing her boots up tight and clutching her cane. She walked out the front door and towards the bleating, tapping her way up the road to the car park. There was a big curve, she knew, and that was easy to navigate because she'd done it before, every time she'd visited. Her dad took her arm, always, but without him she could manage.

Her cane hit the bank before she did—a steep grassy slope, and lumpen. Easy to trip on. It was just a few paces to the fence. A short distance, but she only found out what the ticking was when she reached out and got shocked for her trouble. "An electric fence," she said. "Well isn't that just fucking marvellous."

She still felt guilty, swearing. As if there were someone around to hear her. "I wouldn't mind being told off," said Anna, sucking on the stung finger. "I'd be *happy* to be grounded."

Even the sheep didn't respond to that, though she could hear them just beyond the fence, their quick anxious movements. They bleated again, distressed. Wanting something from her. "Even if I get you out, I wouldn't expect much," said Anna. "If you think I'm going to be the one to shear you, you're sadly mistaken." There weren't any clippers, and even if there were it wasn't like she could see what she was doing with them. "You'd probably lose your ears."

The only thing to do was to follow the fence-line, to try and find a gate. And the only way to do that was to stumble slowly over the grass, trying to keep her balance and listening for the fence. Trying not to fall, because either way was trouble. Down and she'd drop a few paces onto the road, probably break an ankle. Up and she'd fall face first against the electric fence.

"I'm warning you," said Anna. "If I could see, I'd definitely be thinking about mutton right now. You don't know how sick I am of fish."

There were two false alarms before she found the gate, before she could wrench it open with her thrice-stung hand. "Get out, you little shits," she said. "Out! And don't think you're getting anything else from me. I've got nothing for you."

But she couldn't hear any mad rush, not even a little shuffle. "You're the stupidest fucking animals on the planet," she said, but there was no real heat in her voice. It figured—there she was, post-apocalypse, the only person alive that she knew of and doing quite well with it, considering, and she was stuck with geese that flew away from her and sheep that didn't have the sense to make a break for freedom when she gave them the chance.

"Well, the gate's open," she said. "You can all find your way out here and run along the road when

you want to. I'm sure you'll find grass eventually."
There had to be more of them out there, she thought.
More on the farmland, not just these few huddled
at the bottom corner. "You'll have to let them know
yourselves," she said.

She was just about to step back onto the road
when the sheep began to run. One of them knocked
her down as it went past. Its fleece was soft and fluffy.
Another one stepped on her hand.

"I hate you all," she said.

To mark each day, Anna took a piece of gravel from the
car park and dropped it into a mug. She only needed
one cup for herself, and there were fifteen others in the
break room not being used.

On the forty-third day after her father left—the
first mug, the one with the chip on the rim, was nearly
full—there was someone on the radio, someone
talking back to her.

The sound was distant, faint, and she couldn't
make it out over static.

The worst of it was she knew that whoever it was
couldn't make her out either. The sound of another
person was too much for her, and Anna sobbed and
sobbed into the microphone until there was no sound
at all, and there was nothing she could do to get them
back.

When she woke, her cheek was imprinted with marks from the microphone and her eyes were glued shut with salt and swelling.

On the 44th day after her father left, Anna didn't leave the radio. The water boiled out of the jug and she had to turn it off before the element burned out but she was too afraid to leave and fill it again, because whoever it was might radio back while she was gone.

She peed into the jug for the same reason. It'd wash. There was still bleach under the sink.

There was nothing on the forty-fourth day. There was nothing on the forty-fifth day either.

Or the forty-sixth.

Or the forty-seventh.

"I'm going to die alone," she said.

Anna could smell the tides, knew when they were out. The soft-sweet scent of mud was a dead giveaway. Even when it was raining, she could smell it—although the rain made it worse, for the paths were slippery. But she couldn't live on fish forever. Her teeth would fall out, her gums would go soft and spongy. She needed vegetables.

She took the fish bucket with her. It would be difficult, she knew. With the fish, all Anna had to do was to make her way along the path down to the little wharf. She always knew which way was seaward, what with the sound of waves, and she could always find her way back to the lab, back along the path if she kept her hand on the railing and counted footsteps. But for seaweed, she'd have to go out to the rocks. They were slick and slippery and she couldn't see where to put her feet, had no faith in footsteps.

She moved carefully, balancing. Held the bucket out before her, swung it round to check for obstacles. Ran her hands over the rocks, looking for holdfasts and for texture.

Anna didn't remember all the algae she could eat. There was one she knew of. Karengo. A type of *Porphyra*—but she couldn't remember what it was like, how it felt. It could have been anything! A kelp, a red, a brown. She'd hoped that she'd recognise it when the time came but all the seaweeds were foreign under her fingers. Anna knelt with her knees in a tide pool and sobbed until she vomited.

There was nothing to rinse her mouth out with but salt water, so she did that anyway, felt the dry sting of it where she'd bitten her tongue. "I hate this," she said, face wet and feet wet, wet all through and alone with it. "I hate it!"

But hatred wouldn't keep her alive. Anna curled up in the rocks, hid her face in her knees, imagined pineapple to soothe her breathing, and tried to remember.

Feel this, said her father. *Feel how slippery it is. How thin the leaves are.* Sea lettuce, edible as its name suggested, and absolutely unmistakeable under her fingers, like soft oiled cellophane.

Why is it so slippery? she said.

It's only two cells thick. The cells come in sheets, they slide against each other. Like graphite. It lived in the intertidal, in the rocks. Common and unremarkable and *edible*, green she heard. There had to be vitamins in it.

There's another, said her father. *Neptune's necklace. You know that one.* The little beads all strung together, her favourite on the beach because when she found strings she'd pop all the beads as if they were bubble wrap. *Make sure you pop them before you try eating it,* said Dad, because there was liquid inside the vesicles and that liquid was salt and seawater. *Pop them all and rinse it well.*

Anna filled her bucket and made it back to the lab with bruised feet, scrapes all down her legs and her last long fingernails chipped and broken. "What I wouldn't do for a nail file." She sighed. If one of the scientists had kept a manicure set in their offices, she hadn't been able to find it. She had to even them up with her teeth.

She rinsed the seaweed in the common room sink, over and over in cold water until when she bit through the necklace there was only the faintest taste of salt. It hung in ropes, the Neptune's necklace, and she spread them over one end of the table, left them to dry in the sun. "You'll keep a long time, I think," she said. When they were dry enough to rattle, to be crisp under her fingers with bits that snapped off easily, she hung them over the coat hooks by the door. That way she wouldn't have to go out on rainy days. She couldn't afford to catch colds, to succumb to chill. There was still hot water when she turned on the taps and the shower, but Anna didn't know how long that would last. How long there'd be electricity.

She ate the sea lettuce first. Didn't much like it, but it was better than nothing. It rotted easily though, and when dried went down to nothing. "I'll eat you on the day," Anna decided. "Fresh as fresh." It was better than scurvy. Her teeth stayed solid in her mouth, and when she scrubbed them with a small stick she couldn't taste blood, so her gums were all right.

"Looks like there's vitamin C in you after all," she said. That was lucky, though she'd rather have had her pineapple.

She was halfway through the second mug when the radio sparked back into life again. After so long waiting, Anna was afraid to answer. She'd learned that hope was a painful thing; it smelled like hydrochloric acid and deserted laboratories.

"Please don't go!" she said. "I'm here. I'm here!"

She wasn't sobbing really, not again, but her throat hurt, was closing up hard, and she could hear her own voice breaking.

Crackling on the line. Then "What's your name, honey?" said a girl who didn't sound that much older than Anna, and she'd never been so glad to be patronised before. It helped that there was almost as much relief in her voice as there was in Anna's.

There were two of them. Their names were Minnie and Mo. "Short for Moana." They'd been tracking great white sharks, following the migration routes down from Tonga towards the Chatham Islands. "In the middle of nowhere when it all broke out," said Mo. "We thought we were the only ones left." They'd kept going because they didn't know what else to do, and science gave structure to the days.

Their research vessel hadn't come out of Portobello but there was no other home for them now. "What d'you say? Fancy some company down there?"

"Dunno about Anna, but I fancy it," said Minnie. "It'll be a change from you at least." She was good-natured about it, but the two of them were sisters and postdocs in the same field, and Anna could hear that sharing only went so far.

The end of the world was a difficult thing to share.

She was out on the mudflats, at the lowest low tide, when she got turned around and lost. She'd been looking for shellfish; digging for cockles in the sand. The electricity would give out sooner or later, she was sure, but there was driftwood on the beach for fires, enough to cook with so it wouldn't hurt to expand her diet. The shellfish came up easily; there was something satisfying about digging in the sand, although there were crabs in the sand too and she'd been nipped a few times, small pinches that made her squeal.

She'd filled the fish bucket when she stood and realised she was stuck. It had seemed so easy…walk towards the sound of water, and that was the ocean. Turn around and that was shore. But the shore was curved and she was certain she'd walked along as well as down, certain she'd moved further than she should have.

Anna moved slowly, walking towards the rocks she thought, the place where the lab should be—but she walked for longer than she thought she needed to, walked and still didn't feel stone on her toes. She recited her story, to try to hold onto control. "I'm on an island, and there's a bar with cocktails and coffee and cream. There's fruity drinks with umbrellas, and I can smell coconuts…"

She was just about to panic when she heard it: bleating. The sound of a curious sheep. Out of sheer boredom, Anna had started collecting more seaweed than she could eat, and of different types. She'd lugged it up to the car park and dumped it there. "Here, sheepy-sheep-sheep," she'd called. "How about some nice iodine then?"

It was truly pathetic to be so lonely.

"You wonderful greedy little brute," she cried, muddy to her knees and with the fish bucket full against her. She clambered towards the sheep, over the rocks that were closer than she had thought, the distance no longer telescoped by panic. When she reached the path, then the lab, the first thing she did was to take down some of her clean dry Neptune's necklace and feed it to the sheep.

It even let her pat it. "I'm so happy you're here," she said, her fingers deep in its wool. "God, my life."

It was a funny thing, but when Minnie and Mo decided to abandon the end of their shark migration mapping and skip the Chathams to come down south sooner, Anna was furious. All that time hoping and waiting for human contact and it was coming quicker than she liked. No—not quicker than she liked. Quicker than she could respect.

It was the fact that they didn't even ask that annoyed her the most. She knew what had done it. Telling them she was blind had flipped a switch, had turned her from fellow survivor into a child who needed protecting.

"Fuck off!" she spat into the radio, and it was the first time she'd ever cursed at an adult when she knew they could hear her—let alone two of them. "I'm not going to keel over without you, and I don't need any bloody babysitting!"

She'd survived on her own and she was proud of that. From months with the blank emptiness of radio, Anna surmised that it was more than most had done, and no one was taking that achievement from her.

Anna ignored the radio for the next three days, until swearing and pleading and reasoned attempts at dialogue had dwindled into silence and then apology.

"You're right," said Mo. "A week or two more won't hurt. Not when you don't need us to look after you. We'll just follow this big bitch out to the Chathams, maybe see if there's anyone else out there. But once we've finished the study, we're on our way to you."

"If that's all right?" asked Minnie.

"That's fine," said Anna.

It was a week after the mudflats and a day after her last conversation with Minnie and Mo when she decided to pull herself together. The boredom had become intolerable. She might still have some electricity but there was nothing on the radio or the TV. Just static. The lab had a library but none of it was in Braille so she couldn't read it and that was probably a blessing, given that it was likely limited to the history of fish stocks and back issues of marine chemistry journals.

"Still," she said. "This is a science facility. I should be able to do something." She could feed herself. She'd found other survivors. She'd even made friends—if only with sheep, and the geese would come around eventually. (She thought she heard albatrosses on the wind sometimes, and it was a comfort but not a close one.)

"I need a purpose," she said. It was a matter of pride. She'd defended her current capabilities, but that didn't mean she couldn't extend them.

Anna had never been the best science student. She picked up more from osmosis than textbooks. And she could never trust herself in some of the lab rooms—there were chemicals and fume cupboards and equipment she had no idea what to do with, but there were also pieces that she did understand. Old bits of equipment, for basic experiments, for students. "A quadrant's not that exciting," she said, "but it's what you have."

She thought she remembered hearing of random experiments—of the random placing of a quadrant, for surveys. "But I can't record where I am if it's random," she said. She couldn't see the tape measure. "It'd have to be the same spots, over and over," she said. "I could tie ropes." To the wharf and to the rocks, and when she stretched out the rope at right angles she'd be at the same spot each time. There were several places along the little inlet she could pin down that way.

"If I take every shellfish in the quadrant, to the depth of my hand, and count them, I can see how many new ones come when I go back." She'd give it a fancy name of course. *Rate of colonisation of cockles in the intertidal zone outside Portobello Laboratory.* She could keep a record.

All right, so it wasn't going to light the marine world on fire, a paper like that, and there was no one to publish it and no one to read it even, but it would give her purpose. Something to do, something to contribute. Knowledge, in case the rest of the world was alive somewhere. It would show she wasn't useless, that she could survive and be productive.

"When they get here," she said, "I'll finish my piña colada and show them my work."

They'd be scientists, the people who came. And not just Minnie and Mo, because if they'd been able to survive then others would have too…the ones who'd taken the research boats out to sea, back before anyone had heard of plague. And the lab was home. They'd come back to it.

"When they come back," she said, "I'll show them what I can do."

Tea Party

Lauren E Mitchell

We are all, of course, mad here. I am, and Bingo is, and the Count. Chess likes to pretend she's not, but it doesn't stop her from coming to the table when the tea is poured.

She also pretends Chess is her real name, but if there's one thing I'm sure of, it's that nobody uses their real names any more.

Bingo gave me my name, Tally, when he saw the lines of scars on my arms. I called him Bingo because after we'd talked a while it turned out he'd checked off just as much time on the ward, dancing back and forth across the DSM, as I have. Or had. I guess that stuff doesn't count for much anymore. Wherever the doctors did their dying, it wasn't out here, miles-kilometres-light-years from the city. There aren't prescription pads out here. The whole damn world went off-script.

It was our fault, of course. Us humans, who didn't look after the world the way we should have. We spat in the face of Mother Nature, over and over, and eventually she spat right back.

What's left of the world now is about what you'd expect after the earth tried to shake itself to bits, the water rose up and claimed back the land, and whatever was left after that caught fire. Or sometimes all three at the same time.

The last thing I ever heard on the radio, before those signals died as well, was that a scientist somewhere in what was left of the United States had found out that air pollution levels had risen to the point that atmospheric oxygen levels had dropped to nineteen percent, and something or other about carbon dioxide levels being at five hundred and something parts per million, which was why she was not going to be coming into work the next day.

What it means for us is that when we go shopping, the roads are cracked and torn so it's hard to ride along them, and it's harder to breathe than it used to be. What I think it meant for her is that she doesn't worry about breathing at all any more.

Anyway, it's been a year, almost, so who knows, maybe the air's fixing itself, like the ads used to say people's lungs started fixing themselves when they stopped smoking. I haven't seen any scientists to ask. Haven't seen much of anyone, really. I hear things sometimes, late at night when the air's so quiet that the smallest sounds echo for kilometres. Voices, yelling, screaming, laughing. But then Chess says she hears voices during the day, so there's no guarantee that I'm hearing other survivors. It might just be folie à deux. Why not? Might as well share madness as anything else.

Bingo and I are usually the ones who take turns at shopping. We have lists. They rarely get completed. The Count can't or won't talk about what they need, and Chess keeps insisting she doesn't need anything; she's fine. If she's so fine, I don't know why she won't sleep in a bed like the rest of us. Everyone else has regular, mostly easy, orders.

It's my turn to shop today. I check the air in my bike's tyres and get the hand pump to try to combat the slow leak in the back one. If it gets any worse, I'm going to have to find a new bike, or else a new inner tube that comes with really good instructions, because while I'm sure there were a hundred YouTube videos that showed just how to change an inner tube, YouTube got cancelled when the rest of the world did.

Bingo brings me the shopping list. It looks pretty standard; Valium has been at the top forever, but that's one of those things that's really hard to find because other people have already taken it from pretty much everywhere. Anti depressants, anti psychotics, anti epileptics. Exact brand names are not part of the list. Insulin for Bingo. Denture adhesive and some kind of eczema lotion for Nanna. The list goes on.

The bike's saddlebags are empty, waiting to be filled. I buckle the tops closed so that they don't flap and distract me. There really isn't a lot else out here that moves aside from people, which means that small movements could be snakes, and I've already stacked this bike once when I thought a snake was coming at me. Since then the front wheel's been a bit wobbly, but I'm attached to the bike enough that I don't really feel like going looking for another one. Apart from anything else, most bikes made for adults have a whole mess of gears and stuff on the handlebars to deal with. I can't cope with all that.

I can cope with this role, though: breadwinner, bacon-bringer, meds-finder.

"Back soon," I tell Bingo and Chess, who are the only others awake this early. Most people are still in bed. Not that 'most' of our little handful of survivors is all that many to speak of; there are nine of us all up now, less than the hospital used to hold for sure, and less than there were when we started out here.

"Keep kicking on," Bingo says.

The Count is nowhere to be seen. They come and go, especially since we cracked into the arts and crafts cupboard and there are all these lovely bland white walls just waiting to be decorated. I think they'll be fine; there's not a lot of damage they can do to themselves with the cheap plastic deckle-edging scissors. I know. I've tried. I don't know what I was expecting; they barely cut paper.

I go out through the garden because I like it, even though the main ward doors have been broken open for a long time. The garden has potatoes and beans and tomatoes at the moment. We've been trying to grow lettuce but it turns out snails do pretty well in apocalypses. Still, the bit of fresh green we get is good, and even just pushing my bike around the planter boxes that smell of earth and growing and life makes me feel good too.

A shadow looms up beside me as I'm getting on my bike and I nearly fall.

"We're coming," the Count announces, teeth flashing white against dark skin. Sometimes they join me on short jaunts, but this isn't one. I don't know what to do if they can't make it the whole way.

"Oh, hell no. I'm riding at least fifteen kays each way. You'll slow me down."

"We're coming," the Count says again, and then, "Have you considered yoga?"

"How exactly were you planning on keeping up?"

They're obviously ready for this question; they step back into the garden and pull up their own bike from behind one of the planter boxes. It's not Bingo's bike; it's one they've gone out and found, which simultaneously worries me and sets my mind at rest a little. If they can coordinate long enough to go find a bike, maybe they can coordinate long enough to stay on it for a shopping trip. We could use the extra saddlebag space, which I see is something they've thought of, although rather than proper bike bags they've tied a Barbie backpack and a large Pokémon lunchbox to the packrack.

"Why not," I say. "But if we can find proper saddlebags, I'm switching those over."

The Count cheers—quietly, because we're just outside someone's bedroom window here—and gets on their bike. I get on mine, and we head out into the cool early dawn.

I spent a lot of time having trouble being responsible for me. Bingo's name for me, Tally, is a reminder that I'm stuck with. But it turns out it's easier being responsible for other people, even if it's a scary weight sometimes. Chess might think she's so grown up, but even if we don't exactly carry around photo ID any more, I can tell she's not more than seventeen or eighteen. Bingo says he's twenty-three. The Count, it depends on which of them you're asking at the time, but their body's probably mid-twenties. Me, I'm twenty-nine and, while I wish the reason I know where so many hospitals and doctors' surgeries and pharmacies are is because I Googled it, the truth is that I've spent a lot of time sitting in waiting rooms.

This is nicer than sitting in waiting rooms. The Count chatters at me on and off, sometimes asking which way we're headed, sometimes asking if I know about the healing power of mindfulness. Bingo and

I have never been able to work out whether they're echoing something their therapist has said or just taking the piss. Maybe it's a bit of both.

We've been riding for over an hour when they slow down, going from riding in a mostly straight line to weaving back and forth across the white line down the middle of the road.

"Hey. Hey, stop that," I say.

"Thirsty," they say.

"I was planning on a rest stop in another forty minutes. There's a café. It's burnt out, but the tap out back works, and…" I have to stop talking when I realise they're not listening to me and have stopped riding altogether. I put one foot down on the asphalt, the other staying on the pedal. I hate losing momentum. "Look, if you're going to come shopping with me, you have to follow my rules."

"Keep my hands in the trolley? No grabbing?"

"Yeah, pretty much. Now either you can come with me and get a drink in forty minutes, or you can go back and get one at home."

"It's not really home."

"It's what we've got. Are you coming or not?" I don't wait for them to answer, just kick off and start pedalling again, trying to pick up speed and get my momentum back. I do have a small water bottle in my bag for emergencies, and a protein bar that I know from experience won't taste at all like the promised chocolate, but I've travelled most of this route so many times that I know where and when all the rest stops are. Plus, the point is to have space for shopping, not my own supplies.

I hear raised voices behind me, and then a minute or two later the Count catches up with me, back to riding sedately in a straight line, even if it is up the wrong side of the road. Not that anyone's going to be coming the other way anytime soon.

When we get to the café, the Count goes poking around the ruins while I fill my plastic cup from the tap out the back. It splutters a lot and I wonder if whatever source it's drawing from has almost run dry. It's not tank water, so it's not full of mozzie wrigglers or any of the other stuff we boil water to cope with.

Once I've drunk the cupful, I call the Count, but they're distracted by something in the burnt-out building. I'm afraid they'll fall through. I can't help them if they do, and how would I be able to tell everyone else that I'd lost the Count?

"Come on. This isn't a magical mystery tour. We need to keep moving." I've spent nights away from home before, when I had to, sleeping in strangers' disused beds, but I prefer not to. Sterile as everything at home still smells, despite months of mostly disuse, it's more alive than any of the empty, dusty houses out this way. I refill the cup and hold it out to them, and that gets their attention.

"Thank you," they say, and drain the cup. "More, please?"

The tap groans irritably as I turn it on again, and what comes out dribbles reluctantly. I manage to half-fill the cup and pass it to the Count, wondering if this means the water has actually run out here or whether some washer has come unscrewed somewhere and just makes it look that way.

"Here, here, Tally," the Count says, poking my arm with the cup. I realise they've left me half of what I gave them.

"It's okay, you can finish it."

They give me a worried look out of big dark eyes and I repeat myself twice before they'll finish the water. I'm not really fussed about water. I'm looking forward to tea tonight. It may be the one thing I can take for granted, as long as the boxes in the cupboard last. We're getting to the point where it doesn't taste quite the way that it used to—we're on the wrong side of the recommended use by date—but technically so is the whole planet, so the fact that I can have tea at all is still a nice, grounding thing at the end of the day.

I put the plastic cup back in my bike basket beside the torch and the shopping list, and look at the Count. "Are you ready to keep going?"

They nod, getting back on their bike. It's only then that I realise that although their bike helmet is on their head, the buckle is hanging loose, and has been for who knows how long.

I'm reaching out before I can stop myself. The Count is unpredictable in general, but one thing is consistent: they hate being touched. They flinch when my fingers brush the dangling strap and I pull back fast.

"Oh! Sorry," they say, and the buckle snaps shut between their fingers. "Buckle up before you go."

"Right!"

The road safety ad people might not be around anymore, but I'm sure they'd be pleased that their lessons have stuck with those few of us who're left.

It takes another hour and a half to get where we're going, a fairly upscale medical clinic when it was part of the real world, now just another box covered in ash and dust. But it's there, which is nice; the fact is, I could've ridden all this way for nothing. The sign on the front says "dical Gro", and I don't bother to repress a snicker.

"What's funny?" the Count asks.

"A coincidence in homophones," I say, because just admitting it's a dick joke seems crass, and for some reason they absolutely crack up, bike wobbling dangerously even though they're standing still.

I set my bike on its kickstand and the Count follows suit. We both hang our helmets over the handlebars and just leave the bikes there in the half-empty car park. The asphalt is crisscrossed with cracks, but I've found that the further out from the city you go, the less damage there is. Except from the fires, of course. But I think the city shook itself apart worse because of all the buildings to smash against each other. Out here there is this medical clinic, and a supermarket across the road, and we passed a church on the way into town, and then another half dozen shops. Nothing to rattle like dice against each other, to smash down like dominoes.

Most of what I saw of the falling house of cards city was in TV broadcasts before TV broadcasts stopped existing. I haven't had to ride in that direction very far yet to shop, and I hope I don't have to.

The clinic door opens when I push on it, and I squint into the building, then open my eyes properly when I realise it has a skylight and there's actual natural sunlight coming through.

"Tally..." The Count sounds nervous behind me.

"What?"

"How's the light getting in?"

"There's a skylight."

"But all the ash..." They step right up behind me and I can hear their teeth chattering. "It should be dark."

I look up again, carefully this time, and see that the skylight's been smashed out. There's no glass on the floor, though. Someone's been here before us, broken the skylight, and probably looted the place to boot. Great. And the next place on my map, such as it is, is another hour or so's ride depending on how much of a mess the roads are.

There's something coming at us out of the dark. A four-legged thing, spindly, tall, shadow stretching out like a lopsided spider. The Count, shrugging off their dislike for physical contact, grabs onto my arm and clings, whimpering.

"Tally, Tally, what is it?"

"It's okay," I say, not entirely convinced that it is.

"Help me," the thing in the shadows says. "Please. I need—" It falters, and one of its legs falls to the ground with a clatter, leaving it with three. It keeps coming forward anyway, now dragging one leg behind itself, its movements even jerkier now that it's off balance.

The light falls across it and I see the truth: it isn't an it, but a woman. A tall woman with brown hair cut haphazardly short, eyes rimmed with dark shadows, and a crutch under one arm.

"Help me," she says again. Now that she isn't a voice in the dark, she doesn't sound scary, but scared.

"Who *are* you?" I ask.

"I've been alone so long I'm not sure." She brushes her hand across her forehead, pushing a few wisps of hair from her eyes. "Are you the ones who've been looking for me?"

"We've been looking for drugs," I say, and she flinches.

"There's nothing here. It's all been cleared out. Codeine, methadone—"

"Not that sort of drug, psych meds. Is there anything?"

Her face clears and she nods. "Some. Not much. No painkillers." I think she might be lying about that because she says it so quickly.

"Count." They're still clinging to my arm. "*Count.* Bring the bags inside. We need to shop." I shake them off and they go outside, still making worried noises.

"Who *are* you?" she asks, repeating my own question back to me.

"Tally. From East Ward." I point back the way we came. "The private hospital."

"I know it." She hitches forward another two steps. Now I can see the lumpy, misshapen cast on her leg. No doctor put that there. "I'm—I was a nurse."

I can't help but laugh. We could've used a nurse months ago. "And now?"

"Now I'm just a person looking for other people." Her eyes stay wary. "The right sort of people."

"Meaning sane people?"

"Meaning people who aren't out to hurt me." She nods down at her leg. "I got this when I was hiding in the supermarket. I fell and landed with enough junk on me that I could play possum until they were gone."

I can well imagine the sort of people she means, the sort of people who would like to hurt other people, the sort of people who have much better chances of doing so now that laws don't exist and the prisons are all broken. "Did you set that yourself?"

"Nobody else out here to do it for me."

The Count comes back inside carrying my saddlebags and goes back out for theirs, still muttering to themselves. Nurse cocks her head and watches as they go. "Interesting," she says. "Do you know what—"

"We don't keep charts, Nurse," I cut her off. "We don't use the DSM. We have a handful of notes about allergies and prior medications, and that's it. And if you think we can afford to be picky about that shit, then you can stay right here."

I was right before about her being scared, because her eyes go wide when I say that, and she says, "No. Of course. Allergies. I see. What do you need?"

The Count comes in with the Barbie backpack in one hand and my shopping list in the other, and I read out the list. Nurse has a torch of her own and she holds it and directs me around the sparsely stocked cabinets. One of the things I find is yellow boxes of generic diazepam. Chess might be able to sleep nightmare-free for a while with those, if I can make them last.

"We can't just call you Nurse," I say when she comes out with another handful of boxes.

"Call me Florence," she says without missing a beat.

"*Arrogant!*" the Count says, zipping the Barbie backpack shut and opening the Pokémon lunchbox on the waiting room floor.

"Mary, then."

*

Mary doesn't have a bike and couldn't ride one even if she did. I leave her with the Count sitting in the waiting room of the clinic and putter around town on my bike, thinking. Shopping trolley? Not for the distance we have to go. Wheelbarrow? I doubt the Count would help with it, and we still have so far to travel. The easiest solution would be if the buses were still running, but of course they aren't. Arguably, they're now sticking to the timetable better than they used to.

I find the answer out back of the supermarket. A ute with a couple of bales of feed in the back, most of which has been whipped away by the wind. There are ropes and tie-downs. We can bring more than just the saddlebags. If I can make it start, and remember how to drive. My driving history is erratic at best.

About a foot in front of the ute is a sinkhole. Maybe the former owner is in it.

I peer through the ute's driver's side window. The keys are on the seat. It makes me think of my dad pulling up to get petrol at the servo, shutting off the car and dropping the keys on the seat, and tears sting the backs of my eyes. I haven't thought of my parents in months. I can't imagine they're alive. They would have come for me.

I open the door and get in, checking the sun visors for spiders before I sit down. A desiccated huntsman falls out of one. I brush it aside and slip in behind the wheel.

It's been a long time, but I remember how to do this.

The ute barks into life and I shove the gearstick into reverse hastily, very aware of the sinkhole in front of me. I back away from it, then do what's probably a twenty-three point turn—remembering doesn't mean expertise—to face the way I want, and ease slowly out of the car park.

The Count comes running out of the clinic as the sound of the car echoes down the empty street, and even as I'm pulling up they're throwing their saddlebags into the tray and hurling themselves in after them, face aglow.

"Let's go for a ride!"

"Ease up, Count. We can take more stuff now."

Mary comes out more sedately, crutching along, my saddlebags draped around her shoulders. I don't think we'll all fit in the cab, not with Mary's leg to consider, but looking at the way the Count is bouncing gleefully in the tray, I don't think we'll have to.

We take bottled water, cans of food, and economy-sized packs of toilet paper—the last mostly to give the Count something comfortable to lean against. I expect Mary to wait in the ute but she matches every two of my trips with one of her own, lurching along behind a rickety shopping trolley. Despite the looting that must have happened very early on, the supermarket still stinks of rotted fruit and vegetables and meat, and I'm glad to be out of there.

I tie the bikes on top of the ute's cab and then we're off.

It's a little faster than riding. The road is cracked and chunks of asphalt are just missing. Mary looks around at the land to either side of us, green plants slowly peeking through the burnt-black devastation left by the bushfires, and shakes her head.

"It's so bad. How could it get this bad? We've had so many bushfires before, and floods, and we always survived before. Out here, anyway. I can understand the city, sort of, but out here—" Her words rattle out like Rabbit's when he's out of Adderall. "I thought we were better prepared."

"Nobody was prepared for this," is all I can say.

As if it's listening, the earth starts to shake.

We were unobtrusive when we were only ants toiling to rebuild what we had, with nothing fancier than seeds and shovels and bicycles. I am almost definitely being superstitious when I think that the arrogance of daring to drive has pissed off the planet, but whether I am or not doesn't change the fact that the shaking is getting worse.

The Count screams shrilly from the ute's tray, but when I look in the rear view mirror they're clinging tightly to the ropes and look ecstatic.

"*Drive!*" Mary says.

I plant my foot on the accelerator and floor it.

It feels like the epicentre of the earthquake is following us. Mary hangs out of the window.

"It's like an asphalt volcano!" she screams to me.

One of the pieces smashes through the rear window, scattering glass, and she falls silent. The Count is also terrifyingly quiet.

"*Count!*" I yell.

"Faster! Got to get the ice cream home before it melts!"

Maybe they're all right after all.

The needle on the speedo creeps up until we're pushing ninety kays per hour, and still we're not outrunning the earthquake. We're too close to home. I don't want to bring this down on East Ward.

A rattling gargling sound from the engine makes me look down and see the petrol gauge hovering near E. Stupid, *stupid* Tally. Stupid to think this wouldn't happen.

We coast to a silent stop. The earthquake doesn't. It's not done with us. Now the Count is screaming in earnest as the road crumbles under the back wheels of the ute. I frantically try to restart the engine and Mary clings to her seat, knuckles and face white with pain.

I can see the hole in the road behind us. Dark. Deep. Like the sinkhole behind the supermarket. Like something that wants to eat us, with asphalt teeth and a long slippery dirt tongue. The ute tilts, wobbling, sliding, licked backwards.

"Come on, come on, come on," I chant at the engine, turning the key again, trying not to choke or flood it, remembering that the coordination of all these actions is why I quit driving in the first place.

The ute coughs into begrudging life and I turn the wheel hard to the left and accelerate, angling us up and away from the hole. The earth is still shaking under us, but it seems to be quietening.

The Count waves the saddlebags at me triumphantly, calling "Got them!" through the hole in the window. They're back to looking thrilled. Good for them.

We make it another five hundred metres, the ute rocked by the aftershocks but sticking valiantly to the road, before I let it glide to a stop, and put my head down on the steering wheel, scrambling to breathe and only just managing.

"Tally?" Mary asks, tentatively touching my shoulder.

I breathe in, slow count one-two-three-four, try to hold it, give up, and exhale. "Let's just get home."

Chess is waiting out front when we get back, after a painful fifteen minutes of walking, and it looks like she's been standing there a while. Bouncing up and down a little, too.

"Tally!" she says. "Tally, Bingo passed out!"

Oh, fuck.

Nurse—Mary—takes over and it's so smooth it's like she's—I'm stupid, she probably *has* done this a hundred times before. She swings herself along on her crutches, heedless of her exhaustion, into the front waiting area with Chess. Bingo is lying on the floor, in the recovery position, a pillow under his head and a blanket over him.

"You did really well," Mary says to Chess, and to me, "What are his *allergies?*"

"He's diabetic," I say, trying not to bristle—we've been doing fine for a year without *her* help or anyone *else's* help. "But we brought more insulin back."

"I think that's the opposite of his problem." She touches his wrists and neck, thumbs back his eyelid. "Do you have any glucagon kits here?"

"Yeah, we do," Chess says. "Do you need me to get one?"

"Yes, please," Mary says, instead of "no shit, Sherlock", and Chess runs to get one. I know that she couldn't know *that* was the problem instead of not *enough* insulin, but I'm still mad at her.

I go and collect the saddlebags, making a mental note to get the diazepam out of the Count's Barbie bag before Chess can find it. I'd go back to the ute for the other supplies, but I can't do it alone and I'm exhausted. Wound up, but exhausted. Mary is working on Bingo, Chess is standing by for further orders, and all of a sudden I feel totally superfluous.

It's almost time for tea, though. So I go and start the water boiling over one of the three camp stoves that we have set up for cooking. The routine is soothing.

"Tally, you're kicking on," Nanna says. Anyone's guess what her real name is, or was—she looks about a hundred and eleven, so literally everyone calls her Nanna, even Papa. "Tea soon?"

"Tea soon," I confirm, and she smiles, showing her slippy dentures that I finally found adhesive for and really should fix her up with.

"Tea soon!" Mad Hat races into the common room and flaps chequered tablecloths onto the two tables we've pushed together so that we can all have tea at the same table. Room Six follows him in a lot more quietly and sets out the cups.

"How was shopping, Tally?" Room Six asks, giving me a little smile, her slanted eyes crinkling at the corners.

"Good. We have a new person."

"A new...oh." She tugs on her short hair fretfully. "Who?"

"Her name's Mary and right now she's looking after Bingo. He passed out again."

"Oh." She tugs her hair again. "Tally..."

"Yes, Six?"

"If she's here, does someone else have to go?"

"Absolutely not," I tell her, and then I give her the teabags to count out, which makes her happy; she sits at the table earnestly sniffing each bag to determine which ones need to be used first and which might last a little longer.

Nanna, Mad Hat, Room Six; that leaves two unaccounted for.

Papa is asleep in the visitor's chair in his room, which has to be ridiculously uncomfortable. I wake him up and he startles out of the chair and then clasps my hands. "Tally, kóri mou," he says. "Tea?"

"Tea soon. Do you need to use the toilet?" I ask.

"No, no..."

I side-eye him, but he seems to be telling the truth. Good. It's a pain in the arse to lug water in just for flushing. Bingo might be okay with going and watering the trees, but most of us aren't. Or can't.

The last of my patients-flock-family is Rabbit, and he's in the garden carefully weeding around the potatoes.

"Tally, back, kicking on. How'd you go?" he asks, straightening up.

"I got almost everything on the list—" I never admit a perfect shop because then everyone wants everything to be exactly the brand they asked for "—and we have a new person."

"Really?" He drops the small rounded shovel into one of the planters. "Who?"

"Her name's Mary, and she's looking after Bingo right now, but you can meet her at tea time," I say when it looks like he's going to bolt inside straight away. "Bingo passed out, so I'm going to need you to help cook."

"No worries."

*

The water's boiled for the tea. Room Six has put the carefully selected bags in. Rabbit helps me open cans with minimal distraction; we're never short on vegetables, even if the canned ones aren't as good as the few we get from the garden. There are enough potatoes to make mash and for those of us who eat meat there's Spam. If that counts as meat. Debating whether or not it does helps keep Rabbit with me and not off to do something else.

I have my own something else to do before tea time, of course, but that's quicker and easier with the plentiful supplies we brought back. While I fill the tiny meds cups, I hope what I told Six is true: that now Mary is here, it doesn't mean that someone else will have to go. That *I* will have to go. I've been holding this place together okay, but what if the others decide they'd prefer the capability that comes with ironed clothes and a university qualification?

I look at today's shopping. Diazepam. It's so much easier to just take one to blunt anxiety's edge when there's a definite source. This is not a definite source. I am in control control control. I am. I imagine the Count helping me breathe, counting one, two, three, five, seven, making me laugh, unknotting the tenseness in my chest.

The common room smells of hot food when I get back, carrying my nine little cups stacked on my palms, caught between my fingers. Practice makes perfect. Room Six pours the tea, and we're almost ready.

Bingo comes into the common room walking slowly, leaning on Chess, with Mary crutching along beside them. The people who haven't met Mary yet all focus on her, and I hear Mad Hat moan softly when he realises she's a nurse. It's not just her clothes or her posture; she's dug up a stethoscope and pinned her watch to her shirt and while anyone could dress up, on her it looks real. Because it *is* real.

"Mary's going to help out with what she can, just like the rest of us," I say before anyone can say anything. "She helped me and the Count bring the shopping back. There's a place for her at our table, if she wants it."

Mary hesitates, but Bingo and Chess sit down in their places and the extra chair is beside me, so that's where she goes, crutches scraping. "Thank you." Her voice is so soft compared to the voice that spoke from the shadows. "Thank you for trusting me."

"Tea time," Mad Hat says, and he's grabbing for his tiny cup and dumping the pills into his mouth before chasing them with his tea. The others follow suit. Rabbit helps Papa with his. Room Six is fretting with her hair again and Mad Hat helps her with her tea, giving Mary a mistrustful look. She is still going to have to earn her way in; just because she says we trust her doesn't mean we all do.

"We usually say something before tea time," I say to Mary, tipping my own pills into my hand.

"Like grace?"

"Like thank fuck we're still kicking on."

I dump my meds into my mouth and swallow them down with a long drink of tea.

Giant

Thoraiya Dyer

0019.02.04. Username: Rhomboid O8 Cluster, d1 0.234nm, d2 0.266nm.

I've changed my username because I think I'm getting closer to translating my name into Moltorian language.

Not that there's anyone here to call me by my name. Chicken Number 3 is pretty smart for a chicken. She tolerates being stuffed in my sleeping bag, sometimes. But that would be going too far, even for her.

Anyway. Moltorian language. It's to do with calculating the ratios of my constituent atoms, working out what crystal structures they would form under ridiculously high pressures (An indication of the local environment on the Moltorian home planet? They must hate living on our moon!) and then weaving a thin ribbon of a thousand atoms in length or less into the matrices of the reproductive mechanism; a beautiful, twisted tangram of maths and chemistry.

With me (Or any other Earth-life, I suppose?), you'd start with six hundred and fifty oxygen atoms and keep on going, right down to two chlorine atoms and one of lonely old magnesium. I haven't worked it all out yet, but I started with oxygen so I'm more than half done. Did you know that oxygen at that pressure is a gorgeous red colour?

Mother, you named me Sky because you loved the colour blue. On Earth, liquid oxygen is a pale sky blue.

When I work out how to incorporate my thousand-atom name into the propagative crystal the Moltorians use instead of sound, my message to them will be signed off. I'll shoot it from this stupid space station straight into the Sea of Rains where they landed.

Maybe their answer will kill me. But maybe it'll set me free. Me and Chicken Number 3.

It's kind of insulting when you think that you, me, Chicken Number 3 and the sorghum are pretty much all the same in Moltorian.

Or, is it insulting? Maybe the Moltorians were giving us a hint. You know, like instead of calling ourselves American, Chinese, New Western or United Asian, we should all just suck it up and call ourselves Red Oxygen, plural.

Or maybe they just didn't know that we'd be made of the same stuff, smart or stupid, mother or child, because they're not actually chemically identical. Maybe their names are really different and beautiful, just like their bodies could be really different and beautiful. Maybe I'll meet one made of opal. Hydrated Silica by name. Or maybe one made of ruby. Aluminium Oxide with Chromium, Al for short.

Except it doesn't seem like they do short. Names a thousand letters long, and all.

Then there will be that one who's kinkily interested in me. Because I'm mostly water and nitrogen and he is, too. With gypsum hair, graphite fingernails and jadeite eyes. But he won't realise till too late that my nitrogen is organic and his is stinking ammonia. And since he uses bits of broken-off chemicals as words instead of smells, he'll find it difficult to understand what I mean when I say 'smell', but he'll also find it mysterious, and beg me to describe his stink over and over again.

He'll be confused when I tell him his stench is like the chickens', because the word for chickens is the same as the word for me.

And maybe he'll realise that's wrong, because chickens' eggs are for eating and mine are not, and he'll give me another name. Or maybe he'll be kinkily into the chickens, and see no difference between us at all.

The countdown reached zero. Magnets levitated the shuttle, reducing friction against the track. Soundlessly, it surged.

Hugo felt his face become deformed by the acceleration. Unlike the launches of his youth, where he and the other astronauts had squeezed themselves into a kind of giant firecracker and pointed themselves at space, today's launch was a spectacle that couldn't be contained by cinematography. It comprised over three hundred kilometres of mag rail with the near end in Fuzhou and the far end buried in sky over Jade Mountain in Taiwan.

He struggled to stay focused on the monitor. It showed his route across the Taiwan Strait. The water, once blue, was now a patchwork of pale grey floating settlements and lime green algae farms.

Hugo's imagination tried to supply the roar of combustion.

Speed. Silence.

Twenty years had passed since an alien presence began inscribing patterns on the moon. Nineteen since they sent their best chemists and linguists into lunar orbit, along with a robot-collected sample of Moltorian speech, in the hope that it could be made sensible. And if not, if the infectious crystal transformed the Station, killing the occupants, what quarantine could be better than space?

Less than a year after Transl8's completion, well before the occupants could report even minimal success, came the start of the Second American Revolution. Satellites were brought down to keep the masses from communicating. Earth-orbiting stations were collateral damage. High tech installations were swarmed and torn apart in retaliation. China laughed from a distance until its own people joined in.

Nobody knew whether the moon-orbiting men and women, the chemists and linguists, were still alive. Nobody knew if Hugo Bowman was going to be a hero or a gravedigger.

He closed his eyes, fighting to remain conscious. No, launch procedure wasn't like the old days. But then, nothing was like the old days. Fuzhou, the Beautiful City, was certainly not the same. Beautiful? It resembled a box of cheese graters in a catering warehouse sale.

How they'd argued about who could be trusted to go. Anyone who believed in factions, in nations, might deliver that precious sliver of propagative crystal to one side, or use it to destroy the other, no matter that the e-ink was still fresh on the world-spanning treaty.

Most good folk, Hugo thought, could be trusted to put their partners first, and that was why they trusted him. Twenty years ago he'd given Silja his support to leave him, to leave the children, and to go. She'd believed that the aliens were a greater threat than war, that by pacifying the Moltorians she'd be protecting them all.

But the aliens did nothing. While humans killed each other by the millions and billions, aliens made slow scribbles on the moon like limpets in slime on a rock platform.

Hugo wasn't one to criticise. His children, conscripted, had been early casualties. Instead of taking up arms to avenge them, he'd spent most of the revolution camped by their graves, boiling up Illawarra flame tree seeds for poor man's coffee and generally looking too skeletal, ghastly and pitiful for anyone to bother killing.

Mounted propulsion coils hurled the *A. C. Clarke* towards Taiwan where the track finished thirty kilometres above sea level. Vast surges of current liberated him from the clinging fingers of his home planet.

As soon as the launch was complete, the task of disassembling and reassembling the vertical part of the track would begin. Not so onerous as it might have been; the structure was kept rigid not by the world's greatest feat of engineering, but by electromagnets. Electricity was cheaper than steel. The track would eventually extend from Taiwan to Tokyo, replacing shipping routes and supplying ocean communities along the way, but that was not Hugo's concern.

His concern was bringing back the thirteen astronauts, including his wife, dead or alive, with the clear proviso that there was to be one launch, and one launch only.

A swan song for the space program, at least until the world had been rebuilt into some semblance of habitability.

0019.02.05. Username: Rhomboid O8 Cluster, d1 0.234nm, d2 0.266nm.

I take breaks from the translation work in the macro rock centrifuge. The closest to a carnival ride that there is on this whole stupid station.

Obviously it's not safe to switch it on with me in it (but I do it anyway and I haven't died yet). Obviously your ghost doesn't really live in there, telling me how it's going to be when I can stand up straight, for once. Walk on a planet's surface. How my bones will hurt and my teeth will rattle with every step. How slow and fumbling I'll feel and how weight will distract me from the cerebral realm where so much remains to be done.

On the rowing machine, which I've creatively re-imagined (not to mention re-welded), I replay the recording of you. Your eyes are closed. You lick your lips, wanting to taste the salt. Wanting to feel a more punishing muscular burn. You whisper about water beading on skin, about the surge of a wave carrying your crew the last handful of boat-lengths, back to the beach, to carve the yellow sand you see in your mind's eye.

You had nightmares about the Moltorian language eating every last grain of Earth's silica sands. Turning them into something else. You said so.

Superficially, it seems like that would be true, but I'm not so sure, now. There has to be an element of control. Everyone knows when to shut up, if they know what's good for them. There's no noise without silence, after all.

Can't find out their words for "shut up, kid" without talking to them first, though, can I?

*

Hugo saw at once why there'd been no contact between the Station and the outside world: Transl8 had sustained impact damage and the outer shell was broken. Any survivors would have been herded into the Lifeboat, which wasn't the vehicle that the name might have indicated, but instead a sealed inner section.

It could have been an asteroid. Space junk. Or it could have been an incoming message from the Moltorians. Their speech was solid mineral; heavy; occasionally quite angular. Nobody could be sure how the projectile speech had been hurled at Earth in the first place.

Transl8's emergency cascades had been triggered. No transmissions of any kind were permitted under quarantine. Not until an independent team arrived to perform a check and reset.

We failed you, Hugo realised, manoeuvring his hard suit, his extravehicular mobility unit, carefully into the jagged breach. *Nobody came. We thought the problem was at our end, but it was at yours.*

The edges were minimally scorched. Hugo's heart seized for a moment when he saw the floating bodies, but none of the jumpsuited shapes had hips; they were all men.

They weren't turned to stone. It wasn't the alien language that killed them. Just an ordinary collision.

The bodies might have been incinerated if the accident had happened on Earth. Instead, they'd decomposed anaerobically as far as possible. They'd also been baked to blackness. What remained was desiccated, brittle. Hugo bowed his head inside his suit out of respect for the dead, but not before checking their clothing for an indication of nationality.

Six United Asia flags. Nothing to indicate how long they had bobbed about in this broken box, their empty eye-sockets occasionally turned beseechingly towards the distant home planet. Silja wasn't here. She could still be inside, alive, safe in the Lifeboat.

He loaded the bodies into the *A.C. Clarke* before returning to Transl8 Station, heavy-hearted. There, he collected the e-keys.

Hugo reset the system.

His computer and the Lifeboat's, it turned out, couldn't talk to one another. That was unexpected. He would have to swim right in there and see with his own eyes if anyone was left alive.

And then he tried to enter the airlock. Only to discover that somebody else had set a five-letter password.

0019.02.05. Username: Rhomboid O8 Cluster, d1 0.234nm, d2 0.266nm.

Supernova in a shit pump. There is a live human man outside.

Who is it? Why can't I talk to him? Communications

are back up, the system's reset, but his suit's not talking to my jury-rigged computer. I guess anything unexpected reads like a quarantine breach to a paranoid Earthling.

What if he's a quarantine breach?

Should I open the door?

He can't come in unless I let him in.

I can't get out until he lets me out.

Supernova in a shit pump. He's gone and guessed my password.

Hugo's hope soared. The password was "Silja".

She was here. She was alive.

She couldn't be. She would never have chosen her own name for the password. Her own self was never her greatest love; that belonged to the jewel-planet, Earth; its oceans and star-studded skies.

Passing through the airlock into the inner shell, his suit gauges flickered. Hugo steered his wagon through the atrium. It was tempting to bypass the dim corridors of the defunct human habitat and go straight to the Lifeboat, but that would hardly count as a thorough investigation, and shortcuts got people killed in space. Hugo had never taken them and he didn't intend to start now.

The laboratories were locked, but Hugo's guessed password was successful again. He poked through the contents of cabinets and drawers. Equipment, never replaced. Observations, abandoned. There were empty spaces where some of the heavier analytic machines should have been. Either someone had dragged them into the Lifeboat, sabotaging the whole concept of the quarantine, or they had been lost in space. In the library, there were similarly empty benches where computers and e-book banks should have been. There was no dust. No more bodies. No burn marks.

There was nothing.

He walked down a tunnel towards a light. It was the entry to the agricultural terraces. A blinking panel warned him that the terraces remained partially pressurised. Hugo peered through the bright, porthole-shaped window in the door. In semicircular layers under the filtered sunlight, robots were harvesting sorghum.

There was no airlock. Hugo went back to the other end of the corridor, sealed the door there, and rocked back on his heels as gases flooded the tunnel. There would be some further loss of oxygen, but that couldn't be helped, and besides, there would be no need for sorghum after Hugo departed with the survivors for Earth.

He glided face-first through the waving, seeding heads of the ripened crop. It felt strange to be touching it with gloved hands, through five protective layers, feeling almost nothing, but in quarantine mode, the pressure here would be lower than that of his suit. He dared not risk undressing with no airlock and no decompression reference.

There was a grave on the lowest terrace; two pairs of crossed sickles with "RIP" carved into the aluminium handles.

Who was buried there? Hugo wondered if the family would expect him to dig up the remains, which had probably been well-digested by recycling bacteria at this point. Probably not. They were better left undisturbed. A monument in lunar orbit would last longer than one on Earth, anyway.

A check of the animal pens showed the goats hadn't survived, but that chickens in robot-maintained barns with automated feeders still produced eggs that were whisked away by conveyers.

It was time to find out if anyone was alive to consume them.

At the airlock leading to the Lifeboat, Hugo waited patiently while he was imaged, scanned and swabbed. It admitted him at last, and he peeled off his useless helmet and communications cap, so that he could use the bull's bellow he was born with.

"Hello?" he shouted down a white, brightly-lit corridor. "Nǐ hǎo! Namaste! Privyet!"

"Hello?" someone shouted back in the thick, shy guess of the hard of hearing.

An enormous, black-haired, teenaged girl in a hand-stitched smock came towards him down the corridor, a serene human vessel, using one forefinger at a time on hand-holds that neatly fitted Hugo's entire, bulkily-gloved palm.

She had pores like pits in wet sand; white-straight teeth like snapped-off plastic knives in a wide, bow-shaped mouth; Silja's mouth; Hugo's own hands; what was he seeing? How could she—

"Who are you?" he gasped.

She shook her head. Pointed to one ear. Opened and closed her hand like a mouth opening and closing.

"You'll have to speak up," she said.

"Who are you?" Hugo shouted.

"I'm Red Oxygen," she said. "You can call me Skye."

0019.02.05. Username: Rhomboid O8 Cluster, d1 0.234nm, d2 0.266nm.

So. The man out there, Hugo, is my biological father. Really? Yes, really. He's tiny. I thought my father would be tall, like me. I thought I must have gotten my tallness from him.

He likes talking better than reading and typing. Which is annoying. And he's old. He's scary. His crinkly old face is shouting without words or text that I'm going to die some day. I don't want to look at it! I don't want to die. And there's something else really terrible.

Really terrible. Almost as bad as dying.

When Hugo reset the system, a bunch of files opened to me that weren't open before. Starting with the doctor's. That's how I found out, only a few seconds after he opened the door, that Hugo is my dad. It says so in the doctor's files. You were pregnant with me when you came to the Station. Only just. Why did you hide me? They couldn't have missed it unless you lied to them.

That's not the point.

The point is, the doctor said in his last ever entry that he thinks I'll die if I go to Earth. He says I'm tall because I've got a thing called pituitary gigantism, that it's only because of microgravity here that my circulatory system hasn't shut down and given up.

He thinks I'll have to stay here forever.

I'm too big to ever go home.

Mother, why did you lie to me?

As soon as Hugo could get the two networks speaking to each other, Skye retreated deep into the Lifeboat, preferring to talk to him in text; preferring no direct line of sight. It made sense that with a hearing difficulty she'd rather have him subtitled but was being in the same room as her own father really so horrible?

Mum said her family was all killed in the war, her accusing message read. Hugo scrolled around the inside of the communications cap he held in his gloved hands to read the rest of it. *Including my big brothers. Including you.*

She wasn't to know, Hugo typed back, feeling a pang for Silja and for the two boys. He wished there was a video link. He wished she'd speak to him over the audio link instead of typing. He wondered if she was angry. Or if she was crying.

Transl8 has been getting the news feed this whole time, you know.

I didn't know, he tapped back laboriously on his tiny keyboard. *If you've been getting the news feed, then you must have known I was coming.*

I didn't know. The feed was depressing. Earth news is always depressing. I switched it off years ago.

Hugo smiled.

How long have you been alone?

Seven years. They wanted to kill me, the others. I was eating a lot of food. Three times as much as they were eating. They said I wasn't even supposed to be here, that I was eating their share.

Hugo was aghast. He'd barely started formulating a reply in his mind when the second part of her message flashed up.

The doctor was on my side. When he found out that they were going to grab me and chuck me into space, he tricked them all into the outer shell. He trapped them there. Then he used the detonator from one of the missiles. You know. The secret missiles that one of them had smuggled up here to shoot at the Moltorians if they did anything. Like if the Moltorians tried to send another message.

She paused, but Hugo had nothing to say to that. He hadn't known about the missiles. He was dismayed by their existence just as much as the fact that a pack of scientists could turn on a child.

So then there was just me and my mother. When I was twelve, she died. Her bones were all dissolved away. She had kidney failure and she couldn't hold her head up on her neck.

"I see," Hugo said, forgetting to type in his distress. Abruptly, he was the one crying, though he'd known this would have to be the case after twenty years; and he was the one who was angry, because there should have been a way for Silja to return to Earth, but such was the fear of contamination by the Moltorian message that no contingency had been permitted. "I'm sorry to hear that, Skye. But I'm glad you're not...that is, I wonder why...how are your kidneys doing? How are your bones?"

They are fine, thank you.

Silence. How could they be fine? How could she still be alive, after all this time, when Silja had died?

"Skye, do you think I could have another look at you? Do you think we could meet face to face again?"

When there was no reply, he remembered to type the words.

No, she answered. *Not just yet.*

0019.02.05. Username: Rhomboid O8 Cluster, d1 0.234nm, d2 0.266nm.

Your journals opened to me with the reset, too, you know.

How funny that you used the computer like a confessional when the doctor used it like a calculator. We are alike. But I knew that already. Even though you were miniature. Like Hugo.

Now I know why you never told me I couldn't go to Earth. You thought you could solve my problems, one by one, by speaking to me in Moltorian. The doctor helped you. You made a message, a short one, which said the word "bones" over and over. You grafted it into me. I was too little to remember.

Bonesbonesbonesbones, the message said.

Or, more accurately, it said something like, *Calci umcalciumcalciumcalciumcalciumcalciumcalciumca lciumcalciumcalciumphosphatephosphatephosphat ephosphatephosphatephosphatewaterwatersiliconca rbonatezinc.*

You translated the message and you didn't tell anyone except the doctor, because you knew that if they knew the Moltorian language was in my body, I'd be quarantined or killed.

And then they tried to kill me anyway.

Weren't you worried that my whole body would turn into bone? Or the whole Station, for that matter? You could have all died horrible, ossifying deaths. You could have been a murderer. You were so worried about the beaches, Mother. Did you care less about me than about the beaches, or did you care more, to risk everything?

Wait a minute. Hugo's opening your journal. He's reading it. He's going to find out about my bones, and my poor, too-small heart, and then he'll know for sure I can't go with him. But what if he decides that he can't go back, either? What if he decides the risk of contamination is too great? What a rotten place for an old man to spend the end of his life!

There sure isn't room for both of us in the centrifuge. And I don't think I'm quite prepared to share Chicken Number 3.

STOP, Skye texted him.

"Stop what?" Hugo said, startled. He was strapped, vertical-seeming because the moon hung overhead, to an unused bed. The sleeping room had a round window into the terraces and the shadows of the sorghum growing down from the apparent roof made soothing, forest-like silhouettes on the walls.

Stop reading her journals. Just. Go. Back. To. Earth. Now.

Sighing, he pulled out his little keyboard and started tapping.

We'll both go back to Earth, when I've worked out how to make you a suit. Your mother must have had some plan for when a shuttle arrived. How were you going to get from the Lifeboat to the dock?

Read the doctor's records. I can't go with you!

Hugo was quiet for a while, scrolling through the documents. First, he read the medical databases. There, he saw what he supposed Skye had seen: the final entry on her file, which warned of circulatory failure should she experience the full force of Earth's gravity.

But there were other records made by the doctor, too. Secret ones. They could only be read by someone with military clearance in a country that hadn't existed for decades. Hugo was relieved that Skye had not read these; in fact, he deleted them as he read them, trying not to be distracted by such choice entries as:

"0000.02.01. Username: D. Guardian.

During a routine check-up, the Chinese analyst asks me if it isn't a waste of time trying to understand the message. Now that they've got it safely away from the Earth, shouldn't they just burn the rest of it off the surface of the moon like torching barnacles off the hull of a ship? The moon's ours, after all. All those mining ventures that went dark. True, it was only robots that we lost to those parasites, but humans are next, aren't they?

My inadequacy, flung in my face after forty-eight hours. In the whole history of civilisation, no one's been tested, re-tested and tested again the way that this group has. Yet they've all cunningly concealed their motives. The tests are useless. Utter shit. Because of confidentiality, I can't tell anyone what these people are telling me.

I am the useless one. I am the one who is utter shit."

And also:

"0019.11.21. Username: D. Guardian.

This will likely be my final entry. Silja's daughter is eating all the food. Three times the amount that a three-year-old should eat. Glucose test confirms ongoing growth hormone hypersecretion, scans confirm no pituitary tumours. Low gravity is exacerbating her condition and the computer projects an adult height of four metres for little Skye.

And I've gone and made Silja pregnant again, God help us. She won't let me intervene. Chances are it won't go to term, anyway, but what if it does? What if this one's a giant, too? The thought has occurred to everyone else aboard. They want to punish us both for breeding. For finding a little happiness while the Earth burns below. They want to throw all three of us out of the airlock, forgetting the secrets they have spilled to me, each and every one. If they try anything, I'll be ready."

Hugo didn't believe in making spur-of-the-moment decisions. They usually led to disaster. There was no escaping the fact Skye was his daughter, though. His only surviving child. He'd failed the others.

I'm going to sleep, he told her.

You can't sleep! You have to go home!

Hugo sighed and shut his eyes. He hadn't told her that he wouldn't go home without her. That would be rushing to conclusions. After a bit of shut-eye, a bit of distance between him and repeated emotional blows, they'd work out what to do. Together.

Hugo dreamed about an army of magical mice, all pulling together to sew a giant spacesuit with infinitesimally tiny, perfect stitches.

When an ominous shuddering woke him, though, the spacesuit wasn't there.

0019.02.06. Username: Rhomboid O8 Cluster, d1 0.234nm, d2 0.266nm.

I'm going to have to send my message early. My doofus dad thinks he knows what's best for me. Is that what dads are for? Is that why I haven't noticed not having one?

Or are they for dying so their children can live? Because that's what the doctor did and I'm starting to get the same vibe from this one.

His face looks less wrinkly while he's sleeping.

It's a bit scary, rushing to get these last bits done while he's out. Without the Moltorian crystal, some of the more unstable combinations would have set off a bunch of explosions by now. I don't understand it. But I'm coming to trust it.

Just like you came to trust it. Even after the engineer decided to eat some of the Moltorian message to see if it would magically become comprehensible, and was turned to stone for his trouble. Did you think I missed that, in all the excitement of finding out about your love affair with the stupid doctor?

Study anything long enough and it stops being scary, I suppose.

Even space.

Even death.

Hugo opened his eyes to see the shadows of the sorghum-stalks swaying as if in a high wind; robot-arms retreating from the jagged stumps of an ill-cut harvest until their delicate servos could be re-aligned.

"What was that, Skye?" he asked blearily, wetting his throat from the water recycling tube in his suit. She'd told him he didn't have to shout. That if he insisted on speaking there was such thing as volume control.

That?

"The shaking. Have we been hit by something?"

He'd resolved, in the instant since waking, that Transl8 Station was simply too dangerous for her to stay on. For all its relative safety since the threat of other humans had been removed.

Yes, the doctor had predicted medical difficulties, but medicine had progressed in twenty years even in the face of global war. Artificial hearts and vessels could be printed, nowadays, in an hour or less; she would be fine. He was her father. She needed to trust him.

Oh, that. She paused. *No, it was just me using one of the missiles to shoot my reply to the Moltorian message straight at the site where they first landed. I would have waited, let you sleep longer, but it was passing out of range.*

"What? What have you done? What happens when their reply makes a hole in the Lifeboat?"

If that's what happens, it won't be on purpose. I don't think they're trying to hurt us. It's just that we're so fragile compared to them. Like you and me grabbing two fistfuls of sorghum to try and have a conversation with it but pulling it out of the soil by mistake instead.

Hugo felt like it took forever for him to read what she had written. In his astonishment that she'd acted without consulting him, anguish at the increased danger and anxiety at the possibility he might not be able to make her a suit, he let the communications cap float away, pulled himself out of his sleeping bag and bellowed,

"Come here, Skye. Stop hiding. You're my daughter. I want us to talk properly. I want to see your face."

Eventually, she sailed along the corridor, expression sullen, eye contact brief and hesitant. It dawned on him that he'd forgotten her proportions already. He'd anticipated their physical meeting to enforce his authority when it was the opposite. He felt like the child in the room.

She handed him something and Hugo half-expected it to be a written note, in defiance of his wish for words, but it squished when he took it.

"A sandwich?" he said.

"Egg and broom-corn bread," she replied softly. "I save them for birthdays, usually. Celebrations, sometimes. When I make a breakthrough. Today counts. Mother's funeral. The anniversary is soon."

Hugo froze with the sandwich in his mouth. Skye nibbled hers, leaving a bite-pattern in the bread reminiscent of a shark's, and looked up at him with dark, mistrustful eyes. Her long body filled the corridor. She couldn't come into the sleeping room.

"You haven't been hoping for me to come," he said. "You haven't been waiting."

"That's not true. I have been hoping, and waiting!"

Too loud. He resisted the urge to plug his ear canals with his fingers.

"Then what's wrong? Is it too soon? Do you need more time? Because that's fine. I'll need time to make your suit. Will you let me measure you, so I can get started?"

"No reporting to Earth," she said.

He frowned.

"But of course I've been reporting to Earth. Continuously. My suit sends a packet to the shuttle every thirty minutes for broadcasting."

"No. Switch it off."

"Fine."

Hugo complied. He waited patiently to see what would happen, momentarily regretting that he hadn't given her an immediate psych evaluation. Perhaps she'd kill him, given electronic privacy. Throttle the half-swallowed sandwich right out of his scrawny neck. Being alone in space for such a long time was surely too much for anyone to take, much less someone with an obvious hormonal imbalance.

"Check my maths," she said, putting his cap back in his hands, tapping a hand-held device to send him a packet of her own. "Don't show anyone."

"I beg your pardon?"

"My maths, Dad." The word jolted him. His fingers automatically began drawing the cap back over his shaved head. "You used to do more than just float along for the ride, right? You used to do maths?"

"I can have the shuttle's computer check it," he said, scrolling through pages and pages of calculations. "There's a lot here. It would be faster—"

"No. This is the deal. I'll help you make me a suit. But you have to check my maths. Without sending the information to the shuttle."

"Agreed."

Hugo shook her huge hand solemnly, hiding his confusion. Why was it so important to her that he check through the obsolete mathematical work she had done when it was her mother's xenobiochemistry field that she obviously excelled in? Was she trying to prove herself his equal? Was this what happened when children grew up? Did they need to supersede the older generation to take their place in the world?

He couldn't be sure. His boys hadn't grown up, not really. Their bodies had been big enough to fill soldiers' boots, but their brains had been scattered over the dashboards of their supposedly bunker-safe drone-boards before the war had even properly started.

0019.02.09. Username: Rhomboid O8 Cluster, d1 0.234nm, d2 0.266nm.

The suit's finished, Mother.

It doesn't look like yours. Not elegant and of-a-piece, but a patchwork of thermal-blanketing, micro-meteoroid resistant meta- and para-aramids, shuttle-printed metal bearings made from recycling the joints in the other suits, and a closed loop environmental system made from one of the low-grav chicken coops.

Which has halved the number of chickens, but I spared Chicken Number 3, of course, and my belly's not complaining. I don't think Hugo expected a barbecue in space, either.

The point is, I'm leaving you.

Not because I'm going to Earth and you're staying here, a trapped soul making circles around the moon, never arriving, never escaping, till the end of time.

No.

Hugo's going to Earth. That's how I know the suit works really well. I grabbed his little mini-man body and jammed him back into the shuttle where he belongs. And then I bent the wheel when I closed the airlock so he couldn't open it again from the inside.

It's wrong to use force, you told me that once, when the war was raging on Earth, but the rules are different out here. All there is, here, is force. Bodies acting on one another.

So it didn't seem wrong.

He checked my calculations, so I feel pretty confident that once I push this button, the engine I made out of those last four missiles will take the Lifeboat straight to the Sea of Rains, the place where the Moltorians told me to land.

At least, I think that's what they told me. Really, what their message said was: moonlavamoonlavamoo nlavamoonlava.

But I think I translated it right.

I can see the landing site now, clear as the day I've never seen, to the eye that's never been truly naked. I imagine myself standing down there, the rugged Appenine Mountains at my back; the powder-grey ridges of craters Aristillus, Autocyclus and Archimedes ahead of me.

I'll step out of the Lifeboat. I'll walk across that great expanse. The Moltorians will be there, waiting for me.

And that's when we'll part ways. I'll wear the suit that Hugo gave me. I'll take the will to make peace that you gave me.

I just need to work up the courage to push this button, because what kind of crazy person points themselves at the moon and then sets off an explosion right underneath their chair? So much oxygen there, combining with the hydrogen so quickly.

On Earth, liquid oxygen is a pale sky blue.

Spider-silk, Strong as Steel

Samantha Rich

On days when she was going hunting, Emm stayed in bed late.

She woke at the same time as always, but she didn't get up and begin the day. Instead she lay still, staring up at the ceiling and the strips of cloth that hung from a network of strings. She had to get her mind in the right frame on hunting days. Maybe it was superstition, but it hadn't failed her so far.

Superstition kept people alive. If that wasn't true, she didn't want to know.

Emm breathed in through her nose and out through her mouth, picturing what the nest looked like, how far she would have to go to find the silk, how long she would have to do her gathering, how much she could reasonably carry back. The Others had started making shy offers to send someone with her and learn the tricks, under the guise of *helping*, but her answer had stayed the same from the beginning: fuck that, and fuck them.

The Others had put her out to die more than once, until they realised that she could do something they couldn't. Now they wanted to call her a hero, and bring her to live with the rest of them in the tunnels.

It was a little late for all of that.

Danna pushed aside the curtain separating their bed from the rest of their space. Not a house; only the very old remembered houses, and they were dying off fast enough that the word would vanish soon. People carved out a space where they could find it, in the rubble or in the Tunnels if they were luckier than Emm and Danna and Rae. Their space had been part of a larger building once; two walls and part of the ceiling still stood, cut across on a ragged diagonal by rubble. Not a house, but home.

"Do you want something to eat?" Danna asked, standing with her arms folded and looking down on Emm, still tangled in the blankets.

"No."

"Tea?"

Emm shook her head. "No."

"You should have something before you go out."

"I will. Just not quite yet." Emm cut her gaze from the ceiling and looked Danna in the eye. "What do we have ready to go?"

Danna brushed her hair back from her face. "Two big squares that could be blankets or covers to hide under. Three sweaters. And the eggsac you got last time is dried and ready. They should pay a lot for that."

"They *should*." Emm exhaled slowly. "I need to find something just as good this time. It'll be winter soon."

"Winter's good. They hibernate."

It took Emm a beat to recognise that Danna's *them* had switched from the Others, their usual problem, to the Spiders, the much bigger problem that was so present and so eternal that it faded into her peripheral vision most of the time.

"The Others don't have any reason to buy from us then," Emm said, sitting up and scratching at her stumps. She'd gone through a patch of some low yellow plant the day before, taking a shortcut to avoid a patrol of fighters from the Others. Apparently her skin didn't care for the plants. Live and learn, and itch to make sure the learning settled in.

"We won't starve." Danna took Emm's hunting clothes from the hook on the wall and tossed them to her. Hand-knit by Rae, from silk Emm had gathered, they were a fitted sweater and pants in the style Emm needed: knit as a closed pouch at mid-femur, with a layer of leather sewn onto the bottom so she didn't wear through the material too quickly. Spider-silk was as strong as steel, the old ones said, but the threads she gathered were fine enough to need a little help.

Emm was never sure if making the hunting and fighting gear from silk actually helped turn the Spiders' attention aside. In some ways the idea made sense; in others it didn't at all. Still, superstition kept people alive. If she tried to go hunting without the gear,

Danna and Rae would be angry, or a combination of angry, sad, and scared that Emm couldn't bear.

Since the Spiders came, the remaining human population spent most of their time angry, sad, and scared. Like everyone else, Emm could taste the different flavours of emotions, fine gradations at the cellular level. Everyone had a different point where they couldn't stand it anymore.

Dressed, she hopped on her knuckles out of the sleeping area and into the main room, where Rae sat knitting by the stove and Danna was pouring cups of tea. The tea was made of bark and flowers in a combination that only Danna knew. They sold that to the Others sometimes, too, when she was able to make enough. Never the best of it, though. None of them were above tiny, petty bursts of spite. The small emotions proved they were all still human.

She boosted herself up onto a chair and accepted her cup from Danna. "Thanks, love."

"Be careful today." Danna's fingers ghosted through Emm's hair before she turned away to fuss over something in the corner.

Rae looked up from her work for a moment, meeting Emm's eyes. Emm forced herself to drink slowly, to really taste the warm liquid, to remind herself that this was something Danna made for *her*, because she loved her. She was drinking tea made by someone who loved her, in a home that they had carved out with a dearly loved friend, and the three of them were together in the wreck of the world. Always.

She wanted to carry good thoughts like that with her into the nest. It was another superstition, the idea that the Spiders could sense dark thoughts and fear. This belief was even more precious than the rest. It kept her heart alive.

She set her cup aside and nodded. "I'm ready."

"Be careful," Danna said again from the corner.

"Good hunting," Rae murmured, turning at the end of a row.

Emm hopped down from her chair and took her hunting bag from its storage place, hanging from the wall above her board. The board was a low-slung piece of wood, solid and edged in metal, with wheels at each corner on flexible axles, fashioned so that she could lie on her belly and pull herself along with her hands, or sit up and steer with a leather strap in front once she got rolling. She'd had it for years now, as long as she'd considered herself an adult. She knew every nick in the wood, exactly how long it could go between greasing the wheels, the rattling sound that meant she would make a tight corner and the one that meant she wouldn't. She trusted it like she trusted Danna and Rae, and herself. More than she trusted anyone else alive.

The Others had thrown her out to die, more than once. Thanks to the board and her brain, now they came to her and her people with hats in hand. Another bit of spite to get her awake in the morning.

She lay down on the board, settled the bag behind her, and got herself rolling out the door. Outside it was cool, the sun hidden behind clouds and the air restless with breeze. She paused for a few moments, listening for any of the chittering and scuttling sounds that signalled Spiders passing by, or the high bloodless wails that meant they were on the hunt. The Spiders shouldn't be here, according to Rae's scrawled charts and records, but every once in a while she was wrong.

Emm heard nothing but the wind and the cautious squeaking of rats. Lucky vermin, too small for the Spiders to catch unless they walked right into the webs. Too small for the monsters to waste time hunting. Humanity had never been that lucky.

She pushed off and rolled down the path in the direction that led away from the surface space claimed by the Others, around the edges of the entrance to the Tunnels. The paths were still smooth, all these years after they had been roads. In some ways, she wished they had been destroyed, to make it harder for the Spiders to travel, but mostly she was glad they were like this. *She* wouldn't have been able to travel if they were much rougher, and the Spiders had ten legs to carry them over broken ground. Not much could slow them down at all.

She wanted to sing as she made her way towards the nest; her throat was tight with the urge to sing, but the Spiders sensed vibration most of all, and the patterns of human speech and song were things they recognised. Human footfalls, too, the rhythms of walking and running. They knew the visual patterns, but they always seemed to pick up sounds first. If they heard you, they would see you, and if they saw you, that was it.

They'd never picked up on the pattern of Emm rolling on her board, though. There was only one of her, and only in this one place. If the Spiders did have a hive mind, like the old stories said, then she just wasn't enough of a sample size for them to learn from.

Bad for them, good for her. And Danna, and Rae, because it meant she could do these hunts and come back with the materials they used to trade. A group of three alone would never make it otherwise.

Emm picked up a rock from the middle of the path and tossed it aside, then resumed rolling towards the nest. If this really was going to be the last hunt of the season, she needed to bring back the goods. She hoped the Spiders would cooperate. Or— No. She hoped they wouldn't even know she was there. That was her gift to the little cluster of remaining humanity here. She could get in and out invisibly.

The surface grew rougher as she approached the nest, and her easy glide turned into a careful crawl, as she pulled the board along with her hands. She strained her hearing to its limit, listening for sounds from inside the nest above the gusts of wind. At first there was nothing, but as she moved deeper into the structure, Emm heard the soft chittering of mandibles, the click of chitin against other chitin or concrete, and the low whistles the Spiders used amongst themselves.

The nest site had been a building once, one of the tall, elaborate structures with arteries running vertically at the centre and stairwells wrapping upwards in each corner. There were openings along the outer walls, ringed in jagged shards of glass that served well for knives. Emm had collected sacks of it in the past, and Rae and Danna had carefully shaped the pieces and bound them to hilts made of wood wrapped in leather and Spider-silk. Those had traded well, feeding the three of them for a long season. But they should have rationed them out more slowly, instead of flooding the market; all of the Others had one now, and unless she came across a piece suited to a specialised blade, no one would need more for a while.

This year when the Spiders went into their long sleep, she might make her way upstairs and sort through the remnants there, if Danna would come with her for backup. The young were clumsy and less dangerous than their parents, but they hatched hungry.

The whistles grew louder and lower in pitch, and Emm slowed herself with palms flat to the ground, twisting her hips to skew the board towards the wall. She trusted the Spiders' preference for scuttling through open spaces when they could. There were old stories that claimed they partly navigated by the sharp clicking they made with their mandibles, using the echo to identify their distance from obstacles. It fit with what she'd observed in the nest. Sometimes the Spiders veered back and forth, adjusting their path after each click, and then moved straight once they found the centre of the track. Maybe their eyes caught patterns of movement and the echoes helped them steer around things that didn't move. Whatever the truth was, she had learned to exploit it.

Two Spiders emerged into the passageway, and she planted her hands to stop. They whistled to each other repeatedly, moving rapidly down the path without clicking or hesitating. Emm held her breath and kept herself frozen, her shoulder pressed hard to the wall. She had made this venture into the deep, living heart of the nest more times than she could count, and still, seeing them at close range made her chest clench. It left her tasting her own death in her throat.

The Spiders passed by, their whistles fading as they rounded a corner in the passageway. Emm remained still, her fingers tense against the ground. She forced herself to breathe before she moved again, deeper into the nest, where the light faded away almost entirely.

Here, the only way to navigate was by the splashes of dull-glowing fungus scattered across the space. Emm used the faint light to find bits of her real quarry, the Spiders' silk. Once she located a strand, she could follow it inwards, towing herself along by tugging on the silk instead of pressing her hands into the floor of the nest. The ground was soft and warm in a way that made her skin crawl and screams choke themselves off in her throat.

Maybe it was only more fungus. But some instinct in her chest insisted it was flesh, liquefied in the Spiders' bellies or churned to pulp under their limbs. She couldn't push the idea from her mind. She could only keep moving.

She paused again, holding a strand of silk tightly in both hands. She tried and failed to count the sources of the sounds, but gave up and tried to ignore them instead. Emm resumed pulling herself along with the silk and, as she moved, she wound the length of it around her wrist, creating a coil that she could put into her bag once it was large enough to be worthwhile. The knife at her belt was the sharpest she had, just sharp enough to cut through the silk. It had been crafted from a Spider mandible, stolen from a corpse left when the Others had ringed a passage with dry brush, waited for a whistling party of Spiders to enter, and set it all ablaze. It was the one great human victory of Emm's lifetime.

That was a long time ago. Some believed humans were due for a victory. Emm secretly belonged to this camp, although she would never admit it out loud. Rae fell on the other side, believing that all triumphs were behind them and what remained was a quiet slide into endless night. Danna never gave an opinion, no matter how gently Emm coaxed her. She always kept her thoughts as her own.

The strand of silk Emm was following ran out. She slipped the coil from her wrist and put it in her bag, then resumed moving forwards, feeling for another strand. The darkness made her want to close her eyes, but she had to keep them as wide as she could, attuned to the slightest change in the fungal glow, or a shift in the air that was easier to feel on the wet surface of her eyes than on her skin. The fungus grew more thickly around the Spiders' webs, and the presence of prey changed the flow of air around them, just a bit.

Or more than a bit, if the prey was still alive and struggling, but she would be able to hear that.

On her board, she ought to be low enough to slip under the webs, but it would be a pathetic end if she stumbled into one. It was humanity's common nightmare now, the shared horror that stood over everything else in the ruins of the world. The fear of being blindfolded and helpless and slowly suffocating under layers of wet heavy silk, still warm from *inside* the monsters that would kill you, unable to fight, unable to breathe—

Emm came to a halt and gripped the edge of her board as tightly as she could, until the wood dug painfully into her fingers. There was no time for this now. Nightmares and panic had to wait until she was safely back home, until Danna could brush her hair back from her sweaty forehead and whisper soothing things, until Rae could hold her hand in the dark. Giving in and letting fear take over would get her killed, either by blundering into the very webs she feared or by sending her directly into a Spider's path.

She can taste the dull, faintly metallic scent of the Spiders all through her throat and tongue. If feeding them was humanity's common horror, hating them was their common purpose. She opened her eyes to the dark again and moved forwards.

Now that she'd let the nightmare into her head, though, it was hard to push back. She couldn't quite forget that the silk she was seeking on the ground was dry precisely because it had been wrapped around some other poor dying thing, and had been sliced free at random lengths by a careless motion of the mandibles when the Spiders fed. Winding up the silk rubbed death all over her hands.

But she couldn't stop. She gathered three more lengths of silk, none of them as long as she would have liked, and continued deeper into the nest. The air grew stale and heavy, the almost-metal taste nauseating on her tongue. As her hands groped patiently along the floor, she shied away from identifying the shapes she touched any further than *useful* or *not*. Cold practicality could keep her alive as surely as superstition.

Deeper and deeper. She couldn't help but think of it as spiralling downwards into an abyss, though rationally she knew the surface was level. She found dry silk, wound it, stashed it away. She collected things that had a promise of being useful. She listened to the clicks and whistles in the dark and strained to feel any change in the air against her eyes.

She stopped to rest, wiping the sweat from her face on the sleeve of her jacket. She was surrounded by silk, imprisoned. But instead of being spun in hunger, her cocoon was woven with love. It was enough of a difference to matter.

She reached out again, making a slow sweep along the floor with her hands. One more good length of silk and she would call it a day. Not her most successful hunt ever, but not a bad one, and enough to keep them all going. She had hoped to end this season on a triumph, but if life had taught her anything, it was that survival was good enough...

Her fingers brushed against the cool, smooth surface of an object that clicked as it moved against the stone. Chitin.

Spider.

Emm froze, her breath stopping in her chest and her heart tripling its pace. This was her fate, what she'd always known under her skin, the way she knew her darkest fear.

She was going to die alone in the dark, just like everyone else.

She was going to die, here, like this, eaten by a Spider that—

The Spider wasn't moving.

It took a long moment for that to settle in her mind, the realisation that the chitin shell was still under her hand. The click she had heard was dull and hollow, an exoskeleton bumping against stone, not feet skittering or mandibles snapping at prey.

She moved her hand, following the curve of the thing as lightly as she could, barely brushing the surface. It still didn't move or react, and after a moment of exploration, she realised why. She felt a dry, ragged edge, parts of it peeling away to feathery thinness.

It was a moult, a shed exoskeleton, cast aside when a baby monster grew up.

She scooted her board closer and used both hands to explore the rest. She could make out the front and upper portion of the thorax, broken off behind the joint where the second leg would meet, and maybe— maybe, if she was lucky—

She lurched to bring the board forwards, nearly slipping off. Not directly in front of the thorax, everything must be scattered and scrambled by the Spiders running around their lair, but maybe nearby— up against the wall, because it might have enough of a shape to bounce or even roll—

Again, she made a heedless reach into the dark. Pain shot through her fingers as they wrapped around a sharp edge, and she shoved her other hand into her mouth, biting down to keep from laughing. The head. She had found the head, with at least one of the mandibles intact enough to cut herself. Intact enough to craft into a weapon and trade. This made the hunt a success all on its own; this made the whole *season*.

She moved her hand along the mandible, careful not to catch her fingers again, finding first the point and then tracing back in the opposite direction until she reached the base. From there she scouted around, finding that the other mandible was broken halfway along its length.

She got her arms around the head and pulled it up onto the board with her, before sitting upright and clutching it to her chest. She wanted to spit on it. She wanted to smash it. She wanted to kiss it with all the pale, thwarted love the scum of the earth could have for a god.

She had been down here too long.

She put the head into her bag and turned the board around, blinking against the dark. This was always the most terrifying part, retracing her path to the exit. It was why she always kept close to the wall, even though it meant missing out on whatever lengths of silk and bits of useful debris the Spiders might keep at the centre of the nest. Following the wall was the only way she could be sure she would find her way out again.

The urge to hurry was nearly overpowering. Emm had to set her teeth and concentrate on going at a slow, steady pace, stopping to listen every few breaths. Getting careless and getting trapped was another bad, arrogant death. She was going to have a better ending. Dying of old age in her bed with Danna at her side, or setting a fire to stop a Spider advance; those would be worth it. She wouldn't settle for *this*.

She crossed the nest, board length by board length, until she could see her arms moving in the edge of the light coming from the entrance. It wasn't safe to pick up speed, not yet, but her hands moved of their own will, reaching for the surface and yanking the board forwards faster, sending the wheels rattling as they crossed the ground.

Emm heard the rapid clicks coming from behind her and bit down on her tongue hard enough to taste blood. It wasn't a scream she held back, but laughter—the helpless, broken kind.

She slammed the heels of her hands against the ground, bringing the board to a halt. The clicking continued, the staccato rhythm of Spider legs skittering over the floor accented with the off-beat click of mandibles. She wondered what the Spider was saying. Maybe it was calling out a name, like Emm herself coming home from hunting, stepping into the house looking for Danna and Rae.

Spiders didn't have lovers or friends, though. They had their fellow monsters, and they had meals.

Her chest was tight. She opened her mouth wider, struggling to bring in more air without moving her body. The bag holding the silk and the Spider head was wedged under her chest, the edge of the broken mandible digging hard into her ribs.

The footsteps stopped, but the click of the mandibles was so close she felt the vibration on her skin. The Spider was right beside her. She looked out of the corner of her eye and she could see it, the light from the entryway just enough to bring a dull gleam to its exoskeleton.

The Spider clicked again, expectantly, and her heart leaped painfully in her chest, beating hard enough that she could feel it against the broken bit of chitin still jammed against her ribs. Maybe it was this Spider's own former body, outgrown and left in a corner.

She fumbled with the bag, the movement dangerous and stupid but the only chance she had.

The Spider clicked more rapidly, as Emm pulled out the head and shoved it towards the sound. The hollow mandible met the live ones with an impact that sounded wrong to her ears, too bright, too insubstantial, but at least it was something.

The Spider's feet stuttered against the floor, but didn't carry it forwards. Maybe that was how they showed surprise, by dancing in place. Maybe that was how they celebrated catching painfully stupid food. She bit down on another round of frantic giggles and moved the head again, tapping the mandible against the living Spider's.

It clicked one more time, slower, and then moved back into the darkness of the nest. Not far; she could still see it reflecting the light. She moved the head again, wagging it back and forth. Deliberately showing motion in front of the Spiders was suicide, but if it had the look of an old friend saying hello, or a corpse risen from the dead, well, neither of those things was food.

Not food, she thought, shifting her weight on the board, her shoulders aching from holding the head aloft and outstretched. *Not food means not interesting, right? Go away!*

The Spider clicked again, softly, and she heard the patter of ten feet carrying it back into the nest.

She lowered the head slowly, settling it on the board again where her chest would rest. It would dig in even more painfully for the journey home, but she didn't care. It had saved her life; it had earned a little of her pain.

She moved the board along with shaking hands, stopping for breath as often as she'd stopped for caution before. She had always gone out alone when she hunted, steady in the belief that in solitude lived both safety and strength. Now, though, she carried the ghost of a Spider with her, and she would have given anything to have Danna and Rae waiting to meet her at the first edge of sunlight.

She pulled herself to the doorway of their home and rapped out the passcode with one hand, the other braced to keep the board from rolling forwards. The Spider head was digging not only into her ribs, but her throat, exhaustion making her body too heavy to lift and free her voice.

When the door opened, Danna and Rae's hands lifted her up, and the pain eased with every heartbeat. "I made it home," she said, her voice hoarse and choked with dust.

"I knew you would," Danna said. "You're shaking, Emm, what happened?"

"A good hunt," Rae said, looking at the head and the bag of silk. "We'll live another season."

"Yes." Emm nodded, pressing a kiss to Danna's throat, the only exposed skin she could reach. "It was a good hunt, and I'm home. That's all that matters."

Rae closed and locked the door, and Emm moved into the quiet stillness of their own nest, grateful for the lamps bringing light in darkness.

No Shit

K L Evangelista

I'm sitting on the back deck in the humid summer air and enjoying a nice cold brew. My hands are still grimy from today's hard work, but there is no one else around to see. It is nice to have a chance to relax my aching muscles after digging the shallow grave for my parents.

I hadn't wanted to do a shallow grave. I had wanted to do a full six feet—show a bit of respect for the old geezers and all that. But when you're only five feet tall and not very experienced at grave digging, the logistics of it all can be tough.

Let's be clear up front. I didn't *kill* my parents. I loved them. The plague killed them, and everyone else. It swept through fast. One minute things were great, humanity was bustling, and then bammo! There were headaches. There was fever. There were bloody noses. There was screaming and moaning and then there was quiet.

As soon as I heard about it on the news, I rang my sister. We rarely agree on much, because I think she is a well-groomed Barbie soccer mom, and she thinks I am a complete mess. But this time, we agreed on one thing: I should leave my mountain cottage, and travel to the coast to look after Mum and Dad. The traffic was insane, because everyone was trying to reach their loved ones, or outrun the plague, but I made it—just. I had about an hour with them before they died. They were in so much pain I don't think they even registered I was there.

My sister didn't answer her phone after we made our initial plan. She did thoughtfully send a text— "Ella bleeding, Ken gone. My headache's getting bad. Luv u all. XOXO". (Trust Tiana to put hugs and kisses in her death SMS).

I spent the first night after my parents died getting blind drunk. I spent the second night cruising the streets of their coastal town. At first I drove silently, looking for candles, torches, any signs of life. Then I drove loudly, White Stripes blaring, horn honking, lights on full beam. I thought maybe if I was obnoxious enough someone would have to come out and tell me to shut up. There were about five thousand people in this town, and as far as I can tell they are all dead and rotting in their beds.

But at least the deck at Mum and Dad's is nice. Dad repainted it last year. The brass wind chimes play gently in the sea breeze while the sun sinks down to bed. The tang of citronella candles wards off the mosquitoes and also helps mask the corpse stench. Kind of.

When it gets dark, I turn the fairy lights on. Hooray for solar! Not only does it reduce humanity's carbon footprint (guess that isn't a problem anymore), it keeps my beer icy cold and the outside area festive so I can enjoy the end of the world in style.

Just as I am about to go for another beer, a flare lights up the sky. Other survivors! I jump to my feet. It looks like it is coming from a larger city nearby. I get into the car, and speed out of the driveway. On my way out of town, I stop at the cop shop, and then I'm back on the road—now with a handgun tucked into my jacket pocket.

Every twenty minutes or so another flare shoots up and then drifts slowly back down. I turn the headlights off when I reach the city. When I'm sure I know where the flares are coming from, I park the car. I take out the gun, hang some binoculars around my neck (also nabbed from the police station) and trek the last distance on foot. I am possibly a little paranoid, but for a female alone at night, it pays to take precautions.

The other survivors have built up a nice bonfire in the parkland at the centre of town. I stop behind a pair of bins. Now that I have some cover and a decent view of the area, I lift up the binoculars and scope things out.

There are about five or six camping chairs around the fire. Only one of them is occupied. I scan the area carefully, but there is definitely just the one person. The survivor is a man, slimly built, with glasses that occasionally flash in the firelight. He is reading a book

(*Dealing with Change*—ha!), and on either side of his chair are two piles of flare guns. He must have spent his day raiding the boats in the harbour. As I examine him, he looks at his watch, picks up a flare gun from the pile on his right, blasts it into the sky, and then drops it into the pile on his left. The survivor watches the flare drift down and I get a good look at his face. His expression is a mixture of fear, grief and hope.

A mad shriek curdles the air behind me. I startle and the binoculars smash against the bins with a loud clatter. Freaking possum! I hightail it back to the car. No wait. I stop. I run a few more steps then stop again. Dammit! What the hell am I doing?

"Hello?" The man stumbles in the dark towards me. He sees me and slows, still a good distance away. "Hello? It's okay. I'm not going to come any closer. The whole apocalypse experience was weird enough even before I started chasing women through the park at night. Why don't we meet in daytime like sensible people?" He is talking quickly, afraid that I'll run off before he gets his message out. "Have you heard of Bluebottles café? I'll be there, tomorrow from ten. Bluebottles—in the high street."

As I drive back to my parents place I reflect on the events of the evening. Lone survivor man seemed nice. I hope he doesn't think I'm a freak. I really hope he didn't notice my gun.

*

I am late as I pull up to Bluebottles the next morning. The survivor is sitting at a sunny outdoor table and reading another book ("Composting Toilets"). He waves casually, marks his page with a sugar sachet, and stands up to greet me.

"Hi!" he smiles. "I'm Sam."

"Hey," I say. "Jane." We both stand there looking awkward for a moment, and then, when I don't say anything else, he gives a wry smile.

"I don't know about you," he says, "but I need a coffee."

Our table has a vase filled with fresh flowers. Sam begins industriously frothing long life milk over in the serving area. The fridges are empty—he must have cleared out all the consumables that had gone bad. Curious I go check out the back and find the toilets (very important), and a generator, rigged to get power working. His work isn't too shoddy.

Sam calls me back and hands me my short black and a slice of freshly baked teacake. Seriously, when does this guy sleep? I take a swig. *Now* I am ready for some conversation.

Sam takes a sip of his latte and adjusts his glasses. "I'm really glad you came today," he says. "Until last night, I thought…I might have been the only one left. Where were you when you saw the flares?"

"Woolgoolga."

"That far? I wasn't sure how visible they would be." He ponders for a moment. "No one else came last night." Given the ghost town I had experienced, this does not surprise me. "I was hoping that there'd be more. I guess we'll just have to put our heads together and think of a different way to find the others. Locating other survivors will be our top priority—right?"

"Of course." I'd mostly been wallowing in grief and panic since the apocalypse, but I didn't want Sam to think that I couldn't be forward thinking. "What's this?" I ask, gesturing towards the book about toilet composting.

"I found it in the library yesterday." He gently traces the spine. "I think it will be some time before we lose water, but it can't hurt to be prepared. Sewerage is not something I want to deal with."

"No shit," I agree.

He smiles, and I can't help but notice that he has tiny dimples. "We can think of it as an unofficial motto for our group as we rebuild society."

I take a bite of the teacake. It is still warm, with a light and buttery crumb that melts in my mouth. Sam knows how to bake.

While we eat and drink, we sketch out a rough plan which will cover the next few days. It basically involves massive amounts of looting. So it's an *awesome* plan.

We stand up to leave the café, and I wonder if we should shake hands or something. Sam puts his hands in his pockets and looks at me earnestly.

"You do want to stick together, right? Because I do. Want to, I mean. But I don't want to make you feel as if we have to. We don't, if you don't want to." I can see the fear and the vulnerability lurking in his eyes. If I say no, he will be alone again. If I say no, *I* will be alone again.

I punch his shoulder lightly. "Of course we're sticking together. How am I gonna rebuild society without your badass research skills? Read a book?" I school my features into an expression of mock horror.

Sam's posture relaxes. "Reading broadens your life," he says loftily. "Okay, so we'll each grab some things, and then meet up at the supermarket at three."

Looting is fun, although I have to spend way too much time finding some of the electronic gear I want. If only the Internet was still on, I could ask Google! Google knows everything. At least it used to. But since Google is also dead, I am reliant on these slow inefficient yellow-paged directory books.

When I finally rock up at the supermarket, it is behind the wheel of a massive semi-trailer. It has a nice little sleeper cabin in the back, and my gun is now stashed safely in the glove box.

Sam has a Winnebago. With its plush leather interiors and stainless steel appliances, it looks like the kind of vehicle my sister would buy for her family holidays...would have bought for her family holidays.

The Winnebago is stuffed with books and laminators. "It's not immediate survival," says Sam.

"But a lot of these books are important. We have to preserve knowledge for future generations of humanity." He does have some more useful items, including the portable generator he used at Bluebottles. We stow it in the back of my semi.

I show Sam some of the goodies I nabbed. "Spray paint cans?" he asks, clearly sceptical.

"I dabbled in graffiti in high school," I explain "I'm pretty good."

His expression remains politely dubious, so I pull out my ace—a 1000W professional FM transmitter. "Nice!" he says, his genuine appreciation warming me up.

"There is only one thing left before we head out, then: snacks!"

Walking into the supermarket is like climbing into the inside of a bin and licking the sides. The sickly sweet stench of rotting fruit and fetid meat is so strong I can taste it in the back of my mouth.

I glance towards the deli and make a small sad noise. "Bacon…"

Sam takes my arm and draws me towards the aisles. "It's no good, Jane. It's gone…"

We are careful not to take too much of the canned goods—other survivors might come to this store and be in desperate need of food.

Once we adjust to the smell, it's not so bad. It's kinda like being on one of those reality TV shows where you need to grab as many items as possible in five minutes. Baked Beans, yes, chocolate, yes, toilet paper, HELL yes. I'm gonna need every last roll.

"Jane, do you like these cans of SPAM?" Sam calls out from further down the aisle.

"I do not like them Sam I am."

Sam catches on immediately. "Do you like them here or there? Do you like them anywhere?"

"I do not like them from a tin. I do not like them in a bin. I do not like them in a truck. I will never like them, you little—"

Suddenly, I am not in the supermarket. I am on my sister's big blue couch, reading Dr Seuss to my niece. Her curls tickle my cheek as we giggle over the ridiculous pictures.

"Seriously, though," asks Sam. "Do you like SPAM?"

"No," I say. He puts it back. I head to the liquor section to grab some bottles of expensive scotch.

We leave just as the sun starts to set. I pull out my tins of spray paint and tag the building—"Jane and Sam Alive @ 5, 105fm."

Sam scrutinises my work critically. "Is it supposed to be 5 PM? Because you might want that pertinent fact very clear."

"But then it doesn't rhyme properly!" I squish in a little "pm" as best I can.

Sam pulls out a map. "I've been thinking that we should travel just as it gets dark. Hopefully our lights will make us more obvious to other survivors. We'll head north up the highway, and stop for the night when we hit the next major town."

"At the fanciest hotel we can find."

"Actually, my Winnebago. It has two double beds. I don't fancy having to look through hotel rooms until I find one that was unoccupied." Thanks for that grisly image, Sam. But it's a good point. I feel a pang for all those wonderful bathrobes that will never be used again. "We wake up feeling refreshed, do some looting and, er, tag some major landmarks. At five, we perform our radio show, make some dinner and head back out into the night. Then we do the whole thing over again until we hit Brisbane."

I am pumped that we have a plan, and spring into the semi. "Let's hit the road. It's too late to do the radio show tonight and I've already got dinner." I waggle a couple of packets of jerky and chips in his direction.

"That is not dinner," says Sam. "Just because this is the end of the world, doesn't mean you can't have standards."

Halfway to our destination, I regret the jerky and chips. I see a sign for a rest area 10 kays ahead.

"Sam I am, are you there?"

"Roger, Jane-train, what's up?"

"Why are we going so slow?"

"We're going at one hundred." Sam's voice crackles over the radio. "That's the speed limit."

"Yes. And civilisation has ended. So why are we going so slow?"

"Because speed signs exist for a reason, and at night in strange vehicles is not the time to take risks. It would be pretty tragic for the last known survivors to be killed in a car accident."

"We're not driving cars," I point out, as I put my foot on the accelerator. "I'll meet you there."

I leave the semi at a truck stop near the highway (tagging the sign). Then I join Sam in the Winnie and we park in the centre of town (tagging the supermarket). It was a long day. I am asleep before the lights are off.

The next morning, Sam heads out to loot the local library and bookstores while I listen to Vampire Weekend on my sweet new speakers. When he gets back, it is my turn to explore the town. It is depressingly empty.

Sam makes us a nice omelette for lunch—I guess we should eat as many eggs as we can before they all go bad. That afternoon we do our first broadcast.

"Uh, hello?" Sam starts things off. "My name is Sam and I'm with my friend Jane."

I wrestle the handset off him and bellow "We are Sam and Jane, alive at five!" I return the handset to him. "You have to give it a bit more pizzazz, Sam, or we'll lose our listeners."

Sam makes a face at me. "We will be at the Ballina showground tomorrow." He then goes on to list all the other towns we'll be visiting before we get to Brisbane.

"Brisvegas!" I scream from the background.

Sam interrupts the show to scold me. "Seriously, Jane, we don't want to scare people away."

Sam gets back on the air. "I'm going to hand you over to Jane now." I fist pump. "She thinks she has a better radio voice then me, and so is going to give you some step by step instructions on how to buy and set up your own radio." My fist pump turns into a face palm. "Over to you Jane."

We repeat the show three times just in case we get any late listeners, then we are back on the road. I spend the drive to Ballina analysing our performance, and making suggestions on how Sam could improve his radio brand.

Sam drives the Winnie sedately into Ballina. I follow in the semi, honking my horn. We stop at the showground. I pull out some floodlights and connect them to our portable generator. Sam sets up some camping chairs outside, pulls out a book and starts to laminate it ("*Cloudstreet* is a classic, Jane! It needs to be preserved for future generations."). I head into the Winnie and watch a DVD in bed. My gun is snuggled up under my pillow. I have decided to name her Gertrude. I'm not ready to introduce Sam to Gertrude yet—I don't know how he'd react.

Sam comes in after about an hour. "Seriously?" he asks. "Outbreak? You thought a thriller about a dangerous airborne virus was a good choice of entertainment?"

"It's research," I say. "Besides, this movie is a classic. It's not Dustin Hoffman's fault the world ended."

I fall asleep before the end of the movie, and wake up in the middle of the night. Sam is still awake, lying in his bed with a torch and reading.

"No visitors?" I ask.

"No," he says, turning a page.

"Maybe tomorrow. You should get some sleep." Sam takes off his glasses and turns off the torch, and then I hear him shifting around, trying to get comfortable.

"Jane..." he whispers after about half a minute. "Are you still awake?"

"Yeah."

"I can't sleep."

"What's up?" Besides everyone being dead. And the absence of bacon.

"Just...worrying." A lock of hair has fallen over Sam's eyes, and for a moment I am tempted to reach over the gap between our beds and brush it away.

"There were about fifty thousand people in Coffs Harbour," he says. "Eighty thousand if you include the surrounding region. If we really are the only two people left alive in this area...those are really poor odds of surviving the infection."

Poor Sam looks so tense, he could really use a hug. My mum was a good hugger. I remember she asked a lady in the bank once if everything was okay. The lady burst into tears, and my mum just reached out and comforted her, as if she had known her for years.

I have never been that great at hugging, myself. I wish I was better.

"Do you know what a minimum viable population is?" Sam asks. "It is the smallest number of people that are needed for a species to survive over a long period of time. It is a large enough population that we won't be vulnerable to natural disasters, or genetic weaknesses caused by inbreeding. For humanity, the minimum viable population is about four thousand people."

"We should be right then," I say. "There are billions of people on Earth. If one in one hundred thousand survived, that leaves..." It is too late at night to do maths in my head. "... a crapload."

"Sixty thousand, yes. Spread out over the whole globe. Two thousand in Australia. And we'll only survive if we're all together." Sam is talking faster as he goes on. The skin around his eyes is strained. "That's why it's really important we find the other survivors. We have to start building a new community."

I'm not sure I give a damn about the overall survival of humanity. I care about me, and now I care about Sam.

"I reckon there will be way more survivors than that," I say, wanting to make him feel better. "The plague swept through fast. Too fast. It will have burnt itself out before it gets everywhere. There are some pretty remote places that will be safe."

"I hope you're right..." Sam says slowly. "Did you follow the start of the infection?"

"Kind of. It started in Russia. People thought it might have been a bioweapon gone out of control."

"Yes. All of the governments reacted very quickly. They set up quarantines for the infected. Australia shut down all international flights immediately. We're an island, Jane! It shouldn't have been able to reach us. But it did."

"It was too fast!" I say.

"Or too slow. The way it spread—it hit everyone almost at once. It jumped through quarantines like they didn't exist. I think this virus was dormant and spreading for a really long time before the first symptoms appeared."

"Maybe, but so what? It doesn't matter how it spread. What matters is what we do next."

"It might matter," says Sam. "What if we aren't immune to the virus? What if we just caught it later, and it is lying dormant in our bloodstream? Our symptoms could start at any moment."

If I wasn't wide awake before, I am now. I bury my face in my pillows, desperate for the oblivion of sleep. Dad's bloody face and Mum's cries of pain haunt me. I thought I'd escaped that, but it could still be me.

This is the perfect time to try some of that expensive booze.

The next morning my head throbs and my gut roils—alcohol has never been that great for my innards.

Sam has dark circles under his eyes. He forces himself to be cheerful and chatty, but my stomach hurts and I am not capable of making small talk. No, Sam, I do not want some instant coffee. Why would you even bother picking that up from the shelf? I also don't want tea. I rush out as quickly as I can. The brown tide is rising, and I don't want to be near Sam when it strikes.

I spend most of the morning at the mall, within sprinting distance of the nearest loo. The semi is stacked with about one thousand rolls of toilet paper, at this rate that might get me through till next week.

When I feel a bit better, I stomp around the rest of the town tagging the supermarkets in big, red, angry letters.

I return just in time to do the radio show. I can see that Sam is confused, but I'm not about to explain my erratic behaviour.

That night, when we stop, I elect to stay in my little bunk in the semi. Sam doesn't try to argue, he just looks quietly miserable, which is a thousand times worse.

"I'm sorry," he says. "I didn't mean to freak you out last night. I know I don't sleep well. I know it. My mind races, and I worry about one thing after another, and there are so many things to worry about…"

"It's not you," I say, but I know without explanations I am unconvincing. And I am not about to explain.

Everything continues to slowly spiral over the next few days. There isn't a single person at any of the towns we pass through. No one joins our radio show.

Sam is getting a lot of laminating done, and studies his books intently, but doesn't appear to get much sleep. I stop eating and spend most of the days curled up in the semi or on the dunny willing my body to get better.

On the third evening, the CB radio lights up the night with our first caller.

"Hey Sam and Jane."

Sam and I stare at each other in shock. Then we do the world's biggest high five. Our hands cling together afterwards as we jump up and down. I do not want to let go.

Sam eagerly reaches for the radio with his other hand. "You have no idea how excited we are to hear your voice!" he says, giving my hand a last squeeze and then letting go. "We're so glad you got our messages."

"Hard to miss when they're every kilometre along the highway."

"Yeah, I'm very thorough," I say. "What's your name, Mystery Man?"

"Travis. Trav."

"Nice to meet you Trav. Congratulations on surviving the apocalypse. Would you like to meet up, or are you planning on running solo?"

"Maybe in a few days. I've just got into Byron."

"What's in Byron, Travis?" Sam asks gently. The poor man is no doubt checking on family in the area.

"Dairy cows." Or not.

"For real?" I ask.

"Yeah, dead set. I'm from outside of Warwick. I've been driving around this area for a week now, looking for other people. And I haven't found any till now. What I have found is a lot of dead cows. Every single frigging cow in the area is dead and gone. Because of the drought, I guess. I thought there might still be some cows near the coast."

Sam is very excited and goes to get one of his books. "I *knew* this would come in handy!" he exults, while reading key passages out over the radio to Trav on dealing with cattle.

Afterwards, we debrief. "That Travis has a good head on his shoulders," says Sam. "Humanity has had dairy cows for thousands of years. I don't know what we'd do without milk."

I think of sitting at the kitchen bench with my sister and sharing milk and cookies as an afternoon treat. I think of my baby niece lying on her little sofa with her bottle of milk. Trav is indeed a hero.

"I thought there might even have been a few sparks zinging between you guys," Sam suggests.

What. The. Hell.

"Whoa there tiger. I am not going to date Trav." I was just holding your hand five seconds ago. "It's the end of days. Everyone I know is dead, the world smells of corpse and the *last* thing on my mind is romance." My dad always said that if you had to fight, make your first punch hard enough that the other person can't get up. "Just because you have a freaky hang up about saving mankind, doesn't mean I'm going to breed with every new man we meet."

Sam turns pale, and I know I have hit hard enough. I make sure I slam the door loudly on my way to the semi.

We are driving on the highway when my bowels send me an urgent message.

I hit the brakes and bang the horn. "Sam," I radio urgently. "We need to stop. Right now." I pull my semi over to the side of the road. The Winnie is not even properly stationary, but that doesn't stop me—I sprint to the side and wrench open the door to the living area, stumbling in my haste to reach the bathroom. I only just make it in time.

"Jane, are you okay?" I hear Sam's worried voice through the door. He is just outside, and can no doubt hear every humiliating detail.

"No," I reply miserably.

"Is it the plague? Is it some variation of the plague?" he asks.

I am tempted to say yes. "No. It's Crohn's disease. It affects my bowels. Pain and diarrhoea mostly."

"Is it…life threatening?"

"It wasn't. When we had doctors and medicine." I stare at the bloody red bowl before I flush the toilet. "I don't know about now."

"What can I do?"

"For right now, a little space would be great." I can feel another wave coming on, and it is a very thin door.

We make an early camp on the side of the road. Frankly, it is far nicer out here than in the cadaver infested cities. You can take a deep breath without choking on the rot. When we find somewhere to settle down, it will definitely be in the country.

I sit cross-legged on my Winnie bed. Sam has thoughtfully made me a hot water bottle, which I clutch gratefully to my tummy.

"So much for our motto as we rebuild society." I try to smile. It seems like a long time since our first conversation in the café.

"'No shit'," Sam reminisces fondly. "It is still a worthy goal. And we've done okay. There has been a minimum of shit. Less shit than there could be."

"I was lucky today," I explain to Sam, not meeting his eyes. "I won't always make it to the toilet in time. I guess it's better that you're warned before that happens, since you're stuck with me and all."

"Why didn't you tell me?" asks Sam. "I could have helped."

"I'm serving up bum gravy, Sam. It is humiliating. I've never even told anyone outside my family before."

"It is pretty gross," he says. I bury my head in my pillow and try to drown my face so I never have to meet his eyes again. "But it's not as bad as having your testes swell up and double their size."

I am so surprised that I look up from my pillow. "What?"

"Giant. Balls. Yes, that happened to me. When I was in high school. I couldn't wear underwear. I was in massive pain so I couldn't go to school. And I couldn't tell anyone, because you don't talk about testicle problems with other sixteen-year-old boys. It's a rare condition called orchitis." He pauses briefly. "It's what caused my infertility." Whoa! Just...whoa!

Sam sits on the bed and puts his arm around me. "Tomorrow we'll arrive in Brisbane. The first thing we'll do is visit a hospital and find some medical textbooks."

"And go to the hospital pharmacy," I say. "I know what medication to get for my flare."

"I don't know why we haven't been to a chemist before now," says Sam. "We should be stocking up on antibiotics and pain medications."

I lean into him and close my eyes. It is nice to have him here. I get to enjoy the moment for about two minutes before I have to return to my throne.

Our plan to reach the hospital first thing turns out to be a trifle optimistic. Getting around Brisbane is agonisingly slow—cars have stacked up in key areas and are blocking the way, forcing us to find alternative routes. In the end, it is easier to reach our base at

Mount Coot-Tha. We set the area up with floodlights, which should be visible from most of Brisbane. They're rigged to turn on at sunset.

As we make our way to the nearest hospital, we continue to tag signs. Whenever we hit a choke point we can't avoid, we have to get out of the Winnie and drive the cars out of the way. Sometimes the cars are empty, their owners abandoning them as a hopeless cause. Sometimes they are still occupied.

By 5 PM, it has become clear that the hospital itself is a major chokepoint. We consult some maps and decide that we are close enough to walk.

Before we leave, Sam does our radio show while I get a quick dinner together. Sam informs everyone that we are making our way to the hospital, but will be returning to Mt Coot-Tha when we're done. I serve baked beans and toast. I had to pick through the loaf looking for the last few non-mouldy slices, so tomorrow we might need to find a bread maker. I don't really know why I bother eating though, because as soon as I've finished I have to spend half an hour in the dunny while it all comes back out again. Sam tactfully retires outside with his book (*Wool: From sheep to socks*).

By the time we are ready to set out on foot, it is well and truly dark. Our backpacks are mostly empty and ready to be filled with precious, precious drugs. All I'm bringing are the bare essentials—a bottle of water, a roll of toilet paper, a walkie talkie, and Gertrude.

I am carrying a torch, but I don't really need it to see where I'm going. The moon is full, and so close to the horizon that it appears to have doubled in size. It is so pristine, so white. I wonder what is happening to the astronauts up at the international space station right now. Are they stuck up there in orbit until their air runs out, unable to get back to Earth without help?

"Hey Sam," I say. "Check out the moon. It's looking a bit swollen tonight, doncha think?"

"Actually, I was just thinking it looked a bit crappy," he shoots back. And then he stops in his tracks and grabs my arm tightly.

I follow his gaze, and see our destination: the hospital. And all the lights are on.

We break into a jog. I don't know what I'm expecting when I run into the well-lit foyer (Masses of people huddled together with their sleeping bags? An irate administrator wielding a clipboard? A welcome banner?), but I don't find it. All I see is wall to wall stiffs. A lot of desperate people came to the hospital and found nothing but a place to die.

"Hello?" My voice bounces off the walls.

No response.

We start picking our way around the bodies, periodically calling out as we go. It is a bit easier to move once we get out of the foyer, but the dead are still everywhere.

"You know what would suck?" I say. "If that lady zombie turned around and looked right at us."

"Shut up, Jane."

We briefly stop at Gastroenterology for Sam's medical texts, and then find directions to the maintenance areas. Surely the lights in this hospital are still on for a reason.

"Maybe we should split up?" Sam suggests. "We can cover more ground that way."

My heart stops, and then I realise this is what passes for humour in Sam's world.

We find our way to the backup generator, and I inspect it closely. "It's a 1200 KVA diesel. There's no way this could keep the whole hospital powered for more than four or five hours without needing to be topped up with more fuel."

Sam looks at me strangely. "Uh, Jane," he says. "What did you do before the world ended?"

Uh-oh, busted. "I was an electrical engineer."

He makes a small choking sound. "And you didn't feel the need to mention that before because?"

"I didn't want to have to feel responsible for rebuilding civilisation."

"Jane, you need to start opening up more on the important things."

I look back at the generator and return to the topic at hand. "I don't understand why they are using the generator to power the whole hospital. They clearly aren't using everything—this place is empty. They could conserve their power by rerouting some of the circuits and tripping these breakers here."

"Girl, you have no idea how glad I am to hear you say that," says a croaky female voice from just behind my right shoulder.

With a squeal, I stumble back and away. I ricochet off the wall, and then I'm through the door and running out the corridor. I make it all the way back to the foyer when I realise that: (1) Sam is not with me; and (2) that lady was probably in her late fifties and didn't look particularly threatening.

I'm leaning against the wall, panting and attempting to regroup, when Sam arrives.

"Jane, are you okay?" he asks.

"Yep. Just feel a bit stupid. She's not a zombie, is she?"

"No," he confirms. "Not a zombie. Her name is Judith and she is a doctor. I told her we'd be right back. She said, 'Take your time,' which is not the usual zombie M.O."

I sheepishly return to the power room and our new comrade. She is flicking through our liberated medical texts.

"Which one of you needs this?" she asks.

"Me," I say. "I have Crohn's."

"Hmm. An autoimmune." She looks at Sam. "And you? What illness are you bringing with you into this brave new world? Sam looks startled. "Er...nothing? I'm perfectly healthy."

"He did have something when he was a teenager," I volunteer. "Orchidness or something."

"Autoimmune Orchitis?" she queries, and Sam nods.

"What do you have?" I ask on a hunch.

She looks at me as though I have just asked the rudest most invasive question possible, but then relents. "I have MS. Another Autoimmune."

"Do you think that's what protected us from the plague?"

"It is certainly a working hypothesis. It can't be the only factor of course, or there would be more of us. Twenty percent of the population had autoimmune, significantly more than were spared by the virus."

Sam looks distressed. "But if every survivor left has an autoimmune disease… Humanity is FUCKED. Our gene pool is already dangerously reduced. We won't be able to survive this."

Judith shrugs and turns back to the generator. "I haven't slept properly for a week," she says to me. "Help me fix this mess."

"Why should I?" I ask uncharitably.

"Because," she replies, "fifty metres from here are two thousand fertilised embryos. They represent enough genetic diversity to save this pathetic excuse of a species."

Judith's hands shake as she smooths her hair. "I need to make sure they can be kept frozen until we need them." What I have taken for rudeness is actually massive sleep deprivation.

I help Judith reroute the power. She immediately goes to a nearby bunk, promising she will meet us at

Coot-Tha soon. We pick up our medical supplies from the pharmacy and start the long journey back to camp.

"You know what I like about the apocalypse?" Sam says as he drives us up the mountain. "Everyone is basically trying to preserve something. It's not like in the movies where there are always roving bands of armed bandits."

"That's because we're not all fighting for resources," I point out.

"Don't be such a pessimist, Jane! This is clearly a triumph of human nature."

I am excruciatingly aware of Gertrude, sleeping quietly in my backpack. "Yeah, about that..." I say. "There's something here that you'd better see."

Sam looks inside. "Holy Shit, Jane. What the hell?"

I laugh for about a minute. Sam has the best reactions. "This is Gertrude. I've kept her with me because I thought I needed her. But now, I don't think that I do. When Judith appeared right behind me, and I thought she was a real threat, I expected that I would act cool, calmly assess the situation and draw the gun to protect myself if necessary. But I didn't act cool. I panicked. And if I had drawn the gun in that moment, I would have shot an innocent woman and doomed our entire species."

I take a deep breath and pull out my faithful friend. She is a solid and deadly weight in my hands.

"Gertrude. Thank you for your service." I roll down the window and throw her into the dark.

Sam smiles at me. For the first time, I see reflected in his eyes something I have known in my heart for a while.

We arrive at camp, around 2am, tired and ready for a rest. I am not expecting company, and am shocked when a cheer greets us as we pull up.

Seated around the floodlights are a dozen other survivors of the plague. Our fans.

I Will Remember You

Janet Edwards

Day Five

I'd been planning to start my last day alive by sending a farewell message to all my friends, but when I rolled out of bed on the morning of Day Five I found my mobile phone had no connection and my computer wasn't linking to the Internet either. I could hear Mum vacuuming downstairs, the hum of the cleaner mingling with the usual early morning gurgles from the central heating system, so I stuck my head out of my bedroom door and yelled at the top of my voice.

"Mum, is the house phone working?"

The sound of the vacuum cleaner stopped, and there was a brief pause before she called back. "No, Megan. I've just checked and there's no dial tone. Is that a problem?"

"No, it doesn't matter."

"Can I help you with anything else? Should I bring you up something to eat?"

"No, thank you. I'll get my own breakfast in a minute." I worked hard at keeping my response polite. Mum and Dad were ridiculously over-protective about the fact I'd been born with my left arm ending abruptly where my wrist should have been. It was annoying to be constantly offered help that I didn't want or need, but I mustn't snap at them about it today.

I retreated back into my bedroom. Whatever had gone wrong with the phones and the Internet, nobody was going to bother repairing anything now, so I could forget about sending messages.

I felt relieved rather than frustrated, because I hadn't known what to say in my message. The last one of my friends to die had been Caro on Day Three. She'd sent everyone a long rant about the unfairness of her dying when she was only sixteen. That had come across as horribly self-centred given the rest of us were only sixteen too, we were all going to die within the next few days, and the whole human race would be dead by sunset on Day Thirteen. If I was honest about my feelings, I'd probably sound pretty selfish too, but I didn't want to send everyone a message full of fake nobility and lies. The failure of the phones and the Internet had solved the problem for me.

I went across to my bedroom window and pulled back the curtains. It was spring, but it had looked like the darkest of winter days here in Corlforth St Peter ever since the alien armada arrived on Day Zero. One of the vast ships was hanging directly above us, its shadow extending over the whole village and the neighbouring farmland.

I stared wistfully out across the fields to where the sun was shining on the main road in the distance. That road was usually packed with traffic at this time on a weekday morning, but there were just two cars and a death cart heading into the city. People had given up running from the alien ships after what happened to the President of the USA on Day One. If you weren't safe in a remote nuclear bunker under a protective mountain of concrete, then there was no safe place anywhere in the world.

The vacuum cleaner had started up again downstairs. I didn't understand why Mum was spending her last few hours alive doing housework. Did she think the aliens were going to come and inspect our home after we were dead, or was this her way of pretending this was an ordinary day?

I frowned at the row of photo frames on my windowsill. Most of those photos were of me and Alisha. She'd been my best friend, the only one of my friends who lived in Corlforth St Peter instead of the city, and the one person I'd have really liked to say goodbye to, but she'd died on Day One.

We'd both spent Day Zero and Day One at home with our parents, because neither of us dared to go outside with an alien ship hovering over us. I'd started Day Zero by watching television coverage of aircraft and missiles making hopeless attempts to attack the alien ships, and ended it hiding in the cellar while a cloud of fighter aircraft tried attacking the one over our village. Alisha lived over in the new housing estate, so her family didn't have a cellar, and had to cram into the cupboard under the stairs.

By the morning of Day One, it was obvious that nobody had any weapons that could harm the alien ships, so the attacks were abandoned. My parents and I came out of the cellar, and Dad boarded up our two broken windows, while I exchanged panicky messages with Alisha and my other friends about the blue dots that had appeared on their left hands overnight.

All anyone had known then was that the aliens had labelled people depending on which building they were in or near at sunset of Day Zero. Alisha and her family had all only got a single blue dot on their left hands, while my parents both had five of them. It had taken a while for the news to spread about what was happening as darkness fell in places around the world, how all the people with one blue dot on their left hand stopped breathing at sunset. By the time I'd understood what the dots meant, the sun had already set in England, so it was too late for me to say goodbye to Alisha.

I'd had a few bad hours after that. Alisha was dead, and everyone else I knew seemed to be sending me aggressive messages about my missing left hand, demanding to know if I had blue dots on my left arm instead. There'd been something frightening about that barrage of messages. I was still trying to work out whether to reply to them or not, when the television news reports brought an end to it. Some of the Day Twos had tried cutting their left hands off, so the government were publicising cases where someone born without a left hand had died with the rest of their family.

There were no more angry messages after that. I'd even received a few apologies, but it was hard to forget the things people had said, the way they'd acted as if I were as much their enemy as the aliens who'd sentenced them to death.

I rubbed my eyes and turned away from the window. I was glad I couldn't say goodbye to the pseudo friends who'd sent me those messages. Alisha was gone, so it was just me and my parents now. We'd had a lot of fights over the years, as I battled their efforts to smother me with loving care, but I'd be the perfect daughter for these last few hours.

I went to get washed, then took the dress Mum had given me for Christmas out of the wardrobe, held it up against me, and wrinkled my nose. It was a disgustingly girly thing with a pattern of little pink flowers, but…

I shrugged off my pyjamas and wriggled into the dress. It didn't have any buttons or zips, just strategic elastic, which managed to be both considerate and annoying of Mum at the same time. She didn't have to carefully choose clothes like this for me. I could manage buttons and zips perfectly well, even tie shoelaces. Doing most things was possible with a bit of time, thought, creativity, and occasional use of sticky tape, rubber bands, or string.

I brushed my hair, put on some makeup, and sighed as I opened the drawer where I kept my latest prosthetic hand. I knew my parents and doctors kept giving me these things with the best intentions, and perhaps other people found them wonderful, but I didn't. Once I was eleven years old, I'd flatly refused to wear one to school any longer.

The version I called the hook was a bit different, because that could be useful on rare occasions, but the one designed to look like a human hand just got in the way. Why should I have to wear the stupid thing, make it harder for me to carry things in the crook of my left arm, just to make those around me feel more comfortable about my appearance? Everyone seemed to have this peculiar idea that making it look like I had two hands meant I'd been fixed, mended, or cured. It wasn't just that it didn't fix me. It was that I didn't think I'd ever been broken.

Today was a special occasion though. If I was going to play the perfect daughter, then I might as well do it properly. I rolled up my dress sleeve, and secured the hand on the end of my left arm. The awkwardness and the added weight made me cringe, but I pulled my sleeve down and turned to look in the mirror.

I had to admit the hand was unbelievably realistic. It gave me quite a shock seeing my reflection, as if I were looking at a stranger. I was heading for the door when I realised I'd forgotten something. I grabbed a pen from the jar on the bookshelves and made five blue dots on the palm of my fake left hand, then went downstairs.

It was getting close to sunset now. Mum had cooked a special celebration meal. Dad had played along, bringing out two bottles of wine and the Christmas crackers that had been left over from last Christmas, and we'd worn stupid paper hats and laughed at the bad jokes in the crackers.

The meal had been a surprising success, but now the strain was showing. Mum and Dad seemed to be trying to finish both the bottles of wine between them, and all three of us kept sneaking looks out of the kitchen window, checking how low the sun was in the sky.

I swiped the last banana from the fruit bowl, and trapped it between my left arm and my body while I peeled it with my right hand. I had a creepy moment as I realised this would be the last banana I'd ever eat, the last thing I'd ever eat, but I kept stubbornly munching my way through it. As I threw the banana skin in the bin, I heard the church bell start ringing, and bit my lip.

The church bell was the signal Barbara Corlforth had arranged. She'd married the owner of Corlforth House over thirty years ago, he'd died just before I was born, and Barbara Corlforth had been occupying herself by running our village ever since. She organised the bookings for the church hall, ran the church cleaning rota, the pensioners' coffee mornings, the annual village festival, and the monthly barn dances, as well as being president of the flower arranging society, the choral society, and the local history group.

She was naturally organising the village deaths as well. We weren't going to have death lorries coming round like they did in the cities, with men collecting bodies from marked houses and throwing them in the back like rubbish. We were going to handle things ourselves with dignity.

I'd always had an awed fear of Barbara Corlforth's intimidating efficiency, but now I was deeply grateful for it. There'd been horror stories on the television about the death lorries. Pictures of men kicking and stamping on the bodies to get more into the lorry, and tales of them getting caught having fun with the corpses. Obviously the authorities couldn't be too choosy about who they recruited to run the death lorries; most people wanted to spend their last few days with family and friends rather than carrying the corpses of strangers, but I didn't want anyone messing around with my body after I was dead.

I went upstairs to get my jacket. I thought I should let Mum and Dad have a few minutes alone together, so I turned my radio on. It was set to the local station, and someone was screaming hysterically about the whole of the city centre being on fire and people fighting in the streets.

I hastily turned off the radio. I'd always wished I lived in the city, but now I was glad to be in an isolated village. Civilisation was already falling. I'd envied the Day Thirteens their extra few days of life, but perhaps I was better off dying on Day Five after all.

I took off my prosthetic hand for the last time, and threw it savagely across the room. I'd spent the last few hours acting the part of the perfect daughter for my parents, but I wanted to be buried as my real self.

When I went downstairs again, my parents were waiting for me. Dad had a bundle of blankets under one arm, and his other arm was around Mum. We went out of the front door, Dad shut the door with exaggerated drunken care, and we walked slowly down the road. One of the neighbours had been trying to contact the alien ship by painting increasingly desperate messages on the black tarmac, so we were treading on a series of giant lilac, magnolia, and almond letters.

I was feeling muzzy after drinking the wine, and Mum and Dad were swaying by the time we turned down the footpath to the fields. I saw a lone woman with a walking stick ahead of us, struggling to walk on the rough ground. I wondered if I should go to help her, but then I saw two women with torches appear and one of them took her arm. Barbara Corlforth and her trusty band of volunteer helpers were running this with their usual military efficiency.

Once we reached the field, I saw where a neat line of thirteen huge trenches had been dug. The first four had already been filled in with soil. Our trench would be the next one in line, with a bulldozer and some other digging machinery parked next to it. As we approached, a man stepped forward and shone a torch on us.

"Please move on to the far end of the trench and use the ramp there. This end of the trench is reserved for families with babies, elderly, or disabled members who…"

He broke off as he spotted I was missing a hand. "Oh, it's the girl with the… In that case, you can use this ramp."

I sighed and pointed out the obvious. "The fact I was born without a left hand doesn't stop me walking, does it? We can go down the far end."

We headed on to where a sheet of metal formed a rough ramp down into the trench. Once we'd noisily clanged our way along that, there was something unexpectedly soft underfoot. I peered at the ground and saw a layer of straw. Mum and Dad were already shuffling their way further down the trench, so I followed them until we reached another family who were spreading out their blankets. I recognised them as people who lived a few doors away from us, but it wasn't the moment for casual conversation with neighbours.

Dad handed out our blankets, and gestured that I should go in the middle. I spread out my blanket and sat on it. The family next to us were lying down and wrapping themselves up in individual blanket cocoons, but Mum and Dad were sitting and reaching to hug each other with me in the middle. There were more people arriving next to us now, but I didn't turn to look at them.

"Five minutes," called the unmistakeable voice of Barbara Corlforth.

The people next to us settled themselves down and then there was silence for a couple of minutes. "Sorry," I whispered. "I've been a bit argumentative sometimes. About wearing the hand and other stuff."

"We understood," said Dad.

"Two minutes," called Barbara Corlforth.

"Megan, do you remember the summer we spent in Norfolk when you were seven?" asked Mum. "We had a house right on the beach."

"Oh yes," I said. "When we went back three years later, most of the house had fallen into the sea."

"I explained to you about flood defences," said Dad, "and you kept building little walls on the beach with pebbles and sand."

"It was the best summer ever, and it never seemed to rain." I looked up at the dark sides of the trench. They seemed to be closing in on us. I couldn't see the setting sun from here, but we must be down to a few seconds now.

Mum laughed. "Of course it rained. I remember one beautiful day when we decided to have a barbecue and a thunderstorm seemed to come out of nowhere. We had to grab the chairs and the—"

She stopped talking. All the other murmured conversations along the trench had stopped too. I felt Mum and Dad's arms go limp and they fell backwards.

I sat there without moving for a moment. Mum was dead. Dad was dead. Everyone in the trench was dead. I was dead too. I should be lying down, because dead people didn't keep sitting up like this.

I dragged Mum and Dad's sprawling arms and legs into place, so they were lying neatly posed, then lay back myself, arranged a blanket on top of us, and closed my eyes. It was just like when I was very little, and I'd sneak into Mum and Dad's room on weekend mornings, and get into bed between them.

"For I am convinced that neither death nor life, neither angels nor demons, neither the present nor the future, nor any powers, neither height nor depth, nor anything else in all creation, will be able to separate us from the love of God that is in Christ Jesus our Lord," said Barbara Corlforth's voice.

That had to be from the Bible, I thought. It was ideal for this. No angels, no demons, nothing in creation, not even alien ships...

There was a pause before she spoke again. "To Allah we belong, and to Allah we return."

Another pause. "Any other beliefs down for Day Five?" she asked.

"Atheist," said a man's voice.

"No single thing abides; but all things flow." Barbara Corlforth sighed. "It's a pity the vicar was a Day One. I'm probably saying all the wrong things. Megan, you have to get out of the trench now."

I opened my eyes and frowned up at the night sky, with that big, dark section where the alien ship blotted out the stars. Barbara Corlforth couldn't be talking to me.

"Megan," repeated Barbara Corlforth, "I'm sorry but you have to get out of the trench now. We'll fill it in properly tomorrow morning, but we need to put some of the soil in now so the bodies aren't disturbed by foxes or anything."

I closed my eyes again. Barbara Corlforth couldn't be talking to me, because I was dead.

"Andy, can you get her out?" asked Barbara Corlforth.

"Yes, mother."

There was a soft thump from nearby, and someone touched my shoulder. "Leave me alone," I said. "I'm dead."

Hands grabbed me. I'd have fought them off, but I was dead so I couldn't move. I was lifted into the air, someone grunted with the effort as I was passed on to more hands, and then I was lying on the grass.

"You're not dead, Megan," said Barbara Corlforth. "I think you'd better spend tonight at my house."

"No!" I jumped to my feet. "No! I want to go home!"

I ran off into the darkness.

Day Six

I stared out of my bedroom window at a sky that was grey with clouds and brown with the looming bulk of the alien ship. It was early afternoon, and I should be starving hungry by now, but how could I think of eating when it was Day Six and I was still alive? If Mum and Dad were still alive too, then I'd be celebrating, but it was a nightmare being left alone like this. Why wasn't I dead? Had I been such a bad daughter that the aliens...

A volley of gunshots interrupted my thoughts, and I gasped in panic. What was happening? A mob had burned the city centre. Had they come to burn our village too?

I yanked on my shoes with the Velcro fastening so I wouldn't have to mess about with laces, thundered down the stairs, opened the front door, and a male figure caught hold of me.

"Mum said you'd better stay indoors, Megan," he said.

He knew my name, and his face and voice were vaguely familiar. Oh yes, this was Andy Corlforth. There were two other men with him, both holding shotguns. I stared at them for a second, and then turned back to Andy. "I heard gunshots. What's wrong?"

"There's nothing wrong." Andy took something out of his pocket, a thing that looked more like a walky-talky than a mobile phone, and spoke into it.

"Mother, Megan's worried about the gunshots."

"Everything is under control," said Barbara Corlforth's voice. "I can come and talk to Megan now."

Five minutes later, her car pulled up at the roadside and she got out. "There's absolutely nothing for you to worry about, Megan. You're one of the precious few that the aliens are allowing to survive this. You're the future of the human race, and we'll protect you at any cost."

For a second or two, I was totally stunned by her words, and the ringing tone of voice that reminded me of when she'd played the part of Boadicea at the last village festival, but then my brain started thinking again. Barbara Corlforth had reacted too calmly to me not dying with my parents. She obviously knew something I didn't. "What are you talking about?"

"There's been a special information network between the local villages for over twenty years now," she said. "We used it to anonymously pass the word along about sensitive issues. On Day Two, a message came round on the network asking if any other village had an heir. Lots of other messages asked what that meant, and then we worked it out. An heir, Megan. Someone who would survive this. Someone to remember those who died."

She shrugged. "No one knew which village sent that message. The information network was designed to make sure nothing could be traced back to the sender.

There was no more about it on Day Three, but then there was a more detailed message on Day Four. It said that a tiny number of people have no markings on their left hand. The theory is the aliens feel we're too advanced, becoming a threat to them, so they're culling our species but letting a few survive to start again."

I shook my head. "That can't be true. There's been nothing on the news about it."

"The authorities have been keeping it very quiet," said Barbara Corlforth. "They're afraid that any publicity would put the survivors at risk of attack."

I didn't say anything. I refused to believe I'd survive this. The idea of being left alone in an empty world petrified me.

"I made discreet checks," she continued, "and found that everyone in the village was definitely marked for death, except for you with your missing hand. I knew there was only the slimmest of hopes that you were an heir, so I concentrated on organising the burials while I waited for Day Five when I'd know the truth for sure."

She paused. "I called a village meeting at noon today, to tell everyone we have an heir. A couple of people didn't take the news well, and suggested harming you out of jealousy, but I was prepared for that to happen. They were dealt with immediately."

"Dealt with?" I stared at her. "Those gunshots…"

She gave a frighteningly calm nod. "Yes, that was us dealing with the troublemakers."

"But… You can't just shoot people!"

She smiled. "Those people didn't matter, Megan. They'd have been dead within days anyway. This village is incredibly fortunate to have an heir to remember us, and nothing and nobody will be allowed to harm you."

I stared speechlessly at her. Had she shot those people herself, or ordered her volunteer helpers to do it for her? How many people had been killed because they were a potential threat to me? I didn't dare ask.

"From now on," she said in her Boadicea voice, "the efforts of our whole village will be focused on your protection and preparing for your future survival. I've already opened negotiations with the other village that has an heir. You'll stand a better chance of survival with two of you together than alone."

She stopped and frowned at me. "Are you listening to what I'm saying to you, Megan?"

I nodded numbly. Barbara Corlforth had been organising this village for years, and now she was organising the survival of the human race. She was lost in a fantasy world though. The aliens would never have chosen someone like me to live on to rebuild civilisation. I hadn't died with my parents yesterday because I'd made a stupid mistake. I knew what that mistake was now, and how to correct it. I would die tonight.

*

When the church bells began ringing that evening, I was already waiting at the front door. I'd dressed with painstaking care the same way I'd done the previous day, but this time I'd got it right. I was wearing the prosthetic hand, with six blue dots on it now since it was Day Six. This time I'd keep wearing it until sunset. This time I wouldn't reject the hand that symbolised my link to my parents. This time the aliens would let me die.

When the bell started tolling, I opened the front door and went out. Andy Corlforth was still on duty in the front garden, and gave me a startled look.

"I feel I should be at the trenches tonight," I said.

He did a bit of chatting on the walky-talky, before nodding. "Mother says that's a good suggestion."

Andy escorted me to the field and Barbara Corlforth came over to meet us. "Thank you for offering to do this, Megan," she said. "I realise you don't know everyone in the village the way I do, so people will tell you their names before they go into the trench. They know there'll be photos at the farm, but they'll like hearing you actually say you'll remember them."

Photos? Farm? I'll remember them? I didn't understand this at all, but a queue was already forming in front of us, and the first family in line started chanting names at me. I glanced at Barbara Corlforth and saw she was mouthing words at me in the dim light.

"I will remember you," I said.

The family headed off to today's trench and a young couple were next. By the time the third group were talking to me, my brain had caught up with what was happening. These people were all going to die tonight. They didn't just want to know that the human race would continue, but that someone would keep their memory alive. I knew I was telling them lies. I wouldn't be alive to remember them, I'd only come here so I could die where my parents were already buried, but I couldn't mess up their last few minutes alive by saying that.

"I will remember you." I repeated the words over and over. This wasn't a big village, but a thirteenth of its population was here to die today and that was quite a few people. Finally, they were all in the trench, and Barbara Corlforth was giving the countdown again just like yesterday. I closed my eyes when she said two minutes, reliving what happened yesterday, with Mum's voice talking about that summer in Norfolk as the final seconds passed.

"For I am convinced that neither death nor life, neither angels nor demons, neither the present nor..."

Barbara Corlforth's voice was reciting the same words as yesterday. I opened my eyes and walked across to look down into today's trench. All the people there were dead, and I was still alive for the second time. Barbara Corlforth had been right after all. The aliens weren't going to kill me.

I stood there, staring blankly down at the peaceful figures in the trench, and Barbara Corlforth came over to me. "You should go back home now, Megan. We'll bring you a hot meal in a little while."

I turned to look at her. "I'm scared, Mrs Corlforth."

"There's no need to be afraid, Megan." Barbara Corlforth gave me her Boadicea smile. "I promise I'll protect you."

She didn't understand that I was scared of her too.

Day Seven

It was Day Seven, and I was sitting at the kitchen table with Andy Corlforth. I'd spent all of last night thinking things through, and gradually accepted that I was going to live until Day Fourteen. Whether I survived after that or not depended on the arrangements my village made to help me, the negotiations with the other village who had an heir, and whether I cracked under the strain and gave up.

"Mum's talking to the representatives of the other village right now," said Andy Corlforth. "They're having a face to face meeting on neutral ground."

A flash of blue outside the window caught my attention. It was a bright blue budgerigar. People were dying, but not animals, so families had to decide between putting their pets to sleep, or letting them free to survive as long as they could. The budgerigar had obviously been freed. With a lot of hungry cats around, it wouldn't last long.

"What sort of neutral ground?" I asked.

"A restaurant on the main road. Mother will be arguing for you to stay in our village of course, but we may have to make concessions."

I bit my lip. "I don't want to go somewhere strange."

"I understand," said Andy Corlforth, "but it's a question of bargaining power. We still don't know any details about the heir to the other village, but…"

He looked at my left arm and I got the message. My missing hand was a problem when it came to making demands.

"We're setting up the farmhouse at Home Farm in the hope you can stay there," Andy Corlforth continued. "It's perfect. The stream and the old well will give you a reliable water supply, and you'll have open fires, a wood burning stove, candles and oil lamps."

Over at the window, the budgerigar was sitting on the windowsill and pecking at the glass. It must be finding its new freedom terrifying, and wanted to return to the old familiar lifestyle indoors. I could sympathise.

"We'll stock the farm with supplies, and store things in houses all round the village as well. The idea is you'll run the farm as a smallholding with animals and crops. Remember fire will be your biggest danger. You must be especially careful with the lamps and candles at night and in the barns."

He waved his hands to emphasise that, and I automatically counted the blue dots on his left palm. He was a Day Thirteen. Barbara Corlforth was a Day Thirteen. They'd both be with me until the end. That was good. Probably good. I might be as scared of Barbara Corlforth as of the alien ships, but she was on my side.

The budgerigar fluttered further along the windowsill, and tried pecking at the glass again. "I don't know a thing about farming," I said. "I'll have a lot to learn."

"We'll teach you a few basics, and supply you with books. The tinned food will keep for years, so you've plenty of time to get the farm running properly."

I frowned. I'd have to practise opening different types of tins. I could use battery powered can openers for now, but they wouldn't work forever. There should be a way for me to open tins with an ordinary can opener, using something to hold the tin still.

The budgerigar had stopped pecking at the glass, and was now giving me a reproachful look. I gave in, stood up, and went to open the window. It hopped gratefully inside and I closed the window again.

Andy Corlforth sighed. "You can't adopt every abandoned pet in the village, Megan. We're selecting practical animals for your smallholding. Trained farm dogs as well as chickens, horses, sheep, goats, cows and geese."

"I can adopt one impractical budgie," I said. "We had a budgie when I was a little kid. A blue one like this. Can you find me a cage and some birdseed?"

He sighed again. "I suppose so. I don't—"

He was interrupted by the sound of a car drawing up outside. Barbara Corlforth was back. I waited nervously as the front door opened and she came into the room. I didn't like the grim expression on her face.

"How did the negotiations go?" I asked.

"We won," she said. "They instantly agreed to everything we wanted. They've been collecting supplies since Day Two, and they'll bring it all here. They've already handed over their heir."

"What?" asked Andy. "Why would they just agree like that, and give us their heir?"

"Because they were desperate." Barbara Corlforth sat down heavily on a chair as if she was very tired. "Their heir is a six month old baby boy."

Day Ten

It was Day Ten, and I was terrified and exhausted. The electricity had gone off on Day Eight, so I'd moved into the farm. Each day was filled with training sessions about childcare, stoves, oil lamps, making bread, growing crops, and caring for animals. Each sunset I had to endure the ritual at the trenches.

There was a memorial room at the farm, with small photo frames crammed in to cover every inch of wall space from floor to ceiling. On the backs were names and ages and fragments of other details, like the day that people had died. There weren't just photos of everyone from my village, but those of people from the baby's village as well. There was one area of wall still blank, reserved for yet another village, because Barbara Corlforth was searching for another heir. I was sitting at the kitchen table listening to her latest news report.

"There's been a development," said Barbara Corlforth. "We think one of the other villages has had an heir appear. Not a case like you, where they couldn't tell at the start, but a refugee arriving from the city. They won't give any details at all though. That's good in a way. It means they think their heir could survive alone, so it's definitely not another baby, but…"

"But?" I asked.

"It means we have to be the ones who take all the risks," she said. "Give them information about you, when we know nothing about them."

"I understand," I said. "When you were negotiating with the baby's village, they had no choice but to do what we wanted. This time it's the other way round."

She tapped her fingers anxiously on the table. "This could be very dangerous for you, Megan. Have you heard about the rumour?"

I shook my head. I had a wind-up radio at the farm, but I'd been ignoring the outside world for days, keeping myself totally focused on learning everything I needed to keep me and the baby alive. I hadn't even asked about a second outbreak of gunshots two nights ago. "What rumour?"

"The story is that there are a few people who are unmarked, and drinking their blood will make you unmarked too. It's stupid of course, but…" She groaned. "It's possible this mention of another heir is a trap."

If this was a trap, then we'd be handing information about me and baby James to people who believed drinking our blood would save their lives. I knew I should be grateful that I was still alive, but I was living in a nightmare that kept getting worse. Every day, people came to teach me things. Every sunset, I promised those same people I'd remember them, and then watched them lie down in trenches and die.

After sunset on Day Thirteen, I'd be struggling to cope with the farm, and I didn't even have the option of allowing myself to give up and die like everyone else. I had to live, to survive, not for myself but for baby James. Even a five-year-old might have had a chance left with enough supplies of food and water, but a baby couldn't even eat or drink by itself.

It shouldn't be me surviving this, but someone much older, tougher, and more competent. The only thing that was keeping me going was the budgerigars. A second one had arrived at the farm window, and the two of them shared a large cage in my new bedroom. When I woke in the night, shaking with terror that the aliens were saving me for some much darker purpose than death, I'd sit and watch the two birds peacefully sleeping on their perch. They seemed so content with each other in the cage, as if they'd lived together there all their lives. Perhaps they had. Perhaps this was their old cage. Perhaps the two of them had been released, and found each other again.

The thought of the two budgerigars decided me. I needed a companion too. Not a helpless baby like James, but someone to share the work and the pressure of responsibility.

"We have to risk talking to these people," I said. "Life would be so much easier with another heir."

"But it could be a trap." She chewed her lip in indecision.

I had to convince Barbara Corlforth to do this, and to do it now, because we were running out of time and people. There'd been a period of mad activity in the village, with lorries driving in huge quantities of supplies. Now most of the houses were filled with clothes, medical supplies, canned food, soap, a lifetime's supply of thousands of essential items, but their inhabitants were dead. Barbara Corlforth's trusted band of followers had shrunk to a handful.

"We need another heir," I said, firmly. "There's too much work for me. The house. The farm. The baby."

I saw the look on her face, and realised I'd made a dreadful mistake even before she said the words in a cold, flat voice.

"The baby is too much of a burden."

"No!" I cut in frantically, desperate to correct my error. "James isn't a burden. In a few months, he'll be a help to me. Able to bring me food and water if I'm sick or injured."

Barbara Corlforth still looked doubtful. She'd casually disposed of several members of the village because she thought they were a threat to me. It would be much easier to dispose of a baby who wasn't old enough to remember anyone.

"The first few years won't be a problem," I added urgently. "It's later on, when the tinned food starts going bad, that things will get difficult. By then James will be able to help me with the farm jobs, and start learning about how the people in the photos saved us."

I saw her expression flicker. Baby James wasn't old enough to remember anyone himself, but he could be taught my memories. I hated saying the next words, but I knew they were the ones that would finally convince her.

"James will be a pair of hands for me."

I watched her nod, knew I'd won this argument, and went back to my original one. "The benefits of contacting another heir outweigh the risks. We just have to organise this carefully."

Barbara Corlforth nodded. "Very carefully."

Day Eleven

It was Day Eleven. My fake hand had been scrubbed clean of ink and attached to my left arm. I'd had my hair done, my face made up, and was wearing a dress that was a careful compromise between making me look practical and ornamental.

"Their inspector can't know where he is," said Barbara Corlforth. "We blindfolded him and drove him round in the back of a van for hours before bringing him to the meeting point. We'll do the same on the way back."

"I'm still not sure about this whole dressing up thing," I said. "If he spots the fake hand…"

"He won't," said Barbara Corlforth. "It's very convincing, and we won't let him get too close to you."

"But it's not just the hand." I pulled a face. "Is he really going to believe I'm nineteen?"

"Yes, he will," said Barbara Corlforth. "I know you'd have been happier telling the truth, Megan, but once we said you were female and they started talking at last, asking your age and what you looked like… It was obvious their heir was a man. We had to make you sound as attractive as possible, so we said nineteen instead of sixteen."

"And didn't mention the missing hand or the baby." I sighed. "I'm as ready as I'll ever be. Take me to be inspected."

Barbara and Andy Corlforth drove me out of the village to an isolated house. The inspector was sitting in a downstairs room, where the window had a view of nothing but a huge conifer hedge. He tried standing up when he saw me, but two of Barbara Corlforth's helpers shoved him back into his chair again.

"You stay sitting down," said Andy Corlforth in

a menacing voice that I guessed he'd copied from a gangster film. "If you try to touch Megan, we'll kill you."

The inspector gave him an aggressive look. "I just wanted to see the girl's hand."

I lifted my left arm, and held my breath as the stranger studied my palm, then looked me up and down. "Quite pretty," he said. "Lift your skirt a bit higher."

I blinked. "What?"

"I have to report back on the merchandise," said the man. "The top of that dress hugs your figure nicely, but I want a better look at your legs."

I closed my eyes, counted to ten, and reminded myself this wasn't just about me, but baby James. I opened my eyes and lifted my skirt with my right hand.

"Lift the other side too," said the man.

If I tried to do that, I'd give away the fact my left hand was fake. I fought back panic, let my skirt fall back into place, and glared at the man. "You've seen enough. I'm not a lump of meat on display for you."

Bizarrely, the man blushed. "Sorry." He turned to Barbara Corlforth. "All right, the girl looks marketable, so let's talk business. My people have a man, aged twenty, a farmer's son who was training to be a vet."

He paused for a second. "Harry was in university accommodation on Day One, sharing a flat with another student. When the other boy understood the marks on his hand were a death sentence, he tried to beat Harry into telling him how he'd got rid of his own marks, then attacked him with a knife. Harry got a superficial knife wound in the fight but got away. He phoned his family, found his parents and sister were all Day Twos, tried to get back home in time to see them but couldn't make it in the confusion."

I winced. I'd had things so easy in comparison, having that final celebration meal with my parents and being with them when they died.

The man shrugged. "After that, Harry came to... to join his aunt. The farm you've talked about sounds better than our arrangements, so Harry will come to join your girl, but not until Day Fourteen."

Barbara Corlforth shook her head. "He has to come on Day Thirteen so I can meet him."

"That's not going to happen," said the man. "If Harry got spotted then he'd be torn apart. He stays where he is until Day Fourteen, when everyone else will be dead and it's safe for him to travel."

Barbara Corlforth frowned at him. "If you couldn't protect Harry on the journey then... You aren't from a village at all, are you? You're from the city itself."

The man hesitated before speaking. "Yes, we're on the outskirts of the city. I contacted friends in one of the villages, hoping there'd be other unmarked people there, and ended up talking to you."

"And there aren't many of you," said Barbara Corlforth. "Who are you, anyway? Harry's uncle?"

He hesitated again, then the last shreds of the tough guy facade crumbled away so he was just a tired and frightened elderly man. "Yes. There's just me and my wife. We've got Harry hidden in our attic. My wife and I will die tomorrow, but Harry's staying in our attic until Day Fourteen when it will be safe for him to travel to your farm. That's the deal. Take it or leave it."

"We'll take it," said Barbara Corlforth.

Day Thirteen

The sunset ritual had been bad every day, but Day Thirteen was horrific. Barbara Corlforth and her son were the last to go into the trench.

"I will remember you," I forced out the words.

"Be careful with that mini digger," said Andy Corlforth. "I know you've worked out how to manage the lever controls, and you'll have the floodlights to help you with what has to be done tonight, but don't risk driving too near the edge of the trench."

"I'll be very careful, I promise, and…thank you for everything."

"You, and James, and Harry are our future, Megan." Barbara Corlforth gave me an intent look. "Remember us!"

The two of them went down the ramp into the trench. I went to stand beside it, and checked the time.

"Five minutes," I called.

I waited what seemed like both seconds and a century. "Two minutes!"

The final seconds fled past, the sun dipped below the horizon, and now I was totally alone except for a baby crying in a pram. I started reciting the words that by now I knew by heart. "For I am convinced that neither death nor life, neither angels nor demons, neither the present nor the future, nor any powers…"

Day Fourteen

It was early afternoon on Day Fourteen, and I was sitting in the front room of the farmhouse feeding James. I hadn't heated the jar of baby food, because I didn't want to spend too much time in the kitchen at the back of the house. Stupid of me, it wasn't as if Harry would knock at the front door once and then go away if there wasn't an answer, but I was fighting a panic attack.

Last night's dreams about being dragged off to some alien zoo or laboratory had been intermingled with spells where I lay awake worrying about meeting the unknown Harry. I'd considered wearing the hand and the makeup for our first meeting, but felt he should see the real me right away. There'd be the extra shock of baby James too. Barbara Corlforth hadn't mentioned his existence to Harry's uncle, because she saw James as a liability rather than a survival asset.

James didn't seem to care about his food being cold, his mouth kept snapping tightly round the spoon so he didn't miss a single scrap of the orange pureed stuff. He was probably starving. His regular feeding time was two hours ago, but I'd had to leave him wailing in the pram while I finished filling in trench thirteen.

I looked across at the window for the tenth time in ten minutes, and there was an indignant scream from James. I shovelled another load of orange mush into his mouth to shut him up. Six more spoonfuls of baby food and James burped back a bit of orange yuckiness before abruptly falling asleep.

I lifted James into his carrycot, and then went to stand by the window. I'd expected Harry to be here hours ago. I reminded myself that I'd been burying bodies this morning, and Harry would have had bodies to bury too. His uncle. His aunt.

I waited for another hour, listening to the antique grandfather clock in the corner tick away the seconds, before I took the sleeping James outside in his carrycot and sat on the front doorstep next to him. There were a thousand jobs I should be doing, but I couldn't take my eyes off the track leading up to the farm.

If Harry didn't show up, then I'd never know whether some of the Day Twelves or Thirteens in the city had caught him, or he'd decided to go somewhere else. He'd been told the address of this farm, but I had no idea where he'd been hiding. There must be other survivors somewhere, but the wind-up radio hadn't picked up any signals at all this morning, and leaving the farm animals while I randomly roamed the countryside would…

There was something moving on the farm track! A dark blue car. I scrambled to my feet, and found my fingers curling in tension. I was about to meet Harry. Once his uncle had stopped pretending to be a hard and calculating thug, he'd seemed a very nice man. I hoped that Harry would be nice too. Nice enough not to be too angry when he found out that we'd lied to him.

The car pulled up in front of me with an odd jerk that told me the driver was a novice. Harry got out and we looked at each other in silence for a moment.

"Your uncle lied," I said. "You aren't twenty."

He brushed his shaggy, light-brown hair out of his eyes and blushed just like his uncle. "Your people lied first. When they said you were nineteen, my uncle thought it would sound better if he said I was twenty."

The sick feeling in my stomach was slowly easing. Given the odd shape of Harry's nose, you wouldn't describe him as handsome, but he looked dependable.

"So how old are you?" I asked.

"Eighteen," he said. "And you?"

"Sixteen."

He gestured at the sleeping James. "Your people didn't say anything about a baby. He's not yours is he?"

I shook my head. "Another village brought James to us. Do you know much about babies?"

"A bit. My sister was ten years younger than me." Harry gave a shake of his head, dismissing painfully raw memories, and waved at my left arm. "Your people didn't say anything about that either. Will you be able to hold the baby and feed him?"

I held back a sigh. "Yes. I can change nappies too. It's best if you assume I can do everything, and I tell you when something is a problem. Shall I show you the house now?"

He nodded, and I reached for the carrycot, but found Harry had already picked it up and was smiling down at James. Curiously reassured by that, I turned to lead the way into the house, but stopped when a movement above us caught my eye.

"Look!" I pointed up at where the alien ship was rising higher into the air.

"They're going," said Harry. "They're really going and leaving us to rebuild things again. I was worried they were keeping us alive for…"

"Me too," I said grimly.

Sunlight came flooding across the fields as I watched the rapidly shrinking shape of the retreating ship and said the words one final time. "I will remember you."

Afterword from the Editors

Developing *Defying Doomsday*, there were a number of things we wanted to achieve with this anthology.

We chose the apocalyptic theme because, as fans of the genre, we had noticed a distinct lack of post/apocalyptic fiction with disabled and chronically ill characters. Whenever these characters are included, they tend to die or be presented as burdens for the main characters. The idea behind *Defying Doomsday* was to subvert these tropes. Since apocalypse survival fiction so frequently relies on the idea of "survival of the fittest", we wanted to show that there were different ways to survive and different measurements of "fitness" and "worth" than are usually applied.

It was important to us, then, that the stories in *Defying Doomsday* have disabled and chronically ill protagonists. But we also wanted to make sure that these characters' narratives extended beyond this single character trait. We wanted to show that disabled and chronically ill characters have more to offer fiction than tales of their impairments.

There were a plethora of excellent submissions and, unfortunately, we couldn't include them all. Of course, it was also impossible to include a completely representative range of disability and chronic illness. However, we tried to choose stories we felt demonstrated that the experiences of living with disability and chronic illness are varied and complex.

Most of all, we wanted to show that disabled and chronically ill characters can have interesting stories, just like anyone else.

We hope you enjoy their tales as much as we do.

All the best,
Tsana and Holly

About the Authors

Octavia Cade has a PhD in science communication and is currently experimenting on New Zealand's sole seagrass. She actually did some algal research in the Portobello Marine Lab that appears in her story, though never survived an apocalypse there. Her stories have appeared in *Strange Horizons*, *Apex Magazine*, and *The Dark*, amongst other places, and she recently published her first sci-fi novel, the science-history themed *The August Birds*.

Elinor Caiman Sands has had short fiction published in *Cosmos Online*, in the Aurora Award nominated anthology *Strange Bedfellows* (edited by Hayden Trenholm) and on the T. Gene Davis Speculative Blog. She's worked full time as a writer/editor on a commercial popular astronomy series as well as on the British political magazine Progress. When not writing she can be found painting or building diamond-encrusted crowns in digital worlds which is probably about as close to wearing real diamonds as she will ever get. You can find out more about her at her Happy Snappy Gator Bog! Er, Blog: http://ecaimansands.wordpress.com.

John Chu is a microprocessor architect by day, a writer, translator, and podcast narrator by night. His fiction has appeared or is forthcoming at *Boston Review*, *Uncanny*, *Asimov's Science Fiction*, *Apex Magazine* and Tor.com. His story "The Water That Falls on You from Nowhere" won the 2014 Hugo Award for Best Short Story.

A lifelong Amsterdammer, **Corinne Duyvis** spends her days writing speculative young adult and middle grade novels and getting her geek on whenever possible. Her fantasy YA debut *Otherbound* won the Bisexual Book Award and received four starred reviews; *Kirkus* called it "original and compelling; a stunning debut" while the *Bulletin* praised its "subtle, nuanced examinations of power dynamics and privilege." *On the Edge of Gone*, an apocalyptic YA, released in March 2016. In a starred review, *School Library Journal* said, "Insightful, suspenseful, and unsettling in its plausibility."
Corinne is a co-founder of Disability in Kidlit. Find her at www.corinneduyvis.com or www.disabilityinkidlit.com
"And the Rest of Us Wait" is set during the events of *On the Edge of Gone* and some characters overlap.

Thoraiya Dyer is a four-time Aurealis Award-winning, three-time Ditmar Award-winning, Sydney-based Australian writer. Her work has appeared in *Clarkesworld*, *Apex*, *Cosmos*, *Analog* and pretty much every Fablecroft anthology. Her collection of four original stories, *Asymmetry*, is available from Twelfth Planet Press and her debut novel, *Crossroads of Canopy*, first in the Titan's Forest trilogy, is forthcoming from Tor books in 2017.

Dyer is represented by the Ethan Ellenberg Literary Agency. She is a member of SFWA. A qualified veterinarian, her other interests include bushwalking, archery and travel. Find her online at Goodreads, Twitter (@ThoraiyaDyer) or www.thoraiyadyer.com.

Janet Edwards is an English science fiction and fantasy author. Her books include the Earth Girl trilogy—*Earth Girl*, *Earth Star*, and *Earth Flight*. As a child, she read everything she could get her hands on, including a huge amount of science fiction and fantasy. She studied Maths at Oxford, and went on to suffer years of writing unbearably complicated technical documents before deciding to write something that was fun for a change. She has a husband, a son, a lot of books, and an aversion to housework.

You can read more about Janet Edwards and her books at www.janetedwards.com.

Kristy Evangelista lives in Canberra, Australia. "No Shit" is her first professional sale. Like her main character, Jane, Kristy was diagnosed with Crohn's disease when she was a teenager. Unlike Jane, Kristy is not a particularly resourceful person, so in a real apocalyptic scenario she would find herself eaten by a wild pack of dogs on day ten.

Kristy spends her days either struggling with the bureaucracy in her public service job, or struggling to get her children to put on their shoes. She finds that reading and writing is a welcome evening escape from both roles.

Stephanie Gunn is a Ditmar-nominated writer of speculative fiction. In another life, she was a (mad) scientist, but now spends her time writing and reviewing. Her short stories have appeared in anthologies such as *Bloodstones*, *Bloodlines*, *Epilogue*, *Grant's Pass* and *Kisses by Clockwork*. She is currently at work on several contemporary fantasy novels and too many shorter works for her own good. She lives in Perth with her son and husband and requisite fluffy cat (and too many books). You can find her online at www.stephaniegunn.com.

Maree Kimberley is a writer from Brisbane, Australia. She has published articles, short stories, flash fiction and a short children's book. Her work has appeared in *Meanjin*, *Metazen* and *The Big Issue* and in short story anthologies *Impossible Spaces*, *Hauntings and In Sunshine Bright and Darkness Deep* (as Rue Karney). She has a Bachelor of Creative Industries, a Master of Arts and a PhD from Queensland University of

Technology's (QUT) Creative Writing Faculty and her research interests include speculative fiction, neuroscience and posthumanism. An unwelcome guest named Rheumatoid Arthritis moved into Maree's body in 2004. She wishes it'd move out. You can find her on Twitter as @reebee01.

Seanan McGuire is an American author, living on the West Coast (where the rattlesnakes are) and spending most of her time dreaming of rain. She writes a lot of books. When not writing, Seanan enjoys travel, visiting the haunted cornfields of the world, spending time with her enormous Maine Coon cats, and collecting creepy dolls. You can keep up with her at www.seananmcguire.com.

Lauren E Mitchell lives in Melbourne, Australia, with her husband and assorted cats. When she isn't writing she may be working, studying, reading, or wrangling other writers during NaNoWriMo. She is pretty sure her pile of books to be read is going to eat her. If you want to contact her before her inevitable death by unread books, you can find her on Twitter (@LEBMitchell), Facebook (laurenmitchellwrites) or at her website: http://laurenmitchell.net.

Rivqa Rafael is a writer and editor based in Sydney. She started writing speculative fiction well before earning degrees in science and writing, although they have probably helped. Her previous gig as subeditor and reviews editor for *Cosmos* magazine likewise fuelled her imagination. Her previous short stories have appeared in *Hear Me Roar* (Ticonderoga Publications) and *The Never Never Land* (CSFG Publishing). She can be found at rivqa.net and on Twitter as @enoughsnark.

Tansy Rayner Roberts is the author of the *Mocklore Chronicles*, the *Creature Court* trilogy, *Love and Romanpunk*, and *Musketeer Space*. She podcasts on Galactic Suburbia, Verity! and recently started her own fiction serial podcast, Sheep Might Fly. Her eleven-year-old daughter informed her that this was one podcast too many. Tansy's alter ego, Livia Day, writes novels about murder and cake, not necessarily in that order.

Samantha Rich lives in Maryland, USA with a grumpy cat and a cheerful dog. She is a lifelong speculative fiction fan and enjoys running, horseback riding, and traveling.

Bogi Takács is a Hungarian Jewish agender trans person currently living in the US. E writes both fiction and poetry, and eir work has been published in a variety of venues like *Strange Horizons*, *Clarkesworld*, *Lightspeed* and *Apex*. E is autistic and has motor dyspraxia, but e is not a fan of video streaming. You can visit eir website at www.prezzey.net, or follow em on twitter at @bogiperson, where e also tweets short story and poem recommendations under #diversestories and #diversepoems.

Acknowledgements

This book would not have been possible without the help and support of so many people. We'd especially like to thank our amazing Pozible backers, without whom this anthology would not be what it is. Thanks also to everyone who helped us spread the word during our campaign, including Sean Wright at *Adventures of a Bookonaut*, Mieneke van der Salm at *A Fantastical Librarian*, SC Flynn at *SCy-Fy*, Cindy Pon and Malinda Lo at *Diversity in YA*, Elizabeth Lhuede at *The Australian Women Writers Challenge*, Stephanie Gunn, David McDonald of *The Galactic Chat* and *Ebon Shores*, Marisa Wikramanayake, John DeNardo and Sarah Chorn at *SF Signal*, the folks at *Skiffy and Fanty*, Marieke Nijkamp and the team at *DiversifYA*, Mihai at *Dark Wolf's Fantasy*, and Shaheen at *Speculating on Specfic*.

Thank you to all our wonderful authors who have put in so much time and work not only on their stories, but helping us spread the word about the anthology as well. A huge thanks to Robert Hoge for writing our introduction and Tania Walker for our gorgeous cover.

Thank you also to everyone who put in so much work behind the scenes including Alisa Krasnostein, our publisher, Tehani Wessely and Katharine Stubbs.

Finally, we could not have done this without the support of our families and friends.

Thank you to our Pozible backers who include:

- Nick Caldwell
- Grahame Bowland
- Miriam Mulcahy
- Leife Shallcross
- Anne Oberin
- Jessica White
- Benjamin McKenzie
- Sally Koetsveld
- Emilie Collyer
- Chris Currie
- Narrelle Harris
- Suzie Eisfelder
- Gary Kemble
- Jane Rawson
- Robert Giles
- Bron Mitchell
- Kathryn Linge
- Ashley Capes
- Grant Watson

- Jamie Drake
- Alex Pierce
- Scott Vandervalk
- Ju Landéesse
- Liz Barr
- Brendan Ragan
- Catriona Sparks
- Dragonistas Aerie
- Sirocha Bruckard
- Mindy Johnson
- Louise Williams
- Mary Gardiner
- Glenn Jones
- Emma Mann
- John Richards
- Kellie Broadby
- Melina Dahms
- Ricky Buchanan
- Tania Fordwalker
- Rivqa Berger
- Tehani Wessely
- Jay Watson
- Stephanie Gunn
- Corey J. White
- Daniel Luiz
- Jennie Rosenbaum
- Tansy Roberts
- Deborah Biancotti
- Elanor Matton-Johnson

- Karin Landelius
- Kara Chalson
- Ty Barbary
- Helen Merrick
- Katharine Stubbs
- Lara Hopkins
- Joris Meijer
- Jasmine Stairs
- Cheryl Morgan
- Ian Mond
- Mark Webb
- Catherine Green
- Daniel Franklin
- Caroline Mills
- Nicole Murphy
- Shane Nixon
- John Devenny
- Mirabai Knight
- David Versace
- Cory Day
- Karen L Paik
- Louise Hughes
- Howard Copland
- Scott Pohlenz
- Fred Kiesche
- Susan Loyal
- Keffy Kehrli
- Deborah Kalin
- Kirsty Sara

- Jennifer Vail
- Nora Olsen
- Elizabeth Lhuede
- Leonie Rogers
- Robert Hoge
- Russell B. Farr
- Liana Eriksen
- Martin Livings
- Mikayla Micomonaco
- Scott Leis
- Anthony Panegyres
- Juliet Marillier
- B. T.
- Eleanor Smith
- Mieneke van der Salm
- Heidi Stabb
- Elissa Nguyen
- Katrina McDonnell
- Ellen Kuehnle
- Bethwyn Walker
- Tiki Swain
- Terry Frost
- Jessica Gravitt
- Michelle Goldsmith
- Garth Nix
- Anne Mestitz
- Jing Chang
- Maria Spangler
- Bren MacDibble

- Richard Sheresh
- Rowena
- Nick Bate
- Clwedd Burns
- Dame-Sir Rayna Lamb
- Michael Green
- Dante Oberin
- Susie Munro
- Jo Hutton
- Stephen Whitehead
- Kerri Regan
- Chris Bobridge
- David McDonald
- Natalia Denison
- Kathryn Allan
- Paul Laker
- Marie
- Gemma Noon
- Jonathan Strahan
- Jen Rodland
- Phillip Krohn
- Kat Clay
- Rrain Prior
- Nadia
- Amy Flowers
- Andrew Hatchell
- Terry Tuttle
- Kay Buttfield
- Andrea Hosth

- Janelle Barnard Jones
- Lisa Kruse
- Helen Stubbs
- Emily Booth
- Shana DuBois
- Connie Bruckard
- Fred C. Moulton
- grant kench
- Ashton Cartwright
- Rob Irvine
- Rebecca Smith
- Silke Jonda
- Tracy Suraci
- Aaron Ferrell
- Graham Clements
- Sheree Christoffersen
- Jane Shevtsov
- Sarah Yost
- Mark Gerrits
- Wendy Mann
- Donna Maree Hanson
- Rick Keuning
- Timothy Moore
- Aimée Lindorff
- Rebecca Sutton
- anna eidt
- Erin Subramanian
- Abigail Falck
- Richard Leaver

- Navah Wolfe
- Damon Cavalchini
- Tiffany Christian
- Luke Brown
- Bill Racicot
- Justina Ireland
- Lewis Hutton
- Jonathan Craig
- Elizabeth Jones
- Paige Kimble
- Amanda Holling
- Sharyn November
- Brianna Flynn
- Steve Graby
- Yuri Danilovich
- Steven Paulsen
- Hannah Kench
- Katariina Väisänen
- Erika Ensign
- Sarah Cornell
- Belle McQuattie
- Rebecca Raisin
- Terri Jones
- Carol Ryles
- Rachel raisin
- Amie Kaufman
- Leah Goodreau
- Epi Ludvik Nekaj
- Lindy Cameron

- Tiansen Li
- Travis B. Hartwell
- Cassandra Page
- Faith W.
- Len Jacob
- Anne Gibson
- Paul Nasrat
- Kendall P. Bullen
- Nicolas Longtin-Martel
- Angela Slatter
- Margaret Atwood
- Hope L Nicholson
- Carly Kocurek
- Sheila Lane
- Ken Hutton
- Alice Wong
- Larissa Clifford
- Geoff Wales
- Carrie Miller
- Stephanie Bateman-Graham
- Bethany Webb
- Diane Severson Mori
- Paula Palyga
- Catie Coleman
- Steve Sumpter
- Joyce Chng
- Daniel SImpson
- Igel Welt
- Mac Burns

- El Gibbs
- Sylvia Harmon
- Imogen Claire Cassidy
- Ruth Turner
- Daira Hopwood
- Rhonda Elliott
- Heather Berberet
- Amanda Vail
- Leah Cardaci
- Melissa McLaughlin
- Amy Yost
- Laura Topping
- Ruth Long
- E. Guthardt
- Terri Sellen
- Alex Heberling
- Ben Peake
- Nicole Canal
- Sarah Liberman
- Amanda Pillar
- Sue Ann Barber
- Kate Bendall
- He Mianquan Adrian
- Dafydd Williams
- Andy Dent
- Briony Davis
- Chad Hammond
- Lin Simpson
- Glaiza Perez

- Christine Crabb
- Andre Kruppa
- Random Misterka
- Robert Cox
- Pauline Conolly
- Giles Turnbull

About Twelfth Planet Press

Twelfth Planet Press is an Australian specialty small press. Founded in 2007, we have a proven record and reputation for publishing high quality fiction. We are challenging the status quo with books that interrogate, commentate, inspire through thought provoking and provocative science fiction, fantasy and horror.

Visit Twelfth Planet Press at
http://www.twelfthplanetpress.com

Find Twelfth Planet Press on Twitter at
@12thPlanetPress

Like us on Facebook at
http://www.facebook.com/TwelfthPlanetPress

Nightsiders (a Twelve Planets collection)

by Sue Isle
ISBN: 9780980827439

In a future world of extreme climate change, the western coast of Australia has been abandoned. A few thousand obstinate, independent souls cling to the southern towns and cities, living mostly by night to endure the fierce temperatures and creating a new culture in defiance of official expectations.

A teenage girl stolen from her family as a child, a troupe of street actors who affects the new with memories of the old, a boy born into the wrong body, and a teacher pushed into the role of guide, all tell the story of The Nightside.

2012 Tiptree Long List Finalist
2012 Norma Hemming shortlist
Winner of YA Best Short Story and Nominated for Best Collection, Aurealis Awards 2012

Year's Best YA Speculative Fiction 2015

edited by Julia Rios and Alisa Krasnostein
ISBN: 9781922101501

Our goal is to uncover the best young adult short fiction of the year published in the anthologies dedicated to the form, the occasional special edition of a magazine, and individual pieces appearing in otherwise "adult" anthologies and magazines, and bring them together in one accessible collection.

Fans of *Kaleidoscope* will find more tales of wonder, adventure, diversity, and variety in this collection devoted to stories with teen protagonists. The Year's Best YA Speculative Fiction from 2015 includes stories from:

Sarah Pinsker, Shveta Thakrar, Felix Gilman, Genevieve Valentine, Sylvia Anna Hivén, Chesya Burke, Daniel José Older, Erica L. Satifka, Rivqa Rafael, Sean Williams, Leah Cypess, Heather Morris, Cat Hellisen, Sabrina Vourvoulias, Tamlyn Dreaver, E. C. Myers, Marissa Lingen, James Robert Herndon, Joel Enos, Caroline Yoachim, Nova Ren Suma

Kaleidoscope: Diverse YA Science Fiction and Fantasy Stories

edited by Julia Rios and Alisa Krasnostein
ISBN: 9781922101112

Kaleidoscope collects fun, edgy, meditative, and hopeful YA science fiction and fantasy with diverse leads.

These twenty original stories tell of scary futures, magical adventures, and the joys and heartbreaks of teenage life.

Featuring New York Times bestselling and award winning authors along with newer voices:

Garth Nix, Sofia Samatar, William Alexander, Karen Healey, E.C. Myers, Tansy Rayner Roberts, Ken Liu, Vylar Kaftan, Sean Williams, Amal El-Mohtar, Jim C. Hines, Faith Mudge, John Chu, Alena McNamara, Tim Susman, Gabriela Lee, Dirk Flinthart, Holly Kench, Sean Eads, and Shveta Thakrar.